Circles of Fate

Pamela S. Thibodeaux

*And we know that all things work together for good to them that love God,
to them who are the called according to his purpose.* ~ Romans 8:27-29 KJV

CIRCLES OF FATE

by
Pamela S Thibodeaux

Publisher/Distributor:
Temperance Publishing; an imprint of
Pamela S. Thibodeaux Enterprises, LLC
PO Box 324
Iowa, LA 70647

ISBN# 978-0-9896728-8-7

Cover Design: Delia Latham (Heaven's Touch Designs)

Praise for Pamela S. Thibodeaux

"Thibodeaux leads the reader through from the first page to the last without once relinquishing control. She hooks them, holds them, and keeps them enthralled until the last line." ~ Review of **The Visionary** by Delia Latham, author of the "Solomon's Gate" series

*"**In His Sight** caught my attention from the beginning and it made me wonder if I had given all to God as he gave all to me. Thank you, Pamela, for a story that I would readily recommend to anyone who needs that extra encouragement!"* ~ Reviewed by Wendy for Happily Ever After Reviews

*"**Winter Madness** is a wonderful romance and an excellent example of Spiritual growth."* ~Reviewed by Dee Daily for The Romance Studio

*"**A Hero for Jessica is** a good, sweet read charged with attraction but an emphasis on true love. I recommend it to women of all ages."* ~ Reviewed by Violet for LASR

*"**Cathy's Angel** is a short tale that is entertaining as well as inspiring. Well done!"* ~ Reviewed by Marlene for Fallen Angel Reviews

*"Pamela S. Thibodeaux's motto is "Inspirational with an Edge!" Her short story **Choices** lives up to those words and is well worth reading."* ~ Reviewed by Gail for Night Owl Romance

*"**The Inheritance** was my first Thibodeaux work; however, it will not be my last! Her approach to writing about everyday life, while struggling to maintain strict Christian standards and values, is a glimpse into reality which we all must face from time to time."* ~ Reviewed by Brenda Talley for The Romance Studio

*"If you have ever considered Christian fiction bland, then check out the **Tempered Series**. It will be well worth your time."* ~ Amanda Killgore for Huntress Reviews

*"**Lori's Redemption** is fast paced, lots of action, gripping storyline... I loved it. It's gone straight back into my TBR pile."* ~ Clare Revell author of the "Monday's Child" series

"Through Pamela's blessed ability to find God everywhere, even in secular song lyrics, she has written devotions guaranteed to touch the heart and remind the reader of our True Love, the Rose of Sharon." ~ Endorsement for ***Love is a Rose*** by Linda Yezak, Author, Editor Triple Edge Critique Service

Dedication

For Delia & Donna, critique partners, editors and friends....
this book would not **BE** if not for you two.
From the bottom of my heart and soul...
Thank You, Thank You, Thank You!

Special Thanks goes to Liz Bennefeld for helping to pick the winning cover for **Circles of Fate.** Liz Bennefeld, a writer and freelance editor (retired), lives in North Dakota, where she is involved in photographic art and creative writing. A lifetime member of the Science Fiction Poetry Association, she is the editor of its annual online Halloween Poetry Reading and currently serves as Vice President. More on Liz can be found at http://about.me/quietspaces

For MaeBelle & Kay;
my life is much richer for knowing you and yours!

Last but certainly not least, for Keith....God has brought us full circle. Thank you for blessing my life.

Part I

FATE: One's appointed lot: *Destiny.*

Prologue

Todd Jameson paced the tiny room. One moment he cursed his luck and in the next, wished he'd died in the confrontation. He hadn't even been shot at! He'd given up...just like the failure his father always accused him of being. Even the truth of why he gave up didn't ease the sting of guilt.

He plopped into a chair, buried his face in hands that shook. The hair on the back of his neck prickled. Instinct—well-honed by years of life with his father—put him on alert. From somewhere, someone watched. Hidden eyes bore into him.

And it was more than the stupid security cameras in every corner.

He kicked at the chair across from him, muttered a curse and resumed his trek back and forth across the scuffed hardwood. Sunlight filtered in through the dirty window but offered little warmth. Dust danced in the air, stifling his breath. Fear gripped his chest. What was going on and why in the world did it take so long? His court-appointed attorney had said he would try and plea bargain, but for what? One thing was certain, dear old dad would not have to worry anymore. He'd never worry again.

As if he ever had.

The bitter thought twisted Todd's gut. He glanced in the mirror, saw and detested the panic in his eyes. More of the same crawled up his spine. If the wait and the wondering didn't drive him mad, fear and guilt would. He spun on his heel and fought the urge to smash a chair into the glass.

What would happen now?

He stopped mid-pace and turned when the door opened, ushering in a quiet air of authority, along with a man he'd never seen before. The stranger strode to the table and, without a word, gestured for him to sit. Todd hesitated. "No, thanks. I'll stand."

The man took a deep breath and nodded. He strolled across the room toward Todd and extended a hand. "I'm Darrell Champagne."

Again Todd hesitated, confused by the show of courtesy.

Understanding and compassion radiated from the gentleman, encouraging a response. He reached out to shake the proffered hand. "Todd Jameson."

"Nice to meet you, Todd. I've been sent in to talk with you. Your attorney has bargained your case, contingent upon the choice you make, of course, and I'm here to offer you a deal. But first, I'd like to ask a question."

Todd's guard slipped into place against any more interrogation. Every fiber of his being screamed for him to bolt. *Run as fast as you can!* He stiffened, ground his teeth, and held his ground.

"Why did you attempt to rob that liquor store?"

Todd averted his gaze and swallowed the humiliation clogging his throat. "You have the report."

"I want to hear it from you."

Todd walked to the other side of the room, questions ricocheting in his head. *Will he believe me? Would it matter?* He took a deep breath, squared his shoulders, and looked Darrell straight in the eye.

"To pay for my father's burial."

"Why do you think you failed?"

He lifted his chin, unable to prevent the anger that colored his tone. "Because I gave up without a fight. I was outnumbered and I'm not ready to die." Todd allowed his defiant gaze to meet the other man's calm one. "You might call that chicken. I know my father would. The whole idea was stupid and never would have worked anyway. The gun wasn't even loaded."

Darrell moved to where Todd stood and put a hand on his shoulder.

"I don't call that chicken, Todd. I call it smart. Thank you for your honesty. Now let's talk about your options."

They strode toward the table and sat while Darrell outlined the contingency terms the court offered.Despair, hope, and fear collided in Todd's chest. "You call that a choice? Going off to some godforsaken country to fight in a stupid war I know nothing about—and believe in even less?"

"It's more of a choice than you have now. It's a chance at a future."

"It's a chance at death." Todd's jaw clenched. "I just passed up one of those. I'm not interested in another."

Darrell took a deep breath, closed his eyes and pinched the bridge of his nose as though considering his next move. When he addressed Todd again, his gaze was solemn and honest, his voice soft.

"Believe me, Todd. We don't make a habit of sending babies to war. Some of them do go, but it's *their* choice, though only God knows why they make that decision. In your case, however, consider this: If you go...and should you die, your death would be far more honorable than the one you face now if you are convicted and go to prison."

Fear hammered in Todd's chest, belied the sneer on his face. "You mean death before dishonor and all that crap?"

Darrell's eyes flashed at the statement but he never lost his cool. "No, I mean honor, and life. I can promise you will not go to war anytime soon. I'm not saying never, but at least not until you're eighteen or older. The year or more will give you a chance at a life with some honor and respect." He put his hand on Todd's shoulder once more. "Has anyone ever talked to you about God?"

Todd jerked away. His chair scraped the floor and almost toppled over when he got up, fists clenched, jaw rigid. His breath heaved out in short bursts. He glared down at Darrell. "There's no such thing as God. No one, God or otherwise, would take a three-year-old's mother and leave him alone with an abusive, alcoholic father."

"You're right, Todd." Darrell's quiet tone never changed. "But you see, God didn't make those choices. People did. And He's kept you alive until you got into a position to listen, really listen, when someone tried to tell you about Him and how much He loves you. I know others have tried, haven't they?"

Not waiting for a reply, Darrell continued to deliver his message, a message of hope and faith.

Given little choice, Todd listened to what the Army Chaplain had to say. Whether he believed him or not, he took the bait, he took the chance. *A chance at life.*

He joined the Army.

Chapter One

"Here she comes, Miss Shaunna Sweetness!" A voice in the lunch crowd rang out as Todd Jameson sauntered into the Feed Trough Café, picked up a menu, and grabbed the first available seat. *I'll starve before I get waited on,* he thought and watched as the only waitress in sight served a table across the room. With a tray and coffee cup in one hand and a pot of coffee in the other, she made her way to his table, stopping to refill several cups along the way.

Tiny, about five feet tall, she couldn't have weighed more than a hundred pounds. Hair the color of burnished copper fell in thick waves down her back. *What a beauty.* He admired her petite figure as she continued toward him, laughing at the comments and pats the soldiers lavished on her. Todd glanced at the menu, made his choice, and was ready to order when she arrived at his side.

"Hi! Sorry it took so long to get here. Are you ready to order or do you need a few more minutes?"

His pulse jumped into high gear at the salutation, uttered in a breathless, little girl's voice. He looked up into eyes the color of medium-roast coffee, shining with vitality and beauty, and longing tugged at his gut. *The beauty of innocence.*

"Hello, darlin'. I'll have the chicken-fried steak and a beer. Do you have brown gravy or white?"

Shaunna stood mesmerized as the stranger's eyes stared into hers.

Wow! Handsome. The thought danced through her brain and shocked her system. His deep, velvety-rough voice made her shiver despite the warmth of the crowded room. A flush stung her cheeks. She cleared her suddenly parched throat, licked her dry lips, and swallowed hard. "Both."

He smiled. "Good, I'll take the brown."

Her heart pounded and knees weakened, but her lips curved in response. "Will that be all for you?"

He nodded.

"OK, I'll get someone to bring your beer right out."

She had turned to walk away when his voice stopped her. "How old are you, darlin'?"

Shaunna hesitated. For some reason she felt vulnerable, exposed, and foolish—as though he could sense her jumbled emotions. She turned back and looked into his emerald eyes. Her heart skipped a beat—and then another—at the interest she saw there...along with a hint of unease.

"You don't mind me calling you darlin', do you?"

Her buoyant personality rushed to the rescue. She laughed. "Good heavens no! I think that's the only word Army guys know how to use when addressing a member of the opposite sex."

His eyes glowed and her heart tripped over itself. Another blush heated her cheeks. "I'm sixteen. Are you new to the base?"

"Just passing through, darlin'. Just passing through." His voice was soft, husky. Shaunna loved the sound. His was the kind of voice she could see herself listening to for a long time.

"Well, I hope you enjoy your stay here. Let me get your order in." She hurried off, but his eyes remained on her—she felt his gaze...and for some reason, the force of it made her tremble. In the kitchen, she put her tray down and hurried over to the sink. Her hands shook when she got a glass of water and drank it.

"What's the matter?" Her boss, Buddy, eyed her with concern, which only made her blush harder.

"Nothing, I- I'm just...h- hot." She splashed cool water on her face and neck.

A chuckle rumbled low in Buddy's chest. "Well, I'll take that young man his beer. You rest a minute." He smiled, and his eyebrow quirked in amusement when Shaunna flushed again. She averted her eyes at the mere mention of the Army man.

But she still had to deliver his meal. He sighed with obvious relief when she placed the plate on his table. His smile once again weakened her knees. He seemed disappointed because she could not stop to chat with him, but Shaunna was not. She couldn't understand why he affected her so, and was glad to be busy with the lunch crowd.

After he left, she cleaned his table, and couldn't help but remember the color of his eyes and the sound of his voice. Her insides fluttered and she hoped she'd see him again soon.

As Todd made his way back to the base, he decided to give

the Feed Trough Café his business for as long as he was in town. He had three good reasons: good food, cold beer, and a pretty waitress. Honesty made him admit he would go back even if the place served hot beer and rotten food. "Shaunna Sweetness" was a phrase his mind would not stop singing no matter how many times he reminded himself of her age.

At two o'clock he met with his commanding officer, Sgt. Mike Ferel. The sergeant welcomed him to the base, assigned his barracks, and took him to his new quarters. On the walk over, Sgt. Ferel outlined his expectations.

"Not much is required of you, Todd, but to wait for your orders. You are, of course expected to behave in a manner befitting your uniform, whether on or off base. And I'm sure you know quite well your section of the barracks is to be kept clean. One of your superior officers may ask an occasional favor—with which you are expected to comply—but other than that, you're free to come and go as you please as long as you stay within curfew."

Todd listened; glad he would have a little free time. He hadn't used any leave since he enlisted so this would be like a short vacation. He'd already decided Columbus was a fairly decent town. He should be able to find plenty to do without any trouble. Shaunna's image flashed in his mind and he suppressed a groan. *Maybe.*

When the sergeant dismissed him, Todd hesitated and addressed his commanding officer with a salute. "Sir?"

"At ease, soldier. What can I do for you?"

"Well, Sir, I wonder if you could direct me to a dry cleaning service? My dress greens are in terrible shape."

Mike nodded. "There's a dry cleaning service down on Main Street." He hesitated, a frown wrinkling his brow. "Some of the guys have complained about them though. Run by a bunch of foreigners, you know."

He hesitated again, raked his fingers through his hair.

"Tell you what, go talk to Ms. Chatman. She does my uniforms. Tell her I sent you and this is only temporary. She hasn't been taking any new customers, but I'm sure she won't mind. Oh, and Todd, be careful of the daughter," he added, almost as though an afterthought. "She's very protective of her mother. Sick you know."

Barely able to follow his C.O.'s rambling dialogue, Todd smiled, not sure if he "knew" or not.

"They live over in the poorer section of town." Mike muttered something under his breath.

"Uh, Sir?" Todd queried as the Sergeant turned to go.

"Yes?"

"I don't know where the poorer section of town is," he reminded with a grin.

Mike threw back his head and laughed. "That's right, you're new here. I need a vacation." He gave Todd a wink and a good-natured slap on the back.

"Tell you what, I have another meeting soon. How 'bout you go on and get yourself settled. Meet me back at my office at say, sixteen-hundred hours. I'll take you there myself."

Todd decided he liked Mike Ferel and accepted the offer with a chuckle followed by another salute. "Thank you, Sir. You won't have to be a fly after all."

Mike had the grace to wince.

"Heard that, did you?" He chuckled, shook his head. "I *really* need a vacation," he mumbled, then took his leave.

Todd pondered the comment while he put his things in order, then lay down for a brief rest. Dancing eyes and a laughing young face surrounded by a thick mass of shimmering hair haunted his thoughts. Anticipation shivered through him.

He looked forward to his next visit to the Feed Trough Café.

* * *

Shaunna counted her tips while she walked. With trembling fingers, she added a five-dollar bill to the pile in her hand. Her heartbeat quickened and breath caught in her throat with a hiss. Excitement curled in the pit of her stomach. Then she remembered who'd left it, and lost count. Coming to a shaky halt beneath a tree, she leaned against it while newly awakened emotions coursed through her. She pictured his face, remembered his brilliant green eyes, heard his husky voice in her mind, and wondered if this was what love at first sight felt like. Anxious to get home and tell her mother about her day, Shaunna picked up her pace. She envisioned herself graduated from high school, then college and with a better job, one more suited to her purpose in life: *to find a heart specialist who might be able to help her mother.*

As she neared her house, she recognized Mike Ferel's car in the driveway and hurried in, anxious to see him. She entered through the front door, found the living room empty and figured her mother and Mike would be in the kitchen.

"Mom, I'm home!" She called out a greeting. "Hi, Uncle Mike! I had a great day, Mom. I made forty-six dollars in tips. And guess what, I saw this guy. You should have seen him. He was so..." She hesitated on her way to the kitchen.

How could she describe him? Cute? Nah, he was much more than that. "Different." She settled triumphantly on the description as she burst through the doorway.

And there he sat.

Her eyes widened in surprise. The same guy she'd described—no, actually *yelled about*—was seated at her kitchen table. Embarrassment heated her cheeks. If only she could back out of the kitchen and enter again. "Uh..." she stammered. "I'm sorry. I didn't know you had someone with you."

Her mother chuckled. "I take it from all that racket you had a good day?"

Shaunna tore her eyes away from the handsome stranger and gave her mother a hug. "Terrific! How about you? Did you rest?"

Margaret and Mike shared a smile before she answered. "Yes, I rested. I mended a few things and watched the soaps. To tell the truth, I was plain lazy all day."

"Good. That's exactly what you should do, every day."

Mike chuckled. "How about a hug for your old Uncle Mike?" He rose from his seat and opened his arms.

Shaunna turned to him. "Depends, Uncle Mike," she stated with exaggerated politeness. "I don't recall us having any laundry for you. Did you bring some or is this a social visit?"

"Shaunna Denise!" Her mother's admonishment came almost by rote. She was fully aware this same scenario occurred every time Mike came over, a game they'd adopted the first time Shaunna refused work from one of Mike's men. Mom finished her part in the farce as Shaunna threw herself into Mike's arms with a laugh. "Don't be rude!"

"You've grown into a mighty feisty young lady." Mike gave her a mock-stern glare, then turned her to face the soldier with him as the young man stood up. "Shaunna, I'd like you to meet Specialist Fourth Class, Todd Jameson."

Todd's eyes glittered. Shaunna recognized amusement and something else...hope? Did he suspect he was the guy she'd described with such enthusiasm? He offered his hand, and she accepted without reservation, despite a wave of shyness.

"So, we meet again." Todd glanced at Mike, but his gaze returned immediately to Shaunna. He appeared to have trouble focusing anywhere else. "I ran into Shaunna at the café but didn't really have the pleasure of an introduction."

The warmth of his touch sent little sparks of pleasure all the way to her shoulder. She trembled. He gave her hand a light squeeze but didn't let go.

"Shaunna, is it? It's a beautiful name."

A shiver skittered along every nerve ending in her body. Something about the blatant interest in his eyes, and her name spoken in his husky voice... Shaunna smiled and took a deep breath. "Why, thank you. I like it myself, but my mom deserves the compliment. She picked it out." She'd hoped to convey a teasing tone, but her voice shook. She disengaged her hand from his electrifying grasp.

Todd chuckled. "My compliments to her, too." He slipped his hands into his pockets and glanced at her mother. "You know, Mrs. Chatman, I thought you looked familiar when I first saw you. Now I know why. The resemblance between you two is remarkable. Beauty definitely runs in this family." He returned his gaze to Shaunna's.

Her mother flushed with pleasure and immediately began to fuss over Shaunna. "Sit down, dear. Get off your feet. Let me get you something to drink."

Shaunna's sense of responsibility took over. "Oh, no, you don't, Mom. I'll get us all something to drink. You sit down, prop up your feet, and take it easy." Only when her mother obliged, and conversation resumed did she turn to prepare four glasses of iced tea.

As the conversation around her turned to laundry, Shaunna's ears perked up. She didn't like the direction this discussion was headed one bit. She leaned across the table and looked Mike directly in the eyes. Her anger mounted, simmered just below the surface. "Sergeant Ferel."

Mike grinned and winked at Todd. "Uh-oh, here it comes." He then turned to her his tone gone placatory. "A moment ago, it was Uncle Mike."

"Sergeant Ferel." Shaunna maintained her most authoritative voice. "You know darn well my mother is not taking any new clients. Yet every time I turn around, you attempt to bring her some." She slammed his tea down in front of him.

Mike's lips twitched and amusement sparkled in his eyes despite his obvious attempt to adopt a neutral expression. "I know that, dear, and I haven't brought anyone over since you chewed me out six months ago. But Todd will only be here for a couple of weeks, a month at the most. And he deserves our best services, not the awful dry cleaning place. Maybe, if he gets our best, he'll want to come back. We sure could use more soldiers of his caliber around here," he explained in his most persuasive tone.

Shaunna jerked her chair away from the table, plopped into it, and turned to face Todd. "Did Sergeant Ferel tell you about my mother's heart?"

He shook his head.

"Shaunna, there's no need to bore this young man with our personal problems. You shouldn't be so rude!" Mom interjected.

Shaunna's voice and expression softened. "I'm not trying to be rude, Mom. I just want him to know why we are refusing him."

"But Shaunna, you heard Mike. It'll only be temporary. I have very little to do now. It won't hurt me to do his uniforms while he's here. As a favor to Mike." How could her mother always manage to insert a "coax" into a simple expression?

Shaunna snorted and glared at Mike, grateful looks could not kill, otherwise she'd almost certainly have his death on her conscience. "I know how little work you have, Mother. That's why you're able to rest more. And getting the extra rest is why you're feeling and looking so much better lately."

Todd cleared his throat and all eyes trained on him. "It's OK, Ms. Chatman. I don't want to be any trouble for you or Shaunna. I can see she has good reasons for feeling the way she does. I can find someone else.”

“Nonsense! Shaunna worries too much.”

Shaunna eyed Todd with surprise. The way he jumped to her defense filled her with a range of confused emotions. She gazed into his eyes and felt herself weaken. Still, she did not like the idea of her mother doing any more work. “How many uniforms do you have?”

Heat sparked between them, and the ordinary question took on an extraordinary intimacy.

“Four,” he rasped.

“And this would be temporary?”

Todd nodded.

Shaunna hesitated. She did not want to give in too soon, and she definitely did not want any of them to see the real reason she yielded. Something about this man...he was different, exciting. She did not understand at all what made her want to do his laundry. Lord only knew when she would find the time to do it herself, but...she would. She decided the best way to surrender was with reluctance tempered by grace.

“Well, I guess it wouldn’t hurt since it’s only temporary. But you have to promise me you won’t overdo it, Mother. You have to promise to leave his uniforms to me, especially if you’re tired or not feeling well.”

“But honey, that’s ridiculous. You already do more than you should. You work all day and then here at home.”

“No dice, Mom.” She remained adamant. “You promise, or the answer is no.” She sent her mother a firm look, all the while praying her change of heart would be accepted without question. She hoped none of them could see through her façade, especially since she didn't understand what currently transpired within herself.

“I promise.” Margaret agreed without further argument. Relieved, Shaunna sent her mother a mile. The quiet light in the older woman’s eyes said she understood the emotions at war within her only child.

“Really, Margaret, if you're not feeling up to it...”

Margaret shushed Mike with a wave of her hand. “Oh, pooh, I feel fine. Like I said, Shaunna worries too much.”

Shaunna glared at him. “Don't look so surprised, Uncle Mike. I’m not completely unreasonable.” A faint frown tugged at her mouth.

"I never thought you were completely unreasonable, sweetie, and I appreciate it." Mike gave her a wink and a smile.

Todd seemed hesitant—and not surprisingly, surrounded as he was by tension of every nature. "Only if you're sure."

"Of course, I'm sure." Margaret gave his hand an affectionate pat. "Now, you go on and get your uniforms."

"And hurry, before Shaunna changes her mind," Mike teased. "Bring mine too, will you?" Todd disappeared out the door, and Mike turned back to Shaunna as she inhaled a deep hiss of breath. "Now don't worry, honey. It's just a couple of things which have piled up since the last time I came, nothing to fret over," he soothed before she could let loose another tirade on his head.

Her mom reached over and gave Shaunna a hug. "What were you saying earlier dear, something about a man?"

Shaunna flushed. "Nothing, Mom," she mumbled as Todd walked in with his uniforms in one hand and Mike's laundry bag in the other. She stood up and put an end to the conversation. "If you'll excuse me, I think I'll go take a shower before dinner."

Mike rose also. "We should go, too. It's been a hectic afternoon. Margaret, take care of yourself." He kissed her cheek then winked at Shaunna. "You too, sweetie."

"I'll be fine. Shaunna just can't stand it if she's not clucking over me like a mother hen." Love and pride resonated in her mother's voice.

"That's my privilege, Mom. You took care of me all of my life, now it's my turn."

Mike chuckled as Todd took Margaret's hand.

"It's been a real pleasure, ma'am." His eyes glowed with admiration...and something else when he turned his gaze and smiled at Shaunna once more.

Margaret grabbed his arm and escorted him and Mike to the door. "It sure is nice to meet you, young man. Feel free to drop by anytime. In fact, why don't you plan on having dinner with us sometime soon?"

Todd thanked her again and promised to keep the invitation in mind.

They watched the two men leave, then Margaret turned to Shaunna, her eyebrow quirked in curiosity. "Did you want to talk about something, dear?"

Shaunna blushed and headed for the bathroom. "No Mom, not a thing," she muttered, and escaped into the shower.

Chapter Two

Todd stood on the Chatman's porch and waited for someone to open the door. Three days had passed since Mike convinced Shaunna to do his laundry. Not wanting to rush, he'd reassured her yesterday at the café, he was in no real hurry. Today, he had to renege on that assurance because tomorrow he had a meeting with the First Lieutenant in charge at Fort Benning.

Margaret opened the door with a smile.

"Well, hello, Todd. Shaunna's not home yet but come on in anyway."

Todd smiled back. "I figured she wasn't home. But I wondered, Ms. Chatman, if any of my uniforms are ready?"

Margaret breathed a weary sigh and shook her head. "No. I've been a little under the weather since yesterday and Shaunna hasn't had time." She sent him an anxious glance. "I'm so sorry, Todd. I thought you said there was no hurry."

Todd emitted a sigh of his own as Margaret's tired eyes nudged his conscience. "I did, ma'am. But that was yesterday. Uncle Sam feels differently today. I was informed this morning that I have a meeting with the First Lieutenant early tomorrow. I guess I'm lucky to have almost twenty-four hours notice." He hoped his smile would soften the grimness of the words. As inconvenient as it usually was, he enjoyed being kept on his toes by the Army.

Margaret ushered him into the kitchen and fixed them both a cup of coffee. "Well, that's good. I guess. Tell you what, we'll get at least one of them done up for you this afternoon. Have supper with us, and then you can take it back with you."

"Ms. Chatman, please don't let this put you out. I can see you're not feeling well. Shaunna will have my head if you worry over this. Let me take them to someone else," he urged, genuinely concerned for the obviously ill woman and her overworked daughter.

The woman smiled. "It's Margaret, please, and don't be silly. I'm feeling much better, and Shaunna planned on ironing them today anyway."

Todd's heart did a crazy little flip at the thought of

Shaunna's hands on his uniforms. "Well...only if you're sure."

"And I am." Margaret's smile reassured him.

"OK. What time does she get off?"

"Two-thirty."

Todd glanced at the clock over the stove. An hour and a half! His heart soared. He ducked his head, sipped his coffee. He hoped Shaunna's mother didn't see the irrational way he reacted to the thought of her daughter, but from the way her eyes danced and the smile she tried to hide behind her own coffee cup, he figured she did. A flush heated the back of his neck and climbed into his cheeks.

He cleared his throat. "Well Margaret, I'm happy to accept the dinner offer. Maybe I could also walk Shaunna home from work, if you have no objections."

"I don't mind a bit. It would do Shaunna good to relax and enjoy her walk home instead of rushing so much."

Todd nodded. "Is she always so busy? Seems like a lot for someone so young."

"Well, you're not much older than she is. How do you handle the pressures of the Army?"

Todd grinned at the similitude.

"Besides," Margaret continued with a smile. "Shaunna usually runs on a full tank of stubbornness."

Todd chuckled. "Never would've guessed it. Well, I'd better head over there. See you in a while."

Thirty minutes later he sat in a booth at the Feed Trough Café. "Hello, Miss Chatman." He greeted Shaunna with a smile. "How are you this afternoon?"

"I'm fine, Specialist Fourth Class Jameson. And you?"

"Getting better every minute. Your mother gave me permission to walk you home."

A thrill of excitement danced along Shaunna's spine at the thought of him walking with her. "She did, did she? Do I have any say in the matter?"

"Nope, none whatsoever. She also said you wouldn't mind getting one of my uniforms done up this afternoon, and she invited me to stay for supper."

"Oh, really?" She arched an eyebrow and tried her best to look exasperated, though her excitement grew with each statement. "And I guess I have no say in those matters either?"

Todd shook his head with a grin.

"Humph! I guess this is 'Boss Shaunna Around' day." She struggled to suppress the smile tugging at her lips.

Todd chuckled. Was that a glimmer of excitement in his gaze? Was he as thrilled as she about spending the afternoon and evening together?

"Wouldn't dream of bossing you around." He somehow managed a perfectly straight face.

"Well?" Shaunna crossed her arms in front of her. She tapped her foot and waited.

With a toss of his dark head, he laughed. "Please?"

Amusement lit his eyes, along with some other emotion Shaunna had yet to experience. *Desire.* The realization shocked her brain, scorched her senses. Nevertheless, she kept up the banter. "Please what?"

"If you please, Miss Chatman, it'd be my honor and pleasure to walk you home." He adopted a tone of serious persuasion. "And, if it's not too much to ask, I am in dire need of a uniform for my meeting with the First Lieutenant tomorrow morning."

Shaunna sniffed in an attempt at haughty unconcern. "I'll think about it." She gave a sassy toss of her head then turned on her heel and walked away. When he chuckled behind her, she hoped Todd hadn't noticed her shoulders shaking with giggles. A few minutes later, she returned with Buddy Frederick in tow.

"Mr. Frederick said I could leave early, since you are in dire need of one of your uniforms this afternoon."

"Thank you, sir." Todd stood and touched his forehead in light salute to Buddy's authority.

The older man grinned. "You're quite welcome. Make sure my number-one waitress gets home safely and that she doesn't fall into the hands of some lusty soldier," he teased.

Shaunna hoped her boss didn't guess their feelings and put him in the category of 'some lusty soldier.'

"You have my word, sir."

* * *

From that instant, they spent every spare moment together. On the days she worked, Todd walked her home. On the days she didn't, he went to see her. With her mother's permission, he took her out for walks, to dinner, movies, and swimming at the base pool. Laughing and teasing, he taught her how to roller skate and horseback ride. A couple of evenings he showed up with a bag full of groceries and cajoled Shaunna into cooking for them. Their friendship developed and Shaunna found herself head-over-heels in love.

His last night at Ft. Benning proved the most memorable of their shared evenings. Todd came into the café early that morning, unaware his heart showed in his eyes. Shaunna knew by the hint of sadness lurking in those emerald gems, he'd received his orders.

"Well, sweetness, I've got to go."

His voice was soft, and a hint of sorrow darkened the bright green of his eyes. Sadness squeezed her heart. Tears rushed to her eyes. At the gentle shake of his head, she blinked them back. She managed not to cry right then and met him with a smile when he arrived to walk her home.

Silence commanded the walk home, each of them immersed in their thoughts. Gloom surrounded them. The catch in Shaunna's voice when she asked to stop by the bank assisted Todd in making the decision he'd wrestled with all day. He pulled her beneath a tree in the park and took her hands. "Shaunna?"

Her lips trembled. "What?"

Tears stung his eyes. "I hate good-byes."

"Me too."

"Good. Since we agree, I'm not going to see you tomorrow." His finger on her lips hushed her protests. He slid his knuckles over her cheek in a tender caress then cupped her face in his hands. "We'll go out tonight if you want to."

He smiled at the emphatic shake of her head. "OK, but you have to promise me something." He stroked her cheeks with his thumbs and swallowed the hard lump in his throat. "Promise you won't cry. No tears, OK?"

She bit her lip and blinked fast to stem the flood that rushed to her coffee-colored eyes. "OK."

With a ragged whisper of her name, he succumbed to the overwhelming urge to taste the sweetness of her lips. Her flavor filled his senses. He teased her mouth, molded and shaped her lips to his and pulled her trembling body closer. He reached deep for self-control and ended the kiss before it evolved into something more passionate, something undeserving of her.

A soft whimper escaped her trembling lips. She wrapped both arms around his waist and buried her face in his chest. A shiver shook her as he stroked her hair. When her trembles subsided and he gained control over his own rampant emotions, he removed her from his embrace, but allowed his hands to slide up and down her arms in a subtle caress.

"I'd better get you home before your mama starts to worry." He brushed the hair off her cheeks. "Smile for me, sweetness." He brushed a feathery kiss across her lips, and she did. She smiled, though he saw what it cost her. His heart sang at its brilliance and reminded him again of her youth. They walked hand in hand to her door. He kissed her cheek and promised to see her later.

He borrowed Mike's car for the evening, wanting to take Shaunna somewhere special. At first he planned to take her dancing, so he could revel in the pleasure of her in his arms. With a pang, he realized he couldn't, she was not old enough. Against his better judgment, he'd let himself fall in love with a sixteen-year-old girl. So, after dinner he took her to a movie. Once he parked the car, he pulled her close and put his arm around her. She turned to him, her eyes bright with unshed tears.

"Todd..."

He sensed her intentions and silenced her declarations of love with a kiss. "Don't," he whispered and shook his head. His lips brushed hers in a tender caress with each back-and-forth movement of his head.

"I love you!" She choked out the words when he buried her face into his shoulder.

She'd said it, and Todd's heart ached with bittersweet pain. Knowing the grief they would cause, he hadn't wanted to hear those words. He held her and stroked her hair, but never returned the declaration with one of his own.

His orders were to report to Fort Lewis in Tacoma, Washington two days hence, and Todd did not want to encourage her with the fact that he loved her too—more than he'd ever thought possible. Chances were he might not see her again, at least for the next four years. Then there was the war... Knowing Shaunna, if he told her he loved her, she would spend the next four years waiting and even longer grieving if he went to war and didn't survive. She was too young for that.

So he didn't tell her how he felt. He just held her. When her shoulders started to shake, he rocked her in his arms.

"Don't cry. Oh baby, you promised," he groaned and fought back tears of his own.

"I'm sorry, but- but…I don't want you to go!" she wailed. Shudders wracked her slender body.

"I have to go, sweetie…" He crushed her to him and buried his lips against her soft mouth to hush her ragged sobs.

Shaunna whimpered as he pulled her against him, wrapped her arms around his neck, and pressed her body against his. With supreme effort, Todd moved her out of his arms, careful to be gentle.

"Shaunna, we have to stop this," he urged, his voice thick.

"Why?" He could tell she had no idea of the precariousness of the situation.

He stroked her hair off her face. "Because if we don't…" His words lingered and he wondered if she understood what might happen between them. *Not likely.* He kissed her again but kept a tight rein on his emotions. "Because it's time for me to get you home."

She shook her head. "Please, not yet."

Todd took a full moment to consider what might transpire if he honored her request. "Yes, now." He pulled her close for one more kiss.

"Will you write to me?" She pleaded and choked back a sob.

"I'll try," he said with a shrug. He didn't want to appear uncaring or callous. God only knew how much this situation tore at his heart. But he didn't want to tie her down either.

His heart clenched like a tight fist when hurt clouded her eyes. "I don't know what they have in store for me," he explained.

She nodded and bit back another sob. "I'll never forget you."

He smiled and caressed her face. No doubt he'd never forget her either. But four years is a long time when you're sixteen. "Maybe not, but you will get on with your life. Be happy, Shaun, and promise you'll take care."

With a soft sigh, she nodded and moved away so he could

start the car.

Todd didn't take his arm from around her when he drove her home, grateful for each moment he had her by his side. He walked with her to the door and pulled her into his arms. With one last tender touch, he kissed her then turned away. His heart broke into a million pieces at her soft cries, but he did not look back. Instead, he utilized every ounce of strength he possessed and walked out of her life.

* * *

Shaunna brushed the sweat off her brow. She'd finished cleaning the stoves and still had to mop the floor before she closed the café for the evening. Lord, she was tired! Her legs hurt, her back ached and her head had started to pound from the effort it took to pull a double shift. But the physical aches were mild compared to the agony in her heart, which weighed like a lump of lead in her chest. The double shift served as an opportunity to think of something besides Todd, as much as a favor for Mr. Frederick.

His stay at the base had turned out to be the most memorable and happiest time of her life. He'd left a little over a week ago and she missed him—terribly. She leaned on the mop for support and blinked back tears as poignant memories of their last day and night together bit into her heart. Recollections of his kiss still amazed her. Although the kiss was everything her first should be—gentle, tender, sweet, everything she dreamt it would be, remembering it and the subsequent ones they shared wreaked havoc on her body and tortured her mind with thoughts of *what if.*

What if he hadn't had to leave? What if he came back? What if...an endless spiral of downward emotions when she considered, true to his word, Todd didn't see her again after that night. He simply left. No note, no phone call, and no final word, just gone.

With a sigh, she finished mopping and closed the café. Thank goodness school was about to start. Maybe between classes and work, she could get over loving and losing him in the span of three short weeks. Maybe she could get over the pain of her first broken heart.

Chapter Three

Some of Shaunna's spark disappeared after Todd's departure. She ate very little, slept less. The people who cared about her the most, worried. Shaunna didn't realize how much they worried until her mother knocked on her bedroom door nearly five weeks after he left.

"How are you, honey?"

Tears sprang to Shaunna's eyes. She sat up and made room for her mother on the bed. "I'm just tired, Mom, so very tired."

A frown creased Margaret's brow. "Shaunna, I hate to ask you this, but I'm worried sick and I have to know. Are you pregnant?"

Shaunna buried her face in her hands and burst into tears. "No, but I wish I were. At least then I would have some small part of him to hold on to." Wailing, she flung herself into her mother's arms. "Oh, Mama, now I understand what you mean when you say I'm the only part of my father you have left to love."

Margaret rocked her in a tender gesture and brushed the hair off of her face with her fingertips. "No, honey, you don't want to raise a child alone. Trust me, I know. As much as I love you and I would never trade a moment of our life together, single parenting is a very difficult task."

"Tell me again, Mom, the story of my father."

Margaret curled up next to her, leaned back against the headboard, pulled Shaunna into her arms, and stroked her hair as she recalled her own story of love and loss.

"Almost seventeen years ago I fell in love for the first time, the only time, with the most handsome boy I'd ever laid eyes on." She cupped Shaunna's face, stroked her cheek.

"You have his eyes and his hair." A soft smile curved her lips, and then she cuddled Shaunna back against her side. "Sadly, duty called my soldier-boy away and he left before we could get married. He died before I could tell him I carried his child."

"A helicopter crash, right?"

"Yes. His helicopter malfunctioned during a routine training expedition. Without a marriage license to prove you were his, the Army offered no support. So, shunned by my friends and what little family I had, I turned to God. It's been just you, me, and Him ever since."

"You never regretted your decision to have me?"

Margaret brushed her lips over Shaunna's head. "Not once, no matter how difficult things were. I thank God daily for the blessing of my beautiful daughter."

"There's never been anyone else?"

"There have been offers, but for so long I grieved your father and was engrossed in the effort to raise you that I couldn't consider another relationship. Then, with my illness, I didn't have the time or energy to get involved with another man. Besides, not many men would want to be saddled with a sickly wife and another man's child."

"Do you still miss my father? Even after all these years, does his death still hurt?"

Margaret nodded.

"Why, Mom? Why does love have to hurt so much?"

"Love doesn't hurt, honey. Love is a precious gift. The choices we make are what hurt."

Tears spilled down Shaunna's cheeks. "I just wish I could see him one more time, or at least talk to him."

"Would doing so make your separation any easier, especially when you consider the way he left?"

"Probably not," Shaunna conceded. "I guess he didn't feel about me the same way I felt about him."

"I guess not," her mother whispered.

* * *

Joe Taylor pulled his eighteen-wheeler into the parking lot of the shopping center across the street from the Feed Trough Café and emitted a snort of disgust. *I hate Columbus, Georgia—especially being forced to lay over here. The place crawls with soldiers, you can never get a decent motel room, and all of the women are in love with Army men. The only good thing about this town is right across the street where you can get the hottest food and the coldest beer in town.*

His thoughts circled in the back of his mind while he recorded his hours and mileage in the log book. Until recently, he'd worked in the oilfield and had mastered almost every position available—from roustabout to rigger, foreman to operator, in both wire line and pipe testing. Then things started to change in the oilfield and since he never put much store into saving money, there weren't a whole lot of funds to tide him over after his unemployment ran out. So when all other options seemed closed, he learned to drive a truck. He'd been driving for a little over a year and hated every minute of it. There was nothing lonelier than talking to yourself, to some other lonely trucker, or to a neurotic insomniac on a C. B. radio.

The company he worked for hauled hazardous waste. The danger added a touch of excitement to the job, but the only really good thing about it was the pay. Transporting waste paid more than any other driving job and he purposely began to save money. He had bank accounts in almost as many cities as Matlock Truck Lines had terminals. Truck driving had only one other advantage as far as he was concerned—*women*. He'd never met so many different women in his life as he had this past year, *except* in Columbus, Georgia.

He tossed the log book into the glove compartment, climbed down out of his rig, and cursed his luck again. He hated driving a truck and he hated this place. Being forced into both at the same time put him in one sour mood. He suppressed a growl, dusted his cowboy hat against his thigh, and walked across the street toward his destination hoping he could get his dinner before Army men crowded the place. He certainly did not feel like waiting for his food, nor did he relish the idea of fighting...but considering where he was and the mood he was in, both were highly likely.

* * *

Shaunna sprayed the counter with a solvent meant to cut grease and dirt, wrung out her rag, and ran the cloth over the smooth, laminated finish in a circular motion. Her thoughts twirled in her mind in cadence with her movements. While held in her mother's embrace nearly a week ago, she'd accepted the fact that Todd was not a part of her life. *He was gone.* With the exception of one postcard, she had not heard a word from him. To her, those actions proved he did not love her, and she cried herself to sleep for the last time. She'd bounced back somewhat since then, but remained reserved around men she didn't know.

The bell on the door tinkled. She glanced up from her chore and watched a man grab a menu then seat himself at a small table. She sighed, grateful he was alone.

"I'll be right with you."

He gave a terse nod and buried his face in the menu. She put away the cleaning supplies, washed her hands, then placed a glass of water along with a coffee cup on a tray. She picked up the coffeepot and walked toward his table, prepared to take his order. Her guard snapped into place when his low-keyed wolf-whistle reached her ears.

"Well, looky here. Finally, a decent reason to come to this blasted town."

His deep voice rumbled out in a rich southern drawl, and he regarded her with the most striking pair of ice-blue eyes she'd ever seen. Her heart clenched, even as her lips compressed into a thin line.

Not interested.

Careful to keep her expression professional yet impersonal, she took the man's order but remained quiet when he tried to draw her into a conversation. When she brought out his dinner, he asked her how long she'd worked there.

"Almost four months." She kept her tone clipped but polite.

Once again, he tried to draw her into a conversation with him. "Name's Joe, honey, what's yours?"

"Shaunna."

"What a pretty name for a pretty girl. Tell me, Miss Shaunna, why is a good-lookin' little thing like you moping around here without a smile?"

The whole question, including her name, sounded funny laced with his rich accent and she did smile. Nevertheless, she was reluctant to share her personal life with a stranger, so she changed the subject. "I don't recall seeing you before and you certainly don't appear to be in the Army. Are you new to Columbus?"

"No, darlin', I'm just passing through. I drive that rig over there." He nodded in the direction of his parked truck.

Shaunna's heart did a painful little flip at the memory his words evoked. She glanced out the window then back at Joe's comment.

"Uh-oh, looks like the love bug bit then flew the coop. Tell me something, honey, was he a soldier boy?"

Sarcasm colored his tone. She blinked back the tears that rushed to her eyes and nodded.

He shook his head then rolled his eyes in an expressive gesture. "Well, he was a fool. Don't you worry though, if you just lost your last friend, I hereby volunteer to be your next one."

Amusement tinged his voice. Laughter danced in his eyes and sparked a response within her. Shaunna smiled, really smiled for the first time in weeks. Still, she shook her head and inserted a hint of seriousness in her voice. "No, thanks, mister. I've no desire to get involved with someone who's 'just passing through' ever again."

Joe threw back his head and laughed. "Well, at least you're smiling. You need to keep on doing so too, looks real good on your pretty face."

Shaunna giggled. She'd never heard a request for a smile put quite that way and it sounded funny rumbling from somewhere deep in the broad chest, spiced with his heavy accent. Duty called her away as customers began to file in and she was unable to talk to him again until he checked out, but the memory of his cheerful banter made her heart a bit lighter the rest of her shift.

* * *

Todd hung up the phone and walked back to his barracks. It was good to hear Mike Ferel's voice, and even better to know Shaunna and her mother were well. Nearly three months had passed since he left Fort Benning. Less than twenty-four hours after he arrived at Fort Lewis, the Army quarantined him and the rest of his company and put them into isolation to await departure to Vietnam. For nearly two weeks they stayed quartered together with no outside contact. They lived together, slept together, and worked together to build comradeship with the men they would live with, fight with and, very possibly, die with.

They shared practical jokes, funny stories and lives as each man tried to banish the fear they all felt of going to war.

They talked, laughed, and cried for hours on end as each prepared for what would be the toughest test of their strength, courage, and faith. When the tension and anticipation of the wait began to work against them, orders came in that they would not be going to the jungles of Vietnam. However, before the cheers and shouts of gratitude died down, several of the men—Todd included—were hand picked and flown to Panama for Jungle Survival, a course designed to train soldiers in the art of guerrilla warfare.

For eight weeks the soldiers lived, ate, slept, and crawled through the jungles of Panama while playing a very real game of war. They learned to look out for themselves and each other and how to survive under some of the toughest circumstances man could invent. When they thought they had the course mastered, someone would think up another form of torture to inflict on them and then train them to handle it.

It turned out to be the toughest eight weeks of their lives as day after day officers drilled them to expect the unexpected. They learned the most effective ways to watch their comrades' backs, and most importantly, they learned the true meaning of the term CYA: *cover your anatomy.*

During the two-week quarantine at Fort Lewis, Todd spent a lot of time thinking about Shaunna. Had she met someone else yet? Did she miss him as much as he missed her? How could he feel so much tenderness for one young girl? To his recollection, he'd never experienced that particular emotion in his life. He'd always been too busy learning to survive to feel tenderness about anyone or anything.

Part of him regretted not telling her how he felt about her, and part of him argued he'd done the right thing. The thought of war scared the daylights out of him, and he assured himself she was better off not knowing how he felt or where he was going. Then, when he found out Vietnam wasn't in the plan, part of him cursed his own stupidity. Before he could make up his mind to write and tell her of his feelings, he found himself on a plane and in the jungles of Panama. While there, he stayed too busy to think of anything but the brutal training process.

He'd returned today, still undecided as to what to do about Shaunna. As soon as he received clearance to leave the base, he called Mike. He figured the best place to start would be to get a message to Shaunna. Then the ball would be in her court. After all, he couldn't just write after ten weeks and blurt out that he loved her. *Could he?*

The sergeant sounded a bit surprised to hear from him but readily answered his questions about Shaunna and her mother. They talked briefly about his career plans and his decision to join Special Forces. Before he rang off, Todd asked Mike to give his regards to the Chapman's and his address to Shaunna.

* * *

Shaunna threw herself across her bed and sobbed into her pillow. She, Mike, and Margaret were at the kitchen table enjoying a nice quiet dinner when he mentioned he'd talked to Todd earlier in the day...and all of her old pain returned. Todd had been sent away almost immediately after he arrived at Fort Lewis, hence the reason he had not written. He'd returned to the States today, called Mike, and asked him to give them his regards and his address.

With an angry little shriek, she tore the paper with his address in half. Why hadn't Todd tried to reach her at the café? Why go through Mike?

Probably because he thinks of me as family. At least that was the word he used, according to Mike. Family? She fell in love with him and told him so, and he considered her family!

Her mother came in to check on her, and she accepted her outstretched arms.

"Why, Mama?" she cried. "Why didn't he call me, or write to *me* instead of sending a message through Uncle Mike?"

Margaret stroked her hair. "Oh, honey, he's probably as confused about his feelings for you as you are about him."

"I was never confused about my feelings. I loved him and I told him so!" Shaunna wailed. "And he considers me *family*." A fresh wave of hurt assailed her.

Her mother rocked her in a gentle motion. "I don't know what to say, honey. The thought of war does strange things to people. He's been gone quite a while. Maybe he's not sure if you still feel the same way about him. Even though you said you *loved* him. Maybe you need to figure out if that's still true and write to him. And don't forget to pray about it," she urged.

"What good will it do to pray now? God hasn't answered my prayers so far."

"Maybe you've prayed for the wrong thing. Maybe you're prayers are more about what you want instead of what God wants. Remember, sometimes God's greatest gifts are different from what we want from Him."

Shaunna's sobs subsided. Her mother was right. Maybe she did need to think and pray about her feelings before, *if ever*, she wrote to Todd. One thing was certain, she would not declare her undying love until she knew exactly how he felt. She would not make a fool of herself again. Hurt, angry and confused, she cried herself to sleep, emerald eyes haunting her dreams.

Chapter Four

"Well, there you are. How about fetching me a cup of coffee, darling?"

Shaunna looked up into the laughing eyes of Joe Taylor. "How about you going to the counter and fetching your own cup of coffee, darling?" she countered. "I'm on my break and I've got a ton of homework to finish before I get back to work."

Joe grinned. "My, my, have we got an attitude today. Are you this rude to all of your customers?"

"No, only to insolent, lazy Texans who think I should jump at their every beck and call," she stated in mock disgust. His deep, husky laugh made her smile in return.

"Who ever told you I was from Texas?"

She grinned. "No one had to tell me. Only people from Texas talk like this." Her nasally attempt at a Texas drawl reduced her to giggles and had him doubled over with mirth.

"Oh, darling," he choked out. "One thing you Georgia peaches will never master is a Texas drawl." He reached over to brush a strand of hair off her face.

Shaunna flushed at the way her skin warmed at his touch. She slid her notebook inside the textbook to mark her place then rose. "Where would you like to sit?"

Joe slid into the seat across from the one she'd vacated. "Right here, if you don't mind."

She sighed. "I'll get your cup of coffee and you're welcome to sit there, but I really need to finish my homework."

"I won't bother you," he promised.

She got his coffee, placed the mug in front of him and slid back into her seat.

"Can I help you with anything?"

She shook her head. "No, the work isn't hard. I just have a lot to do in a little bit of time."

True to his word, Joe kept quiet while she continued her schoolwork. His mind raced back to the first time he met Shaunna, nearly six weeks ago, and he pondered the reasons he'd readily accepted two more runs to Columbus in such a short span of time. Something about this little waitress made him want to return to the place he detested most in the United States. She pulled at his heart and mind, and he found himself falling deep and fast, getting more emotionally involved than he'd ever allowed himself to get.

A waitress appeared to refill his cup. He thanked her with a smile and shook his head when she inquired if he wanted anything else. Shaunna never looked up from her work. The waitress disappeared and left him alone with his thoughts.

Statistically he was another product of child abuse in a time when abuse ran more and more rampant. Thrust into a selfish world from day one, he grew up hard and fast. His mother was a whore who worked in bars and strip joints to support her drug habit. His father, the latest jerk she hooked up with. At fifteen, he ran away. He traveled through the back woods and small towns of Texas and Louisiana, lived from hand to mouth, avoided the police at all costs, and hoped against hope his mother did not care enough to report him missing. For two years he ran. He worked wherever he could and did whatever he had to to put food in his belly and clothes on his back.

Across the aisle, Shaunna closed her book, gathered the others together, stuffed them into a book sack and regarded him with a smile.

"Thanks for being so quiet."

"You're very welcome. Wish I could help you, though."

She shook her head. "Like I said, the work isn't difficult, just a lot more than I bargained for. You'd think by the time I reached the twelfth grade, I'd know all I need to know."

He laughed. "I doubt we ever know all we need to know. What time do you get off?" Her tired sigh concerned him.

"Not until ten or later. I close tonight."

"Should you work so late on a school night?"

"Normally I don't, but Julie asked me to switch with her this evening. It's her little brother's birthday."

"So that's the new girl's name...Julie?"

She nodded and rose from her side of the booth. "Pretty, isn't she?"

He chuckled. "Not as pretty as you. Mind if I hang around and walk you home?" Her smile touched him like no other had before.

She hesitated, nibbling at her delectable bottom lip. Then she smiled. "No...I don't mind." She walked away then, and started tending to the customers as they poured in.

Joe ordered a plate of supper and stayed as long as he could stand the crowd. He left then, but not before he promised Shaunna he'd be back at ten to walk her home. Settled in his hotel room, he turned on the television, but couldn't concentrate. His thoughts rambled along the path they'd taken when he sat with Shaunna at the café.

At fifteen he ran away from home. At seventeen, he obtained his first real job in the oilfield. He started out as a roustabout and worked his way up in the industry as far as he could. His reputation as a reliable, hard worker kept him employed, clothed, and fed. Determined to make something of himself, he took correspondence courses to get a high school diploma and was considering college courses when the oilfield took a nosedive. A strong sense of self-preservation and determination aided him in learning to drive a truck when he was not able to find other work.

He'd avoided three things while on the run in his early teens—booze, drugs, and women. As he matured, his dislike for drugs remained strong, but his opinion of booze and women changed. Whiskey and women just seemed to go together. He kept a tight rein on his taste for whiskey, but never lacked for female company. Though he showed them little respect, they always went out of their way to fall at his feet.

Except Shaunna.

Her innocence, combined with a maturity most women twice her age lacked, attracted him like a fly to honey. Normally, he had little regard for women. He did not hate them. In fact, he loved them, every one of them. Still, the way they threw themselves at him disgusted him and reaffirmed his opinion that women were put on earth for the sole purpose of satisfying men. But Shaunna...she was different. When he watched her work and saw her put those soldiers in their place when necessary, he felt more than desire or plain interest in her. He felt respect. Respect and tenderness. He'd never associated either of those feelings with a woman before, but they filled his heart whenever he thought about her and Joe found himself falling in love for the first time.

He arrived at the café before ten o'clock and welcomed the cup of coffee she placed on the table before him. When she was ready, he walked her home and said goodnight with a kiss on her cheek and a promise to see her the next morning before he left town.

* * *

Shaunna paced the floor of the emergency room, waited for some word on her mother's condition, and hoped for a word from Joe.

The winter chill seeped in through the cracks and crevices of their apartment and Margaret had developed a cold. Despite the medication she took, the cold continued to progress and now bordered on pneumonia. Shaunna ignored her mother's protests and called an ambulance, then directed them to the hospital instead of the charity clinic. Now all she could do was wait.

After their arrival, she called Mr. Frederick to let him know what happened in case she could not make it in to work the next day. He told her Joe had called earlier to say he was on his way to Columbus. She wrapped her arms around herself, closed her eyes, and wondered if wishing would make him magically appear.

Over the past couple of months, their relationship had developed steadily. He spent as much time as possible with her when he was in town, and Shaunna found the emerald eyes which had graced her dreams were a lot less vivid and usually replaced by ice-blue ones.

She'd heard from Todd only a handful of times since the first postcard right after his arrival at Fort Lewis and his subsequent call through Mike. She wrote to him a couple of times, but they seemed to have less and less to say to each other as each became immersed into their separate lives. News that the war would end, and the condition of the soldiers as they returned, kept him alive in her dreams—usually bad ones. When she awoke, she always sent a prayer for God to keep him safe wherever he was.

She heard footsteps behind her and turned, right into Joe's open arms.

"How is she?"

Shaunna shrugged. A soft sob escaped her. "I don't know."

"From the looks of it, you're not doing so hot yourself."

Concern edged his voice. He pulled her into his arms and pressed her face into his chest.

Shaunna sighed in relief as his strong arms wrapped around her in a protective gesture. She slid her arms around his waist, rested her head against his chest, and gained strength from his solid embrace.

"I'm just worried," she mumbled into his shirt.

"Yeah, sure." He pushed her gently away from him and gazed into her eyes. A frown tugged at his mouth.

Shaunna suppressed a moan. She must be quite a sight with pale cheeks and dark circles under her eyes.

Joe confirmed her thoughts with a groan. "Worried, tired, emotionally and physically drained." He brushed the hair off of her face. "Shaunna, baby, you're going to have to slow down. Quit work, or at least work fewer hours than you do now. Otherwise, you're going to push yourself into an early grave."

"I can't slow down. I can't afford to, especially now." Even *she* could hear how tired she sounded.

"Let me help you," he urged.

Shaunna closed her eyes, buried her face in his chest once more, and silently begged him to shut up. Now was neither the time nor the place for such a discussion and she definitely didn't want a lecture.

As she and Joe grew closer, and he learned more about them and their situation, he had offered to help out in any way possible. Unwilling to take advantage of their budding relationship, Shaunna always refused his offer. Now, she was not sure how much longer she would be able to do so, and it bothered her. Her independence made her feel secure and self-confident. She relished those things. Even though social security would pay some of the bills, this little trip to the hospital would almost certainly demolish her savings. All of her hard work was going down the tubes. *I. V. tubes.* Besides, as hard as it was to admit, Joe was right. She was tired.

She shrugged mentally. It didn't matter. Nothing mattered, except her mother. She would gladly work the next fifty years to pay off the medical bills as long as her mother was OK.

The doctor arrived and informed them that with constant antibiotics and hourly treatments, Margaret would pull through, though he was worried about her heart. The pneumonia and labored breathing had not helped the disease which causes the heart to weaken, but it seemed Margaret had enough strength of will to compensate for her weak heart. She would be in the hospital for at least three days so he could keep a close watch on her condition and administer the vitally important medication. He promised to keep Shaunna informed if there was any change.

The next few days were hectic. Between school, work, and the hospital, Shaunna stretched herself to the limit. At night she fell into an exhausted slumber only to be robbed of the sleep she so desperately needed by nightmares.

At the insistence of Mr. Frederick, her mother, her mother's doctor, Mike, and Joe, she took some time off from work.

Joe appointed himself as her guardian and took a week off also. He took her home from the hospital and threatened her with unbearable consequences if she dared to disobey everyone's strict orders to rest.

Exhaustion battled with stubbornness and won. She pleaded, and he allowed her to take a long, hot bath, after which she climbed into bed and fell into a deep sleep.

Joe reveled in the pleasure and opportunity to sit and watch her sleep long and hard. He'd learned so much about Shaunna and her mother in the last few months. He'd learned of Margaret's plight and struggle to raise Shaunna alone and understood, even envied the relationship she and her mother shared. Though Shaunna's refusal of help upset him, he understood her desire for independence. How much longer could she retain her hard-earned independence? And how much longer could Margaret hang on to her health for her daughter's sake?

When Shaunna awoke, he made her stay in bed while he prepared a tray of food and promised to let her get up when the tray was empty. Youth, health, and rest had her back to normal, but she heeded his concerns and did only minor house cleaning to prepare for her mother's release from the hospital.

Chapter Five

Shaunna heaved a huge exhale and stretched out on her lounge chair. The week of paid vacation Buddy offered after one year of service was a great gift and she opted to take that week between the end of school and graduation. She caught up on all of the housework and laundry early so she could rest and relax the remainder of her time off. After graduation, she would be ready to start back to work refreshed and with renewed vision and purpose. A thrill of accomplishment raced through her as she thought about the upcoming ceremony when she would finish school with honors despite the rough year past.

A smile played along her lips as she recalled the last few months.

With her mother still weak from her bout with pneumonia, Christmas had been a bit subdued. Still, Shaunna managed to buy her a thick, fluffy robe and slippers despite the hole in her savings from the medical bills. Joe was not in town, but he called her, as promised. In fact, he'd called her almost every day since she agreed to let him have a telephone installed in their apartment.

The early months of the New Year proved to be fruitful. School became easier and with time her mother's condition improved somewhat. She had Mrs. Frederick to thank for that.

Millicent, or "Millie" as she preferred to be called, turned out to be as much of a lifesaver as her husband. They had grown close since Shaunna started her job at the café and when the older woman offered to sit with Margaret while she was at school and work, Shaunna accepted. The only thing which bothered her about the situation was that Millie would not accept any monetary compensation for her efforts.

The lesson she taught was that a little bit of charity never hurt anyone, and this kind of help was exactly what friends were for. Shaunna learned to be a little less independent and a little more open to the help others offered and she realized they offered the help out of love and not pity. Millie also took it upon herself to do some of the housework for Shaunna while Margaret rested. Shaunna repaid this overture by keeping a four-point grade average as requested by the sweet lady.

The three women became very close friends over the months and Shaunna found it nice to be able to relax and rest more when she was home. The free time also enabled her to spend more quality time with Joe when he was around.

Her mind raced in another direction as she thought about the way their friendship developed over the past few months. The walks, the movies, dinner at her house, and the talks they shared. The most memorable evening was the night of Joe's twenty-seventh birthday....

He knew and agreed her mother should not be left alone yet, so he brought over a bottle of champagne to go with the cake she baked. With her mother as chaperone, they reveled in each other's laughter, which, with the aid of tiny bubbles, often turned to giggles on her part.

Shaunna had splurged and bought him a hatpin for the cowboy hat he wore when not in his truck. Though inexpensive, the gift cost her much more than she could afford but she threw prudence to the winds and purchased it anyway. A blush covered her cheeks when she handed him the tiny package. "It's not much, but I want you to know that nothing in the world can compare to the value I put on your friendship."

He gazed at her for a long moment before he opened the gift with shaking hands. She heard his sharp intake of breath when he pulled the shiny gold object in the shape of the state of Georgia from the box. A tiny diamond chip marked the location of the city. He stared down at it for a long time and she, ashamed she was unable to get him something nicer and shy about giving him a gift in the first place, misread his scrutiny as disappointment. Then he smiled and the unmistakable light of love in his eyes made her heart soar.

"It's beautiful." He cupped her face in his hands. "But you shouldn't have. Just having you celebrate with me is more than gift enough."

The huskiness of his voice sent shivers down her spine. He placed his lips on hers in a tender gesture. A moan escaped her when the kiss deepened and she felt him shudder. His lips clung and molded her mouth to fit his. She trembled in response when his hands traveled lightly down her back and urged her closer to his hard body.

An indiscreet cough from Margaret brought them back to

their senses. He ended the kiss and buried her face in his chest.

"Happy birthday." Her thick, shaky voice came out in a mumble.

He responded with a throaty chuckle as she quivered in his arms.

"It sure is, darling, it sure is," he replied, his voice just as thick.

The chatter of mockingbirds brought Shaunna's mind back to the present. A cool breeze ruffled the hair off her shoulders. A rush of warmth enveloped her when she thought about the emotions Joe's kisses evoked. Tightness began in her lower belly and pulled at her very core, and she wondered what it would be like to have him hold her when she felt like this.

A gust of wind rustled through the trees and slapped her senses back into reality. Embarrassed at her thoughts, she rose from the lounge chair, went inside, and took a shower. Though innocent, she was neither stupid nor naive. She knew those feelings were desire, pure and primitive. Every time she thought about Joe they intensified and left her a pulsing mass of sensations. What would it be like to make love with him? The tepid water eased her fevered mind and body and helped put her feelings in perspective and she scolded herself mentally.

Sure, she cared about Joe. She cared a lot, but did she love him? She felt desire for him, but was that love? Were love and desire one and the same? Regardless, she knew the result of giving in to those feelings and there was no way she would subject herself to what her mother went through as a young girl, no matter how much she cared.

* * *

Joe sat in Matlock's terminal office and waited for the office manager to finish the paperwork he'd requested. Although he'd missed Shaunna's seventeenth birthday, he determined not to miss graduation night. The office door opened, and he turned.

"Well, Joe, looks like you get your wish. Here's the paperwork to prove it. Man, I never thought I'd see you, of all people, so totally smitten with one woman. If you can call her that," he amended with a chuckle. "More like robbing the cradle."

Joe reached for the papers, grinned. "Makes two of us,

Bob."

"Well, she's sure got you hooked."

Joe hesitated, reveled a moment in the depth of his feelings for Shaunna. "I gotta tell you; this girl has more maturity in her little finger than most women twice her age. I mean, the way she handles the curves fate throws at her is amazing."

Bob arched a brow at him. "Really?"

"Yeah. You know I told you about the rough time she and her mom have had. Well, Shaunna just rolls with the punches, picks up where she left off and keeps on planning and dreaming. She is one determined little lady. Even though she can't attend college in the fall as hoped, she's already looking forward and saving for it sometime in the near future."

Unless I can sell her on another idea for her future.

Joe kept that thought to himself. He and Bob shared a few more pleasantries then he left the office and headed to Georgia. He arrived with moments to spare and accompanied Shaunna and Margaret as well as Mike Ferel and the Fredericks to the graduation ceremony. When it was over and they returned to the apartment, he asked Shaunna out to dinner.

"I don't know," Shaunna hesitated. "Mom?"

"Go," Margaret insisted, "I'll be fine. I'm just going to rest anyway. There's no sense in you two being stuck here."

"No one feels stuck, Mom. I don't want to leave you."

"That's right," Joe agreed.

"Nonsense. You deserve a night out, honey. I won't have it any other way."

"Will you at least let me call someone to sit with you?"

Margaret heaved a tired sigh and agreed. Shaunna called Millie who came without hesitation. Joe told her where they would be, and she promised to call should anything occur.

While they waited for their food, Joe presented her with two gifts. "One for your birthday and one for graduation."

The first, a beautiful birthday card, contained a piece of paper which stated a transfer he'd requested was under consideration. He watched her expression sober then brighten when she realized he would be transferred *to* Columbus, which meant he would be here more than gone.

"This is wonderful!" She placed the paper and card back into the envelope with great care. "When will you know for sure?"

"A couple of weeks, I guess. Open the other one." He pointed to the box on the table.

Shaunna opened the package to reveal a tiny gold band engraved with her school insignia and the year and set with a garnet. Tears sparkled in her eyes, and she leaned in to kiss his cheek.

"This is the most beautiful graduation ring I could have imagined. Thank you."

Joe took the ring and slid it onto her finger. At the same moment, he presented her with another gift.

Speechless, all Shaunna could do was look at the box in his hand. She had never received so many wonderful things in one night and was almost afraid to open another one.

Joe placed his hand over hers. "Before you open it, I want you to know how much I love you."

His words sent a horde of butterflies straight to her stomach and she knew deep in her heart what the box contained. With trembling hands, she removed the ribbon and lifted the lid. A tiny, heart-shaped diamond sparkled up at her from its velvet nest. A sob stuck in her throat when she met Joe's brilliant gaze.

"I love you, Sweetness. Marry me and let me take care of you and your mother for the rest of my life."

The sob escaped, tears followed. Unable to speak, all she could do was nod her head and cry.

With a throaty chuckle, Joe pulled her into his arms. "Is that a yes?"

She trembled, unable to contain her emotion. Burying her head in his chest, she managed a muffled reply through the huge lump in her throat. "Yes."

Before either could say more, a waiter appeared at the table. Shaunna had an emergency phone call. She rushed to the phone where Millie informed her that her mother had suffered a severe heart attack and was enroute to the hospital.

"Buddy and I will meet you there," Millie promised.

She slammed the phone down, wringing her hands, and begged Joe to hurry and pay their tab. The emergency room was a blur of activity when Shaunna rushed in with Joe right behind her. The Fredericks and Margaret's doctor met them as they burst through the doors.

"Where is she?" she demanded. Dr. Turner stemmed the

flow of questions before she could utter them. He took her by the arm, led the two of them into a private office and urged Shaunna onto a chair.

"Shaunna." The doctor's voice was haggard, sending a shiver of fear up her spine. He cleared his throat. "She's very weak. I want you to be prepared. Shaunna, honey, there is nothing we can do for her anymore. Do you understand?"

The world tilted. The magic of the evening slipped into the horror of a nightmare. The only thing real about the whole situation was Joe's strong arm supporting her.

"How long?" She swallowed the lump of tears in her throat. He shrugged and shook his head, but she saw the truth and the sadness in his eyes. Shaunna bit her lip, squared her shoulders and swallowed hard. "I want to see her," she demanded, and rose.

Dr. Turner led them into the room where her mother lay. Shaunna closed her mind to the ghastly scene before her. Her mother was pale, so *pale*, with machines hooked up to her everywhere. She fought back a momentary surge of panic, blinked back tears, and took her mother's hand. *It was so cold!*

"Mama." She whispered into the soft whirr and whine of machinery. "Mama, I'm here."

A smile crossed Margaret's face before she opened her eyes. "Shaunna." She raised her hand to stroke Shaunna's cheek. "I'm so sorry, baby," she whispered.

Shaunna shook her head, blinked hard to staunch her tears. "There's nothing for you to be sorry for," she choked. "You rest now."

"I love you," Margaret rasped. "And I'm so proud of you." The effort to speak brought on a fit of coughing.

Shaunna held her mother upright while she coughed then laid her back down with a sad little smile and squeezed her hand.

"I love you too, Mama." Her whispered words were raspy with unshed tears. "I'll always love you." She began to cry in earnest. "Mama, please don't die. Joe asked me to marry him. He wants to take care of us. We have a wedding to plan. I need you, Mama." Sobs tore through her, shook her shoulders. "Mama...please..."

Margaret took a deep, harsh breath. "Joe?" She reached a weak hand toward him. When he took it in his, she met his gaze.

"Take care of my baby."

Tears shone in his eyes. He swallowed hard and laid his other hand atop the one he held. "I will."

Shaunna pressed her mother's hand to her cheek, brushed back her hair. Margaret smiled and closed her eyes. She whispered Shaunna's father's name with her last, frayed breath. The heart monitor's beep, beep, slowed then lapsed into one continuous sound and Shaunna realized the last word her mother spoke was her father's name. "No! Mama, no! Oh, God! Please, no!" She wailed, and then screamed the word again. "Turn it off!" she cried and covered her ears. "Someone please turn it off."

When the machine grew silent, she pulled her mother into her arms, buried her face against her neck and rocked. Wretched sobs tore out of her body in painful torrents. *Dead!* Her beautiful, brave mother was dead, and her heart recoiled at the anguish. The initial searing pain turned into a dull, horrid ache and her sobs subsided. The nurse tried to move Margaret out of her arms.

"You need to let go now."

She shook her head, clung to her mother's lifeless form, and sobbed. "No, please."

The nurse turned to Joe. "You've got to get her out of here."

The muscles in his throat convulsed. Joe nodded and swallowed the thick clump of tears clogging his airways then put his hands on Shaunna's arms. "Come on, honey."

She turned pain-filled, tear-drenched eyes to him, and clutched her mother tighter against her breast. "I can't leave her."

Joe pried Margaret from her grasp and laid her back against the pillows. "I know it's hard." He grabbed her hands before she could take hold of her mother again. Oh, how he wished he could bear the pain for her! "But there's nothing we can do now."

She gazed up at him and the devastation in her eyes tore at his heart.

"Please, Joe, don't make me leave her here. I want to take her home. She needs to come home."

"You have to leave her," he insisted, and pulled her into his arms. "Let's go, Sweetness, I'll take care of you now." He picked her up off the bed and carried her from the room.

Shaunna buried her face into his neck and sobbed but let him take her from the room.

The Fredericks followed them home, where Joe called Mike Ferel. Mike came at once, but not even he could console Shaunna. She sat with her arms wrapped around her waist, rocking while muffled sobs shook her slender frame and a steady stream of tears poured from her eyes.

Chapter Six

In the days which followed, Mike watched helplessly as Shaunna walked around in a haze. He helped Joe make funeral arrangements with the money from social security, along with the rest of Shaunna's savings and their own contributions.

People came and went but someone stayed by Shaunna's side every moment after Margaret's death. Soldiers whom she knew by name only made Mike proud when they offered to be pallbearers. Shaunna accepted, grateful her mother would be buried with some dignity. The service was simple and beautiful, but when one of the soldiers pulled out his trumpet and began to play Amazing Grace, Shaunna's composure ripped to shreds. She turned in Joe's arms and buried her face in his chest. Her entire body shook from the force of her sobs. He wrapped his arms around her in a protective gesture.

The Fredericks clung together, but Mike stood alone. He'd loved Margaret Chatman and even though she never gave him reason to, he believed she loved him also. When the service was over he took Shaunna's hands in his and gazed into her pained, haunted eyes.

"This may not be much consolation right now, but I loved your mother."

"I know," she choked.

Mike smiled and brushed his knuckles across her cheek. "No, honey, I loved her. I asked her to marry me, several times."

Shaunna's eyes widened in surprised shock. "She turned you down? Why? You're a wonderful man."

Mike shrugged. "She didn't think she could be a proper wife, whatever that meant. I tried to make her understand her illness didn't matter to me. I loved her and wanted to take care of her...and you." He tried not to sound bitter. "But you know how stubborn she was, always concerned about someone else."

Shaunna nodded. "That's mama, selfless to a fault." Another wretched cry tore from her throat. "Oh, Uncle Mike!" She threw herself into his arms and soaked his shirt with tears.

Mike held her tight and consoled her with tender words until the tears subsided. "Promise me, if you need anything,

anything at all, you won't hesitate to call. I love you, Shaunna."

"I love you too." She tightened her arms around him. "I promise."

With one last hug, they vacated the graveyard, and each left a huge part of their lives behind.

* * *

Shaunna dragged herself out of bed, brushed the hair off of her face, and went to answer the insistent knock at the door. Two weeks had passed since her mother's funeral—two horrible, lonely weeks of empty days and agonizing nights. Though he'd fought hard not to, Joe had to leave almost a week ago to make a cross-country run. He called her nightly but that only served to enhance the emptiness of her life. She had not gone back to work. Both Mike and the Fredericks checked on her every day and urged her to get out of the house, to visit, or even stay with them, but she couldn't pull herself out of the pit of despair which filled her heart.

With a weary sigh she opened the door, surprised to find Sheila Jones, the social worker who'd handled their welfare case for the past several years. She heard the woman's gasp and knew she must look a fright with her dirty, unkempt hair, gray skin, and dark circles beneath her eyes. She'd lost weight and her clothes hung on her body, rumpled and untidy.

"How are you, dear?" Sheila's tone was gentle. Kindness softened her gaze.

Then she stepped into the house. Eyes widening, she whirled around, taking in the place. Horror froze her expression and anger chilled her eyes.

For the first time, Shaunna noticed the condition of her home. There were rules about cleanliness in their government-subsidized apartment. Regular inspections had been a part of her life as long as she could remember. A flush of embarrassment heated her cheeks.

"Uh, Miss. Jones," she stammered and picked clothes up off the couch so they could sit. "I'm sorry the house is in such a mess," she apologized in a ragged little voice. Her lips trembled, eyes filled with tears. "I just haven't felt like doing anything."

Compassion once again filled the other woman's eyes.

"It's OK." Sheila patted her hand for reassurance. After a moment's hesitation, she took a deep breath and spoke.

"Shaunna, honey, there's something I have to discuss with you. There's a woman with a set of twins in terrible need of a home. She's escaped from a very abusive relationship and she and her two little boys are at the women's shelter."

Shaunna stared at her. Why did she need to hear this tale? Wasn't she sad enough already?

"Well, Honey, since it's just you now and this is a two-bedroom apartment..." The caseworker's words trailed off.

Shaunna gasped and shook her head as the meaning of Miss. Jones' visit reverberated in the air. She felt the blood drain from her face. Her stomach churned. She reached for Sheila's hand, clutched it with what little strength she could muster. Sheila patted her hand but instead of being comforted by her touch, Shaunna's skin crawled. She jerked away when Sheila pressed a piece of paper into her hands and tried to reassure her.

"Now, don't worry. I've talked to a real nice couple, people who have helped many children like you, and they're willing, anxious even, to take you in and be your foster parents."

Anger leapt within her heart, drove her to her feet. Shaunna threw down the paper and faced the woman on her couch.

"Get out." She gritted the words through clenched teeth. "This is my house, where I grew up. And now, just like that—" She snapped her fingers for emphasis. "You're going to kick me out and put me with foster parents? I don't think so. I don't need foster parents, thank you very much. Good day, Ms. Jones." She walked to the door and held it open.

Sheila grabbed her by the arm, forcing Shaunna to look at her. "Listen, Shaunna, I really hate to be the one to do this, but I have no choice. This is a government home, and you are only one person in a two-bedroom apartment. We are hereby serving you notice. This is a court order." She pressed another piece of paper into Shaunna's hand. "You have to be out in sixty days."

"I won't," Shaunna bit out. She forced herself not to tear the paper in half and throw it in Sheila's face.

"You will. You have to." Sheila's voice softened. "Call the people, Shaunna. At least meet them. Give them a chance."

With as much dignity as she could muster, Shaunna lifted

her chin and jerked her head toward the open door.

Sheila sighed. "I'm truly sorry it has to be this way. If I can be of any help, please don't hesitate to call me."

Shaunna swallowed hard but refrained from comment as the caseworker walked out. She slammed the door on the woman's departing figure then turned to look around at what had been home her entire life.

This is unreal! It can't be happening! First Mama and now my home?

With a sob, she crumbled to the floor. "Oh, God, why?"

They'd never been overly religious. Her mother was shunned as a young girl by her family, friends and church. Yet Margaret had instilled in Shaunna a deep belief in God. She taught her to pray when she was a little girl and urged her to continue to do so as she got older. Now she questioned God. She wanted to know why. Why did He take her mother from her? Why would He allow her home be taken from her now?

She pulled herself to her knees and began to rock to and fro while she blubbered her fears. Clasping her hands to her breast, she began to pray, really pray, for the first time in her life. "Oh, God, help me. Forgive me of the sins I've committed against You. Comfort me now, but, most of all, Lord, help me."

As she knelt, a sense of peace enveloped her, as though a giant hand stroked her hair in the same soothing gesture her mother always had. God's presence surrounded her, and she heard His whispered words of comfort. Faith sprang to life in her heart.

Shaunna opened her eyes. Her mother's Bible lay on the table beside the couch where it had rested for years. She reached for it and dropped it. The Bible opened as it hit the floor. She picked it up and Psalm Twenty-three caught her eye.

Yea, though I walk through the valley of the shadow of death, I will fear no evil; for Thou art with me; thy rod and thy staff, they comfort me... Surely goodness and mercy shall follow me all the days of my life: and I will dwell in the house of the Lord forever.

"That's where Mama is now," her heart whispered.

For the first time in two weeks, Shaunna smiled, even as tears streamed down her cheeks. Tears of relief, peace, and joy cleansed her troubled soul.

"Thank you, Lord," she said aloud. "But what am I going to do now?"

She sat quietly with her eyes closed and held the Bible. Faith grew in her soul, a flame of hope ignited in her heart. A thought wormed its way into her mind and grew until she knew exactly what she would do. She would survive. By the grace of God, she would fight the system and she would win.

Rising to her feet, she gently eased the Bible back into place. Something shiny beckoned from the table and she recognized the Sacred Heart medal her mother had often worn. A frown creased her forehead. The medal had been missing for quite a while. Her mother had looked for it and prayed about it for months before she died. Shaunna picked up the necklace, gasping when it seemed to grow warm in her palm and vibrate in her hand. She smiled again, convinced her mother's medal was a gift, a sign that the Lord had heard her plea.

Strength soared through her as she slipped the treasure around her neck. By the time Joe called that evening she had scrubbed the entire apartment, done all of the laundry, showered, dressed, eaten, and read several more scriptures from the Book of Psalms.

She sat at the table and surveyed her list of things to do the next day. When the phone rang, she picked up the receiver with a smile. "Hello, Joe."

"Hi, doll. How'd you know it was me?"

She chuckled at the surprise in his voice. "Well, since you make it a habit to call at exactly nine o'clock each night and it's that time now, I felt safe to assume you were on the line."

His low chuckle lightened her heart.

"You sound good. Feeling better?"

"Well, if you consider the events of the past few weeks and the fact I received an eviction notice this morning, hand-delivered mind you...yeah, I'm feeling much better."

"What?" Concern tightened his voice.

"I'll explain when you get home. When will that be, anyway?"

"Soon, I hope."

His tension could be felt over the line.

"I knew I should have told them to shove it when they wanted me to take this stupid run." The love and concern in his voice lifted her heart another notch.

"It's OK," she assured. "I'm going to check on my job tomorrow. If you can't catch me here, try the café."

Shaunna hung up the phone with a glow around her heart. She was not alone. She had Joe and her friends...and she had God. How truly blessed she was! She bowed her head to thank Him.

Later she crawled into bed while clinging to her Bible and, for the first time in two weeks, she slept peacefully, and with a sense of purpose for her life.

* * *

Shaunna awoke with a tiny flame of hope flickering in her heart. Before she arose, she prayed and read from her Bible. Afterwards she bathed, dressed, and ate a light breakfast. Then she left with a list of things to do imprinted in her mind.

Her first priority was to see Buddy about getting back to work. He welcomed her with open arms and assured her the job waited. They worked out a new schedule which included a small raise. She would return the next day. She requested some boxes and promised to pick them up a little later in the day.

The second item on her list proved to be a little more difficult. She arranged to meet with Sheila Jones to find out what, if any, options were available to her. Sheila ushered her into the office and waved her into a chair with a smile.

"Well, you certainly look much better today—more like the healthy, robust girl I've watched grow into a lovely young woman, instead of someone on the verge of a nervous breakdown."

Shaunna flushed. "Ms. Jones, I'd like to apologize for my behavior yesterday. I..." Her words trailed off when Sheila held up her hand.

"There's no need. I know the past couple of weeks have been difficult for you."

"Thank you," Shaunna breathed.

"Now, what can I do for you?"

"I want to know what I can do to stay in my house."

Sheila shook her head. "I'm afraid there's not a thing you can do, dear. You are one person in a two-bedroom apartment."

"Are there any one bedroom apartments available?"

Again, Sheila shook her head. "Not at the moment. Did you call the number I gave you yesterday, talk with the people?"

"No, ma'am. I wanted to see if there were any other options first."

Shaunna tried not to fidget when Sheila drummed her fingers on the desk as though in deep thought. A breath she hadn't realized she held escaped when Sheila smiled, and a hint of excitement lit her eyes.

"When the judge issued the eviction notice, he took into consideration the fact that you are seventeen and how you've worked to support your mother these past years. That's a good sign. I believe if you petitioned the court for emancipation, he would grant it."

"What's emancipation?"

"That's where you are declared an adult despite your age. If granted, the court would have no say in where you live or what you do, unless you get into trouble with the law or something."

"You really think I have a chance?"

Sheila shrugged. "I won't make any promises, but it's worth a shot." She picked up the telephone and made an appointment for Shaunna with an attorney in the Legal Aide department.

Mr. Humphrey gave her his undivided attention when she explained her circumstances. He agreed at her age, and considering what her life had been like, she was too old to live in a foster home, even for one year. He then advised her to find an apartment since there was no way she could avoid moving and to get back to work. Her chances of getting what she wanted were greater if she could show a judge that she could support herself.

Shaunna left his office a bit discouraged, but optimistic. She approached a small church and stopped in hopes the peace and quiet would help her gather her thoughts and renew her strength. The pastor of the church listened to her story, offered up a prayer for guidance and strength, then left her alone. As she sat in a pew, the tranquil atmosphere seeped into her soul and soothed her worrisome thoughts. Faith and hope stirred in her heart. Everything would be all right. All she had to do was to have faith and believe.

Back at the Feed Trough, she picked up a newspaper,

poured herself a glass of tea and sat down to do some figuring. With estimates of what her income would be, not counting tips, she picked up the want ads and began to search for an apartment. She was still hard at it when Buddy passed by and saw the frown on her face.

"What's the matter, honey?" Concern laced his gruff voice.

Shaunna sighed and rubbed her weary eyes. "I need an apartment, but everything's so expensive. The Housing Authority needs my two bedrooms. Since I'm only seventeen and they have no one-bedroom apartments available, they're going to put me in a foster home unless a judge grants me emancipation. At the rate this is going, that's highly unlikely." Despite her best efforts, a hint of desperation colored her tone. "I'm too old and have been through too much to have to move in with strangers!"

"No luck?"

She frowned. "No. Everything is either too far from here or too expensive. Even with the raise you gave me, I'll hardly be able to afford rent and utilities—never mind eating."

"You could always eat leftovers from here." Buddy chortled at the frown she bestowed upon him.

He turned to walk away, hesitated, and then twirled back to face her. "I know what!" Excitement edged his voice. "We've got an apartment over our garage. Millie and I have never thought about renting it before. I always figured it'd be my escape whenever I was in the doghouse."

She rolled her eyes and grinned. "Like you're ever in the doghouse."

He chuckled. "Nah, just seemed too inconvenient, you know, to have strangers live so close. But you're not a stranger. I'm sure—no, I'm positive Millie won't mind if you live there...unless you want to live with us?" He rattled on, enthusiasm enriching his tone. "That's where you belong anyway, with friends. It's not furnished but I'm sure we could work out something."

Shaunna perked up. "I'm not worried about furniture. I have furniture."

Now it was Buddy's turn to frown. "That may be another problem. Although we have a huge garage, the apartment is small. There may not be enough room for all of your stuff. But maybe..." He thought another minute, tapped a finger against his chin. "We've needed to clean out the garage for some time now. In fact, Millie's been after me to do it for ages. Maybe we could find room to store what you can't use."

Shaunna shrugged. "What I don't need I'll get rid of. Don't worry, I'll manage." A ring of confidence strengthened her voice for the first time since she'd shared her situation with her boss.

He hung the 'Be Right Back' sign and locked up the café so they could go look.

Millie welcomed Shaunna with open arms. She listened to her dilemma and Buddy's plan and became just as enthusiastic as her husband. At first she insisted Shaunna live with them, but Shaunna liked the idea of the apartment. Excitement coiled in the pit of her stomach as she took the stairs to the living quarters above the garage. Though tiny, the apartment contained a kitchenette/living room, a bedroom and a small, but full bathroom. In the bathroom there was a hook-up for a washing machine, but none for a dryer. Buddy offered three solutions to the problem. She could get a set of apartment-sized stackable units, use their dryer or the clothesline. The more they talked, the more excited everyone became.

"How much?" Shaunna asked, anxious to get the details ironed out and start the move.

"Honey, we can't charge you rent," Millie protested. "We're just glad to be able to help you."

Buddy nodded his approval.

"But I can't let you do that," Shaunna argued. She had to make them understand her predicament. "As much as I appreciate your intentions, I have to rent it. I have to prove to a judge I can support myself. You not charging me rent will only prove I'm dependent on you."

"How much did you plan to spend on rent?" Buddy asked.

She remembered how slim her allowance would be and grimaced. "Well, I'd like to work my budget around my salary only. That way I can use my tips for unexpected expenses and hopefully be able to put some up for the future."

"Smart plan," Buddy said. "But I think the utilities may be tied into the house. If I'm right, it'll sure make things a lot easier on you." A walk around the garage confirmed his theory. "Puts a whole new light on the subject now doesn't it? How much do you think we should charge her for rent and utilities, Millie?"

Millie paused as though she gave the idea serious consideration. The amount she suggested bordered on insult.

"That's a rip-off," Shaunna snorted, and then bit her tongue. These people were her friends. They were only trying to help, even if it meant cheating themselves and patronizing her. "Look, I know you two want to help and I love and appreciate you for it. I really do. But that's just not fair to you." Her counteroffer was much higher.

"Don't be ridiculous or stubborn!" Buddy proved much less effective in biting back temper than she. "You're stretching your income to the limit. Besides, we're not making a penny on it now. Make me another offer."

Shaunna crossed her arms over her chest. So he wanted to haggle. A smile tugged at her lips. She hadn't had a good argument in a while. She made another offer. He shook his head. They haggled back and forth until she capitulated at what seemed like a reasonable yet fair amount. "You are one tough cookie. I'm not sure I want you as a boss *and* a landlord."

He shrugged, his expression smug. "Your choice."

"She has no choice." Millie surprised them both with the vehemence in her tone. "I won't have it any other way. And if she argues too much more, I'll just go see the judge about legal guardianship of her until she turns eighteen."

"Oh, Lord, now I've got both of you on my case." Shaunna laughed and then hugged the little woman beside her. They talked a while and ironed out the details of cleaning and moving. Buddy revised her work schedule to allow her plenty of time to do both. She returned to the café, gathered up her boxes, hurried home, and called Mr. Humphrey. The attorney was thrilled for her and encouraged by the news. He told her to keep in touch and to bring the Fredericks with her to court. He gave her a tentative date but promised to confirm with her later on.

Shaunna sank onto a kitchen chair, overwhelmed by the events of her day. She may have accomplished a great deal in two short days but there was a lot more to do before it was over. Fear swept through her. Fear of moving, fear of change, fear of being alone. With a sob she clasped the medal which hung around her neck and prayed for the strength to handle it all.

Peace enveloped her as it had yesterday. A surge of strength which far surpassed her own filled her spirit. When the phone rang at exactly nine o'clock that evening she once again answered with a smile. "Hello, Joe."

"Hi, Sweetness."

They talked for a while and each went over their day. Joe informed her he would not be home as soon as he hoped. When the company said 'cross country' they weren't kidding. He had to go to Missouri, then Ohio before he could even consider Georgia.

"So, you'll probably be all settled before I get back, and I wanted to take care of you."

Confidence rang in her voice when she informed him she could take care of herself. "But I love you anyway," she assured.

"Boy, I'm glad to hear that!" Joe chuckled before he hung up the phone.

* * *

The clock buzzed at exactly six o'clock a.m. Shaunna jumped out of bed the minute the alarm sounded. She showered, dressed, and brewed a pot of coffee. Her stomach lurched at the strong black liquid, but she needed something to do, and eating was out of the question.

Today was the big day. The Fredericks were due to arrive at her house any minute and she tried to curb her anxiety. They would meet with her attorney, then go to court at nine o'clock.

During the past two weeks, she had been too busy to think about the upcoming court date. She, Buddy, and Millie had cleaned and painted the apartment and Millie helped her make new curtains.

Each evening she sorted through seventeen years of accumulated stuff and made arrangements to either give away the things she didn't need or trade them for what she did. She gave away her bedroom suit but kept her mother's, feeling the double bed would be a lot more sensible—especially when she and Joe got married. She invested in a small trunk to house a few personal mementos of her childhood and of her mother.

Although the apartment was small, she determined to make it cozy and comfortable and was excited about the whole move. Now all she had to do was convince the judge she could manage on her own. The atmosphere brightened another degree when Mike Ferel arrived.

Shaunna walked toward him, arms outstretched, and greeted him with a hug. "Hi, Uncle Mike. Thanks for coming."

Mike nodded. "Hope I can be of some help. I'm sorry I haven't been around much, darling. It's just hard, you know."

Shaunna's eyes filled with tears at the emotion in his tone, but she blinked them back and smiled. "I understand. I'm forced to get on with my life. You should, too."

Mike smiled—a sad little smile which did not reach his eyes.

"I'm glad for you, honey. But I'm a lot older than you are. It's not as easy for me. I loved her so much." His voice broke, and he choked back a sob.

Shaunna's heart ached for him. She pulled him tighter in her embrace. "You're not old, Uncle Mike," she chided. "If I weren't already engaged I'd marry you myself."

Mike couldn't help but chuckle at her insistence. "And if I were twenty years younger, I'd definitely give old Joe a run for his money." He brushed his knuckles across her cheek. "Thanks honey, I need to know you understand and still care."

"You know I do." She reassured him with another hug. "And I want you to come over and have supper with me soon." Mike nodded then walked with her into the courtroom when her attorney signaled for them to enter.

Judge Hawthorne listened attentively when Shaunna's attorney explained why she wished for emancipation. He seemed impressed with her life story and even more impressed with all of the people, Sheila Jones included, who rallied to the belief that she could make it on her own. He expressed pride in the fact someone so young could cope with such adversity and still have the self-respect, pride, and strength Shaunna exhibited. The fact that she would live in the same yard as her boss and his wife seemed to strengthen his decision when he granted her petition to live on her own. He informed her, however, since she had lived in the welfare system for so long and was not yet eighteen, Sheila Jones would stay in contact and keep him apprised of her situation.

A thrill of triumph raced through Shaunna, and she thanked him when he rose from his seat and exited the courtroom.

Chapter Seven

Shaunna worked her thick hair into a French braid and hoped it would make her a little cooler. She leaned on the sink, stared at herself in the mirror, and took in the tension around her mouth and eyes. She closed her eyes and took several deep breaths in an effort to calm her nerves. It had been one hellacious day.

In the past three weeks her life had gone smoothly. She moved into her apartment with only one problem—she was not able to transfer the phone, which was in Joe's name, over to her new address without his signature. Joe called the telephone company in a useless effort to get them to bend the rules. Since he never stayed in one place long enough for Shaunna to get the necessary papers to him she was unable to get his signature, and as a result had no telephone. Unless he was lucky enough to catch her at the café, she rarely got to talk to him.

Unable to hear his voice nightly, she leaned heavily on the Lord for companionship and the Bible for strength and found comfort and solace in the words she read. She discovered first-hand the depth of Jesus' love and compassion. Today, however, was one of those days when she desperately needed to hear Joe's voice to soothe her frazzled nerves.

She took one more deep breath, washed her hands, and headed back to the kitchen, determinedly refusing to look around, lest another unhappy customer detain her. She heaved a sigh. The hot weather must have everyone on edge.

Buddy met her at the counter. "Shaunna, there's a customer at table seven. I need you to wait on him, please."

"I sure hope he's in a better mood than the last one."

Buddy shrugged. "Well, he did seem a bit moody, so I thought I'd better send you over instead of the new girl."

"Thanks," she muttered. "All I need today is one more irate customer."

He chuckled. "Cheer up. Only a few more hours and you're through for the day."

She rolled her eyes heavenward. "Thank God."

"No, thank Buddy. I make the schedule," he teased, and chortled at the sassy look she gave him.

The banter alleviated her tension a little and she picked up her pad and pencil then squared her shoulders. "Well, here goes nothing."

"Smile," Buddy ordered. "It'll make things a whole lot easier."

"Right." She mumbled a reply, and then walked toward the customer slumped in his chair at table seven. A baseball cap covered his head and concealed what little of his face he hadn't buried in the menu. The man's uncommunicative posture set her teeth on edge.

"May I help you?" She hoped she didn't sound as agitated as she felt.

"Humph," was the grunted reply. "I don't see what I want listed on this menu."

Shaunna inhaled a hiss and mentally counted to ten. "Tell me what you want, and I'll see if we can make it for you." She summoned the sweetest voice she could muster.

"Turtle soup," he growled.

Shaunna's stomach did somersaults at the images her mind conjured up. *Turtle soup? Ugh!* She shuddered, swallowed hard, and sent up a silent prayer for her stomach to behave. A soft sigh escaped as her mind reeled. As if this day wasn't bad enough already, now her mind played tricks on her. He sounded like Joe. *At least from what I can remember.* But Joe would never be that grouchy. Besides, all Texans sound alike, she concluded mentally.

She took a deep, calming breath, forced her thoughts into some semblance of sanity and tried again to get his order. "I'm sorry sir, but we don't serve turtle at all. Is there something else I can get for you? Our dinner special, maybe?" Her taut nerves made it hard to be polite.

"I guess I'll just have coffee," he replied with a grumpy snort. "And you." His voice softened and he lowered the menu with a grin.

Shaunna's weary brain took a moment to register what he said—and who said it. "Joe Taylor, I ought to slap you plumb out of that chair!" Instead, she grinned and threw herself into his arms for a much-needed hug.

Joe stood up with a chuckle, his arms open wide. "Man, oh, man! Had I known I'd get a welcome like this, I'd have come home a lot sooner," he teased.

He noted the trembling of her body when he gave her a tight squeeze.

"I've missed you," she breathed.

"Missed you, too, Sweetness." He lifted her hand to his lips. At the sight of the engagement ring on her finger, his heart soared. He brushed his lips over her knuckle. "I'm glad to see you're wearing this," he whispered.

"Yes." Her eyes lowered, a flush colored her cheeks. "I've been wearing it."

When he left a little over a month ago, he had no idea what Shaunna did with the ring or how she felt about marrying him. In the loneliness of his rig, he often wondered if she held him accountable since he'd taken her away from her mother on the night of Margaret's heart attack. The question tortured his heart and mind but, afraid of what the answer might be, he never voiced it aloud.

He kissed her hand again, then pulled her against his chest.

"When did you get in?" she asked.

"About an hour ago. When do you get off?"

"Not until five o'clock."

"That's almost three hours from now. Think you can leave early?" He didn't want to whine, but it had been so long... "I've got a desperate need to hold you in my arms," he whispered.

Shaunna trembled against him. He could see her need was just as strong, but she shook her head.

"I can't, not today. We've been busy beyond belief and I'm trying to train a new girl." She reached into her pocket. "Here's the key to my apartment. Why don't you go on over there and rest. I'll be home as soon as possible. We can visit then."

"How about if I stay a while? At least then I can watch you work, maybe talk some."

"Oh, I wish you could. I'd love that. But please, not today."

Joe didn't like the tired look on her face. "Been that rough?"

Shaunna nodded. "The new girl is nervous which is making her clumsy. She's getting on my nerves, big time. Customers have been complaining left and right all day." She rubbed her temples, heaved a sigh. "But she's young, I'm sure she'll be all right in a couple of days. If she stays that long."

Joe knew how difficult it was for them to keep servers. He chuckled and stroked her cheek and hoped his next words would make her smile. "And you're so old."

Instead of the smile he hoped for, she buried her face in his chest. "Today I feel old. A million years old."

He slipped his arm around her waist, pulled her close. "Well, darling, you sure look good for a million-year-old broad." His voice didn't come out quite right, but what the heck. Warmth curled through his fingertips and sent sparks of heat up his arms when he caressed her spine. Shaunna trembled then pushed herself out of his embrace. A flush colored her cheeks and brightened her eyes.

"Go away."

"Walk me out?"

She did and kissed him goodbye at the door. He hoped his return lifted her spirits and enabled her to work the rest of her shift in a much lighter frame of mind.

Joe made his way to the Fredericks house and visited with Mrs. Frederick before he headed up to Shaunna's apartment. He opened the door and stepped into the living room then noticed the tiny kitchenette to his left, painted a pale, sunny yellow. Curtains with a bright, print pattern covered its single window.

The living room, small and cozy, sported almond-colored walls, and off-white trim. A loveseat and Margaret's rocking chair were the only pieces of furniture in the room. A tiny trunk covered with a frilly cloth served as a table between them. The flowered curtains on the window matched the print of the loveseat. Across from the furniture, the sewing machine cabinet served as a stand for the television. Above that hung a set of shelves which held books, pictures, and knickknacks he recognized.

The bedroom, large in comparison to the other two rooms, and the connecting bathroom were decorated in pale green and peach and large enough to house the washer and dryer unit. He smiled to himself. The whole place was so *Shaunna* that he felt right at home.

He took a shower and cleaned up after himself then washed and dried his clothes. If he didn't, Shaunna would want to do it for him, and there was no way he would allow that this evening. Tonight, he planned to reacquaint himself with his fiancé. He turned on the television and tried to rest but the loveseat wasn't very comfortable for his large frame. Reluctant to mess up her crisply made bed, he went into the kitchen.

An idea formed in his mind, and he decided to act on it. He made a trip to the grocery store to pick up a few things—roses...candles...wine. Tonight, would be special.

He loved to cook but being on the road so much inhibited the use of his culinary skills. Tonight, would be different. Instead of taking Shaunna to a restaurant where he would have to share her with the crowd, he would cook for her, a candlelight dinner with wine and roses. The thought of the evening ahead put a song in his heart and a smile on his face.

He met Shaunna at the door when she entered the apartment, pulled her close, and kissed her. "Umm, I've wanted to do that for a long time." He covered her lips in another heated embrace. "I could eat you up right now," he whispered. He left a trail of kisses down her neck, nuzzled her slim throat, and reveled in the feel of her in his aching arms at last.

"Yeah, well I think we need to slow down." She pulled away from him.

"Why?" He voiced the husky inquiry even as he pulled her against him for another kiss.

Shaunna trembled as his mouth caressed hers, but then she pulled away and warded him off with a slight shove. "Because, Joe. I'm all hot and sweaty and grubby."

"Beautiful." He silenced her protests with his lips while he stroked her back until she relaxed in his arms.

She trembled as she surrendered to his tenderness and Joe suppressed a chuckle. *Sweetness clothed in flesh.* He took her by the hand and led her toward the bedroom. At the door of the bathroom, he turned to her. "Your bath, madam," he drawled with a graceful bow.

Shaunna smiled. She walked eagerly to the tub and ran her fingertips through the warm water. "Umm, perfect," she murmured, then reached up to unbutton her uniform.

Joe leaned against the doorframe and wondered how long it would take her to remember he was still there. *Not long.* With a blush she turned her back to him. He couldn't suppress a deep chuckle when he went to her.

"Ah, Sweetness," he whispered, and ran his hands down her shoulders to her hips. "Need me to wash your back?" He wrapped his arms around her waist and pulled her firmly against him.

Shaunna moaned softly—and blushed harder. "No," she whispered, her tone thick.

He didn't release her.

"Joe, please..." He couldn't tell if the words were a plea for him to stop or a cry to continue. He held her trembling young body in his arms and knew exactly what he wanted. With slow intensity his hand moved up from her waist, tenderly massaged its way to her chin. "Please what?" he asked and nuzzled her ear with his mouth.

She slumped weakly against him. "Don't," she whimpered, and reached up to stop his hand from its sensuous torture.

Joe fought the urge to press his advantage. With a soft hug, he placed a kiss on her cheek and left her alone. Back in the kitchen he paced the floor in an effort to stop his imagination from its wild ramblings. With supreme effort, he stayed away from the bathroom, determined to let her enjoy her bath in peace. A short time later, the bedroom door shut and he assumed she was getting dressed, so he poured them each a glass of wine. When he turned to bring the wine into the living room, Shaunna stepped out of the bedroom. He stopped in his tracks. His breath caught in an audible hiss, and his heart somersaulted.

Thick copper-colored hair fell in a silken mass of waves across her shoulders and down her back. A turquoise T-shirt enhanced the golden sheen of her silky skin. His eyes dropped to her bare feet and traveled up slim legs to her shapely hips encased in blue jean cut-offs.

Shaunna's body tightened in response to the blatant desire in Joe's eyes. A slow burn began in the very core of her being. Liquid fire raced through her veins. Heat raged between them, stealing her breath and leaving her gasping. She crossed her arms over her chest, embarrassed by her body's intimate response to the look in his eyes.

"Joe, don't look at me like that." She forced the words past her tight throat.

He heaved a deep, shaky breath, and then shook his head as though to clear his mind. "Can't help it, you're too beautiful for your own good," he muttered, and walked to where she stood. "And my peace of mind." He handed her a glass and covered her lips in a tender caress.

His kiss sent conflicting messages through her body. She trembled. "I can go change," she offered. "Put on something a little less revealing."

His grin made her think of the rogues and pirates she read about in romance novels.

"What? And spoil my chance to look at those legs?" He ran a hand up her thigh. "You have the most beautiful pair of legs I've ever seen." His hoarse whisper traveled her nerve endings, setting them afire...then he captured her mouth in a long, lingering embrace.

The kiss ended when he groaned. "Besides, it's too late to change now. I've already seen you. And don't you know I'd want you no matter what you're wearing?" He nuzzled her cheek.

Shaunna had no idea how or even if she should answer such a question. She shrugged, took a sip of wine, and refrained from comment. "You're not planning on getting me drunk and seducing me, are you?" Her voice quivered, whether from desire or fear she wasn't sure.

He grinned again. "Doesn't sound like a bad idea. Do you know how sexy you are and what you do to me?"

She shook her head and took a deep appreciative whiff of the aromas filtering in from the kitchen. "No. But I do know how hungry I am."

Her matter-of-fact reply must have brought him down to earth somewhat, because he chuckled.

"Trying to change the subject?" he teased. "Besides, I don't think I'd have to get you drunk to seduce you. I doubt it'd even be a seduction. Would it, Sweetness?" He bent to tease her ear with his mouth.

Again, she offered no reply to what seemed like an unanswerable question.

Joe chuckled at her obvious dilemma. Shaunna promptly stuck her tongue out at him and broke the spell. He tossed his head back with a laugh, took her wineglass and put both down. He took her in his arms, cupped her face in his big hands, and nibbled gently at her mouth.

"Don't worry, Sweetness. I won't seduce or force you. But

promise you'll marry me soon, 'cause I don't know how long I can keep that vow."

Shaunna's heart thrilled at his words. "I promise. But don't you think we should make plans first?"

He nodded then led her into the kitchen. "Over dinner."

Shaunna served them both. She then clasped his hands with hers and gave thanks to the Lord for his safe return and their food, then released them with a gentle squeeze. They talked over dinner and while cleaning the dishes.

Around ten o'clock Buddy knocked on the door. He offered Shaunna the next day off and became insistent when she refused. At Joe's encouragement she relented, glad she had such a considerate friend for a boss.

Buddy backed out of the door then turned to Joe. "The back door's open, Joe. Blankets and pillows are on the couch. Make yourself at home."

"Thanks Buddy, but don't go to any trouble. I can sleep in the rig."

Buddy shook his head. "No need to sleep in there when you don't have to. You just come on in." He left before Joe could offer any more arguments.

Joe grinned at Shaunna and winked. "That way they can keep an eye on me."

She blushed when he pulled her against him. He held her for a while, and then, out of respect for her and the Fredericks, he left, with a promise to see her early the next morning.

* * *

Shaunna fidgeted with the strap of her white satin gown, tied the silk bows of the matching robe and gave her hair a final once-over with the brush. She looked in the mirror, noted the fear and excitement in her eyes and the flush on her cheeks and shook her head. "This is ridiculous," she whispered. "This is what you wanted, right?"

Her reflection nodded. "It's just that, I never realized how big and strong he is."

"And you're afraid."

Again, her reflection nodded.

"Well, one thing's certain; he's going to have you

committed if he finds you talking to yourself."

She giggled and winked at the woman in the mirror. "You're right. But the dangerous thing is, you're talking back."

She shook her head, washed her hands and splashed cool water on her face, then took a deep breath and opened the bathroom door. With a glance over her shoulder, she blew her reflection a kiss. "I guess we're all a little crazy."

She walked out, unsure if she was more nervous, or just plain naïve and foolish.

* * *

Joe stripped off his suit jacket, tossed aside his tie, and wrestled out of his boots. He turned down the covers on the bed and waited for Shaunna in the living room. He'd thought this day would never end, first the wedding, then the reception. He remembered the way she looked in her white, lacy sundress dotted with pearls and his heart skipped a beat. Her thick hair curled into huge ringlets down her back. A crown of baby's breath held her tiny veil in place but didn't hinder the sun's rays which bounced off the copper highlights and turned her locks into a fiery mass.

Buddy and Millie stood up for them and Mike gave her away. The ceremony was simple and beautiful and blessedly short, but the reception seemed to drag on forever. The only hint of sadness which marred the day was Margaret's absence. They went to the cemetery and Shaunna placed her bridal bouquet on her mother's grave. She sat quietly, whispered words of joy and pain and he stood by until she took his hand with a smile.

Now, at last, they were alone. They'd decided against renting a motel or going away, but opted instead to spend their first night together in the bed they would share forever.

Anticipation crawled through him and left a slow burn in its wake. His hands shook, palms sweated. Instinct warned she would be nervous, possibly even scared, and he resolved not to rush her too much. Even if he had to wait to make love with her, at least he would sleep with her in his arms as he'd longed to do for what seemed like forever.

He sensed movement behind him—her footsteps, muffled by the thick carpet—and turned around. His breath lodged in his throat. She stood an arm's length away, a vision for his hungry eyes. Her hair streamed down her back in thick, silken waves. A white satin gown clung to youthful curves and revealed just enough silky skin to make his mouth water and his arms ache with want. His resolve slipped to a dangerous low point. He closed his eyes and committed the picture to memory, then with a deep breath opened them and consciously commanded control over his senses.

"You are so beautiful. Shaunna, love, come here." Barely able to force his thick voice past his tight throat, he opened his arms to her.

Lured by the seductive invitation in his eyes and the huskiness of his voice, Shaunna moved into his arms and trembled as fire began to melt the icy tension within her. His arms wound around her. She wrapped hers around his neck and molded her body to his.

Joe cupped his hands on her waist and stepped back, and she could tell he fought hard to control the desire raging between them. She clung to him wide-eyed, her lips tender from his kiss, and trembled violently when his hands moved across her back and over her shoulders then slid down her arms and up again to cup her face.

"Oh, look at you," he groaned, and stroked her cheeks with his thumbs. "Don't be afraid." His voice was soft, husky. His mouth captured her lips in a kiss designed to banish the fear he surely saw in her dark eyes.

"I can't help it," she mumbled when he released her lips. "I want to please you and I don't know what to do." Embarrassment colored her tone and heated her cheeks.

He kissed her tenderly, her lips, her cheeks, her eyes. "You don't have to do anything right now. There's not a whole lot different about tonight compared to the other nights since I came home."

"Nothing except you're not leaving, and we'll probably follow through on what you've instigated every night these last two weeks." Tension made her throat ache, her voice tremble.

A soft chuckle rumbled deep in his chest and escaped his smiling lips. He ran his hands over her shoulders and down her back. "We don't have to."

"Really?"

Indecision flashed in his eyes followed by disappointment. She smiled and rose up on her toes to kiss him. "Might as well. I hear the first time is always the worst anyway."

"Who says? I plan to make this a night we'll both remember," he promised in a husky voice as he swung her up in his arms and carried her into the bedroom.

Chapter Eight

"What?" Todd Jameson's hand trembled so hard the phone he held threatened to slip through his numb fingers. He wiped a sweaty palm down his thigh and grabbed the receiver then switched ears. The anguish in Mike Ferel's voice made the pleasantries they shared the first few minutes of the call seem like a distant conversation.

"I'm sorry, Todd, to be the one to tell you this, especially after what you've been through this last year."

He'd spent nine months at war, nine months facing and dealing with death, but not even those things prepared him for the death of his hopes and dreams in nine short minutes. "When?"

A heavy exhale preceded Mike's answer. "Margaret died six months ago. Shaunna married three months after."

She said she loved me. He hadn't meant to utter the thought aloud, but somehow the words slipped past the knot in his throat.

"She cried a long time after you left, didn't understand why you never wrote or called."

Though his voice held no accusation, Todd heard the chastisement in Mike's tone. "I..."

He blinked hard and cleared his throat. "What was I supposed to do, blurt out my feelings over the phone or in a letter and ask her to wait? I thought she was too young to go through that, especially with the war and all. Not knowing if, *when,* I'd get sent over there was hard enough on me; she didn't need that on her heart. What if I didn't come back? I couldn't fathom putting her through such an ordeal. Not with all the responsibilities she shouldered from her mother's illness."

"I'm sorry."

Todd raked a hand over his face. "Is she happy? Is he a good man?"

"Seems to be."

The other line in Mike's office rang.

"Look, I hate to cut you off..."

"I understand. We'll talk again soon." Todd hung up the phone and walked back to his barracks, his shoulders slumped in defeat. His head hurt with the finality of it all. The truth in his mind battled with the love in his heart and made his head reel and stomach churn. A wail of despair rose within him, and he fought back a groan. He plopped down on the bunk, buried his face against his knees and covered his ears with his arms in an attempt to quiet the voices in his head. He began to rock back and forth.

"Oh, God!" He choked on a sob. "Why?"

Why had he gone to war? Why had he not told Shaunna how he felt? Why had she married? Why, after so long, did it hurt so much?

"Fret not, and be not afraid."

The words entered his thoughts with such quiet authority he wondered if he actually heard them. Calmness seeped into his heart and mind and stilled the angry, confused voices within.

He'd experienced this sense of tranquility one other time in his life, while on night-watch in the field. Except for crickets and nocturnal creatures, the air was so quiet you could almost forget there was a war going on. He lay on his belly, cradled his gun, listened for any sound, and watched for any movement. From deep within the dark silence, Todd heard what sounded like someone weeping. He'd called out to his fellow guard, but the guy heard nothing. In those moments Todd wondered if there was a God and if it was He, crying over the hideousness and insanity of war.

Now he wondered if God spoke to him or if he was going quietly insane as he'd seen others do.

He stretched out on the bunk once more and let the memories unfold as they had numerous times over the last year.... Sixteen-year-old Shaunna working as a waitress to help support her ailing mother... Her laughing coffee-colored eyes and thick, copper-colored hair...*the sheer beauty of innocence...*

His heart thudded then clutched. Those memories had kept him alert, *had kept him alive,* while in the jungles of Vietnam. A sob escaped. Todd dragged a hand over his eyes, willed his tumultuous thoughts into some semblance of control, and realized he would have to get on with his life. He wasn't the first nor would he be the last to experience the heartache of love and loss. He had to learn from one of the biggest, dumbest mistakes in life*: Never put off saying what needed to be said.*

Never assume things won't change.

Things change, people change. Life goes on. Now he must go on, determined he would not make the same mistake again. His heart reasoned with his mind to learn his lesson and chalk it up to experience, but all the reasoning in the world couldn't banish the pain.

Only time would do that.

* * *

Mike Ferel leaned back in his chair with a sigh. The hollow sound of Todd's voice made him sick with regret that he'd had to share the news of Margaret's death and Shaunna's marriage with him so soon after the horrors he'd already encountered in his young life.

He felt an odd sense of familiarity toward Todd. Their lives were a lot alike, almost parallel to one another, except for the age difference. Maybe that's why he related to the boy so much. Both had been orphaned and left alone at a young age, and both had chosen the Army as a way out of their circumstances. Both had gone to war.

He rubbed his knee and remembered his one and only tour of Vietnam. He'd been there three days when he stepped on a land mine. Whether sheer luck or a miracle, he only lost half of his right leg. Too young to accept the fact he was disabled, he opted to remain in the Army as long as needed or allowed.

He'd come to Fort Benning and spent the last ten of his fifteen years training and preparing men and boys for war. A war, by the grace of God, he never returned to although he still had nightmares of the devastation. He still heard the cries of the wounded and dying in his dreams.

The anguish in Todd's voice brought back his own pain over losing Margaret, and he ached for the boy he'd grown so fond of in such a short time. He tried to force his mind to more pleasant thoughts. It refused, ran in circles instead, from one painful memory to another. With grim determination, he walked out of his office and went to visit Shaunna, in order to reassure himself she was fine. The ten-minute drive did little to ease the turmoil of emotions, but they lightened the moment she opened the door and greeted him with a hug.

"Hey, Uncle Mike. How are you?"

Mike shook his head, smiled. "Not bad for an old man."

Shaunna hugged him again. "How many times do I have to tell you? You're not old and if I weren't already taken, I'd marry you myself."

Mike laughed and stroked her cheek with the back of his hand. "Keep saying it and maybe one day I'll believe it."

"Would you like something to eat or drink?"

He shook his head. "Just wanted to check on you, see how you're doing."

A flush filled her cheeks. Her eyes danced.

"I'm fine. Never felt better. No morning sickness or anything."

"That's grr...wait, what did you say?"

She laughed and the sound sent peals of joy through his system.

"We found out for sure this morning. Joe is ecstatic."

"Wonderful! I've got dibs on spoiling him."

Shaunna giggled. "You'll have to take that up with Buddy and Millie."

An hour later he left. Though delightful, the visit enhanced the emptiness in his life, and he regretted not having children of his own. Angst filled him as he wondered why the two women he'd ever truly loved preferred someone else.

His mind drifted back to another time, and he remembered a girl from long ago. She had preferred someone else, and it cost her her life. Margaret had preferred the memory of Shaunna's father and had died with his name on her lips. Mike wondered how love in that degree would feel and knew he couldn't hold a grudge toward either of them any longer. He closed his eyes with a sigh and did what he should have done long ago. He prayed.

"God, I know You're there. I'm living proof of something greater than man. I can only assume it's You. I know Margaret is up there with You now, too. If it's not too much to ask, tell her I'm sorry. I loved her, but she was too afraid to love me back. Tell her I understand now. And I forgive her. And, Lord, if it's not too much to ask, will You forgive me? I know I'm not worth a plug nickel, but I surrender. I can't seem to do anything with my life. Maybe You can."

Peace enveloped his soul.

"Thank you," he whispered and vowed to encourage Todd to move on and not miss out on the precious gifts life had to offer—love, family, children.

Chapter Nine

Joe Taylor pressed the phone to his ear. "Shaunna, can you hear me?" The static in the lines made her response almost impossible to understand. The one thing he did understand was she was crying. *Again.*

"What?" He cringed at the bad connection.

"I'm sorry about the fight last night," she sobbed.

"Me, too. It's OK, Shaun, we'll talk when I get home. All right?" He thought he heard a mumbled agreement before the line went dead. With a muttered curse he slammed the receiver down and restrained himself from jerking the thing off the wall.

Dejected, he tugged insulated coveralls over his jeans and T-shirt then made his way through the blinding snow to the lounge across the street from the truck stop where he'd showered, changed, and eaten.

"Come on in!" A hearty voice from the bar invited. "What'll it be? First one's on the house," the sultry-eyed barmaid offered as he perched on a stool.

"Whiskey, straight up."

A low hum sounded in her throat. "That'll warm you for sure. Mighty cold out."

Joe snorted. "Too cold for my blood." He downed the shot she placed before him.

"Mighty glum looking there, fellow. Where's your Christmas cheer? Just a week away y'know."

Joe nodded and gestured for her to pour him another drink. "Yeah, and from the looks of it I'll be stranded here in this blasted blizzard and not get to be with my family again this year."

She tut-tutted. "So goes the life of a trucker."

Joe twirled the whiskey glass and watched the amber liquid dance along the rim. "Yeah, and if that ain't bad enough, I've already missed my wife and son's birthdays, my wedding anniversary, *and* Thanksgiving." He slammed the shot glass down on the bar. "All because of this stupid job."

The barmaid eyed him. "Careful there, guy, those don't come cheap."

"Sorry," Joe muttered.

"Would you like another or something to chase it with?"

Joe withdrew a fifty-dollar bill from his pocket and threw it on the bar. "Keep 'em coming till this runs out. Water chaser."

Bill, another trucker who worked for the same company as Joe, climbed up on the stool next to his. Joe flagged down the barmaid.

"Bring my buddy here a drink on me, please, ma'am."

"Thanks, Joe."

"Talk to the wife before the phone went dead?"

Bill nodded. "Yeah, man. Who'd've thought marriage would turn out to be such a drag?"

"Tell me about it, especially with this job."

Drinks flowed steadily between the two as they discussed the pains and disappointment of marriage and life in general. When the barmaid announced closing time, Bill paid for them each a pint to go and he and Joe stumbled across the street to their trucks.

Joe climbed up into the cab, kicked off his boots, struggled out of the coveralls, and loosened his jeans. He picked up the whiskey and took another drink. The strong liquid burned all the way to his stomach. He wondered why life had to be so hard.

Heck, his own mother didn't want him.

The thought twisted his gut as he remembered the one time he tried to visit her since he ran away at the age of fifteen. That was almost a year ago. He'd thought about her a lot since Shaunna's mom, Margaret, died, but it wasn't until Joey was born that he realized he wanted her to know her grandson. He wanted some sort of a relationship with his mother and thought maybe having one would round out their lives and help Shaunna with raising the baby while he was gone so much.

With that concept in mind, he looked her up and found her spaced out as usual on booze and drugs. He told her about his wife and son and attempted to make peace with her. He even offered to pay for rehabilitation and provide her with a decent place to live. She rejected his efforts.

Disillusioned, he decided to never try again.

* * *

Shaunna experienced a ripple of relief followed by a wave

of depression when she realized she was not pregnant. No matter how much she wanted one, a baby was the last thing she needed right now, especially with the current state of her marriage. She fought back tears.

Life is not fair!

A knock interrupted her pity party. Shaunna splashed water on her face, dried her eyes and hands, then went to open the door.

"Well?" Millie Frederick stepped over the threshold and shut the door.

Shaunna shook her head and tucked her hair behind her ear.

Millie drew her into her arms. "I'm sorry, honey. Maybe next time."

Shaunna sighed, stepped out of her embrace, and put the kettle on to boil. "Probably for the best, all Joe and I do is fight right now anyway."

Millie's eyebrow arched in concern. "About what? If you don't mind my asking."

Shaunna shrugged. "Everything. His job, the apartment, me going back to work."

Millie frowned. "Buddy isn't going to let you work if he knows doing so will cause problems between you and Joe."

Shaunna set out cups, saucers, instant flavored coffee, and a box of assorted herbal teas onto a tray. "I know. Which is why I haven't asked."

The kettle began to whistle. Shaunna poured water into their cups then carried the tray into the living room and set it on the coffee table. She waited while Millie chose her tea, then prepared coffee for herself. She took a sip, swallowed the knot of tears in her throat. "I never thought marriage would be so difficult. I mean, we were so blissful the first year or so. We laughed and loved and learned so much about each other. Then Joey came along. I thought life would be perfect and we'd always be the happy little family, but Joe's changed so much I hardly know him anymore."

"Changed how?"

"He's just so..." Shaunna's voice trailed off as she searched her mind for the right word. "I don't know...it's like he doesn't care about anyone or anything but himself and his stupid job.

The more he's gone the less he seems to understand the full extent of the stress involved in raising a child—the fears and joys, the wonders, and heartaches—and most of the time, he doesn't seem to care."

"I imagine him being gone so much is rough on both of you," Millie murmured.

Shaunna grimaced. "What an understatement. He's always gone when I need him the most. Holidays, birthdays, and anniversaries mean nothing to that stupid company. Here it is late spring, and we haven't spent more than a month together since before Christmas—which he missed. *Again.* Then, when I mentioned I'd like to go back to work, he had a conniption fit. Said all he wants is his wife at home to take care of him and the baby so *he* can enjoy his family when he has the chance."

She put her cup down with such force the whole tray rattled. "As if I'm not entitled to a life outside of being a wife and mother! He's selfish and chauvinistic and I'm sick of it!" she shrieked then burst into tears.

Once the torrent passed, Shaunna scraped the tears away and mumbled an apology.

"It's OK," Millie soothed. "I wish I had some words of wisdom to share. Buddy and I never had children, and I've never wanted to work, so we haven't faced the same issues as you and Joe. But I will say this, you two need to stop fighting and talk this out. Communication and compromise are key ingredients to a successful marriage."

"I just don't know what to do anymore."

Millie patted her hand.

"Pray, honey. Read and find out what the Bible says about being a good wife and then, when Joe has been home a couple of days and y'all are relaxed and at peace, talk to him."

"I will," Shaunna promised.

Three days later her vow to be a godly wife blew up in her face. She'd been out running errands and returned to find Joe home. Her excitement at seeing him again waned the moment she opened the door to find chaos where order once reigned.

She stumbled over Joe's duffle bag which lay open right inside the door. Clothes spilled out of the canvas tote in a foul heap on her clean floor. Bags of snack food, trash, and his log books were scattered over every available surface.

"Where've you been?" he bellowed from the living room.

Shaunna took a deep breath and prayed for calm. "Running errands."

"Where's Joey?"

Her temper strained but Shaunna answered in as polite a tone she could summon. "With Millie."

"What's for dinner?"

Heat spewed through her veins. "What's for dinner? No, 'hello,' 'I missed you,' or anything? Just 'what's for dinner?' I'll tell you what's for dinner, Joe Taylor. Whatever you can find at the nearest restaurant!" She picked up the duffle bag and flung it out of her way. "And pick up your junk before you leave! I am not your maid. I am not your mother, and I refuse to clean up after you anymore!"

Joe uncurled his long frame off the loveseat, every nuance of movement indicative of the battle about to ensue.

"You're my wife and that's what a wife does. Besides, if we had a real house with a laundry room, I might have some place to put my *junk* when I come in."

Shanna stormed into the living room and went toe-to-toe with him. "That's bull and you know it! There's a dumpster in the driveway, a dirty clothes hamper in the bath room, a trash can under the kitchen sink, and you could have set, not *thrown*, your log books on the counter. And for your information, God created woman to be a man's help mate, not his slave!"

"God created woman to take care of the home and children while man toils by the sweat of his brow to provide for them."

Shaunna threw up her hands. "That's not true. Marriage is about working together to provide a home for each other and our children. As it is now, you're always gone and when you are home, all you do is sit around while I wait on you hand and foot. Well, no more! If I'm going to wait on people, I'm going to get paid to do so."

Joe grabbed her by the arm. "Don't you dare start with that again. You are *not* going to work! There's no need for you to. I make plenty of money."

Shaunna whirled away and stomped her foot in agitation. "It's not about the money; it's about having something to do besides change diapers all day and someone other than a two year old to talk to! I've worked for Buddy since I was sixteen years old, pestered him for a year before that, and Millie is like a mother to me. You know this, yet you want Joey and I to move clear across town where I don't know a soul so *you* can be more comfortable when you're never home to begin with. Why don't *you* find a different job then we can find a house together and be a *real* family!"

A low growl sounded in his throat. Joe spit out a curse.

"You think I *like* being gone all the time and then spend every waking moment home arguing with you? Let me tell you something, Shaunna Marie. I *hate* this job as much as you do! I've called other companies, sent résumés, and followed up, but no one offers the same benefits I have now."

"My mother and I never had a drop of insurance or any of the benefits you hold so dear, but we had love and happiness, and we were *together*. Which is more than you and I have, so trust me when I say I'd rather have *a family* than the biggest or best benefit package!"

Joe raked a hand through his hair, cursed again.

"Maybe so, but I will not take the chance of you or my child having to settle for substandard health care because of your idealistic dreams of what a family is and what a husband should do." He stepped around her and in less than three strides stood in the kitchen. He turned to face her once more, his eyes narrowed into shimmering slits of icy blue flame.

"You want to work, fine. Work. *After* you do the laundry, clean the house, and get dinner on the table." He kicked his duffle bag for emphasis. "I'm going to pick up my son and take him to the park. We'll be back when we get back," he said, then stormed out of the apartment.

Shaunna collapsed onto the love seat. Every nerve in her body quivered like a bowstring drawn and ready to fire. She raked trembling hands through her hair, rubbed her throbbing temples and took deep breaths to quell her churning stomach. The tears came, slow at first then poured. Wrapping both arms around her waist, she buried her face into her knees, and rocked while sobs tore through her in painful torrents. Spent, she curled up on the tiny couch and tried to pray.

"So much for compromise and communication, Lord. What now?"

Peace washed over her. Shaunna arose and walked over and picked up Joe's duffle bag. She stuffed the clothes back in it then carried it into the garage below where her washer and dryer were now housed. Sorting through his laundry helped her sort through the emotions roiling in her heart, and she determined to try again to be the kind of wife God intended and Joe needed her to be. By the time Joe and Joey returned, his clothes were clean, folded, and stacked in the bag, which she'd also washed and dried. Her kitchen was back in order and dinner simmered on the stove.

* * *

Shaunna sat on her bed and thumbed through the photo albums she kept stored beneath it and wondered how, in heavens name, she was supposed to continue existing in the black hole her life had become. She'd gone to work alright. Not because she wanted to but because she had to.

Two days after their last argument, Joe left on an overnight run and hadn't come back.

That was six weeks ago, and Shaunna still did not know where they stood. In the last couple of weeks, they were able to talk civilly, but nothing had been resolved. Joe was still not home, nor did she know if he was going to come back.

What she did know was he lived in a small town south of Columbus, and he was on vacation this week. The reason she knew this was because three days ago he called and wanted to pick up Joey for a few days. Encouraged and thinking this would make things easier between them, Shaunna agreed to let Joey go with him.

The way they talked around each other, like polite strangers instead of husband and wife, hurt but at least they talked instead of screamed. That in itself was an improvement, and Shaunna hoped this time alone and Joe's time with Joey would give them each room to breathe and to decide what they, or rather what *he*, wanted.

She knew what she wanted.

She wanted her family back.

She buried her face into her hands and succumbed to the hot, cleansing tears pouring from her heart and soul. "Oh, God," she sobbed. "I know You hear my prayers. And I know *You* know what's best in this situation. It's obvious I don't. I don't know what to do! Please help me. I miss him so much," she admitted, and realized for the first time she missed her husband as much as her son.

As usual when in distress, the presence of the Lord calmed, and gave her the strength to go on, to face her day, and to challenge fate with a smile and confidence she found herself hard-pressed to exhibit. She knew God would not forsake her, and that He knew what was best. He would solve this problem according to His unfailing, holy will, and all would be well.

So, with confidence in Him, she took a long, hot shower and dressed for work.

Work was the last thing on earth she felt like doing.

Work. She would give it up if given the chance to make her marriage, her life, whole again.

Work, she knew, was not the real problem between her and Joe. The real problem was communication, or rather the lack of it, and stubbornness and pride. Sins they were both guilty of, pride being the most destructive—pride that caused them to want the other to see and accept their point of view no matter the cost.

The cost was too great, and she would do whatever it took to have her family back.

But then again, going to work sure beat the heck out of staying home alone.

She braided her hair and dabbed a little make-up under her eyes to conceal the dark circles beneath them. With a reluctant sigh, she left the apartment and hoped the walk to the café would revitalize her. The warm sun, cool breeze, smell of flowers, and sound of birds singing did much to ease her troubled soul, and she faced another day, determined to conquer it with faith.

Chapter Ten

Todd Jameson stared at his orders in disbelief. Dread and excitement collided in his chest. His hands shook, heartbeat quickened, palms sweated. He took the orders and went to meet with his commanding officer.

He handed the papers to the lieutenant. "I think there's a mistake here, I didn't list Fort Benning as my choice of bases."

Lieutenant McCormick glanced through the papers in his hand. "No, Sergeant, you did not. However, it looks like that's where you're going."

"Why?"

McCormick shrugged. "It's where we need you."

Todd leaned forward, palms flat on the lieutenant's desk. His eyes narrowed, temple throbbed, jaw muscle twitched. "I thought one of the rewards of reenlisting would be the base of my choice."

McCormick threw the orders on the desk, rose from his seat, and drew himself to attention, his hands clasped behind his back. "Something wrong with Fort Benning, Sergeant?" he asked through gritted teeth. "If I recall, once upon a time you requested that same base."

Todd ignored the anger in his C.O.'s eyes and the alarm which sounded in his brain. "Right. Once upon a time. Not this time. I was under the impression I'd get my choice of bases."

"You're offered a choice. There's no guarantee you'll get it. Now, I'll ask you again, Sergeant, is there something wrong with Fort Benning?"

Todd heard the tension in the lieutenant's voice, saw it in his face, and realized he walked the fine line bordering insubordination. As McCormick stepped from behind the desk, Todd stood at attention and forced his voice to be calm. "No, sir, Fort Benning is a fine base. It's just not where I'd choose to spend the next four years of my life."

McCormick snorted. "I don't understand you young punks with your high expectations. Despite your exemplary record, Sergeant Jameson, it seems you have a problem understanding that you are under the divine authority of the United States Government. Your only choice, son, was in joining the Army. The rest is up to Uncle Sam and Uncle Sam says he needs you in Columbus, Georgia, so I'd suggest you get packed. Any more questions?"

Todd bit back the angry retort which sprang to mind. "Just one more, sir," his voice crackled with tension. "Do I have any other options?"

"Sure, you can quit."

Todd snorted. "Probably too late for that now, too. Right?"

McCormick shrugged with a smug smile and nodded. "Right."

Todd suppressed a growl. He and McCormick never did get along. He'd bet his last dollar McCormick had everything to do with these orders. *The arrogant jerk.*

With a gesture resembling a salute he strode from the room. Back in his barracks he remembered his brief stay at Fort Benning, Georgia four years ago and the girl who had haunted his mind ever since.

Recollections of Shaunna sent an ache through his entire being; her smile, her laugh, her innocence. Regret ripped at his soul as memories filled his mind...the sweetness of her voice when she declared her love, the anguish of her sobs as he walked away, the agony when he found out she'd gotten married, the sharp stab of jealousy when he learned she'd had another man's child.

They'd shared a moment in time, but a moment was all it took to remind him of his lost childhood, his lost innocence. Somehow, be it by grace or a miracle, the gift of sharing in her innocence gave innocence back to him. For he could never recall a time he laughed or loved so much in his entire life as he had in the three weeks he spent at Fort Benning, Georgia.

Yet, despite all that, despite the pain and the years—years of war and strife, of separation and regret—he wondered if any female would ever do for him what Shaunna had. She'd made him feel young and carefree. She'd made him feel twenty-one.

In return, he gave his heart but like a fool he never told her. Instead, he made her promise to get on with her life and, despite her vow to never forget him, she'd done just that.

Less than two weeks later Todd walked toward the Feed Trough Café. He'd been in town three days and had put off going to the one place he desperately wanted to be. "Might as well get it over with," he muttered to himself.

He knew there was no way he could live in the same town with Shaunna for four years and not run into her, especially since she worked at the best café around and was like a daughter to the best friend he had.

He paused in his tracks when he caught a glimpse of her through the café window. His heartbeat quickened. Even though her back was to him, there was no doubt it was she. He knew it instinctively. His body knew and responded. The thick curls he remembered so vividly lay in a French braid down her back. Her hips tantalized as she cleaned and wiped the tables. Old feelings and desires ran rampant through his mind and heart. His blood simmered. He took a deep breath, opened the door, and walked in.

Shaunna turned from her task at the tinkling of the doorbell. Her eyes widened in surprised shock as a ghost from her past walked toward her. She felt an unfamiliar longing from deep within. Tears rushed unbidden to her eyes. Her heart constricted with the pain of remembering, in one heart-wrenching moment, the joy and pain of loving and losing him all within the span of three short weeks.

"Hello, Shaunna."

His voice was soft and husky. There was something about the look in his eyes—longing, need. Hunger reached deep inside and sent an answering shiver through her body.

She stood, mute, and stared at the man in front of her, unable to fathom the emotions screaming through her soul.

Todd!

His name reverberated through her entire being. Emotions began to surface and identify themselves, fear, loneliness, anger, pain, *love.* Emptiness engulfed her.

Life is not fair!

The thought surged through her on the knife-edge of anger. She grasped it. Anger was much preferable to the ache clamoring in her heart.

"For someone who considered us family," she almost choked on the word, "you sure never bothered to contact us. You weren't even around when Mama died."

A horrified gasp escaped when hurt glazed his emerald eyes and she realized the unfairness of her words. Regret ripped her heart. "I'm sorry," she whispered and reached out to touch his arm. "I'm sorry, Todd. That was unfair and uncalled for."

Todd accepted the apology with a nod. A tiny smile tugged at his mouth. "I missed you, too."

His grin broadened when a hint of a smile curved her lips. "I was, am, sorry to hear about your mom. I wish I could've been here."

Shaunna had no reason to doubt his sincerity. Even so, tears filled her eyes. Concern flickered on his face.

"What's wrong, Sweetness?" he asked.

Shaunna's heart did an irrational little flip at his use of her nickname. She was deemed 'Shaunna Sweetness' on the first day she started working at the Feed Trough more than four years ago. Some still called her that. Others shortened it to 'Sweetness.'

Though the name didn't roll off anyone's tongue quite like it did his.

The concern reflected in his gaze, assured her he noticed the ill-concealed circles beneath her eyes and the sadness which lurked in the dark depths. She took a deep breath, blinked back the tears, and attempted a smile.

"Nothing. You just caught me having a bad day. Welcome back. When did you get in? Can I get you something?"

Her voice was soft and held a false note of cheer. Disbelief clouded his expression, leaving no doubt Todd saw the ruse for what it was. He refrained from comment or question, and sat and answered in a thick voice, "Just coffee, please."

Shaunna brought his coffee and offered him a menu. He declined with a shake of his head. He stirred a spoon of sugar in the strong black liquid and looked up into her eyes. She could almost hear the questions reflected in his gaze, the same ones that echoed through her mind and wrenched her heart. She turned to walk away. He reached out and touched her arm. She trembled in response.

"Stay for a minute."

His low voice beckoned. Hunger flamed in his eyes. Again, Shaunna felt the familiar pull from deep within. His touch was like fire, his voice like satin. His eyes glowed like polished emeralds. She hesitated for a moment, unable to resist his offer. *Unable to resist him.*

Silence stretched between them as neither knew what the

other wanted to hear.

"How've you been?" he asked.

She shrugged. "OK."

"Heard you got married."

She nodded but refrained from comment.

"Well, how's it going?"

A tiny, insincere smile touched her lips. "OK," she replied, and swallowed hard the lump which clogged her throat, grateful he didn't voice aloud the disbelief flickering in his gaze.

Todd groaned and she felt his frustration. This conversation was headed nowhere and getting there fast.

"You look good. Married life must agree with you."

"I have a son," she said and hoped to steer the conversation away from her marriage.

He arched an eyebrow at her. "Heard that too. How old is he now?"

"Two."

He rolled his eyes in exaggeration then grinned. "Is he terrible?"

Shaunna knew he referred to the childhood syndrome for which two year olds were famous. She shook her head with a smile. "Oh, no, not my son," she stated in mock horror. "He's wonderful."

"And you're not prejudiced," he teased.

"Not me," she denied with an emphatic shake of her head.

Need coiled with desperation, and crawled through him as Todd sought to remain on a safe topic of discussion before he blurted out his love for her. "Where is he?"

Once again sadness clouded her eyes.

"He's with his dad," she said, and he knew she danced around the truth. Unspoken words echoed loud and clear. Something was wrong with her marriage. He remained quiet and hoped she would elaborate. An uneasy silence hung between them when she opted to say no more, and he dared not pry.

"Oh, well..." the false cheer was back in her voice. "Guess I'd better get on back to work."

"Yeah, I can see y'all are swamped," he teased, unwilling to let her go just yet.

Shaunna could not suppress her answering smile which danced in her eyes and lit up her entire face. His breath caught in

hope through her. She never thought she could miss someone as much as she missed her baby, and her husband, this past week.

"Hey."

A hand out of nowhere touched her. She gasped, stumbled, and fell right into Todd's arms. His boyish grin curled through her heart and made her smile.

"Well, just fall on in here, darling."

Unable to resist his roguish grin, she laughed. "You startled me," she accused and stepped out of his scorching embrace.

"I'm sorry."

Shaunna grinned. She'd wondered where he'd been these last few days but wasn't willing to think about how much she had looked forward to seeing him again. "You don't look sorry," she teased and willed her thoughts to behave.

Todd laughed and her thoughts rocketed into turmoil once more. *He is so different from Joe.* His five foot eight inches wasn't near as tall or as broad as Joe's six-foot frame, but he was every bit as attractive, perhaps more so.

His dark hair fell in thick waves across his forehead despite its short length and she had to force herself to keep from brushing a stray lock off his face. Sensuality lined his every feature, from the deep green eyes framed with thick, black lashes to the full sensuous lips which smiled easily and often. His voice had a velvety-rough quality and sent shivers dancing down her spine whenever he spoke. He possessed an aura of sensuality most men she knew tried hard to feign. Though not tall, he was muscular and well proportioned for his height.

Shaunna could not help but remember what it felt like to be in those strong arms. She felt a tremor of want followed by a wave of embarrassment at her blatant appraisal of him.

Todd chuckled at the blush that rushed to her cheeks, his thoughts just as appraising. She was every bit as beautiful as he remembered, and more.

Her hair hung in thick, shiny waves down her back, blinding in its brilliance. Her petite, five-foot figure seemed a little fuller. Her breasts strained at the uniform in a way far more enticing than he remembered. Though not fat, she had filled out with a maturity that drove him wild with wanting. Her eyes sparkled with interest and excitement, a big difference from the sadness he saw lurking there three days ago, and he wondered if his return was what had her looking so happy.

"Where are you going in such a hurry?" he asked.

"Home."

"Mind if I walk with you?"

Shaunna shrugged. "Not at all." She turned and led the way to her apartment.

A nostalgic euphoria enveloped him as Todd remembered the summer four years ago and the many times he walked her home. He had to restrain from slipping his arm around her waist. A flicker of hope flared in his heart.

He often wondered why he never got over his feelings for Shaunna. He tried. Lord knows he tried. Sometimes he even thought he succeeded. Like the time he dated one girl for six months. Rebecca was sweet but she could not compare to Shaunna. No one affected him the way Shaunna had, and her memory continued to haunt him.

Even now she disturbed his whole being. All he could feel was an ache in his soul because he still loved her. The fact she was married didn't seem to make a difference either. He felt a stirring of desire every time he thought about her, which had been often since he learned of his assignment in Fort Benning. As he walked next to her, desire more than stirred, it resembled a tidal wave threatening to engulf him. The separation between her and her husband gave him hope that he could tell her how much he loved her and say the words he should have said four years ago.

"So," he began, "what are your plans for this evening?"

"To take a six-hour bubble bath. How 'bout you?"

Todd stopped in mid stride. "Six hours! You're going to shrivel up like an old prune." He sucked in his cheeks liked he'd sucked on a lemon.

Shaunna laughed. "Oh, well. That's the breaks. What are you doing?"

He shrugged. "Depends."

Her eyes widened at the husky note in his voice. "On what?"

"Fate."

Shaunna smiled and shook her head. "What's fate got to do with anything?"

Todd felt the familiar pull of desire tug at his mind. He didn't want to scare her away, so he shook it off. "Has everything to do with my plans. Let's see, I've got the whole afternoon and evening ahead of me. I'm young, healthy, good looking..."

His voice softened and he whispered something intimate and primitive. She blushed, her expression a comical mix between total surprise and absolute shock. With a shriek she punched him on the arm.

"And terrible," she added to his long list of attributes.

He chuckled. "That, too," he agreed, then continued when they resumed walking. "So, what are you going to do after your six-hour bath? Not that you're going to have much time left in the evening to do anything." He paused at the foot of the stairs leading up to the apartment.

Halfway up the steps, Shaunna stopped and turned. "Aren't you going to come up?"

He shrugged. "Didn't know if it was proper. Besides," he wriggled his eyebrows, "enjoyed the view."

Shaunna rolled her eyes, unable to suppress a grin. "You're impossible. I don't care a flip about what people think. Come on in."

Without hesitation Todd bounded up the stairs, two at a time. "Nice place. Small, but nice."

"Thanks." She smiled and waved him to a stool beside the snack bar.

He preferred to stay close to her when she walked into the living room. "So, are you going to answer my question?"

"What question?"

This time he rolled his eyes in a pretense of aggravation. "Hello, earth to Shaunna." He pinched her ear. The simple contact sent shivers through him. His voice lowered a notch. "I repeat, what are you going to do after your six-hour bath?"

"Oh, that question. Well, I need to clean this place up a bit and I have a new book I want to read."

His lip curled and he snorted. "Read? My word, you sound like an old woman. Besides, you should clean before you take a bath. Not that it looks dirty to me."

"I am not an old woman. I'm a young woman. A young, *married* woman with a child," she reminded him. "Besides, my baby will be back tomorrow."

"Well, one thing's for certain, that little bitty guy is not old enough to appreciate clean floors and dust free furniture," he countered.

Shaunna smiled. "But I'm his mother," she explained in a tone usually reserved for the young or dense. "I appreciate clean floors and dust free furniture, especially when he picks something up and puts it in his mouth."

He relented with a laugh. "Well, shoot, can't argue with you there. But it's still early. Why don't you whiz through here with your magic dust broom, then take your bath, only make it one hour instead of six and I'll pick you up at five. We'll go out to eat and catch a movie. Or go dancing. How long has it been since you've been dancing?"

"Gosh, I don't even remember the last time. I'm not even sure I remember how."

"It's easy," he assured and took her into his arms while he hummed a tune. "You just fall on in here, like you did earlier, and move to the music. Like this." He edged her closer and danced around the little room. Giddy from the feel of her, he exaggerated his movements—teasing, seductive. He took her by the hand and twirled her around. Unprepared for the sudden change, she stumbled.

He caught her before she could regain her balance and held her for a moment, his gaze locked with hers in a heated embrace. "See, it's easy," he assured in a husky voice and forced himself to release her. She emitted a nervous little giggle that made him smile.

"You're crazy," she accused. "Go away. I'll have nothing to do with a crazy man."

"If I'm crazy, it's your fault. Come on, go with me."

"My fault? Oh, go ahead, blame it on me. As if I don't have enough on my shoulders..."

"You have beautiful shoulders," he interrupted, his tone silky while his eyes roamed over her in an intimate gesture. The look in her eyes suggested he walked in dangerous territory. Her voice and expression turned serious.

"I can't, Todd."

He sobered. "Why not?"

"Because I'm married."

Todd knew anger would get him nowhere and bit back a

snarl. He grabbed her hand, fingered the ring. "I'm under the impression he's not hanging around where he's supposed to be." He couldn't hide the thread of annoyance in his voice. The truth had to come out. She had to admit Joe was not in the picture before she would ever consent to go out with him.

She frowned. "So, we're having some problems. My going out with you will not solve anything."

He ran his hands up her arms, rested them on her shoulders and hesitated, knowing his choice of words would count a great deal in her decision. "We're old friends, right?"

She nodded.

"Friends who haven't seen each other in years."

Again, she nodded.

"So, let me, as your friend, take you out to dinner or something. We'll order in, stay here, and talk or whatever. You can't stop living just because y'all are having some problems. You can bet he hasn't."

"Two wrongs don't make a right, Todd," she insisted, then turned and hurried across the room to answer the phone.

Todd's curiosity turned to anger when he heard the anguish in her voice as she spoke.

"What do you mean you're not bringing him home? A run to Louisiana, how long will that take? A week? Wait! Who is he with? You can't just leave him with some stranger! Joe! Bring my baby back now, before you go!"

With a shriek and a curse, she slammed the receiver back in its cradle. A furious little sob escaped her.

The knife-edge of anger cut through Todd followed by a thin ribbon of hope. The way her husband treated her infuriated him, but at the same time, the few days it took Joe to go to Louisiana and back might give him the time he needed to show her how much he cared.

He clenched and uncurled his fists to ease the tension coiled in his gut. He walked to where she stood, put his hands on her waist, and turned her to face him. "At least you can skip the cleaning for tonight." He kept his tone light in an effort to recapture the mood they shared moments ago. "Come with me," he coaxed. "It'll be fun. I promise to be good and to get you home early if that's what you want."

The anguish in her gaze tore at his heart. She bit back a

sob, blinked back tears, and attempted a smile. At her obvious indecision he frowned. "Are you gonna say yes or am I going to have to drag you out of here kicking and screaming?"

She shook her head, chewed on her lip. "I can't."

He cocked his head to one side. "That does not compute," he stated in a robotic tone and tapped his head for emphasis. His antics succeeded in wringing a tiny laugh from her.

"You're going to drive me crazy unless I agree, aren't you?"

He grinned, nodded. "Yep."

She rolled her eyes. "All right then, go." She shooed him toward the door. "I'll be ready by five, no make it six."

He took her hand and raised it to his lips. "Until then..." he breathed and felt her tremble.

With a song in his heart and a smile on his lips, he left.

Two hours later he arrived at Shaunna's and waited for her to open the door. When she did, every ounce of anticipation in his blood chilled. "What's wrong?"

Shaunna sniffed and bit her lip. "I can't stand this!" She buried her face in her hands and burst into tears. "I have no idea where my son is, or with whom, and I don't know what to do."

Todd grabbed her hand. "Let's go."

She frowned at him. "What? Where?"

He urged her a step closer. "We're driving to where he lives and finding your son if I have to tear the town apart."

She hesitated. "Wait, we can't just barge down there and knock door to door until we find him."

Todd raked a hand through his hair. "You're right. You have no phone number or anything?"

She shook her head. "We've been fighting for so long, and it was such a relief to have a civil conversation with him, that when he asked to pick Joey up for a few days, I didn't think to ask for any of that. I had no idea he'd leave him with a virtual stranger to go out of town."

"A stranger to you maybe, but not to him."

"What do you mean?"

Todd grimaced. "Shaunna, do you honestly think he would leave his son with someone he didn't know, hadn't known for quite some time?"

He knew the moment she realized what he meant. She paled. Tears rushed to her eyes. Todd held her while she cried.

Every shudder and sob tore at his heart, but he dared not shush her. When the weeping subsided, he ran his hands over her back and shoulders in a soothing gesture.

"OK, let's think this through. What about the company he works for, I'm sure they'd have his information."

She brightened. "They might, I never thought about that."

Todd followed her back inside the apartment and waited while she called the company and obtained the information she sought.

Shaunna's hand trembled when she dialed the number dispatch gave her. A woman answered. "Is this where Joe Taylor lives?" she asked.

"Who wants to know?"

"This is his wife. I'm..." She looked at the phone in disbelief then turned to Todd. "She hung up on me!" Her whole body quaked, and fingers shook so hard it took three attempts to redial the number. "Please don't hang up; I just want to know if you have my son!"

The woman hung up again. Furious, Shaunna banged the receiver into its cradle, a foul name escaping in a screech.

Todd took her by the hand. "C'mon, we'll go to the police and see if they can help us find out whose number it is and give us an address."

Shaunna stuffed the paper into her purse. On a whim she gathered her and Joe's marriage license and Joey's birth certificate. Thirty miles separated the towns where she and her husband resided.

The drive felt like a hundred.

Todd stopped at the first convenience store within the city limits and asked for directions to the police department. He pulled into the location and squeezed her hand in a gesture of support. Shaunna gave him a weak smile then climbed out of the car and entered the building.

"May I help you?" An officer behind the counter asked.

"Can you assist me in locating an address and tell me who lives there?"

The officer shook his head. "I can try. What seems to be the problem?"

Before Shaunna could answer, Todd stepped up beside her. "Her estranged husband took their son, and we're trying to find him."

"Do you have divorce papers or a custody agreement?"

Shaunna shook her head. "No."

"Well, then, the boy's not kidnapped. The father has as much legal rights to him as the mother."

"But he's left my baby with someone I don't know and gone out of town..."

"Out of state," Todd interjected.

"Yeah, out of state. I only want to find my son, make sure he's OK, and take him home."

The officer grunted. "I understand your situation, ma'am, but unless we have proof the boy is in danger, there's nothing we can do."

"That's just it! I don't know if he's in danger or not! I don't even know where he is. All I have is this phone number and when I tried to call and find out, the woman hung up on me."

"Give me the number. I'll see what I can do."

Shaunna handed him the paper.

He glanced at the number then back at her. "I know this woman and can assure you the boy is safe."

"Would you please call anyway?"

He nodded.

Shaunna waited while he put the call through and identified himself to the party who answered. Tension curled up her spine when the officer arched an eyebrow at her.

"Really? Oh, I see. Well thank you for your help," he remarked and hung up.

"What did she say?"

"She said you gave her fiancé permission to have the baby for two weeks and have been harassing her since he left town today for work."

"That's not true!"

"Did you give him permission to take the child?"

"Yes, but..." Her words trailed off when the officer held up a hand to signify silence.

"There is nothing we can do, ma'am. The lady assured me the child is fine, so you need to go on home and resolve this with your ex-husband. And don't try to contact her again or she may file harassment charges against you."

"That's ridiculous!" Shaunna slammed the paperwork

she'd brought along with her on the counter. "This is *my* two-year-old son we're talking about. How can his father be her fiancé when he's still married to me?"

The officer drew in a deep breath.

Todd grabbed her by the elbow. "Calm down, Shaun."

Shaunna turned on him in an angry whirl. "Calm down? How can you expect me to calm down when this harlot has my baby?"

"Listen to the gentleman, ma'am," the officer said, an edge to his soft voice. "Otherwise, I might have to haul you in for harassment myself." He raised a brow in Todd's direction. "Consider this fair warning. If I find out she's called and bothered this lady..."

Todd took a firm grip on Shaunna's arm and jerked her up short. "She won't."

Shaunna slumped, sobs wracking her slender frame. "I just want my baby," she sobbed. She turned back to the officer. "I won't bother her, but will you *please* call her back and make sure she knows how to reach me should an emergency arise?"

The officer emitted a low growl, dragged a hand over his face.

"Please? He's only two."

He heaved a sigh, picked up the phone again, and made the call.

Shaunna relayed her telephone number and address and offered an apology to the woman via the officer then thanked him. When she turned to leave, he called her name. The softness in his tone sent a shiver of hope through her.

"Yes?"

He handed her a business card. "Look, I'm sorry I can't do more for you but like I said, I know this lady very well and I can promise your son is safe. However, if you want, I can occasionally check on him and let you know how he is doing."

Shaunna heard the emphasis he put on 'occasionally' and nodded. Her lips trembled, tears clouded her gaze. "Thank you. Thank you *so* much!" She took the business card and left. All she could do now was wait, and pray, and trust God with the safety of her son.

Chapter Twelve

Todd prepared for the evening with care and anticipation. *Tonight, was the night.* At least he hoped it would be. He'd restrained from pushing Shaunna too soon into a more intimate relationship, but his need for her neared the breaking point. He wanted her more than he'd ever wanted a woman in his life. More than that, his love was stronger and deeper than desire. He'd wanted to tell her, but the words wouldn't come. He tried to show her in numerous ways, still he felt as though she looked at him as nothing more than a friend and was at a loss on how to let her know his feelings went much deeper than friendship.

But maybe tonight...

He bounded up the stairs to her apartment and waited, albeit with a bit of impatience, for her to open the door. When she did, he thought he'd drown from the flood of need coursing through his veins. Drawn away from her face with a big gold barrette, her hair hung in soft curls down her back. Both the tank top and the white lacy over-shirt enhanced the silkiness of her skin. Her jeans clung to her hips and legs...a virtual feast for his eyes. He bowed and kissed her hand. A blush filled her cheeks and added a rosy glow to her tanned complexion and a sparkle to her dark eyes. He turned her hand over and pressed a soft kiss on the inside of her wrist. Her pulse leapt into high gear beneath his lips and he suppressed a chuckle. No matter what she said, her body responded to his touch. Another surge of desire sliced through him.

"Ready?"

Shaunna arched an eyebrow at him. "Do I look ready?"

A roguish glint lit his eyes, impish smile tugged at his lips. His gaze traveled over her in a look as potent as an embrace, added heat to the warm, balmy air.

"Most definitely."

A shiver shook her from head to toe. Shaunna hesitated. *Maybe being with him tonight isn't such a great idea.*

She and Todd had visited almost every evening since that first night after they drove to the neighboring town where Joe lived and talked with the police. He'd told her of the extensive training he received over the past four years—a jungle survival in

Panama, Arctic training in Alaska, and desert training in California although he could not, and would not disclose any specific details of his job.

The aura of mystery surrounding him sent shivers of fear through her heart and made Shaunna glad he was bound by a code of honor which required secrecy. She refused to dwell on the depth of the emotions between her and Todd. They were friends. Farther than that, she refused to think, refused to consider how deep the friendship went. She enjoyed his company and was grateful for his loyalty. He'd held her while she anguished over the prolonged separation from her son. She, in turn, offered comfort and solace when he relived the horrors of Vietnam. They needed each other and God knew she hadn't felt needed in a long time. Still, she'd hesitated in going on an actual date with him until tonight, and here he was, in rare form—teasing, seductive—and it was barely six o'clock.

The situation with Joe sent anger roiling through her system. He said he'd be gone a week at most and here it was nine days later, and she hadn't heard a word from him. Even though she'd heard from Officer Brady often, attesting to Joey's well being, and even though he'd reported seeing Joey for himself, she still had no idea who had her son.

To heck with it! I'm going and I will have fun! If Todd's in an exceptional mood, I'll handle any situation that comes up when the time arrives.

She locked the door behind her, took his hand, and they walked down the stairs.

The dimly lit, smoke-filled club welcomed them with open arms. Todd found a table and signaled for a waitress. He ordered them each a drink then reached over and took her hand in his. Shaunna shivered when he traced tiny circles in her palm then brushed his thumb over her wrist in a sensuous gesture. They sat in electrified silence as the band finished the song and began another. Shaunna couldn't stand it. The tension between them was so thick, so hot. She needed to move. She rose.

"If you don't get me out on that dance floor, I'll find someone who will."

He needed no more persuasion. With a grin he tossed a bill on the table, told the waitress to bring one more round when their glasses were empty and to keep the change. He took

Shaunna's hand and led the way to the dance floor.

"Was that a threat?" he queried and held her tight.

Shaunna gazed up at him, surprised at the unnerving response of her body to his embrace. Her return smile was meant to drip sweetness. "I don't know about you, but I came here to dance."

"Well, look around, honey. There are plenty of men in here aching to oblige you. Be warned though, you will not escape these arms tonight."

His voice, soft as a caress, sent tiny shivers along her spine. He urged her closer as the music slipped into a buckle-shining slow song. Each song, each dance, every moment in each other's arms intensified the feelings between them until their senses hummed like high-tension wires.

Todd stroked her back. His fingertips left trails of fire wherever they touched. His breath heated her neck and fanned the flame of intensity that sparked between them. Though the noise drowned out his words, his body language spoke loud and clear. He slowed their movements to an almost standstill. In the midst of a dance floor full of couples, they were alone in a vortex of emotions, aware of nothing but each other.

Todd cupped her face in his hands and kissed her. Tender. Thorough. Hopeful. She melted against him, emitted a soft whimper. His gaze searched hers. His name whispered through her lips in weak protest.

"Shh." His mouth brushed hers with every shake of his head. "Don't say anything," he urged in that gorgeous, velvety-rough voice. He urged her closer, if that were possible. The low vibration of his tone shuddered through her. "Just feel what you do to me."

She felt. Boy, did she ever feel. His heat devoured her, scorched every thought from her mind, and consumed every nerve in her body until she burned with him, for him. He didn't give her time to utter a word but closed his mouth over hers in another heated embrace.

Before she could think or protest, he led her off the dance floor, past their table, and out into the warm summer night. He wrapped his arms around her, devoured her lips and once more obliterated all thought from her mind. His arms wrapped like steel manacles around her waist, lips molded and shaped hers to his until each ragged breath he took robbed her of much needed oxygen. Had he not held her so tight, her legs would have buckled and left her in a useless heap on the ground.

Shaunna gave up all hope of reasonable thought, any thought. Her response to him was as natural and instinctive as the very breath she took. She slipped her arms around his neck and unconsciously molded her body to his passion-hardened one. Wave after wave of pleasure rippled through them, left both breathless with need. She gasped for air and pushed at him.

"Todd, stop, please."

"Why?" His lips traveled back up her throat in a greedy quest for her lips.

"Because..."

His mouth silenced her protests. His sensual assault never ceased while he dug into his pocket for the keys, then unlocked the door and guided her onto the seat. He climbed in next to her, traced her jaw with his fingers then nuzzled her lips with his. His hand massaged her neck and shoulder. He whispered words of love and desire punctuated by the brush of his lips over her ear while he drove, as fast as he dared, to the small apartment he rented off base. She was out of the car, into his arms, and ensconced in the apartment in one swift, not-so-subtle move.

With supreme gentleness, he picked her up and carried her to the couch, kicking his shoes off as he went. He set her on the edge and knelt before her, unbuckled the sandals she wore and removed them from her feet. Trembling fingers stroked her ankles and calves. His hands moved with feather softness up her thighs and over her hips to her waist and left hot trails of fire where they lingered. All the while his husky voice battered her heart with tender exaltations. His lips moseyed across her cheek to tease her ear. He uttered soft words of praise at her sweetness.

Shaunna could have cried with the intensity, the onslaught of emotion raging through her senses. With a tug on his dark head and a twist of hers, she offered her lips to his ravenous mouth. A hum of pure pleasure ripped through her when he accepted without hesitation.

An insistent voice wormed its way into her conscience and nagged her to stop this while there was time, insisted she back out now, while she could do so with her self-respect intact. She couldn't suppress it, or ignore it. When Todd sat back on his heels and jerked his shirt off, she placed a firm hand on his chest. "Todd, *no,*" she said, her voice soft but determined.

"What?"

"I can't."

Pain and anger collided in his gaze, his eyes darkened to a dangerous glow. He reached for her. *"What?"*

She rolled out of his grasp, away from his touch. "No. I just can't. Please...please don't hate me."

She slid off the couch, turned away from the angry confusion in his eyes, and walked to the window, her head bowed in shame. How could she have let this get so far out of hand and how on earth could she turn away now?

She just knew she had to.

"Why?"

His raw voice dug into her heart and made her feel about as low as dirt. A silent sob shook her slim frame. "I just can't."

Todd felt as though he would suffocate. He couldn't breathe. He was numb. Dying. Dead.

He staggered to his feet and walked toward her. "Shaunna," he moaned, his voice ragged and reached out to stroke her hair. He turned her around, tilted her face with his hand, and waited until she raised tear-drenched eyes to his.

"Please don't do this to me. Don't deny me this night in your arms. Don't deny yourself any longer. I love you."

She swallowed her tears and clasped her hands over her chest then shook her head as if to deny his words.

"Please. Don't say that. It only makes this harder."

He hated the desperation in his voice, despised the desolation in his soul when he whispered, "It's true."

She shook her head again.

A sudden rage swept through him and he forced himself not to shake her. "You can bet that whoever's good hands little Joe is in, big Joe has been in also."

This time it was he who regretted words so carelessly spoken.

Tears rushed to her eyes, but her chin lifted in a defiant tilt. "Maybe so," was all she said, but her eyes said much more. She turned away.

"That still doesn't make it right. Besides it's not Joe I'm concerned with. It's Him." Her eyes lifted heavenward. "I made my vows before God. It is *He* I can't disappoint."

Todd sighed, defeated by something he could never fight. "I'm sorry." He raked his fingers through his hair. "Oh, Shaunna..." His voice hitched as he struggled for control. "The last thing I want to do is hurt you."

"I know," she whispered and the raw emotion in her voice seared his soul. "It's OK. Take me home."

"I will." He hesitated then turned her to face him again. "But, Shaun?" A gentle finger lifted her chin. He waited until her gaze met his.

"Let me hold you awhile longer. I won't force or even try and persuade you to make love, but please don't rob me of the opportunity to hold you while I have the chance."

She hesitated but a moment. Her eyes spoke volumes and he knew she could not deny the feelings that raged between them—a war between love and passion, right and wrong. With a sigh she surrendered, walked into his arms, buried her face into his chest, and nodded.

Todd enveloped her in a fierce hug. "Thank you," he whispered and kissed her hair, her eyes, and her lips. He picked her up, carried her back to the couch and cuddled, his intentions changed; this need just as strong.

Chapter Thirteen

Joe Taylor unhitched the box trailer from the cab of his eighteen-wheeler in the transport yard then drove to where his son stayed with his girlfriend. When told to make the run to Louisiana almost two weeks ago, he did so with a great deal of reluctance. He had been on vacation and was due to bring Joey home to Shaunna. Convinced the trip was an emergency, he made the stupid run. While there, he drove south to Thibodaux and talked to his former employer, Mr. James Garrison who owned and operated a wireline and pipe-testing service. Joe had worked for him for several years in the past. Thrilled to see him, James offered Joe a job. Ecstatic, he accepted, anxious to get back to Georgia, give his notice and make moving arrangements. However, when he called the company, they extended the run from Louisiana to Texas.

While in Port Arthur, he decided to try one more time to see his mother. Finding the dirty little apartment where she lived empty, he sought out the landlord. The man reeked of whiskey.

"Yeah, what'cha want?"

"I'm looking for Katherine Taylor. She used to live in that little apartment."

"I know who she is. You that boy of hers?"

Joe nodded.

"Well, she ain't here no more."

"I can see that. Do you know where she is?"

"Don't see as it makes no difference now, seeing you ain't been around in damn near fifteen years. Broke her heart, leaving like you did."

"Look, Mister, I don't need a lecture from you. Do you know where she is or not?"

"Yeah, check out the church cemetery."

"What?"

"Look, boy, I might be drunk, but I don't stutter. You heard me. On the corner," he called out when Joe turned to leave.

A suffocating feeling enveloped Joe as he walked toward the small Catholic church on the corner. He walked through the cemetery and stopped at a grave which could not have been more than a few weeks old. Engraved on the headstone were the words: *Katherine Taylor, alone no more. May she rest in peace.*

Regret, more profound than he'd ever felt washed over him in great, heaving waves. "Mama," he whispered. A hand on his shoulder startled him. Joe turned to look into the eyes of a priest.

"You must be Joe."

He nodded. "You knew her? She told you about me?"

"Come inside, son. We'll talk." He turned and led the way into the church rectory.

Joe stood in awkward silence as the little man moved around the small kitchenette and poured two glasses of lemonade. He placed them on the table, gestured for Joe to sit, then introduced himself.

"I'm Father Jacobson. I met your mother three months ago when she attempted to commit suicide. I was at the hospital visiting a friend when the paramedics brought her in. Once they stabilized her, I introduced myself. When she got out of the hospital, I talked with her often. She told me about you a few days before she died."

"Did she tell you why I left?"

"She told me everything, son. I know this may be hard for you to understand or believe, but she loved you. She deeply regretted your estrangement."

"Did she tell you I tried to visit her? A couple of years back. She rejected me, sent me away."

The priest heaved a sigh. A sad little smile curved the corners of his mouth.

"She told me." He reached over and touched Joe's hand. "She regretted that, too. I want you to know something. It may make things easier for you. She found peace at the end. She made her peace with God. She accepted His forgiveness and forgave herself and you. She died peacefully in her sleep. Now, if you'll wait here, I have something for you."

Joe nodded.

When Father Jacobson returned, he placed a box on the table in front of Joe and put a hand on his shoulder.

"I have to get ready for Mass. Stay as long as you like. Join us if you want to. If not, remember this: Through the love and grace of the Lord Jesus Christ there is peace and joy for even the most troubled soul."

Unable to speak, Joe nodded his thanks. The priest exited the room and left him alone with the box and his thoughts. With trembling hands, Joe removed the top. What a waste, he thought, a whole lifetime summed up in the contents of a shoebox. His heartbeat stumbled when he picked up an envelope with his name on it. The packet contained his birth certificate and a letter. His breath came in short, frantic gasps as he read...

My darling son, I hope someday this letter will find its way into your hands and into your heart. I am so sorry for all the pain I've caused you. I love you and I hope someday you can find it in your heart to forgive me. I've found peace now, in Jesus. My greatest regret is that you're not here to share it with. Please know, no matter what, I love you and will be with you always. Your mother...

She'd signed the note in a weak scrawl.

Blinded by tears, Joe made his way out of the rectory. He walked past the graveyard to his truck. He was about halfway back to Georgia when the sobs started, slowly at first, then with more force as the letter echoed in his mind and heart. He realized the depth of emptiness in his soul and in his life.

The enormity of the mistake he'd made in his marriage hit him with the force of a Mack truck on a Volkswagen. He pulled off the highway and wept. Shame and guilt filled him. He felt dirty, so dirty. Easing back onto the road, he drove to the nearest truck stop and headed straight for the shower. He closed his eyes and let the hot water cleanse his body and refresh his mind and soul. His mother's words echoed in his heart. *I've found peace in Jesus.*

How he longed for that peace. He knew who God was, knew Shaunna prayed all the time. He opened his heart and mind and promised himself, and God, if he got one more chance, he would never forget Him again. He would do whatever it took. Even if it meant he had to crawl on his knees and beg, he would apologize to Shaunna. If she forgave him, he would take her with him to Louisiana and never hurt her again.

There was one catch to his plan. Vickie Lewis.

He'd met Vickie in a bar about the time he and Shaunna began having trouble. The tension in his marriage made him feel inadequate as a father and a husband and he began to drink more than he ever had before. In the past, he stayed away from alcohol.

Now he couldn't seem to get enough of it. During one of his drinking stints, he went to bed with Vickie. After the first time, it got easier, at least when he drank.

When the guilt first set in, he consoled himself with more booze. What began as a vicious circle, too soon became a way of life. It was easy. And fun. No wife. No kid. No responsibilities.

He stayed on the party wagon until Vickie forced him to make a choice. That's when he left Shaunna. He started a fight with her to ease his conscience and justify his actions.

The first couple of weeks with Vickie were sheer alcoholic bliss. He did not have to think. All he had to do was work a little, drink a lot, and party the rest of the time. The bliss lasted about a month. The constant partying grew old, and Joe became disgusted with it all. He threw out the bottle and vowed to never touch the stuff again. And he hadn't. Then he realized how much he missed his son and his wife. He decided to start with his son.

When he called Shaunna and asked to pick Joey up for a while, she surprised him by agreeing. Thrilled he could make a fresh start, and possibly have a relationship with his son, he planned to keep him, a week. At the end of that week, when he realized just how much he needed Joey, he had to leave him with Vickie and go to Louisiana. The rest, as they say, is history. Now he had to make another choice. This one was simple.

He stopped at the first rest area he came to and called Vickie to have her pack up Joey's things. He did not know how he would break off their relationship, but he knew the first and most important thing would be to get Joey back to Shaunna. He did not want the baby caught in the crossfire if Vickie tried to make his leaving difficult.

She hadn't. When he arrived at her apartment, he was surprised and glad to find she had Joey's, and his, things packed. She cried when she told him about the phone call from Shaunna and the police, how it made her realize they were wrong, and that she did not want a ready-made family. She wanted her freedom. He was all too happy to give it to her. He loaded up his truck and drove straight back to Columbus.

Now, he had to convince Shaunna he'd changed enough that she'd want to leave her home and move with him to Louisiana.

* * *

Shaunna's smile wavered when Todd entered the café and ambled toward her. He had not wanted to come here today, to see her. Not yet. But some demon in his heart and mind drove him. He put his hands in his pockets and forced himself not to reach out and touch her. The anguish in her eyes ripped at his heart.

He accepted her offer of a cup of coffee then invited her to join him while she was on break. They sat in tense, wary silence for a minute then she reached over and touched his hand. His fingers closed over hers.

"I wish I could explain how I feel about you...But the truth is, I don't even understand it myself," she admitted in a soft voice.

Oblivious to everything except the raw emotions between them, Todd kept silent.

"From the first time I laid eyes on you, I never understood the feelings you aroused in me, how they could run so deep, so strong. Everything happened so fast. Then you were gone." Her lips trembled, voice clouded. "I missed you so much."

A muffled groan escaped him when she reached up and wiped a tear off her cheek. "Shaunna, please," he whispered, the ache in his heart reflected in his voice.

Shaunna shook her head. "Then Joe came along," she continued, her voice thick with unshed tears. "At first I didn't want to have anything to do with him, especially when he said he was *just passing through'*."

A tiny smile tugged at the corner of his mouth as he remembered the time he spoke those words to her. Her lips curved in response. She took another deep, cleansing, breath.

"Anyway, he kept coming back. I had more time to get to know him, to grow to love him. He was there when Mama died, when I needed him. Please try to understand. My marriage is not over. Not yet anyway. Its unfinished business and I can't think of anything else until it's resolved."

Her voice broke and she swallowed a sob. "Please," she whispered. "I never want to hurt you."

"I know." His voice sounded as husky as hers. "I'm not blaming you. It's my fault. I should have told you years ago how I felt."

"Why didn't you?"

He shrugged. "Stupidity, pride, fear. I thought you were too young to wait. Then there was the war."

"I told you I'd never forget you and I didn't. Even being married I thought of you often and prayed for you. Had I known how you felt, I would've waited."

"I was too scared or maybe just too proud to ask. Thought it was wrong, especially if I went to war. I couldn't imagine putting you through that. I..." His words trailed off when the bell on the door tinkled. They turned in unison to see Joe walk in with Joey.

"Des Mommy," the little guy said and struggled in his father's arms for Joe to put him down.

A sob escaped Shaunna and she bolted from the booth. She met him halfway across the floor, dropped to her knees, picked up her baby, and hugged him to her breast. Sobs wracked her body as she clung to her child, rocking him back and forth.

The real man in her life is back, Todd thought. *And his father with him.* His heart sank despite the fury in his veins.

Todd rose, tossed a five-dollar bill on the table and walked toward the door. He paused beside her, reached out and stroked her hair.

Shaunna trembled, took a deep breath and lifted tear-drenched eyes to his. Her gaze begged for understanding. Without breaking eye contact, he cupped her cheek in his hand and brushed a tear away with his thumb. A tiny smile tugged at his lips. Her eyes glowed and he knew she understood he loved her, completely and unconditionally.

Which only complicated matters.

His smile broadened for a brief moment. With a gentle nod and a tender wink he turned to leave and stood toe to toe with her husband, eye level with his broad shoulders.

Todd clenched his fists to keep from putting his hands around the man's throat. His angry gaze lifted to meet the challenge in Joe's eyes. He saw love there, and sorrow. And fear. Fear that he might be too late. Todd knew the battle was on, and, chances were, he'd lose. Still he stood tall and proud, and determined.

For a moment, neither man budged. Eyes clashed, each

willing to fight for the woman they both loved.

Todd lowered his gaze and Joe took a single step back to let him pass. Both knew the other wouldn't back down, and it was not fair to put Shaunna through any more turmoil, especially when she was so torn. Todd made his stand and Joe stood up for what belonged to him. Now it would be up to her.

A wave of emptiness engulfed Shaunna when Todd walked out of the café without so much as a glance back. Guilt and shame for the hurt she caused him, ate at her heart, and she fought to hold back another deluge of sobs. Joe's voice brought her out of the pit she sank into. "What did you say?"

"I asked what time you get off and if you have any plans for this evening. I'd like to discuss something with you."

Shaunna's heart hardened and she wondered if this was the end. What did he want, a divorce? Looking into his eyes, she doubted it. That, too, served to complicate an already complicated situation. She stifled a sob. "At five and no, I don't have any plans."

"Would you mind if I wait at the apartment until then?"

She did not need or want him watching over her shoulder for the rest of her shift. Shaunna shook her head. "That's fine." With Joey in her arms, she stood to her feet, gave him a final hug and a kiss and attempted to hand him back to his father.

Joey cried out when Joe's hands closed over his tiny waist. He clung to her and buried his face in her neck. Shaunna jerked him away from Joe, trembling from the emotions rioting within her soul. Buddy, in his infinite wisdom, picked that precise moment to stroll into the room.

"Hey. What's all the fuss here?" He tickled Joey's cheek.

"He needs a nap but doesn't want to leave his mama," Joe answered.

"That's understandable," Buddy remarked. "It's slow around here anyway, so go on home with him, Shaunna."

Shaunna nodded and turned toward the door.

Joe hesitated long enough to thank Buddy.

"Thank me by straightening out this mess," Buddy replied.

"Exactly what I came home to do."

They rode home in tense silence. Shaunna wondered what Joe meant by his closing remark to Buddy but was too upset to ask. Her mind circled on all the possibilities. They arrived at the apartment and Joe took her by the arm and guided her up the stairs.

Shaunna put her fussy child in his crib. *Where he belongs,* she thought with a fierce stab of protectiveness. She stroked his silky blond hair, reluctant to leave his side. The gesture calmed her frazzled nerves even as it calmed Joey's restlessness. A few quiet moments alone with him was all she needed. She kissed his head, whispered a prayer then took a deep breath and went to hear what Joe had to say.

She didn't really want to talk to him now. She was too confused, and hurt, and angry. But she had no choice. She had to find out what he wanted before she could consider how to get on with her life.

Chapter Fourteen

Shaunna came home from work to find candles, roses, and wine. Joe had arranged with Millie to keep Joey for the night so he and Shaunna could settle their differences once and for all.

She relaxed for a few minutes in the warm bath he'd prepared for her then emerged ready to talk. They chatted for a few minutes, then Joe handed her a piece of paper that demanded she make up her mind about the state of their marriage. She gazed down at the lab report which gave him a clean bill of health, something she insisted he obtain before he even thought about touching her. The statement obliterated him from any physical traces of his affair, but it could not stop the sharp stab of pain in her heart. Anger followed.

"Well, thank God for small miracles," she bit out and tossed the paper at him. "I guess this makes it all OK." Anger flared in his eyes, but Joe bit his tongue.

"No, it doesn't," he replied, his tone mild. "I know this doesn't absolve me from all guilt, Shaunna. It doesn't change what I've done, but nothing can do that. What more do you want from me? I've already apologized and promised you it will never happen again. I haven't touched you in days. I went to the doctor, like you insisted. And now, when I give you proof I'm clean you throw the report back in my face. I don't know what else I can do. What do you want from me?"

The agony in his voice and sincerity in his eyes forced her to bite back the angry retorts which sprang to mind. Joe reached for her. She stiffened.

"I can't erase what I've done, Shaunna. I can't change the past. God knows if I could, I would. All I can do is assure you, once again, it will never happen again. I don't know what else I can say or do to earn your forgiveness. But I know this much, our marriage will not work if I'm the only one trying."

Shaunna jerked out of his grasp, still angry. Angry with him for what he did. Angry at fate for the curves it threw in her life and angry with herself for not being able to let go of the pain, bitterness, and unforgiveness, in her heart.

"So, I guess I'm supposed to take this piece of paper and your word and run off with you to some God-forsaken place in the swamps and believe we'll live happily ever after?"

Shaunna knew she was being unreasonable, but in her heart she hadn't heard the right words yet. The right words to ease the pain of his infidelity and to trust him again, even a little. She had no idea what the *right words* were, but she knew he hadn't spoken them.

Joe shook his head and clenched his fists instead of reaching for her again. "We don't have to move. I won't take the job if you don't want me to. We can stay here, and I'll keep driving if that's what you want. You name it and I'll do it. Just don't say it's over between us. But, before you say anything, I want to ask one question."

He lifted her chin and waited for her to look into his eyes. "I've wanted to ask this for days, but I couldn't. I have to ask it now. This guy you were with the other day, what does he mean to you?"

Anger erupted at the mere nerve of him to mention Todd at this moment, or *any* moment for that matter. Her shoulders stiffened, teeth clenched, hands curled into tight fists. "I haven't slept with him if that's what you mean."

"That's not what I asked. I have no right to ask you that after what I've done," he admitted. His voice remained soft, and she could tell by the pain and guilt in his tone he believed her.

"What I want to know is how you feel about him? Is he the reason you can't or won't forgive me? Is he in the way of you giving our marriage another chance? And, if you do decide to give us a try, can we give it an honest shot with him so close?"

Shaunna felt the fight leave her. Those were the right words...that no matter what else he thought, he hadn't judged her relationship with Todd. Even if it bothered him, he wouldn't ask about it.

No matter what Joe had done, she had married him for better or worse. Regardless of how much she loved Todd, and she did love him, she would have to make a choice. In that moment, she knew this was what she'd prayed for and what God intended when he created marriage. She also knew she could not deny the love she and Joe once shared, no matter how confused she felt now. And Joe was right; she would not be able to give her marriage an honest try if she constantly ran into Todd. Both her marriage and Joe deserved a chance. For the sake of their child, she had to try and recapture the love she once shared with her husband.

Her shoulders slumped in defeat as wave after wave of emotions washed over her. Pain. Fear. Resignation. *Love*. A soft sigh escaped, tears slipped from her eyes. In the last four days she'd argued, fought, screamed at, and talked with Joe, but not once did she cry. Now she couldn't stop the tears pouring from her heart. Tears of pain for what they lost, tears of hope for their future, tears of grief over what she knew she had to do.

The choice was made.

Hope raced through Joe's heart at the first tear and grew when she began to shake as silent sobs wracked her small frame. "Shaunna?" he whispered, his voice thick. "Are we OK? Can we try again? Do you forgive me?"

She nodded.

Her forgiveness cleansed the remains of guilt from his heart for the sin he committed against her. Relief swept his soul. "Thank you. Thank God."

He drew her into his arms. When her sobs subsided, he cupped her face in his hands.

"I love you," he whispered, and skimmed his lips over hers. "I am so sorry. I swear I will never hurt you again," he promised then kissed her eyes and cheeks. His mouth took possession of hers for the first time in months. His lips remained soft, insistent, urging a response from her while he held his passion in check.

Shaunna began to tremble. A soft whimper of surrender escaped as he awakened the desire asleep within her, the desire which had raged and been banked a few nights ago in Todd's arms. Where that was wrong, this was right. So right.

She pressed into him, shy at first, then urgent. Joe murmured sweet words of love and desire as his mouth devoured hers. He rose and lifted her in one smooth gesture then carried her to their bed. The lovemaking which ensued was a gentle rediscovery of the love they once knew, a tender reawakening of the passion that had existed between them, and a subtle recommitment of their marriage vows.

* * *

Shaunna awoke before dawn, wrapped in her husband's arms. She slipped from the bed and prayed. *Oh, Father, thank You. Thank You for the blessings in my life. Thank You for bringing them home safe to me. Thank You for answering my prayers.*

God's peace filled her, and Shaunna knew she'd made the right choice in forgiving Joe and accepting him back into her heart. Later, however, in the harsh light of day, faced with Mike's anger and fears, she experienced doubts about her decision to remain with Joe. She sat in silence while he paced his office.

"How can you let him do this to you?"

The angry edge to his voice pierced her heart. "He's my husband."

"But he's taking you away from your home. From the people who love you. From the place you were born and raised!"

"My home is with my husband and my son." Her lips trembled and she fought back tears. She and Joe were moving to Louisiana.

"Did you tell the Fredericks yet?"

She stifled a sob, blinked hard to stem the tears gathering in her eyes. "Yes. Buddy is trying to find a replacement and Millie hasn't stopped crying."

"They love you, and so do I."

The anguish in his voice tore at her heart. She buried her face in her hands. Tears leaked through her fingers.

"Leaving here is the hardest thing I've had to do in my life, next to burying Mama."

Mike groaned. "But why, honey? Why?"

Shaunna's mind did a quick, desperate search for an answer to appease him and quiet the doubts which plagued her heart. "He's my husband, the father of my child."

"Do you love him?"

Mike walked over to where she sat, knelt at her feet, and cupped her shoulders in his hands. In all the answers she gave him, not once did she say she still loved Joe and she knew her lack of assurance concerned him.

"Look at me, Shaunna," he insisted and continued when she raised her gaze to his. "Please, honey, don't go if you have any doubts."

Her jaw hardened with determination, chin lifted a notch. "I can't keep Joey from his father. I never had a father. He will."

"But do you love him?"

Shaunna took a deep ragged breath, raked her fingers through her hair and avoided Mike's gaze. She knew she loved Joe but how much, she was unsure. All she knew was she had to do what was best for her family. The move would be difficult, but life had never been easy for her. She knew she needed to convince him, and herself, her decision was a good one and the right thing to do. She dragged the heels of her hands down her face, emitted a weary sound, and locked her gaze with his.

"Yes, I love him."

Mike shoved to his feet and whirled away with a snort. "What about Todd?"

Her chin lifted a notch, eyes narrowed. "That's a cheap shot and an unfair question. I never promised Todd anything."

Defiance fled, strength deserted her. She buried her face in her hands and sobbed again then raised a beseeching gaze to his. "Please, Uncle Mike, don't make this any harder than it already is."

Pain flashed in his eyes, his shoulders slumped in defeat. Mike groaned. "Come here," he urged and opened his arms.

Shaunna struggled for control and walked into his embrace. Mike clasped her to his chest and asked once more, "Are you sure this is what you want?"

She nodded. "I'm sure I want to try."

He heaved a resigned sigh and brushed the hair off her face. "OK. OK. The most important thing in the world to me is your happiness. If leaving with Joe makes you happy, then I'll stand behind you. Do you want me to tell Todd for you?"

She took a deep breath and hesitated, tempted to worm her way out of that situation. She knew she couldn't leave without some explanation, and allowing Mike to explain for her was both cowardly and selfish. Besides, she wanted to see him, *had* to see him one more time. "No, thanks, that's something I'll do myself. There is one thing you can do for me though..."

She paused, about to make the hardest request she would ever make. Although she knew by the look in Mike's eyes he knew what was coming. He cupped her face in his hands.

"What, darling?"

"Take care of Mama for me." A sob caught in her throat.

Mike brushed her tears away. "I will," he muttered and held her next to his heart. "Promise me you'll call and write often."

Shaunna heard the tears in his voice, felt the sob shudder through him. She placed her hand on his cheek, then her lips.

"I promise. Goodbye, Uncle Mike," she murmured then turned away from the closest thing to a father she'd ever known. She hesitated outside his door, heard when his knees hit the floor and the sobs wracking his frame but couldn't turn back, knowing if she did, she'd never be able to say goodbye to him again.

She left Mike's office in search of Todd. She passed his apartment and noticed his car parked there but not his motorcycle. She felt a momentary surge of panic. He could be anywhere, and she had no idea where to start her quest. Mike's offer echoed in her mind, but she ignored the temptation to give up, turn around, and go home. Her heart ached with determination as she set out to find him.

She passed the airstrip, recognized his motorcycle parked on the side of the road. Then she saw him. He stood alone, hands in his pockets, and stared at the smoke trail of a laser jet. She noticed the dejected slump to his shoulders and knew deep down in her heart *he* knew it was over between them.

She parked the car, got out, walked toward him, and wondered what to say. What *could* she say to ease the pain she would cause?

Todd heard the car door slam behind him and knew it was her. He knew even before he heard her say his name and felt her hand, soft on his arm. Her touch seared his flesh, his muscles quivered. He took an uneven breath and jerked away but didn't turn to face her.

"You're leaving." He'd been on his way to see Mike when he'd overheard their raised, angry voices. He hadn't meant to eavesdrop but hadn't been able to tear himself away from the door until he heard her say she still loved her husband.

"I'm sorry," she whispered.

He turned, and the pain in her eyes cut him like a knife. "But I love you," he whispered, his voice so thick he could hardly get the words past his raw throat. She shook her head, as if by sheer will, she could deny his words, could change his mind. He grabbed her by the shoulders, gave her a slight shake.

"Yes! I've always loved you. From the first time I laid eyes on you."

She spun away. Her fists clenched, breath gasped in and out in jagged pants, and eyes flashed fire when she turned back to face him.

"Oh, no, you don't, you're not going to lay all of this at my feet! You never told me you loved me! You told me to go on with my life. You made me promise! It's too late to tell me now!"

Todd took a step back before he either shook or kissed some sense into her. "It's not too late. You're just not giving me, giving us, a chance."

Tears filled her eyes. She didn't try to stem them but crossed her arms over her chest as though trying to contain her shattered heart. "I can't. Don't you understand? I have to do what's right." She choked back a sob.

"How do you know it's right?"

"I just know. I'm so sorry I've hurt you. I never wanted to hurt you."

A single tear escaped his eye and spurred her into action. She groaned and reached to wipe it away.

"Oh, don't. Please, don't." She cupped his face in her hands. Her lips quivered. "This is killing me."

Her pain, as deep and raw as his, cut through him like a sword. Todd emitted a harsh cry of her name, dragged her into his arms, and buried his face in her thick mass of hair.

The pain of losing him again, this time by choice, was more than Shaunna could bear. She wrapped her arms around his waist, buried her face into his chest, and drenched his shirt. "I wish I didn't have to make a choice, I wish I could love you both."

Todd drew in a sharp breath. He swallowed hard, groaned, and hauled her against him. "I know. Don't cry, baby. Please, I can't stand it when you cry like this."

When her sobs subsided, he cupped her face in his hands and brushed the tears off her cheeks. "Are you sure this is what you want?"

Shaunna didn't want him to see how unsure she felt so she closed her eyes, took a deep breath and nodded then bowed her head, ashamed of the hurt she knew she caused. She knew he was not satisfied with her response when he gave her a slight shake and demanded she look at him.

"Promise me you're sure or I won't let you go."

She would have to convince him, or he'd never let her leave. She also knew he'd see through anything less than complete honesty.

"Oh, Todd," she whispered, her voice urgent. "I wish it were that easy. I'm sure I have to try. But I want you to know something..." She hesitated, unsure how to say what she needed to say. "If things were different, if he weren't so determined, if nothing was left between us, if I didn't think there was a chance, I would stay." Her eyes searched his for some sign he understood.

A ghost of a smile played around his sensuous lips, he nodded. "I know," he whispered. "And I understand," he said and gathered her close once more.

She should leave. Shaunna knew Joe waited for her, but was unable, unwilling, to end it, to end them, just yet. She held him firm in her embrace, committed the feel of his body to heart.

"I have to go," she whispered, then clung, not yet able to turn him loose.

"I know," he answered and tightened his arms around her. With a sigh of surrender, he stepped away, loosened his hold but rubbed her back and shoulders in a tender gesture.

"Don't look back," he whispered then dropped his hands to his side, clenched his fists.

She saw the struggle in his eyes, felt it in her heart, as each fought not to grab hold and cling. They gazed at each other, read the naked truth in each other's eyes.

Neither wanted to be the first to walk away.

Shaunna touched his face, traced his features...his eyes, his jaw, his mouth. A shiver shook her when he held her hand and pressed his lips to her fingertips.

"I almost wish we had made love the other night."

Almost?

The word echoed between them like a silent scream. The despair in his eyes slashed her heart another degree. He shook his head, swallowed hard.

"Know this. If we had, you would not leave here today."

She stroked his cheek, her smile tender, bittersweet. "Take care of yourself. Please," she whispered then placed her mouth on his.

Lips met on a sigh, breaths mingled on a sob. Each of them committed the kiss to heart and fought not to cling to the other. With a final touch, a last trembling smile, Shaunna did one of the hardest things she'd ever done in her life.

She left.

Part II

DESTINY: *Fate.*

Lives forever entwined with velvet chains.

Chapter Fifteen

The sun began its descent: blood red, bright, and hot on a glorious May afternoon. Though low in the western sky, its brilliance filtered through the branches. Huge trees lined the gravel road, provided shade, and perfumed the air with the scent of magnolia and pine. An occasional breeze added a hint of honeysuckle to the aroma and offered relief from the stifling Louisiana heat.

This was Shaunna's favorite time of day, right before dusk but still early enough for a nice, long ride. She kicked her feet out of the stirrups and loosened her grip on the reins, then leaned over to pat her horse on the neck.

Smokey snorted and nibbled at the soft grass along the side of the road. Shaunna chuckled and gave him his head, knowing he was ready to walk after the exhilarating run upon leaving home. She lifted her arms overhead and stretched, enjoying the peaceful country road. A serene smile played upon her lips as she contemplated the joy of life.

Almost six years had passed since she, Joe, and Joey moved to Louisiana, and Shaunna couldn't remember a time when she was happier than she was right now. Her mind wandered back over the years and how they'd grown since coming here. The first year was the hardest. They'd fought a lot. Fought, loved and learned, then settled into a comfortable realm of marriage, one of peace and harmony.

And now?

Now, life was an endless bowl of cherries, without so much as a single pit. Well, maybe just one. If only her husband stayed home more than two weeks at a stretch. Other than that...

Oh, well, guess you can't have it all.

The thought made her laugh. If what she had wasn't *it all*, she didn't know what else there could be. Heck, if it got any better she probably couldn't stand it! Another laugh escaped, swallowed by the rustle of trees as a gust of wind lifted the hair off her shoulders.

She raked her fingers through her hair, thanked God for her life, and promised herself she'd take Joey to the beach tomorrow. *Saturday.* One more week and Joe would be home. A thrill of excitement raced through her as she thought about her husband, and what his homecomings were like. Pulling Smokey's nose out of the grass, she kicked him into a trot, then a gallop.

She leaned forward, buried her hands in his mane, and urged him into a run, thrilling when he chomped down on the bit and obeyed the grasp of her legs and the sound of her voice. Faster, until her hair streamed out behind her, mixing with his dark mane, and she felt as though she and her horse were one.

Oblivious to her surroundings, Shaunna didn't hear the car approach from behind. The squeal of tires, blast of a horn, and spray of gravel and dust brought her to her senses.

Spirited on the best of days, Smokey jumped and neighed with fright as the car sped by, missing them by a hairsbreadth. Shaunna clung to his neck. Her legs tightened. She grabbed the saddle horn and held on as he reared and bucked once more before her voice reached his ears. "Easy boy, easy."

After he settled down, she slid from the saddle and clung, trying to still her racing heart. Her legs threatened to buckle beneath her. Nothing like this had ever happened. She'd never experienced the helpless terror of losing control of her horse and trembled from it. She petted and stroked and soothed the animal, then checked his legs and hooves for any sign of injury. She heard the car door slam and footsteps but couldn't let go. Smokey snorted and pawed the ground in agitation. She continued to stroke his face and neck while murmuring in a desperate attempt to calm him before remounting.

Todd Jameson slammed his car to a halt and cursed his luck. *The perfect ending to a perfectly wretched day.* From the time he got out of bed this morning, late, nothing went right and now this. He leaned his forehead on the steering wheel, forced calm to his raging nerves, and prayed no one was hurt. He'd never seen anyone riding on this road before, and he hadn't seen them this time until he drove right upon them. His hand shook and he fumbled with the door handle. He climbed out of the car to go check on them.

"Are you all right? I swear I never saw you."

"Well, I guess you didn't. I'm surprised you saw anything with the way you came flying down here."

Thank God she wasn't hurt, Todd thought, giddy with

relief. From the tone of her voice, she was angry as all get out, but not hurt. "I'm sorry. I really didn't see you. Is there anything I can do?"

She turned on him in an angry whirl. "I think you've done enough already!" In her ire, she gave a rough jerk on the bridle and further upset her already irate horse. With a shrill neigh he reared. She stumbled as the big horse wrenched her off her feet. "Now look what you've done!"

Though delayed by shock, Todd reacted instinctively. He grabbed the horse's bridle with one hand and her arm with the other and yanked her away from the threatening hooves. Shoving his shoulder into its chest, he backed the horse up a step as Shaunna lost her footing and, with a yelp of frustration, landed in a heap on the ground.

"Whoa, boy, whoa," he quieted the agitated animal. Getting the horse under control, he turned to the woman at his feet. A wealth of emotions surged through him, his mind whirled. He reached down to help her up. "Are you all right, Shaunna?"

Shaunna's eyes widened in surprised recognition, a smile broke through the fear in her expression. "Todd!"

Emotions rioted within him. Desire heated his blood. Anger brought on by years of pain, loneliness, and regret obliterated all thought. He thrust her away then gave her a slight shake. "What are you doing here? Where's your husband? It's obvious the idiot still has no sense, that's way too much horse for a woman! You could have been killed!"

Fury replaced every other emotion in her eyes at his unfair, unwarranted attack. Shaunna jerked out of his grasp.

"I'll have you know my husband has plenty of sense," she replied, heating up and spilling over. "Smokey would never hurt me. It's idiots like you who drive like maniacs that would hurt or kill me."

The icy tone of her voice helped cool the erratic beat of his heart as anger gave way to the need to feel her body pressed against his. Todd jerked her to his chest and seized her lips in a bruising kiss.

Shaunna struggled in his grasp. "Stop it! How dare you?" she muttered, swiping the back of her hand across her mouth as though she could erase the imprint of where his lips bruised hers. Tears sprang into her eyes, a visible shiver shook her. Grabbing

Smokey's bridle, she rested her head against his face. He nuzzled her and emitted a low, soft nicker.

Chastised by the hurt in her eyes, Todd ran his fingers through his hair. How on earth was he ever supposed to forget if he ran into her every time he thought he'd gotten over her? Remorse seeped in, replaced the anger and frustration in his soul. "I'm sorry," he whispered, running his hand down her back. "That was uncalled for. Are you all right?"

"I'm fine," she muttered.

"Shaun." He sighed. "I didn't mean what I said. I don't know what came over me. I was just shocked to see you and upset over what happened. Are you sure you're all right?"

She nodded.

"What do you say I help you fix that cut?"

"What cut?"

He pointed to a cut on Smokey's side right beneath the stirrup. "That one."

A gasp escaped her as Shaunna reached trembling fingers to touch it. It wasn't deep but bled profusely. She threw the stirrup over the saddle and hooked it to the saddle horn so it wouldn't rub the horse's raw flesh.

"C'mon," Todd urged in a soft voice. "I don't live far from here. I'll help you treat it."

Taking a deep breath, she nodded.

"Put your saddle in my car. I'll go slowly enough for you to keep up."

Todd watched as she did as he suggested. Holding Smokey, he offered her a leg up. She declined with a shake of her head and with very little effort, mounted the big horse, careful of his injury.

Once they arrived at his house, she slid off the horse's back and again examined the cut on Smokey's side. Dust mixed with sweat and blood caked the abrasion. Todd retrieved his first-aid kit from the bathroom and handed it to her. He watched as she doused the cut with peroxide and examined it again.

"Doesn't appear to be deep or long enough for stitches." he said. Relieved, he handed her a tube of antibiotic salve. "I don't know if this will help."

She shrugged and applied a liberal amount to the cut. "It can't hurt. Now, how am I going to keep the dust and gravel out of it until I get him home? A band-aid is not going to work."

"Hang on. I've got an idea," he said, then handed her a piece of gauze big enough to cover the cut. Having trotted back into the house, he emerged with an old sheet and tore a wide strip off of it. It barely went around the big quarter horse's girth. "OK." He tore another strip and tied the two together. "What's a little bitty thing like you doing on such a big horse anyway?" he asked, while she wrapped the cloth around Smokey's belly.

"I raised him," she replied with a hint of pride in her voice.

He handed her the water hose to wash up then went inside once more. He returned with two glasses of iced tea and handed her one with a grin. "Peace offering."

She accepted with a smile and settled beside him on the porch. They sat in silence for a moment, sipping the cool liquid.

They turned to face each other and asked in unison, "What are you doing here?"

She giggled.

"You first," he insisted with a chuckle, curious to know why she was in the same town as he.

She grinned. "I've lived here for almost six years now. What's your excuse?"

"I live here, too." Questions crowded his mind. He asked them all at once. "Where's your husband? How's your son? How've you been?" His voice softened as he gazed at her. She hadn't changed a bit in the past five, almost six, years, but grown more beautiful.

Shaunna trembled at the softness in his eyes. With a smile she answered his questions in the order he'd asked. "Working. Terrific. Wonderful." Her voice quivered as she gazed at him. A tremble skittered along her spine as she remembered the feel of his hands on her skin and the taste of his lips. *The magic is still there.* Shaunna felt herself leaning toward him, anticipating his kiss.

Todd's breath caught in an audible hiss. He cupped her cheek and whispered her name.

Heat rushed to her cheeks. She turned away, sipped her tea, and attempted to calm her racing pulse. The silence between them became awkward, strained. Shaunna cleared her throat and got up to leave.

She saddled Smokey, careful of the bandaging. Todd

untied the reins from the porch rail and held the horse still while she climbed up on him, then passed them over the horse's head and slipped the leather straps to her. Her flesh burned where his hands brushed hers, a tremble skittered down her spine.

They gazed into each other's eyes, neither knowing what, if anything, they could say after all this time.

With a smile and a nod, Shaunna turned Smokey around and headed for home.

Chapter Sixteen

As soon as Todd picked the glasses up off the porch, the full impact of the afternoon hit him. Six years? Anger pummeled through his veins. What in the world was Mike thinking? He knew Shaunna had lived here for six years and he sent him anyway?

He stomped into the kitchen, slammed the glasses down on the counter, grabbed the phone and punched out the familiar number. He didn't know where Mike was coming from but he intended to find out. Teeth clenched, fingers drumming on the counter, he waited for the call to go through and Mike to get on the line.

"Todd, my boy! How's it going?"

For the first time in his life, Todd wished he could strangle his friend. "It was going great, Mike. Until today." Sarcasm thickened his voice. "Bet you'll never guess who I ran into this afternoon. Or do you already know because you planned it all along?" The tenuous hold on his temper snapped. "Damn it, Mike! What on earth were you thinking?"

"Whoa, what are you talking about?" Mike interrupted, confusion evident in his tone.

Todd raked his fingers through his hair and struggled to get a grasp on his whirling thoughts. "I ran into Shaunna today. What on earth were you thinking? You knew she's lived here for the past six years and yet you still sent me here. I thought we were friends." He moaned, the ache in his voice evident as pain crashed in.

"Now wait a minute. I remember telling you she and her husband used to live there but they moved out of Thibodaux. They live in some little town called Shivens, uh, Shuffens, uh..."

"Chauvin?"

"Yeah, that's it."

Todd moaned. "Chauvin is about thirty miles outside of Thibodaux."

Mike groaned. "Oh, no, I didn't know, Todd. I swear. I've never been there. Shaunna always came home for visits, and I never looked it up on a map. I mean, ask me and I can tell you where every Army base in the United States is located, but colleges offering ROTC? Ninety percent of them offer it and I can't begin to tell you where they all are. I promise I never would have told you about the position had I known. Wait a minute, what are you doing in Chauvin?"

His anger abated but pain continued to throb through his system. Todd leaned on the doorframe. "I leased a house out here last week. You want to hear the best part? As far as I can tell, my house is less than five miles from hers."

Mike gasped. "Oh, boy. You want me to get you out of there? I can send a replacement. Maybe transfer you to another college," he offered.

Todd rubbed his tired, gritty eyes. His mind mulled over the options as Mike spoke. "I don't know, Mike. I've been all over the world and never felt at home like I do here. I like it here. See what you can do. Call me. I'll make up my mind later."

"OK. You haven't found some sweet little Cajun girl to help you forget?" Todd heard the strain in Mike's voice as he attempted to ease some of the tension on the line.

"Lacey." A groan accompanied her name and Todd consulted his watch. He should have been gone an hour ago.

"Pretty name," Mike remarked. "Knowing you, she's as pretty as her name."

"She is. Very pretty. Special, too. She's deaf."

A soft chuckle preceded Mike's words. "Well, at least you don't have to worry about her talking back. You'd always have to worry about that with Shaunna."

"Don't be crude, Mike," Todd growled, unspent anger laced his tone.

"You know me better than that," Mike chided, his tone soft. "Just trying to lighten the mood a little."

Todd buried his face in the crook of his arm with a sigh. The whole afternoon had been a horrible strain on his emotions. Simply holding the phone was an effort. "I know, buddy. I'm sorry. I never thought I'd run into her. I mean, I didn't know she lived so close to the city. I didn't realize it would be so exhilarating and yet devastating. Besides," he forced his thoughts back to the other girl at hand. "Lacey has a language all of her own and she argues plenty."

Mike chuckled. "So, how did you two meet, and how come I haven't heard about her yet?"

"Met her my first day at work. Leaving the class room, I backed right into her and made a complete mess of all her things. I bent to pick them up and we bumped into each other again. She landed in a heap on the floor." Todd laughed at the memory. "Oh man, she was a sight. All flushed and tussled."

"I'll bet."

"Took a few minutes for me to realize she's deaf and to understand she wanted my help on a class assignment. Been friends ever since." Todd's heart clutched. "Now what am I going to do? It's obvious from one meeting I'm not over Shaunna."

Mike's exhalation spoke volumes. "I don't know, guy, but we'll get it figured out. I'll call you in a few days."

They rang off. Todd tried to relax while he took a shower, but his mind whirled with implications and possibilities. The fact Lacey was a student and, he, an instructor had made it easy for him to resist the temptation to cross the line from friends into a more intimate relationship with her, but both of them felt the desire. She'd even made a point to remind him often she wouldn't be a student forever and they looked forward to the time when they could explore the possibility of a real relationship.

Tears pricked his eyes and burned the back of his throat. Todd raked a hand over his face and slapped the water off. He jerked a towel off the rack, rubbed it over his body and through his hair then wrapped it around his waist. He turned on the hot water in the sink to shave and caught a glimpse of himself in the mirror. Haunted eyes. Pale skin. His hand closed around the razor, and he fought not to smash a fist into the mirror. The incident today made it clear that, although his relationship with Lacey was the closest he'd come to getting deeply involved since Shaunna left Georgia six years ago, he did not love her with the same passion, the same fire he felt for Shaunna.

How he managed to shave without scraping the skin off his face he'd never know. With a heavy heart and grim determination, he left to do what he knew had to be done.

Break off his relationship with Lacey.

Lacey opened the door before Todd could knock, worry etched in her expressive face. Todd knew he had some tall explaining to do, though he had no idea where to start. He attempted to smile. "Hi," he said with mouth and hand.

His heart twisted at the fear and confusion in her eyes and he knew without a doubt he was about to hurt her. Better now than later, he thought, hating himself. And Shaunna. And Fate, the real witch in the whole miserable situation. The air around them became strained, awkward. He spoke again.

"Sorry I'm late. Can I come in?"

She stepped back from the door and allowed his entrance then turned to face him. "Being late is not a problem," she signed. "Why you're late may be." She attempted a smile, failed miserably.

Todd's stomach did somersaults at the ordeal ahead. In the nine months they'd known each other, Lacey had taught him a great deal about sign language, and he taught her more about reading lips and expressions. Together they established their own style of communication. Therefore, he knew she could read right through his strained smile.

His mind raced as he wondered how and where to begin. Raking his fingers through his hair, he sighed. "There was an accident this afternoon."

The fear which had plagued Lacey the past few hours escalated when she gazed into Todd's face. He'd changed somehow, and her heart sank into her stomach. *Someone else.* The thought twisted her heart and mind like a knife. *Not again!* Her heart cried out as she rejected the thought. Todd was different. He wouldn't do that to her.

Experience had taught Lacey to never give too much of her heart to a man. Once they got tired of waiting for what they desired, mainly sex, they seemed to not want or need her anymore. From the beginning she'd sensed something different about Todd. He was a good man, honest and sincere. A man of honor. Although their relationship hadn't ventured beyond that of good friends, she'd felt secure in their feelings for each other. Just last week he'd given her a dainty gold chain from which hung a tiny diamond. A promise, he'd said, that one day his kiss would be more than a brush of lips across her cheek or forehead.

A surge of anger tore through her. "An accident? What did you hit, a cat?" Her lips thinned, chin trembled. "Tell the truth, there's someone else, isn't there?" she accused in short, angry gestures.

Todd grimaced but shook his head no.

She saw through that too. Swallowing her tears and her pride, she slapped him. "You lie! I thought you were different, but you're not. You men are all alike. Can't wait to get in the sack or get tired of waiting. Then you leave. But, I gotta hand it to you. You were a lot more patient than most." She jerked the chain off and threw it, hitting him in the chest.

Todd didn't even attempt to catch it, but grabbed her hands instead, pulling her to him as a tear slid from her eye. She struggled in his embrace, but he held on. Even though she couldn't hear, she felt his chest rumble with words.

Grabbing the pen off the table by the door, he turned so she could see the tablet where he wrote in large letters: *No!!!*

Still holding her hands, he turned her to face him. "Lacey, please," he spoke distinctly so she could read his lips. "Please. Let me explain."

The haunted look in his eyes neutralized her anger. *Something's wrong.* Lacey knew she would not find out what unless she let him tell her. Jerking out of his embrace, she led the way into the kitchen and motioned for him to sit, then walked over and opened the refrigerator. Grabbing two beers she placed one in front of him and opened the other for herself. She hated beer but had a feeling she'd need this one.

Todd suppressed a wry grin when she placed a can in front of him and sat with the other clasped in a tight grip. She popped the top and foam spewed forth from the cold brew. She took a gulp, grimaced, and waited with an expectant look on her face, so he began his story. "Ten, no twelve years ago, I met this girl..."

In the time it took to relate the story of him and Shaunna, Todd realized the similarities in their personalities were what had drawn him to Lacey. In looks they were opposite, but in character they were so much alike it was uncanny, almost eerie. Shaunna was rich, vibrant. Every pore of her being spoke of vitality from the rich hue of her hair to the dark, expressive eyes. Lacey was tiny, fragile, with an ethereal quality about her. Her fair, almost translucent complexion, silvery blond hair, and deep violet eyes added to her otherworldly appearance. Both women possessed an insurmountable amount of strength and determination, and both had overcome obstacles in their lives to which many would succumb.

Pushing his beer away, he reached over and brushed the

tears off her cheeks. Lifting her chin, he gazed into her eyes. "I'm sorry, Lace. I never want to hurt you."

Lacey smiled and reached over to give him a hug. "Thank you for being honest with me," she signed. "What a beautiful story. Love like that is rare."

He snorted. "Or only happens in those novels you like to read."

Laughter lit her features. "Outside the love of God, I haven't known much love in my life. Not the kind you have for her. The kind of which authors write, poets pen, and artists sing. The kind expressed in the Bible. Gives me hope that one day, God will bless me with a man who loves me as deeply as you love Shaunna."

Todd shook his head. "I don't understand how or why I still love her or how to get over her, but I do know I can't love you the way you deserve to be loved." He raked his fingers through his hair. "God knows if I could, I would. You are so beautiful, Lacey—inside and out."

Lacey stroked the cheek she'd slapped earlier. For once she wished she could talk and tell him she did understand. She cupped his face in her hands until she had his full attention. "It's OK," she signed. "I do understand. And it's OK. We can still be friends, can't we?"

Todd's breath stuck in his throat. Her continued friendship was more than he could hope for. He searched her eyes, surprised at the love and understanding he saw there. "You still want to be my friend?"

Lacey's shoulders shook with a silent giggle. "Yes! You need a friend, don't you?"

Todd grinned. "God knows I do."

She sobered. "I have to tell you something."

Todd knew Lacey well enough to understand that when she got a certain look on her face, like the one she had now, whatever she said would be full of knowledge and wisdom. She always amazed him with this trait of hers. Something deep, something spiritual lived in Lacey, and he had learned to listen, really listen, when she was like this. She continued talking in the language they'd perfected between them.

"There is a reason, a purpose behind why you two always run into each other. I don't know what it is yet, but I do know it's true. The Bible says in Ecclesiastes there is a time and a season for every purpose under heaven. Revelation will come, Todd. You just have to be patient."

"I wish I had your confidence."

Light radiated from her. "Confidence born of faith."

Todd sighed. "I'd love to have that kind of faith."

She smiled. "Be careful what you pray. Faith is usually honed by fire and shaped by trials and tribulations."

"Tell me about it, Lacey. I know you were abandoned at birth and grew up in a convent, so you've had a foundation in God from early on. My mother died when I was three and I was raised—or rather raised myself—in a single-parent home with an alcoholic father. I knew nothing of pride or honor or even stability, until I joined the Army, and even that was out of necessity and not by choice."

"What do you mean?"

Todd dry washed his face, the memory as sharp as if the event had happened yesterday. "It was either join the Army or go to jail."

Her eyes widened. Shock clouded her features.

"Jail! *You?*"

He chuckled. "Yeah, me. My father had died, and we had no money, so I thought I'd rob a liquor store to pay for his burial."

"My word, you're lucky to be alive!"

Bitterness twisted Todd's gut. He snorted. "Not lucky. Stupid and foolish. Wouldn't have worked anyway, the gun was empty. When the police arrived, I gave up without a fight, just like the failure dear old dad always accused me of being."

"How old were you?"

"Seventeen."

"Then I'd say you were *not* stupid or foolish but brave and wise. Much better to surrender and live than make a mistake that might cost your life. It's obvious the judge saw it that way too when he gave you the option to join the Army. And now look at the man you've become."

Love and pride shone through her and for the first time in his life Todd felt something other than shame and guilt when he thought about his past. "So what other trials and triumphs have you experienced that have made you so strong?"

Lacey rose and offered Todd another beer, choosing water for herself. Once seated, she told him the story of a young girl who'd been shunned all of her life because she was deaf. An undetected ear infection had damaged her eardrums. Surgery could not correct the problems caused by neglect, so Lacey lost all hearing. For years others treated her with disdain because she could not communicate her needs or wants. Nor could she show her love or appreciation when she received the slightest bit of encouragement. Emotion punctuated her features and sharpened her signs, but what amazed Todd the most was the lack of bitterness in her expressive eyes.

"When I was about ten a new nun entered my life. Sister Mary Katherine Bishop brought understanding and compassion to the convent. She took me under her wing and taught me sign language, then showed me how to read and write. Under her tutoring I developed a burning desire to catch up and within two years I could read and write as well as the other children my age. Under the Sister's gentle guidance, I learned the real meaning and depth of God's love and I never doubted Him until the day Sister Mary Katherine died in an automobile accident."

Lacey stopped, brushed tears away and continued. "I was fifteen when that happened and it took a long time to understand the Sister's purpose had been fulfilled. God sent her to help me and to help the other nuns and children at the convent to grow in love, patience, understanding and kindness. And I knew, with the love and guidance of God, I could do and be anything I wanted to. So you see, Todd, all things do work together for the good of those who love God and are called according to His purpose. You've got to believe that and not give up. Trust Him completely even when you don't understand what's going on."

"I don't know how patient I can be. It's crazy, Lace, the circles of fate in our lives."

She nodded. "I know. But just wait. I'll wait with you."

"Thank you," he whispered, then signed. A gentle light shone from within her. She enfolded him in her embrace. Todd clung to her warmth, grateful she still offered it.

Chapter Seventeen

After leaving Lacey's, Todd drove around for a while before going home. He went out of town and down to the Gulf shore. He walked in the sand along the beach and wondered what on earth was going on. He wondered and questioned God, searching for some kind of answers, some clue as to why he and Shaunna's paths always crossed, why their lives entwined.

Getting no revelation or insight, Todd did the only thing he could think of; he went home and dug out his Bible. Beginning with Ecclesiastes, he read the scripture Lacey talked about. Then he read further, until he felt a burning desire to read the entire book.

Each evening he set aside time and engrossed himself in the word of God, amazed at the steadfastness of God's love for His people. Like his love for Shaunna, it seemed never-ending, unshakable, and strong. He spent many evenings with Lacey discussing what he read and, again, she amazed him with the depth of her faith.

He was convinced some deeper reason existed, some divine purpose for his feelings for Shaunna, and for the fact he could never forget those feelings. He believed there was some unknown reason for the circles fate played in their lives. Though he didn't know what it might be, he believed one day the answers would come. Until then he could only wait. Wait and trust God that he didn't go crazy in the mean time.

The most memorable and important lesson he learned was the absolute necessity of salvation through Jesus Christ. He'd heard it all before and many times during his eight years in the Special Forces, he'd trusted God with his life. But never before had he trusted Him with his heart. Never had he known the importance of a personal relationship with Him. There were still moments when he doubted it was real or possible. When overcome by uncertainty, all he had to do was look at Lacey's life and remember her story to believe something unseen made her as strong and as gentle and kind as she was.

* * *

Every day for the next couple of weeks, Todd drove home from work, hoping for, and at the same time fearing, a glimpse of Shaunna. Nothing could stop the whirlwind his thoughts were in. They ran around in circles, giving him hope and yet, confusing him. His shoulders slumped with disappointment because he hadn't seen Shaunna, and yet his heart lightened with relief.

How could someone be relieved and disappointed at the same time?

His thoughts were so full of Shaunna he could envision her every time he closed his eyes. He could see her, feel her, and his whole body ached with response. He groaned in frustration. He changed clothes and took his daily run trying desperately to clear his mind. It didn't work. He took a shower then tried to read. Not a chance.

"Lord," he groaned in frustration. "What am I going to do?"

Patience was the answer, and Todd nearly choked on the irony of it. Patient, how? Leaving the confines of his house, he drove over to Lacey's knowing he could find peace at her home.

Lacey welcomed Todd with open arms and a smile. She could read him like a book and knew he'd had a rough day. His face was taut, his eyes haunted. Holding him, she felt the familiar stirring of desire he aroused in her without even trying. Woman's instinct told her he needed a friend, someone to ease the pain and frustration he felt. Jealousy made her want to make him forget Shaunna if only for a little while. She knew how much it hurt because she felt the same hurt for him. Maybe not as deep or as strong, but she felt the pain of loving someone and knowing you couldn't have them.

Since that night almost three weeks ago, Lacey had prayed daily for God to help her deal with her feelings for Todd. She knew her task was to bring him closer to the Lord and she prayed for the strength to conquer the physical response Todd elicited in her. Today, God seemed to be silent.

Lacey knew sex without marriage was a sin. She also knew the devastating effect that particular sin had on her life. The lesson had cost her dearly the first and only time she gave in to desire. She was eighteen, fresh out of school, new to life outside the convent and she thought she was in love. She never forgot the pain and shame of giving herself outside of marriage. Nor did she forget the unconditional forgiveness of God when she turned to Him after her love was thrown back in her face.

Since that first demoralizing encounter with a man five years ago, she withheld herself. That, too, cost her more relationships than she ever imagined it would. Men got tired of waiting and moved on to easier conquests. Except Todd. Todd never pressured her. Remembering his patience and tenderness, she felt an ache in her being which went far deeper than the physical, but it was her body that responded to having him in her arms.

She nuzzled the skin showing above the open collar of his shirt, stroked the taut muscles of his chest and back. She felt his chest reverberate as a moan ripped through him. His arms tightened around her.

Todd groaned and forced her to look at him. "Lacy, don't." He knew she could read his lips.

She just smiled, her eyes deep pools of love.

Todd wrestled with the temptation to capture her mouth with his, pick her up and carry her to the bedroom. Gazing at her passion-flushed features, he regretted he could not love her as completely as he wanted, as honestly as she deserved. Desire died a quick death. He knew he could take her now and ease the ache in his body, but doing so would create a gulf between them. He stepped out of her embrace. The hurt in her eyes cut him like a knife. Todd took her in his arms once again, this time to comfort. He stroked her hair and hated himself for the tears she shed. When her sobs subsided, he tilted her chin with his finger. A tender smile tugged at his mouth. He brushed his knuckles across her cheek.

"I care too much to use you that way, Lace."

He didn't have to explain. She knew. Fresh tears filled her eyes. She blinked them back and nodded. "I know. I wish it were enough."

They clung to each other until the passion subsided. In its wake developed the warm glow of friendship, of love deeper than normal human capacity, one far more profound than physical expression could ever accomplish.

* * *

As the would-be lovers battled their feelings on land, another, more evil, struggle was uprising in the Gulf of Mexico.

About one hundred miles off the shore of Galveston, Texas, a crew-boat radioed an oilrig, with an S. O. S. that they were having engine trouble. The rig responded with an invitation to dock until help arrived. The boat tugged along until the workers tied it to the platform.

Dressed in black and wearing masks and gloves, the gang boarded the platform bearing guns. They took all valuables, watches, rings and tools, harassing the workers and robbing them of everything including their pride.

The oilfield hands watched, helpless with fear, until the boat raced out of sight. They couldn't even radio for help. The crooks had destroyed the short-wave radio on the rig before tossing it into the water. They gathered together in the galley and prayed the injured would survive and someone on shore would soon realize they hadn't heard from the rig and send help. If that failed, their only hope was to wait until crew change and pray their relief got there safe and on schedule.

* * *

Unaware of the uprising, oblivious of the impending danger, Shaunna sent her husband off to work. A contented smile played along her lips as she stretched languidly, remembering the night of loving which always preceded Joe's return to work; loving meant to keep them both satisfied until his return three weeks from now. Though she enjoyed every minute of his two weeks home, she didn't like him being gone three weeks at a time. But it was his job, a job he loved. With a sigh, she wrapped her arms around his pillow. Holding it, she drifted off to sleep, and dreamed she held his strong, hard body instead.

* * *

Once again, Todd saw Shaunna out riding. He wondered what she'd been up to these past three weeks. He knew she recognized him when she pulled Smokey up short, turned him around, urged him to jump the ditch and brought him to a sliding halt alongside the car.

The entire maneuver took a split second which seemed like an eternity to Todd. In his mind's eye he could see her fall off the big horse and trampled beneath his hooves. He glared up into her smiling face when she bent down to bid him hello.

Slamming out of the car, he exploded. "Are you crazy? Pulling a stupid stunt like that! You shouldn't even be riding such a big horse, much less jumping ditches with him!"

Shaunna laughed down into his tense face. "Well, hello to you, too," she teased. "Don't worry about me. I've been riding him since he was old enough to carry me. I know what I'm doing."

Todd snorted. "And how long is that, two, maybe three years? And that makes you an expert rider?"

She chuckled. "Expert, no, but I bought him when he was six months old. I raised him and broke him. I know him well enough to know my limitations. Besides, I had a good teacher."

Her soft voice reminded him, it was *he* who taught her to ride. "Yeah, well that was a long time ago," he muttered as the rest of her words took on a different meaning than what she said. Limitations... Those she imposed on herself and those imposed by her marriage vows. There was no threat or warning in the statement, only fact. In a voice as soft as velvet, she reminded him no matter how deep the feelings ran between them, she was off limits.

A fact I'm painfully aware of.

Todd resisted the urge to pull her into his aching arms. Such an action would serve to complicate an already complicated situation.

He knew by the softness in her eyes, Shaunna recognized his struggle. He could tell she felt it too when she tightened her grip on the reins and backed Smokey up a step.

She leaned toward him, a wicked gleam in her eyes, a smile tugging at her mouth. "Got your blood pumping though, didn't I?"

"Being in the same state as you keeps my blood pumping," he muttered under his breath.

She clicked her tongue and edged the horse closer. "What?"

He scowled up at her. "I said if you fall off and break your neck, I'll leave you for the buzzards."

Shaunna's eyes widened in mock horror, and she bit back a smile. "Todd Jameson, you should be ashamed of yourself," she scolded, her tone playful.

"For what?"

She giggled. "For telling such a blatant lie."

Todd was not immune to her infectious laughter. He chuckled. "Witch."

"Well, look here, he can smile," she remarked with exaggerated surprise.

Todd eyed her, not sure how to handle her being so close and yet, so untouchable.

"How about a glass of tea?" he offered without thinking of the consequences of them being alone at his house.

"Thought you'd never ask," she remarked. With a sassy toss of her head, she turned Smokey in the direction of his house and kicked him into a gallop.

Todd groaned. "What in heaven's name possessed me to do that?" he asked himself with a muttered curse, as he climbed back into his car and followed her.

Shaunna walked Smokey to cool him off while Todd went inside and prepared them a glass of tea. Loosening the cinch on her saddle, she dropped the reins so Smokey could graze in the soft grass near the porch and joined Todd on the steps.

They sipped in silence. The air around them sizzled with emotion. Shaunna trembled when his arm brushed hers. She turned, handed him the empty glass, and with a shy smile, thanked him and left.

Todd sensed her disappointment that they could not communicate for the feelings raging between them. He too, wondered why he got so tongue-tied when she was around—like he had no brain, only emotions. Love and desire, deep, strong and white-hot, clamored within him and he wondered again how on earth to cope with her being so close.

Chapter Eighteen

Three days later Shaunna and Todd ran into each other again. As before, she was out riding, and he was on his way home from work. Noticing each other, about the same time, they smiled and waved. Todd stopped his car and Shaunna rode over to greet him. Once again, he invited her over for a glass of tea.

They sat in tense silence for a few moments then turned to face each other. "What...?" they asked at the same time. The incident made them laugh and broke the tension between them. Being a gentleman, Todd insisted she speak first.

"Well, there's something I've been dying to know since the first time you ran into me."

He grinned at the hint of laughter in her voice. "What's that?"

"What are you doing here?" Her laughing brown eyes and teasing voice belied the rudeness of her words.

He chuckled. "I'm an ROTC instructor at Nichols State."

"Since when?"

Todd answered her question and the conversation which ensued reflected on their lives over the past six years. He told her of some of his assignments while still in Special Forces. When she asked why he decided to get out, he replied, "Eight years in Special Forces is a long time. A person starts thinking about his own mortality, especially since I survived those eight years without a single injury. I just didn't know how much longer my luck would hold out."

The truth in his words and his tone of voice sent shivers through her soul, and Shaunna sent up a silent 'thank you' to God that he was safe and got out in one piece. Todd asked about her husband and son.

"Well, Joey's almost eight now, going into the third grade. And Joe's fine. He works offshore. Twenty-one on, fourteen off."

"Wow, he's gone a lot."

She smiled and answered the questions in his eyes. "Yeah, but he loves it so much more than driving a truck. Our first year here was the hardest. Poor Joe, I put him through hell, but he persevered," she admitted.

Todd snorted. "Hell was too lenient after what he put you

through."

Shaunna's smile was wistful. "No one deserves that much misery."

Again, he snorted. "How can you say that?" He couldn't hide the pain and anger in his voice for what he, too, had suffered at Joe's hands.

Shaunna understood how he felt. "It's called forgiveness, Todd. I had to forgive him and myself and get on with my life. Otherwise, I might have thrown away the thing that mattered to me the most."

Hurt glazed his eyes then they softened with understanding. He stroked her cheek, his smile tender.

"I'm glad it's worked out for you, Shaun. Really."

She pressed upward with her shoulder and snuggled her face into his palm. "Me, too. Leaving was difficult, but we managed and survived. Now we're happier than ever. And Todd, I'm glad to see you, to know you're OK. You don't know how many times I thought about you, and worried. Especially when I'd hear our Army was involved in a skirmish somewhere."

Todd's smile widened and a sound, part chuckle, part groan, escaped him. He brushed his thumb across her lips then withdrew his hand from her face. "So," he breathed, "tell me more."

"What do you want to know?"

"Every single thing you've done the past six years."

She giggled. "That might take a while, and I've got to get home. Mary will be back soon with Joey."

"Who's Mary?"

"Mary is a combination of Mama and Millie Frederick. She's my friend, housekeeper, and business partner."

He grinned. "She sounds like quite a character."

Shaunna laughed. "She is. Mary was our neighbor in the small apartment complex we lived in during the first two years in Thibodaux. With Joe gone like he was, and me unable to go home as often as I wanted, Mary became my friend and confidante. When I found out her husband died in a boating accident and her son in Vietnam, I began to realize how selfish and ungrateful I'd been toward Joe and toward God." She drew in a breath and sipped her tea.

"I realized I should get down on my knees and thank God

every day I still had my husband and son, and we were together. Mary's love for God, her peace, and strength helped me through that first awful year away from home and was a great influence on developing my faith."

Shaunna finished her tea and set the glass between them then drew her knees to her chest and wrapped her arms around them. "As the second year passed, Mary taught me a great deal about God, and even more about cooking and baking. When she confessed she'd once owned a small bakery but lost it after the death of her son, I approached Joe about opening a shop of our own. Knowing we'd be moving soon, we decided to do private catering instead and formed 'Shaunna's Sweets.' We cater small parties and weddings, providing all of the food and desserts needed for the occasion."

Todd cocked his head. "I remember seeing or hearing that name somewhere. 'Shaunna's Sweets'.... Should have put two and two together considering your nickname at the café back in Georgia."

A sweet flush tinted her cheeks. Todd grinned. "I'll never forget the first day I walked into the Feed Trough." He closed his eyes, inhaled. "I can still see people spilling over from every booth, hear the conversation and laughter mingling with the aromas in the air—bacon and eggs, ham and onions, hamburgers and French fries, fresh coffee. Thought I'd starve before I got waited on. Then out rings a voice... *Here she comes, Miss Shaunna Sweetness*'... and you walked in from the kitchen, a coffee pot in one hand, tray in the other." He chuckled, shook his head. "Captivated me, and I haven't been the same since."

He gazed at her a moment, saw the softness in her eyes and resisted the urge to take her in his arms.

Smokey shifted and stomped his feet, breaking the spell between them. Shaunna slid off the porch and consulted her watch.

"It's after four o'clock, I gotta go! I might not beat them home after all. You managed to keep me here longer than I should have stayed." She untied Smokey's reins and vaulted into the saddle.

Todd chuckled, put his glass down, stood, and walked over to her, reluctant for her to leave. "Wish you could stay longer."

Forever would be nice.

He bit his tongue to keep from blurting out that thought. Unspoken longing surged between them. She backed Smokey up a step.

"Thanks for the tea."

Emotion colored her tone, and he could tell she, too, struggled with the desire to stay and the need to leave. He nodded, fought not to restrain her further.

"See you around," he said, his tone indicating he had no intention of being in the same state, much less town, hell, *neighborhood* as she, and not see her.

She nodded. "Later then." She turned Smokey in a whirl and kicked him into a gallop.

Shaunna slowed Smokey to a trot when she turned the corner from Todd's house. Anxious as she was to get home to Joey, she needed a few minutes to pull herself together. She wondered about her feelings for Todd and worried where they might lead. She was happily married, but a single look from those beautiful emerald eyes still made her insides flutter. She had no doubts about her love for Joe. Nor did she doubt her ability to remain faithful to him. What she didn't understand were her feelings for Todd and why they ran so deep. After all this time and all they'd been through, why was she still so drawn to him? Why did he still affect her so? She loved Joe. They were happier now than they'd ever been. So, why did she still feel so much for Todd?

Shrugging her shoulders, she cast the thoughts from her mind. The subject was getting too deep for such a beautiful afternoon. Putting her horse away, she hurried in to hear all about Joey's adventures at day camp.

* * *

During the next two weeks, Shaunna ran into Todd a couple of times. Each time she accepted his offer of something cold to drink, enjoying the friendship that rekindled and grew between them.

When Joe came home they took Joey to Astroworld in Houston, Texas for his birthday. Mary took the week to go on a retreat with her church group.

When Joe's two weeks off were almost up, he and

Shaunna heard about the piracy in the Gulf. The situation seemed to grow and worsen in a few short days. By sheer luck, or the grace of God, they hadn't heard of it until on their way home from Texas. Not wanting to fight in front of Joey, Joe refused to discuss the situation until they got home, thereby putting off the confrontation he knew would occur.

Unwilling for him to put himself in more danger than his job already entailed, Shaunna voiced her objections when he started getting ready to return to work. The arguments between them continued, coming to a head the night before he left. Shaunna wanted him to quit his job. He refused.

"It's all I know, Shaunna, besides driving a truck. You want me to quit and get a driving job?"

Shaunna knew how much he loved his job and how much he hated driving a truck. So, she tried a different approach. "We've got enough money to support us for a while. You know I can always do more catering, maybe even open a restaurant, anything. We'll manage. Just don't go back, please. You don't have to quit, just tell them you won't go back until this is over."

"Do you honestly think you can get enough catering to support us? Think honey, how much do you turn down?" At her hopeless shrug and frown, he continued. "It would take too long and too much money to open a restaurant. We couldn't do it without me working to help out until we showed a profit. By then all this will be resolved, so calm down. It's bound to blow over soon. These fools are either going to get caught or get tired of pushing their luck. Either way, this nonsense will be over sooner or later."

The logic in his arguments angered and frightened her. "I only hope it's sooner and not later and no one gets killed in the meantime. How can you expect me to calm down? Calming down is not the problem. Staying calm for three weeks while you're out there in the middle of the Gulf with a bunch of idiots acting like Robin Hood just may prove to be a little more difficult." Her voice rose to a hysterical pitch. "How do you know this'll all blow over? Can you guarantee when you leave, you'll come back?"

"Robin Hood?" he chuckled, hoping to ward off another tirade.

His laughing infuriated her further. "Well, what would you call it? The only thing the authorities can assume is they're selling everything or shipping it overseas. No one knows why they're doing it, only that they are. And we both know the definition of assume!" She stomped her foot in frustrated wrath, a tear sliding off her cheek. "Joe, please," she pleaded, fear replacing her anger. "Please don't go."

"I have to go. Now calm down before you make yourself sick. I haven't even left yet." He hauled her against his chest. "I'll be OK."

"How do you know? You just don't care!" she cried. Jerking out of his arms she stormed into the bathroom, slammed, and locked the door. Angry, frustrated sobs shook her.

Joe stood rooted to the floor listening to her heart wrenching sobs. With a ragged groan, he walked to the door. He hated fighting. No matter what the outcome, he always seemed to lose. He knocked. "Shaunna, open the door, honey."

"No!" she spat. "Go away. Go on to your precious job."

He rattled the knob, his patience strained. "Come off it, Shaunna, and open this door before I break it down!" At her angry retort, Joe slammed his palm on the door. He clinched his fist and refrained from putting it through the thin, hollow wood. He turned away, determined she would be the one to end the fight this time. A feeling of utter helplessness overcame him at her continued sobbing. "I'm sorry, Shaun. I don't want to fight with you. C'mon, open the door," he urged.

She fumbled with the lock, opened the door, and went straight into his waiting arms. "I don't want to fight either," she sobbed. "It scares me. What would I do if something happened to you?"

Joe ran his hands up and down her back. "Nothing's going to happen. I won't let it," he assured. He carried her to their bed, his lovemaking gentle and achingly tender.

* * *

July loomed before her like a gaping black hole. Shaunna walked along the dirt road in front of her house. The latest news report echoed in her mind. The condition in the Gulf had become explosive. No one knew when the pirates—as the media dubbed them—would strike again. Joe hadn't been gone, more than three days and she was already a wreck. Her mind whirled. Her heart ached. She walked on, wondering how on earth she'd get through eighteen more days of this without hearing from Joe and knowing he was safe.

Chapter Nineteen

At five minutes before twelve, a knock sounded on Todd's classroom door. He opened it, surprised to find Lacey standing there. He smiled and signed 'hello.'

"Can I buy you lunch?"

A frown creased his brow. "Thought you had class."

"I skipped," she confessed, an impish light in her eyes.

"Bad habit to get into," he chided.

She shrugged. Laughter danced in her eyes. "If you're going to fuss at me, I'll withdraw my offer."

Todd couldn't resist her teasing. With a smile, he dismissed his students, left campus, and followed her to a park where she spread a blanket beneath a giant oak tree. A picnic basket held fried chicken, potato salad, iced tea, and homemade cookies.

"When did you do all this?"

"This morning. I played hooky all day," she confessed, a tempestuous grin tugging at her lips.

Todd's sense of discipline reared its head. "Lacey Johnson, skipping class is bad enough, but all day? What's gotten into you?"

Her grin turned into a giggle. "Spring fever."

Unable to resist her mood, Todd chuckled. "It's July, too late for spring fever."

She shrugged. "I've always been a late bloomer."

His laughter stuck in his throat when she placed a hand on his chest.

"I love it when you laugh."

Todd took her hand, squeezed. "You're incredible. You know that?" he asked, grinning when she nodded and ran her fingertips across his lips and down his throat.

"Will I see you tonight?"

He sensed the passion bubbling beneath the surface of her innocent, playful mood and hesitated in answering. His gut twisted with need. Knowing he'd be grasping at a substitute for the woman he really wanted, he struggled with the impulse to throw propriety to the winds and fulfill the needs of his flesh.

"We'll see. I'm not sure what's going to happen the rest of

the day."

Lacey lowered her gaze, but not before he saw the hurt. Resentment oozed from her every pore but not for long. She lifted shimmering eyes to his.

"Well, you know you're always welcome."

It always surprised him how incapable Lacey was of feeling anything but pure love. He smiled and resisted the urge to press a soft kiss upon her brow. "I know. Thank you."

They spent the next hour and a half laughing and teasing until Todd went back to work and Lacey went home.

At four-forty-five, Todd turned the air conditioner up a notch and loosened the top button of his shirt as he headed toward home. The day had been full, taxing, and he was ready for it to be over.

Though not well educated outside of the Army, he had a wealth of experience to rely on when teaching, and this semester, this particular class, kept him on his toes, drawing heavily on his experience. Although some days were more difficult than others, he enjoyed the heated discussions that evolved during the two-hour course.

He always managed to either get a rise out of or a good laugh from his students. Either way, he made them think. And they made him think. Though it wasn't always easy, he found it stimulating, often fun, and he loved it.

He chuckled to himself and slowed his car as he approached the turn off to his house. As was his habit, he scanned the area, hoping to get a glimpse of Shaunna. He hadn't seen her in a couple of weeks, and, if he calculated right, her husband would be back at work, and she would be out riding. His heartbeat quickened in anticipation. He'd come to expect her visits, to look forward to them and to having her near.

He didn't expect, however, to see her walking, oblivious to her surroundings, with a haunted look on her face. Todd halted his car and jumped out. "Shaunna, what's wrong?" he asked, taking in her tear-streaked face.

Shaunna took a deep breath and swallowed hard but couldn't seem to answer. A cloud of despair surrounded her and stifled the atmosphere.

"Are you OK?" His brows drew together, a frown tugged at his mouth. "Where are you headed?"

She shrugged. "Walking."

"You've been walking quite a while," he guessed, considering how far she was from her house. "C'mon, I'll take you home."

Shaunna didn't object when he guided her into his car.

Realizing he was closer to his house than hers, Todd drove there. He didn't like the condition she was in. He'd give her something to drink and a chance to pull herself together before he took her home. Leading her into the kitchen, he urged her to sit down, asking again what was wrong.

Shaunna shook her head and reached for the glass he extended toward her. She closed her eyes as the warmth of the brandy spread through her. Her hand trembled, lips quivered. She suppressed a sob but couldn't stop the tear which dripped down her cheek.

With a muffled groan, Todd gathered her into his arms.

Shaunna slipped her arms around his waist and sobbed into his chest. Having her this close was like the answer to a prayer. Todd tightened his hold and stroked her hair in a soothing gesture. Each muffled sob tore at his heart. Cupping her face in his hands, he kissed the tears off her cheeks and eyes. His lips found hers; heart soared when she didn't protest.

Shaunna drew him closer. White-hot sensations streaked through him. The kiss changed from gentle comfort to raw hunger. All of a sudden, she struggled from his grasp.

"Todd, no," she pushed herself away from him. "I have to go!"

"Wait!" He took a deep, ragged breath, trying to still his raging senses. "I'll take you home."

She shook her head. "It's OK. I'll walk."

"No," he insisted. "It's too far."

She didn't argue, simply went out and climbed into his car. He followed at a more sedate pace.

Todd couldn't help but remember her response to his kiss but apologized anyway. "I'm sorry, Shaun. I only wanted to comfort you. Guess I got carried away."

"Thank you," she said, her smile tender, eyes glowing with emotions and feelings.

Feelings better left unspoken.

Todd dropped her off when her house was in sight and

went home. Once there, he couldn't bear to stay. The house seemed unpleasantly empty now. He changed clothes and left for Lacey's where he knew he could forget for a little while. Lacey welcomed him with a smile. Todd's heart lightened. Just knowing she was there, still his friend, helped his frame of mind.

"I didn't think you were coming over," she said.

He remembered the mood she'd been in earlier and grinned. "You didn't get my message?"

She frowned and shook her head. "What message?"

"Telepathy," he teased. "For the past half-hour I've been using ESP to send you a message. Guess you weren't tuned in."

She smiled at his teasing and shook her head again. "I've been studying."

He nodded in approval. "As well you should, especially after playing hooky all day."

"Yes, Professor Jameson," she agreed, her eyes laughing into his. "Are you going to fuss at me or help me study?"

"Both," he admitted with a grin then chuckled when she rolled her eyes.

* * *

The days passed horribly slow and Shaunna's frame of mind worsened. If she could just talk to her husband! Dragging her fingers through her hair, she glanced at the calendar. *A week.* He'd only been gone a week. "I knew that without looking at the stupid thing," she muttered aloud. "How on earth am I going to get through another two weeks of this?"

She buried her face in her hands, the images in her mind wreaking havoc on her senses. "Oh, God," she sobbed. "Please keep him safe and bring him home to me."

As usual, when in distress, Shaunna felt the hand of the Lord soothing her troubled soul. Until her imagination took over again, torturing her with images of her husband being robbed or killed.

She glanced at the clock on the stove, noting the time. It would be hours yet before Mary returned with Joey, who was on a nature hike with his Cub Scout den. Her eyes drifted until she gazed out the patio door. The pool sparkled in invitation. Without hesitation she donned a swimsuit.

She worked herself into near exhaustion, hoping the exercise would alleviate some of the tension she felt. Dragging herself out of the pool, she collapsed into a heap on the towel she'd laid out before diving in. The sun warmed her skin, soothing her frazzled nerves and she drifted into a weary slumber.

* * *

Todd drove toward Shaunna's house. "This is a big—no, a *huge* mistake," his mind insisted. His heart disagreed.

It had been nearly a week since he last saw Shaunna. A long, torturous five days, and that concerned him. He had no right to worry about her. Whatever upset her was none of his business. Her life was none of his business! But he couldn't help it. He loved her. It was as simple and as complicated as that.

He loved her.

That alone gave him the right to worry.

Parking in front of the house, he noticed one car in the carport and prayed it belonged to her. With a great deal of courage, a whole lot of determination, and absolutely no common sense, he strode to the door and rang the bell. He wondered what he would say if Mary and not Shaunna opened the door. What if Joey opened the door? He groaned but refused to walk away. Ringing the bell again, he waited.

Satisfied no one was home, he walked back to his car. Relief and disappointment wrestled within him. A reflection caught his eye. His curiosity aroused he walked around the house. What he discovered aroused more than his curiosity.

Shaunna lay beside the swimming pool, a skimpy bikini clinging to every curve of her beautiful body. Her sun-kissed skin glistened like silk.

Todd's heart leapt into his throat. Taking a deep, shaky breath, he leaned on the fence, his eyes feasting on the sight of her. He called her name, hoping she'd stir. An eternity passed before he got up the nerve to call out again. When she didn't move, he began to worry. He tried again, holding his breath when she picked up her head, brushed the hair off her face and rolled onto her back.

His heart beat a tattoo in his chest. *She's all right. Leave,* his mind insisted. He couldn't. Entranced, he walked to the gate, found it locked.

Ignoring the voices in his head, he jumped the fence and walked in a daze toward her. His breathing became labored, his palms sweaty. He felt like a junky, craving something he shouldn't have, and yet, having no control over the hunger. If this was madness, then he was insane.

With trembling fingers he touched her cheek, whispering her name. He froze when she snuggled her face in his palm, smiled, and opened her eyes which widened in shocked surprise.

"What?"

He silenced her protests with trembling fingers. "Don't fuss at me," he pleaded. "I tried to leave. Honestly."

"How did you get in here?"

"Jumped the fence," he admitted with a sheepish grin.

She shook her head. "You're crazy."

"You're beautiful," he countered in defense. "So beautiful," he breathed and traced her lips with trembling fingers. His whole being ached with want.

Her eyes darkened, she pushed his hand away. "Don't."

He stood up, pulling her to her feet. "You're right," he conceded. "I'm crazy. You're a drug and I'm addicted. I know I shouldn't want you. I know it's wrong." He sounded frustrated and angry even to himself.

"But I can't help it." His voice softened. "I just can't," he admitted and stroked her cheek. Her eyes pleaded with him to stop this madness and end the conversation, implored him not to kiss her.

Shaunna felt as though she were drowning in a sea of emotions. Sheer force of will enabled her to drag her eyes away from his hypnotic gaze. She took a deep breath, reached for the towel, and wrapped it around herself. Todd's eyes glittered with humor at the modest gesture. Her chin lifted a notch, teeth ground in frustration. "What are you doing here anyway?"

"I've been worried and wanted to check on you."

"I'm OK."

He snorted. "You don't look OK."

"Thanks a lot," she muttered, frowning when he grinned. Rolling her eyes, she talked about the situation in the Gulf of Mexico, explaining the fear for her husband.

"Making yourself sick won't solve anything," he chided in a gentle tone.

"I know, but I can't help it. I love him."

He nodded. "I know," he whispered and stroked her cheek. "Don't worry. I'm sure he'll be OK." Tearing his gaze from hers he turned around.

Watching him walk away, Shaunna felt a familiar longing, a familiar pain. Calling his name, she walked toward him.

His eyes feasted on her, as every step brought her closer to him. With a tender smile she opened the gate and thanked him for his concern.

Her words echoed in his mind as Todd drove home. He knew she loved her husband, didn't expect less. But he also knew she loved him, had from the beginning. Though she refused to voice the love aloud, he felt it every time she looked at him with those beautiful coffee-colored eyes. Desire flamed within his soul as he dwelt on how beautiful she looked today, and the way she felt in his arms. Something between a groan and a whimper sounded in his throat, slipped through. *How am I supposed to stay sane with her so close and so untouchable?*

There was no answer to the question repeating itself in his mind. All he could do was wait and see what fate had in store for them this time.

Chapter Twenty

Joe walked toward the galley to get his supper. Lord, it had been a long day! It's been a long ten days, he thought, wondering again how Shaunna was holding up. Knowing her, she was a wreck from worrying. Maybe Mary could keep her calm, he thought. Thank God for Mary.

Mary's calm presence was the catalyst to Shaunna's emotional one. Shaunna was high-strung, passionate about everything and everyone she cared about. He walked along, gazing up at the full moon, smiling to himself as he thought about his fiery young wife. Suddenly, the sky lit up. An eerie orange glow followed by plumes of smoke clouded the clear summer sky. An explosion! The Gulf waters seemed to churn and its sea floors to shake with aftershocks.

He gathered with his coworkers around the radio to see what they could find out, concerned about those on the rig about twenty miles east of the one they were on. As reports of the explosion aired, everyone was relieved to learn they would be going home until an investigation was completed. Though it would cost the oil company a slight fortune in production, they would not risk the lives of any more men until they uncovered whether or not the so-called modern day pirates were responsible for the explosion.

* * *

Shaunna sat in the den playing cards with Joey when a news bulletin came over the television: "An oilrig has been reported to have blown up. No details have been provided as of yet. Stay tuned, we'll keep you informed as we find out more. Once again..."

Her heart plunged to her feet. A deep-seated fear began to gnaw at her. With an imploring look at Mary, she pasted a smile on her face and finished the card game with as much enthusiasm as she could summon, then urged Joey into the kitchen for a snack and hurried him up to bed.

Assuring Mary she should go to bed also, Shaunna returned to the den and turned the television back on. The only new news was that the company—the same one Joe worked for—was shutting down all of their offshore rigs in the immediate area and bringing the workers in until the facts were compiled, and the explosion explained. All she could do now was wait and pray her husband would come home.

Back and forth across the carpeted floor, Shaunna paced. Her mind careened between fear and hope as she counted the reasons it might take so long to hear from Joe: *they couldn't get helicopters out this late, there were a dozen or more rigs, no news is good news.*

Her mind whirled, fear ate at her heart. The clock struck midnight. Two hours, she moaned. Two hours since she put Joey to bed, two hours since she turned off the television. She stopped pacing and listened. The house was quiet except for her labored breathing as she tried to quiet the fears within her heart and mind. The thick carpet on the den floor muffled even the sound of her footsteps as she resumed her pacing. Panic grew with each passing minute, with each tick of the clock. As it chimed one o'clock, Shaunna dreaded the coming day.

Oh, God, she prayed. God, please, she pleaded, fighting down her rising hysteria. In her agitated state, she inadvertently closed herself off from the soothing presence of the Lord. The fear alone wasn't what drove her crazy but the waiting. The waiting and not knowing. The phone rang and Shaunna all but jumped out of her skin. She grabbed the receiver before it could ring a second time.

"Joe?"

"No, Shaunna. It's me," Todd replied. "I heard the news. Are you all right? Hear anything yet? Anything I can do?"

"Just pray," she choked. "Pray to God he's safe."

"I will. Hang in there, Shaun. It'll be OK," he assured her in a soft, tender tone.

The clock chimed on the half-hour then again at two am. Shaunna wrung her hands, her nerves stretched so taut she ached. Four hours. Four hours, which seemed like a lifetime, had passed since she first heard the news of the explosion. Exhaustion numbed her mind and body, but fear wouldn't let her go to bed. Her mind raced in circles wondering what she would do if her husband didn't come home. She shook her head and pressed trembling fingers to her throbbing temples. *No! I won't even think like that!*

A vehicle turned into the driveway and the reflection of lights danced off the walls. Her breath came in shallow gasps. Shaunna tried to still her racing heart. This was a nightmare, the vehicle an unknown terror. Who was it? She bowed her head and refused to look, determined to wait until the unknown person came to the door. She heard his key in the lock and burst into tears of relief. *Thank you, God!* She flew into his arms as Joe reached for the light.

Joe hauled her against him, shushing her ragged sobs. He stroked her hair, back, and arms.

"I was so worried," she sobbed, stepping out of his embrace. She began to tremble with the intensity of emotions coursing through her. Fear. Relief. Love. Need. Reaching with a trembling hand, she touched his face, his cheek, and his lips. "Oh, God, I love you so much."

Joe groaned and tugged her to him. His mouth pursued hers in a fierce kiss, one designed to banish all fears from her mind, and show her how much he loved her also.

* * *

A week passed before the company called Joe back to work. A week he and Shaunna spent loving and playing, strengthening the bond they shared. Though saddened at the loss of life, both were relieved to know faulty equipment and not the pirates caused the explosion.

Although no one saw neither hide nor hair of them since before the explosion, the situation surrounding the modern day privateers puzzled the authorities, and everyone hoped they had quit while they were ahead. Whatever their reasons for robbing the rigs, it was stupid and dangerous.

Reluctant but relieved, Shaunna sent her husband back to work after the investigation reassured her of his safety. The explosion was an accident, and though his job involved a certain amount of danger, she knew it was important to him, and no more dangerous than being on the road for days or perhaps weeks at a time. She vowed not to worry during the next two weeks.

* * *

With a sigh, Shaunna withdrew the last batch of cookies from the oven. Hosting a swimming party for Joey's Cub Scout den had turned out to be a major event. With a spatula in one hand and a potholder in the other, she brushed the sweat off her brow and smiled at Mary, who looked just as tired but as happy as she. She placed the cookies on a large serving tray and grinned. "Now I know why I don't have a house full of kids," she told her friend. "I didn't know six boys and one man could eat so much."

Mary chuckled. "And I didn't know they could drink so much either. This is the second pitcher of fruit punch since lunch." They laughed in unison and took the snacks outside where shouts of joy greeted them.

"Slow down now. Quiet! This is not a zoo." David Farley, Joey's den leader, admonished the horde of boys under his command as they abandoned their volleyball game and ran toward the table. "Where are your Scout manners?"

"We left them on the field," one of the boys quipped, and brought a round of laughter.

"OK, settle down now and thank Mrs. Taylor," David insisted.

They obeyed in unison. "Thank you, Mrs. Taylor."

Shaunna laughed. "Why, you're welcome. I've enjoyed it immensely despite all the noise."

"Aw, Mom, you love it and you know it," Joey countered. His eyes glittered. "Best party you've ever catered I bet," he challenged with a grin. Turning to his friends, he continued. "My mom's a caterer. She makes food for weddings and things." His chest puffed with pride.

"Joey, it's not gentlemanly to brag."

"Why not? You're the best."

Shaunna shook her head and slipped away as the boys resumed their rowdy conversations. She welcomed David Farley with a smile and nod when he walked up beside her. Leaning his elbows on the fence, he regarded her with merry brown eyes.

"I'd like to thank you again, Mrs. Taylor. I was running out of ideas to keep these guys occupied. It was great of you to have us all here. Each of the boys will receive a badge for swimming today."

Shaunna laughed. "Well, as you can see, my son has a way with words. I didn't have much choice in the matter. However, you are quite welcome, Mr. Farley."

"David," he insisted with a grin.

Shaunna smiled in response then turned to greet Smokey, who'd walked over to nudge her on the neck.

"Beautiful animal," David remarked.

"Thank you. He's my baby. Yes, he is," she crooned.

A high-pitched whinny and the assault of hooves on wood coming from the barn diverted their attention.

"Goodness, what an eerie sound," David remarked.

"That's Joe's horse, Satan, aptly named I assure you. The proverbial one-owner horse. He'll let us feed him but that's about it. He's gentle as a lamb for Joe the minute he steps onto the property, but otherwise, he's a devil of a horse. No pun intended." She laughed, scratched Smokey's ears and nuzzled his nose. "But this sweetheart is mine, aren't you, boy?" she queried. Smokey nickered and stomped his feet, telling her in his own way he'd had enough of the noise for one day and longed for a nice, long run. Shaunna whispered a promise to take him out soon.

David chuckled. "Looks like you could use that ride yourself," he remarked. "Go on, take him out."

"I was contemplating whether it would be unreasonably rude of me to do so," Shaunna confessed, warmth rushing to her cheeks.

He laughed. "After what you've done for us today, I'd say it was the most un-rude, sanest, thing you could do. If I weren't used to these boys, I'd be begging to join you."

Shaunna's lips curved in response to the humor in his gaze. "Tell me, David, what on earth possessed you to become a Cub Scout leader? All those boys..." She rolled her eyes in an exaggerated manner. "All the noise."

He shrugged. "I love kids. My utmost desire was to sire a basketball team. Life just didn't work out that way. Being an only child is lonely."

Shaunna frowned. "Don't you have two sons?"

David laughed. "Yeah, I do. *I'm* an only child."

An embarrassed flush heated her cheeks, but Shaunna laughed with him. "And what does Mrs. Farley have to say about a basketball team?"

David's smile wavered. "My wife died three years ago."

Shaunna gasped. "I'm so sorry."

David shook his head. "It's OK. You didn't know," he answered, his smile warm.

"It must be awful," Shaunna remarked.

David nodded. "Pretty rough, especially on Josh. Jason was four when she died, so he didn't understand what was going on. But Josh was seven. It was harder on him. He watched her suffer for so long." He shrugged. "But life does go on. And it does get easier with time."

Shaunna looked over at the ten-year-old boy who acted as lifeguard, referee, and coach to the five boys in the den. Compassion constricted her chest. "Well, you all feel free to come over anytime. Jason and Josh are more than welcome to stay over with Joey. But, please, limit the visit to you three."

David chuckled. "Aw, come on now. You mean you really didn't like having us all here?"

Shaunna heaved an exaggerated sigh. "I loved it. Joey loved it. But I have no desire for a basketball team. I like things a little quieter and a house full of boys is not my idea of quiet."

David laughed and went to gather up his boys. Once everyone left, Joey pitched in to help clean up after which Shaunna escaped for her ride.

* * *

The reins dangled as Smokey walked with his nose buried in the soft grass along the side of the road. Shaunna trailed her fingers through her hair and stretched, embracing the warm summer afternoon. Already in its descent, the sun filtered light through the tree branches overhanging the road. Taking a deep breath, she leaned forward and gave Smokey a hug. She enjoyed the smooth gait and gentle clip-clop of his hooves.

Her legs swung free and she wriggled the toes of her bare feet, glad she hadn't taken the time to change clothes and saddle up. It'd been a long time since she rode bareback and she relished the feel of his silky coat beneath her legs.

She murmured to her horse, laughing when he pricked up his ears and snorted. Both were relaxed after the run they'd indulged in when first leaving the confines of home.

Noticing Todd's house down the road, she smiled to herself. What better way to end the day than with a visit with her very best friend? Picking up the reins, she urged Smokey into a trot. Nearing the driveway, she pulled him over to the side of the road as a car backed out. Her heart crashed into her stomach when the woman behind the wheel blew Todd a kiss and waved before driving off.

Chapter Twenty-One

Todd laughed and waved, then watched Shaunna approach on her horse. His heart skipped a beat at the stricken look on her face, of which he felt certain she was unaware. He sighed and once again thanked God Lacey remained his closest friend. He'd never have made it this long without her. He smiled up at Shaunna when she halted Smokey beside him. "Hi."

"Who was that?"

He arched an eyebrow, grinned. "You mean the girl in the car?"

She made a face at him. "No. I mean the ghost on your porch. Never mind. It's none of my business anyway."

He chuckled. "Jealous?"

"Yes."

If the stricken look on her face gave any indication, the admission came straight from her heart because she had no time to consider an answer before she blurted it out.

"I mean, no. I have no right to be jealous," she answered.

There was no use denying it or trying to hide it. He knew. His grin widened. "You have no reason to be jealous either," he insisted, his voice as soft as the touch of his hand on her knee. His heart did an irrational little flutter at the quick flush of pleasure on her cheeks and the shiver which shook her slender frame.

She chewed on her lip then placed her foot on his chest. "Get," she insisted with a gentle shove. "Get your hands off of me. I did not come here to wrestle with you."

His response was automatic. With a lunge, he hauled her unceremoniously off her horse and into his arms. "What did you come here for?"

"To escape. I've been invaded all day by a slew of boys ranging in age from eight to ten. This is the first bit of peace and quiet I've had since dawn. So, get your hands off of me and offer me something cool to drink," she ordered with a smile, and pushed herself out of his arms.

"Yes, ma'am," he replied with a chuckle. Taking Smokey's reins, he led the way to the porch.

Shaunna sank onto the steps and sighed with relief when

he brought her a glass of tea. Laughing, she told him about her day. She finished the tea and handed the glass back to him. "Well, guess I'd better go. Thanks."

The excitement in her eyes set fire to Todd's blood. He placed a restraining hand on her arm. "But you just got here," he protested, reluctant to let her out of his grasp, out of his reach, out of his sight. "Stay a little longer."

The touch of his hand and the longing in his eyes turned Shaunna's bones to jelly. Pain suffused her heart. *This will not work.* Her heart cried out in anguish. Her smile trembled. "I guess plain friendship between us is impossible," she remarked, her voice thick.

She saw the denial in his eyes and knew he refused to listen, to hear, and to believe what she said.

"Nothing is impossible if you want it enough," he countered.

Desire darkened his gaze. Shaunna swallowed hard and blinked back the tears filling her eyes and clogging her throat. Her heart broke. She was losing him.

Again.

"This is," she whispered, the ache in her heart reflected in her tone. "I can't do this to you, to me, to us. There's no hope for a relationship between us. We're going to end up hating each other."

Todd ignored her attempts to make him understand and see reason. He shook his head, stroked her cheek. "I could never hate you."

"Why?" The throb in her voice deepened. "Why can't you just find someone to make you happy?" *And leave me alone,* her heart added. "Then I wouldn't feel so guilty all the time."

Todd shook his head. "I don't know," he growled, suddenly angry. He gave her a slight shake. "Don't you think I've tried? Don't you think I've asked myself that same question a million times? Trust me, I've tried," he insisted. "Come close, too. Lacey, the girl who just left, is very special to me. I've known her since I came here. And, believe me, for a while there I thought I'd finally found someone to make me happy, someone to make me forget how much I love you. I thought I had a real chance with Lacey, until I saw you again." His voice softened. "It's hopeless, Shaunna. I love you and I can't help it. I love the way you walk, the sound of your voice, the way you smile."

"Don't," she croaked.

He continued, oblivious to the pain he caused. "I love the way the sun bounces off your hair." He stroked a silky handful. "I love the way your eyes shine when you're happy or flash fire when you're mad. I can't help it, Shaun. Lord knows I've tried, but I can't change the way I feel about you. I don't want to hurt you, or cause you trouble, but..." His voice trailed off.

The pain in his eyes and the desperation in his voice added to hers. "No!" She jerked away from him. "Don't say that! It's not right. Can't you see?" Her chin jerked up a notch. Resolve hardened her jaw.

"I don't love you," she insisted through teeth clenched as tight as the fists in her lap.

His eyes narrowed. He jerked her into his arms and closed his mouth over hers in a fiery kiss, drowning out her protests.

Shaunna struggled, afraid of what was happening between them, of what might happen, and desperately afraid of losing herself and her control. She pushed at him but he tightened his hold. His mouth bit into hers, his arms held her trapped her against his hard body until she ached from fighting his embrace.

The feelings he evoked in her were impossible to control, impossible to resist. Desire surged through her like wildfire. With a soft sigh of surrender, she slipped her arms around him. Her hands traveled up his back. Her fingers sank into the luxurious thickness of his black hair.

Her response drove Todd wild. Passion coursed through his veins like hot, molten lava. His hands roamed over her back, his senses swam at the silkiness of her hair brushing across his arm. "Shaunna," he breathed. "Shaunna..."

He wrapped one arm around her waist and the other hand in her thick tresses then kissed her tenderly—her lips, her eyes. He nibbled at the corners of her mouth, his lips worked their way across her cheek, to her ear. "Tell me again you don't love me."

Tears filled her eyes, spilled over. She took a ragged breath. "Don't do this to me," she begged. "Please don't make me hurt you."

Todd wiped the tears away with a brush of his thumb over her cheek. "You won't hurt me, Shaun. You love me," he whispered and stilled the shake of her head with a firm hand.

Conflicting emotions battled within him. Compassion, love, and desire waged a war within his conscious, wreaking havoc on his senses. He mumbled her name again and crushed her to him. His lips possessed hers. She trembled.

"Love me," he whispered. "It'll be OK, Shaun. I'll never hurt you or demand more than you can give," he promised in a husky whisper. "No one will ever know. I swear." The emotions screaming through him rendered him senseless. "I love you," he groaned, not caring his need had reduced him to begging.

The impact of what he asked of her cooled the blood faster than ice water on a fire. A strangled sob escaped Shaunna. She jerked out of his grasp, her hand connected with his cheek. "Don't you dare say that to me. I love my husband and I would know!"

Reality crashed in. "Oh Todd," she gasped and reached for him.

Todd grabbed her wrist, the full weight of the whole incident trampling on his soul. He'd asked—no, *had begged*. She responded, heatedly, then rejected him. She'd slapped him!

He stepped away from her, his eyes narrow, jaw muscle throbbing. "Don't ever slap me again."

"I'm sorry," she whispered and reached for him again.

He jerked away from her touch. "Just go, Shaunna. Now," he insisted when she hesitated.

In one fluid motion, she untied and mounted her horse. "I'm sorry," she said in an almost inaudible whisper. Without waiting for a response, she swung Smokey around and kicked him into a gallop.

Todd stood motionless, watching her leave. Tears stung his eyes and rolled unchecked down his face. Oh, God, what now? he thought, running a hand through his hair. He swiped at the tears. His face stung where her hand had left its imprint.

The cold shower he took did little to ease his fevered mind and body. He grabbed a sandwich and cola and left the house, knowing no matter where he went or what he did, nothing would erase the memory of what happened. That would be emblazoned on his heart and mind forever.

Chapter Twenty-Two

The next few weeks passed with explicit swiftness. Between Joe's days off and getting Joey ready for school, Shaunna didn't have much time to dwell on the incident with Todd. Once school started and Joe returned to work, the whole thing came back to haunt her. She began avoiding even accidental contact with Todd, riding at different times of the day and in a different direction. Her efforts to put him out of her heart and mind failed and she found herself in tears more often than not.

Mary walked in one day to find her a wreck. Her nerves frayed, her stomach revolted at the slightest thought of food, her eyes red and swollen from crying, which enhanced the dark circles beneath them from lack of sleep.

At her gentle insistence, Shaunna told her the story of her and Todd. The whole story including the fact they'd spent time together. To her utmost surprise and relief, Mary believed her when she insisted they had not slept together.

Shaunna felt a huge sense of relief after talking with her friend, and it was Mary's advice and Scripture that encouraged her to *avoid the appearance of sin* which convinced her to steer clear of contact with Todd.

* * *

Todd, too, went out of his way to stay away from her, but not because of advice from a friend or a Bible Scripture. It was his choice. And he was miserable. He ate less and drank more than normal, more than he ever had, and it showed. He lost weight and his complexion took on an unhealthy pallor. Even his work began to suffer because he spent most of his time cursing himself for his weakness, weakness that was out of character.

The Army advocated strength, pride, and honor, and in one moment of passion, he'd thrown all of those away. And he'd lost Shaunna. *Again.* That alone made him sick with regret.

He knew she would never consciously decide to cheat on her husband. He didn't expect her to. He wanted her, true, but not with guilt and condemnation. The fact he'd given her a choice did little to ease the remorse and shame he felt for putting them in such an awkward situation.

For once in his life, Todd identified with his father's addiction to alcohol. The craving, the desire, the overwhelming need to have one thing could drive a person to do strange and stupid things. Kneeling in the student chapel on campus, he thanked God for the understanding, repented of his unforgiveness and pride, and forgave—really, deep down forgave his father for what he went through while growing up.

The lesson was a difficult, but necessary one, and Todd committed it to heart. After almost three weeks of self-condemnation and regret, he crawled back from the pain of losing Shaunna yet again. As usual, when the turmoil settled, he found himself irrevocably drawn to her.

Late one evening, he drove past her house. The whole place was dark with the exception of one light and he longed to know if it came from her bedroom.

As if bidden by his thoughts, she appeared at the window. Even from his car, he could sense her pensiveness as she reached up to pull the shade. *No,* his heart groaned, *don't pull it yet.* Again, as though tuned with his thoughts, she responded. She leaned against the window and gazed up at the sky. He could feel her anguish and his whole body responded. His arms ached to hold her, and he had to force himself to remain put. Desire, ever ready, sprang to life, unaware it would go unexpended yet again.

The next afternoon, Todd drove straight home after work, hoping he'd see Shaunna, which was unlikely since she hadn't ridden out this way in weeks.

Restless and edgy, Shaunna had decided on an early ride. Her heart leapt into her throat and her insides fluttered at the sight of Todd's car. Hands shaking, she reined Smokey to a halt.

Todd rolled the car to a stop, turned off the engine, and climbed out. "Hi. How's it going?"

His eyes swept over her in a look as potent as a caress then captured her gaze. Shaunna shrugged, not trusting her voice.

"Everyone's OK?"

Her mouth curved into a strained little smile. "Fine."

He took a step closer. His eyes searched hers. Shaunna knew by the concern in his gaze he noted the tension in her face and the paleness of her complexion.

"Are you OK, Shaun?"

Her smile felt even more strained than before. She took a deep, shaky breath and shrugged. "I'm OK. I guess." She swallowed hard and blinked fast to contain the tears that rushed to her eyes.

"Really?" he asked, his voice soft, thick. "I'm not. I've been a wreck. I want to apologize, Shaunna."

"Shh," she admonished and leaned down to touch his lips with trembling fingers. "Don't blame yourself. I have a feeling this situation has been out of our control from the very beginning."

"Maybe so," he agreed. "But that does not excuse my behavior. I'm sorry."

The huskiness of his voice brought tears to her eyes. "No need to apologize," she insisted, tearing her eyes away from his probing gaze. "It's as much my fault as it is yours. I should have known, with what we feel for each other, plain friendship wouldn't work. It was stupid and..." Her voice broke. "And naive of me to think otherwise."

With a strangled sob, she jerked Smokey around.

Todd's reaction was automatic. Grabbing the bridle, he stopped her departure. "No, it wasn't. Shaunna, don't turn away. Don't end it like this," he pleaded.

"There's no other way," she said, her voice a broken whisper. "I don't understand this situation. I don't know why life throws us together then forces us to tear each other apart. Don't you see?" she cried. "I can't keep putting you through this, and I don't know how much longer I can resist you. I don't want to have an affair!" she admitted, unable to suppress a sob. "We'll only end up hating each other."

"No," he groaned, "I could never hate you. I love you, Shaunna," he whispered, then pulled her off her horse and into his arms.

Nearly three weeks of anguish erupted in violent force and Shaunna clung to him, wretched sobs wracking her frame.

Todd stroked her hair and back. "Shh, please don't cry like this. You know I can't stand it when you cry. I'm sorry I behaved so stupidly." A bitter little laugh escaped him. "I used to pride myself on my self-control. Stupid," he muttered with a shake of his head. "I lose every ounce of self-control when I'm around you."

He held her tighter. "I am so sorry, I'll never hurt you like this again," he promised. "But, please Shaunna, please don't do this. Don't ignore me. If friendship is all you can give, then I'll accept and count my blessings you still care enough to offer it. I can't bear not having you in my life at all. Not now. Not knowing you're right down the road."

Squaring her shoulders, Shaunna stepped out of his embrace and looked into his eyes. Honesty, love, and pain shone from deep within his troubled gaze. Dragging the heel of her hands down her face, she raked her fingers through her hair, undecided what to do about his request. Could she stay away knowing he, too, lived just down the road?

The answer rang loud and clear in her heart: *No*.

Then what? she asked herself. What am I going to do? She pleaded with God for understanding, for direction. He kept silent. She knew the choice belonged to her since God would never interfere with her free will. Scriptures floated through her mind, giving her the strength to make the right decision.

"I won't ignore you, or avoid you," she told him in a soft, tremulous voice. "I can't do either and stay sane, but we also can't see each other all the time. The Bible states we should avoid the appearance of sin." The hurt in his eyes pierced her heart like a knife.

"You've already begun to hate me, haven't you?" he asked.

She shook her head and stroked his cheek. "You know I could never hate you any more than you can hate me," she admitted with a sad little smile. "That's why this is such a necessary decision. Don't you see? If we're constantly together, we are constantly tempting fate. And that..." she struggled with her choice of words. "Witch already has us over a barrel."

Acceptance flashed in his eyes. He brushed his lips across hers in a gentle kiss then backed away. "OK. I'll let you set the pace. You're welcome to come over any time you want. And please do."

Tearing herself away from his haunted green gaze, she mounted her horse and turned Smokey toward home.

Todd stopped her again. "Shaun?"

The ache in his voice sent a shiver of longing through her soul. She gazed down at him. "Don't." She shook her head for emphasis.

He urged her toward him. "One kiss."

She couldn't resist him any more than she could resist breathing.

His lips met hers softly—searching, hungry, pleading.

Though shaken by his kiss, Shaunna felt at peace over her decision to limit their visits but to stay in Todd's life, if only as his friend.

Todd wasn't so lucky in finding peace. He knew she was right, but he couldn't help but feel like the loser in the whole situation. He tried the cold shower trick as he often did after being in Shaunna's company, and as he'd come to expect, it still did him little good. He left the house, determined to find someone, somewhere to ease the sting of loneliness.

As usual, he ended up with Lacey. He ran into her at a little nightclub they frequented, shooting pool with some people he had never seen before. Grabbing a beer, he joined them.

Lacey felt torn when she saw Todd. She could tell by the haunted look in his eyes something had happened. Again. *I don't want to hear it,* she thought with an angry shake of her head. For a moment she hated the woman she'd never met. Hated both her and fate for taking away the one man she honestly thought would be hers. As the night wore on, she could sense his restlessness. It became all too apparent when one of the guys she'd been laughing with kissed her on the forehead. Todd stood up and took her by the arm.

"Time to go, Lace."

She shook her head. "I'm not ready to leave."

He tightened his grip.

"Hey, buddy, don't look like the lady wants to leave with you."

Todd turned, his eyes narrow slits.

"And how would you know what the lady wants?"

Lacey felt the tension and moved between the two men, pushed Todd away. "How dare you!"

Todd tugged her close. "Stop it, Lace."

She jerked free from his grasp. "No. You stop it. I don't want to deal with this situation tonight. I came here to have a good time. If you're ready to leave, then by all means do so. But I'm not ready to go, and even if I were, I'm not sure I'd want to leave with you!"

From the way she swayed on her feet, Todd guessed she'd had too much to drink and shouldn't be driving herself home. It tore at his heart. Lacey was not a drinker.

"Suit yourself," he signed with a shrug. He turned on his heel and strode toward the door, intending to wait by her car all night if necessary so he could see her safely home. He looked back and watched the guy pull Lacey toward him and attempt to kiss her. She struggled and turned her face away. She didn't hear the man's muttered curse. Todd did. He walked back to them and wrenched her out of his grasp. With a bellow of rage, the man took a swing at Todd.

"Your biggest mistake, buddy," Todd growled. He shoved Lacey aside and pinned the guy up against the wall, one hand wrapped around his throat, the other gripping a cue stick.

People gathered in a circle around the two men, waiting, watching, and betting on which would win the confrontation.

"If I ever see you near her again, I'll kill you," Todd muttered.

Lacey grabbed his arm and dragged Todd off the other guy. With an angry push, she shoved him away. Her hand connected with his cheek with a resounding slap.

The guy snorted. "Looks like the lady made her choice," he said with a leer and reached for her again.

Lacey shook her head and jerked away from him. "I don't want either of you!" she signed.

"Don't know what you're saying, sweetheart," he slurred. "But I'm sure I'll have fun finding out," he insisted and grabbed her arm.

Todd wrenched him away from Lacey and sent him sprawling across the pool table with a backhanded fist. "Don't try it," he warned in a soft voice, his eyes narrowed, when the guy struggled to get up. Taking Lacey by the arm, he led her out of the club, past her car and to his own.

She jerked away from him. "I can drive."

"Don't think so, Lace."

"Curse you, Todd Jameson!"

He nodded. "Curse me all you want, but you're not driving," he insisted, and helped her into his car. "Things are bad enough. I will not have your death on my conscience."

Lacey sat in subdued silence while he buckled her in and drove to her apartment. Guilt and shame filled his heart. Remorse washed over him in sickening waves when he declined her invitation to stay a while, and she cried.

Todd held her to his chest, hating himself for what he put her through. Tears filled his own eyes as he looked down into her's, swimming with hurt. "I'm sorry, Lace. I wish I could forget her and love you like you deserve, but I can't. God knows I've tried. I can't blame you for hating me. I'm sorry. I'll go. And I'll leave you alone. If that's what you want."

Her sobs increased but she shook her head. "Please, Todd, stay. I can't bear to be alone right now."

With a reluctant sigh, he took her key and opened the door. He led her to the couch and cradled her, as ragged sobs shook her tiny frame. After she cried herself to sleep, he carried her to the bedroom, laid her on the bed, and removed her shoes.

The next morning, he awoke to the smell of breakfast. Rolling off the couch, he was greeted with the sight of her showered, dressed, and cooking bacon and eggs. He walked up behind her and slipped his arms around her waist.

Lacey drew comfort from his embrace. She'd awakened a long time before she took a shower and started breakfast. In the silence of the dawn, she'd cried and prayed to God for forgiveness. Now she wanted Todd's. She turned to face him.

"I'm sorry, Lace. I don't mean to hurt you," he said before she could sign a word.

She stopped him with a shake of her head. Tears gathered in her eyes at his tender words and Lacey hated herself for her selfishness and jealousy. She knew he had no control over his feelings for Shaunna. She was just upset and jealous because she hadn't found someone to love her like that yet.

She hugged him to her, shaking her head. "No. It is I who should apologize. It just hurts, here." She touched her heart. "But I know, in here," she put a fist to her stomach to indicate a gut feeling. "There is someone for me, someone who will love me like you love her. I'm sorry for getting so angry and behaving rather badly last night. Will you forgive me?"

His eyes searched hers and she knew he was, once again, at peace about their relationship when he nodded, kissed her forehead then signed, "There's nothing to forgive."

She wrapped her arms around his waist and hugged him to her then, with a smile, handed him a plate of food.

Chapter Twenty-Three

Shaunna dragged herself out of the pool. She tried to relax, hoping to get her emotions under control before Joe got there, but her mind continued its torturous circles. She'd seen Todd a mere handful of times in the two weeks since they talked. The visits were short, polite, awkward, and left them wanting. The effort to maintain friendship was strained when all they wanted to do was hold each other. Though they never went farther than a brief hug, Shaunna always left feeling guilty. Guilty for not being able to resist him, guilty for being in another man's arms, and most of all, guilty for the pain she knew he felt.

Pain she caused.

As a result, she grew frustrated, angry, and depressed. She knew staying away was the proper thing to do, the only thing to do, but it was killing her, killing them, and she didn't know how much more she could take. Thank God her husband was coming home today. She needed to be held and loved, by him. She dove back in and swam, hoping to calm her agitated mind and spirit. That's where she was when Joe joined her.

"Hello darling," he greeted, his lips covering hers in a thorough kiss.

Shaunna wound her arms around his neck and kissed him with all of the pent-up emotion in her soul.

"Wow," he breathed. "I missed you too," he whispered, teasing her ear with his mouth.

A sob shuddered through her and she clung to his strong frame. He eased back, his gaze honed in on hers, darkened with concern.

"What's the matter, Sweetness?"

Shaunna looked away, blinked furiously, and swallowed hard. "Nothing."

He picked her up, set her on the side of the pool, and settled himself in front of her. "You sure?" he asked.

She sighed, leaned into him, and rested her head on his shoulder. The time for truth had come. But how much truth? How could she tell him what really bothered her? Would he understand? Be furious? Jealous? Would he be able to trust her if he knew the truth and how difficult a time she had in resisting

Todd? Would he understand that, although she loved him with all her heart, another man entrapped her soul, a man she'd loved long before she ever met him? Someone she'd loved forever.

She gave herself a mental shake. How stupid! What man would understand that? She took a deep, cleansing breath and prayed for strength and guidance.

"I guess I've been a bit depressed lately, and I really missed you this time." It was the truth. Not the whole truth, but the truth, nonetheless. A bit of truth she hoped he could accept.

Joe smiled and rubbed her back. "I missed you too, angel," he confessed, then frowned. Something in his memory clicked. An image fleeted then gelled. Instinctively he knew. The pieces fit. The unease he'd been feeling since his last days off, the tension she tried to hide then, the turmoil she was in now. It was at once foreign and yet, achingly familiar. He took a deep breath, shaking with the realization. Suppressing a groan, he held her close. Fear and jealousy rocked him to the core. He didn't want to know but had to ask. "Would someone with black hair and green eyes have anything to do with the way you're feeling?"

He saw the fear and pain in her eyes. *And the truth.* Tears welled in the dark depths.

"How did you know?"

His heart ached at the soft question. His hands dropped from her back, burning, as though he'd held them over a fire too long. He shrugged. "I passed him one day while he was jogging. He looked familiar but, until now, I didn't know how I knew him. What's he doing here, Shaunna? What's going on?"

She shook her head, reaching for his hands. "Nothing, I swear Joe, nothing is going on between us."

He jerked away. "Then why are you so upset? Is something wrong with Joey, or you, something you're not telling me?"

"No. No." Shaunna rubbed her temples. "He's an ROTC instructor at Nichols State. We ran into each other a couple of months ago, purely by accident. I was out riding. He flew around the curve and spooked Smokey." She shrugged and took another deep breath.

"At first it was nice to see him. It was all so innocent. We spent time together..."

"I'll kill him," he interrupted through gritted teeth.

"No!" She cupped his face in her hands, forcing him to

look at her. "No, just talking." Her hands dropped but not her eyes. "But then, it got harder to maintain mere friendship. I swear, Joe; I have not slept with him."

"But you want to?" Another question he didn't want answered but had to ask.

"No." She whispered as though afraid he would see through the denial if she protested too vehemently. "We had a big fight. He wanted more. It was stupid and we both knew it would never happen, but we fought anyway." She lowered her gaze.

"Then, we met up again while I was riding. He apologized, said if friendship was all I could give, he'd take it." She shook her head. "I don't know what to do. I don't understand the feelings I have for him. I never have. Especially loving you the way I do. Please Joe, you've got to believe me. It's hard enough dealing with this confusion and guilt, but I promise, I will never hurt you that way." She touched his cheek. "I love you."

Her eyes begged him to believe, to trust. "But you love him more?"

"No, not more."

"But you love him?" Anger and jealousy goaded him into asking.

Shaunna couldn't answer. She wouldn't lie to him and answering would incriminate her more, hurt him more. She swallowed the lump in her throat and bit her trembling lip until it bled. Suppressing a sob, she lowered her head, ashamed of the hurt she knew he felt. *It's not fair! I didn't ask to see him again. I haven't done anything wrong!*

But she was wrong, she realized. She loved a man other than her husband, and, though she refrained from acting on that love, she couldn't deny it.

Joe shook his head. "I don't understand, Shaunna. If you don't love him, and you've made up your mind you're not going to sleep with him, why are you so torn up?"

She shrugged. "I don't know," she admitted with a sob.

"Oh, God," he groaned. "Now how am I supposed to go off shore for three weeks and not worry about what's going on between the two of you?"

"Please, Joe," she begged. "You've got to trust me. I love you. I couldn't bear it if you didn't trust me. I have not and will not sleep with him. Your love and trust is what has kept me from doing so. If I don't have that, what's the use in fighting it?" Unable to hold back any longer, she began to cry.

Jealousy exploded into rage. He pushed away from her. "Why don't you just go for it, Shaunna?" he hissed slapping the water.

She flinched, paled. *"What?"*

"Go for it," he sneered. "Sleep with him. Spend the night, or the week. Maybe then you'll get him out of your system."

Shaunna stiffened. Though warranted, the accusation in his voice infuriated her. She'd pleaded for him to understand, begged him to trust her. This is what she got? She scrambled to her feet and glared down at him. "You want me to go now or wait until you leave?"

"What?"

"When do you want me to go to him, Joe? Oh, and another thing, what if it backfires? What if I can't *'get him out of my system,'* as you so delicately put it? What if it makes me want him more? What will we do then?" Turning on her heel, she headed toward the house.

Joe lunged out of the pool with a growl. "Don't you dare!" He grabbed her by the arm and flung her around to face him. "You're mine, Shaunna! Mine, and I won't share you! You understand?" he asked, giving her a slight shake.

She couldn't stop the tears welling up in her eyes or prevent them from falling. "I never asked you to."

For the first time since the start of the conversation, Joe felt fear. Not that she would betray him, but that he'd lose her because of his selfish pride. He made a mistake once and she had forgiven him. Now she fought to not make the same one. She'd been honest with him, asked for his understanding, his trust. He had to give it to her otherwise he'd risk losing her. He lifted her chin with his finger and urged her to look at him.

"I trust you," he assured. "Promise me you'll stay away from him, Shaunna."

She nodded her assurance, but it wasn't enough. "Say it, Shaunna. Promise me you won't go near him again."

She locked her gaze with his. "As God gives me the strength, I will stay away from him."

He knew it was the best she could offer. Odds being what they were, she would see him again. Sometime, someplace, but he knew she would not deliberately seek him out. He wished she could promise more but took what he could. "OK," he whispered, rubbing her back. "OK. I believe you. I trust you. Let's forget about him."

"Thank you," she whispered, relief evident in her tone and posture. She wrapped her arms around him, clung.

"I love you," she whispered covering his lips with hers, soft, gentle, then urgent, demanding.

He responded heatedly, anxious for assurance of her promise in the best way he knew. "I've been thinking lately," he whispered. "About a girl, one with chestnut hair and blue eyes."

Her smile did not quite meet her eyes. "You've met another woman?" She made a feeble attempt at teasing and failed. Her lips trembled.

He grunted and gave her braid a gentle tug. "Yeah, a mermaid. Don't be silly," he scolded, determined to make her smile and forget her depression. "I'm talking about a little girl," his voice softened. "A baby," he suggested in a voice so masculine it made her shiver.

A baby. The suggestion echoed through Shaunna's entire being. It had been a long time since she thought about having another child. There were times in the past six years when she desperately wanted a baby, and times when she just as desperately didn't. Now the idea was very appealing.

A baby. Her heart swelled with excitement. She ached at the thought. Her arms ached to hold it, breasts ached to feel the gentle tug of her child nursing, body ached for the act to conceive. One thought filled her mind: *What better way to assure him of her love and fidelity than to give him another child?*

She hugged him closer, covered his lips in a melting kiss. Soft whispers of kisses flowed between them as they made their way up the stairs.

Two hours later they awoke with a start when Joey burst into the room.

"Oh, boy, Daddy, I'm glad you're home! We're having open house at school tonight. Can we go?"

Anger at being so rudely awakened failed Joe as he looked into the eager eyes of his son. Still, he made an attempt to correct Joey's manners. "You know better than to barge in here without knocking young man. Where are your manners?"

Joey dropped his eager gaze. "I'm sorry. I was just so glad you're home, I guess I forgot." He lifted innocent brown eyes to his father. "Please, can we go?"

"We'll see." Joe tried to remain firm. He really did. "Now get outta here before I change my mind."

"Oh, boy!" Joey lunged at him, gave him a quick hug. The boy ran to the door then turned teasing brown eyes to Joe. "I knew you'd say yes." His grin held all the triumph of youth. He ducked out of the door moments before Joe's pillow hit it.

Shaunna's restraint broke. With a howl of laughter, she struggled with him as Joe turned and pinned her beneath him. "What's so funny?" he demanded.

"Nothing," she giggled, imitating the look Joey gave him. "And you want another baby?" she taunted. "You're too soft."

He silenced her teasing with his lips. "I can't help it. He looks at me with those black eyes of yours and I'm a goner," he admitted with another kiss.

"I can just about imagine how tight a little girl will have you wrapped," she teased.

"One thing's for sure, if she's anything like her mother, I don't stand a chance," he admitted in a husky voice then hushed her giggles with his mouth.

Chapter Twenty-Four

Flashing lights in the room signaled someone was at the door. Lacey glanced out the window, surprised to see Todd's car in the drive. Nearly three weeks had passed since the last time he came over. They saw each other on campus, and he'd told her about his talk with Shaunna, but other than that, he stayed away. It was his way of dealing with the feelings still apparent between them. By avoiding being together, he felt as though he could keep those feelings in perspective and not take advantage of her or their friendship.

Lacey prayed daily for the strength to overcome the desire she still felt for him. She knew making love would solve nothing, would make things worse, and wouldn't keep him by her side. In the end it would probably destroy their friendship, which was the last thing she wanted. She opened the door, welcomed him with a smile and watched as he went straight to the refrigerator for a beer. She declined one with a shake of her head.

Todd opened the can and took a long, soothing swallow, then walked over and kissed her on the cheek. "I've missed you."

"I think you've just missed my beer." She meant the words in jest but realized her teasing had the opposite effect when a flush darkened his cheeks.

"Some great friend I am, coming around only when I need a shoulder to cry on," he muttered, his face hard.

She stroked his cheek hoping to ease the tension evident in every plane of his face. "You're a wonderful friend who's going through a rough time. I would be very upset if you didn't come over when you need a shoulder. That's what friends are for."

"Yeah, wonderful." Sarcasm oozed from every pore of his being. "How wonderful can it be having me bellyache all the time over another woman? In fact, how smart is it to be in love with another woman when I have you? It's stupid. I'm stupid. This whole blasted situation is stupid. I must be the biggest idiot in the world being in love with a married woman."

"Stop it! You are not stupid! You loved her long before she got married."

She knew by the flash of emotions in his gaze her admonishment did little to ease his frustration, anger, or jealousy.

"Yeah, well those feelings should've changed when she got married."

He took another swig of beer and slammed the can down on the table. "All I know is I'm sick of the whole blasted situation. I wish I could just forget her and get her out of my mind before I lose it." His expression softened. "And you."

He reached for her, and Lacey went willingly into his arms. She held him for a moment then stepped back, gazed into his eyes, and then lifted her hands to continue their conversation. "The heart doesn't lie, Todd. You could make yourself try and forget her, but she'll come back to haunt you. You love her. Deeply. I believe she loves you too. You're both just caught up in some vicious quirk of fate. It'll work out, I promise, and you'll be glad you're available when she does come to you. Besides, I wouldn't want you that way. I couldn't live with you knowing you never really got over her. But I'll be your friend. I can promise, as long as my friendship is wanted or needed, I'll be here for you."

Lacey's smile was gentle. Her eyes were alive with an inner radiance. Peace and love which came from her knowing the love and peace of the Lord. *Peace which surpassed all understanding.* Todd longed for such peace. Sweet Jesus, he needed that peace!

"How come you always know what to say?" He cupped her face in his hands.

She smiled and shrugged.

"You're beautiful. You know that?" He smoothed the hair off her face.

She nodded, an impish light in her eyes. "Feel better?"

He did. A whole lot better. "Yeah," he said with a nod.

She grinned. "Good, then you can clean up your mess," she teased, indicating the smashed can and spilled beer on her table.

Todd looked from the table to her laughing eyes and felt the world lift off his shoulders. He chuckled. "I'm company. Guests do not pick up after themselves."

She shook her head in quick denial. "You've been here more than twice. Around here, that makes you family."

Todd had no choice but to clean up the mess.

* * *

At Open House, Joey's teacher had nothing but praise for him. Shaunna accepted it with grace, Joe beamed with pride. She reintroduced him to David Farley who was there with Jason. They talked a few minutes, then Joey dragged them across the room to look at some pictures he'd drawn.

A few minutes later Shaunna slipped her arm through Joe's. "Let's go," she whispered.

Joe looked down into her dark, shining eyes and nodded in agreement. Four hours had passed since Joey woke them this afternoon. Four hours of tender kisses, subtle looks, teasing touches and electric gazes. Seeing the bold invitation in her eyes, he wanted nothing more than to take her home and spend a rapturous night with her. He'd never felt the overwhelming, insatiable need he felt for Shaunna this night. He knew where it stemmed from but refused to think about it. He had no choice but to trust her. So he banished the demons of doubt the only way he knew how. He loved her many times until they fell into an exhausted slumber, clasped in each other's arms. He awoke the next morning to find her soaking in a hot bath. Padding over to the tub he reached for her, wincing as the hot water stung his hand.

She slapped it away. "Get!" She groaned, glaring at him through half-closed eyes.

He chuckled. "Let's go to New Orleans for our anniversary."

"Today?"

The doubts were back, haunting him in the bright light of day. He refused to give in to them. "Yeah, we'll leave as soon as we can and be back in a couple of days."

He wanted her alone, away from this house, this town, and away from the threat to their happiness.

After discussing their plans with Mary and Joey, they packed up and left. Arriving in New Orleans, they lunched in Jackson Square before taking a carriage ride through the French Quarter. The next day they toured Bourbon Street and the St. Louis Cathedral and ate beignets at Café Du Monde. They walked hand in hand along the river and enjoyed a riverboat tour of the most romantic city in Louisiana.

When the time came, Joe returned to work secure in her love. He trusted in the strength of her commitment and believed her faith in God would enable her to withstand temptation and stick to her promise to stay away from the man whose name he didn't even know, didn't want to know.

Chapter Twenty-Five

Joe awoke with a start. In hazy confusion he brushed the sleep from his eyes, trying to figure out what woke him. He listened, his ears tuned for some sound, some noise to blame for waking him in the middle of the night. What he heard brought him instantly awake.

Nothing.

No clanging noise of drilling, no hum of the wire-line unit. Everything was silent. A shiver of apprehension raced up his spine. Something was wrong. Reaching up to the bunk above him, he shook Sam awake.

"What is it?" Sam groaned.

"Listen."

The absence of noise brought Sam instantly awake. He rolled out of his bunk and collided with Joe in his haste to put on shirt and boots. Before either could reach the door, it burst open. Two men wearing masks and holding guns rushed into the room.

"What the...?" Joe backed up until his knees hit the edge of his bunk.

"Shut up! We want your valuables, watches, rings, tools, everything. We want it all or someone's gonna get hurt. Goes for wedding rings too." Though the facemask muffled the intruder's voice, his demands, punctuated by a waving pistol, were perfectly clear.

Silence, thick and tense, filled the room as a sense of helplessness overwhelmed them. A feeling Joe never liked. Caught at a disadvantage more often than not while growing up, he adopted a motto similar to that of a famous Tennessee sheriff: *Walk tall and carry a big stick.* Anger at his own helplessness urged him to act. With deliberate ease and caution, he ran his hand along the wall until he grasped the object of his intention, a hickory stick the size of a small baseball bat.

Wrapping his hand around it, he felt a surge of adrenaline. The odds were still uneven but better. "Duck, Sam!" he shouted at the precise moment he swung the club at the pirate closest to him.

The sickening crack of either skull or stick filled the air as Sam dove under the bed.

Taken off guard, the pirate's companion fired a shot in the general direction where Joe stood. Within a split second, Joe lay on the floor alongside the man he hit. He watched Sam reach for the gun which flew from the fallen pirate and lay within inches of his face. His hand closed over the weapon, and he shot. His target hit the floor with a groan and a thud.

He scrambled out from under the bed, raced to the door and locked it then knelt at Joe's side. "Joe, you idiot! What on earth were you thinking?" He grabbed a sheet off the bed and pressed it to Joe's stomach.

Joe groaned. "Had to, Sam," he whispered. "Someone had to put a stop to this nonsense. Let them know they couldn't keep taking advantage of people."

"Oh, God, Joe, that was for the Feds to do, not you!"

Joe shuddered. "Sam?" His voice was a mere whisper.

"I'm here, buddy. Save your strength."

Joe shook his head. "Sam... Tell Shaunna," his voice broke as another surge of blood rushed from his body to soak the sheet and Sam. "Tell her I love her...and Joey."

"Shh, don't talk. Hang on, buddy," Sam urged. "Hang on and you can tell them yourself."

Joe gasped for breath. "Tell her, Sam...Promise," he begged, and coughed, closing his eyes. "Sam...?"

"I promise," Sam whispered.

With one last shuddering breath, Joe slid from Sam's embrace into oblivion.

* * *

Shaunna awoke to the insistent ringing of the doorbell. She slipped into her robe and made it down the stairs as Mary opened the door to a policeman.

"Mrs. Taylor?"

"I'm Mrs. Taylor," Shaunna said.

"I'm sorry, ma'am, but you'll have to come with me. Your husband's been in an accident."

Shaunna felt the blood drain from her features, her knees threatened to buckle beneath her. Her knuckles whitened from the strain of her grip on the banister. "What kind of accident? How is he?"

The questions were automatic, useless. She already knew the answers in her heart. They lay like a lump of dead weight in her chest. She sank down onto the bottom step and waited for his response.

"I don't know, ma'am. All I know is I'm supposed to come get you and take you to the hospital."

Shaunna heard the pain and regret in his voice and knew the words he spoke were not the whole truth. She nodded, then rose and went to her room to dress. Closing the door behind her, she ran into Joey in the hall.

"Where are you going? Why's that cop here?"

Shaunna saw the fear in her baby's eyes and stood rooted to the floor. How was she going to tell him? What should she tell him? She sighed. There was no way to cushion the news. "I'm going to the hospital. Daddy's been hurt," she told him in a soft, tender voice.

"Wait! I'm coming with you."

"No!" Shaunna winced at the hurt and confusion on her son's face. She hugged him to her breast. "Not tonight. I'll take you to see him tomorrow," she promised, stroking his silky blond hair.

With a muffled sob, he put his arms around her waist. "Tell him I love him."

She nodded, silent tears filling her eyes. "I will."

Sam met her in the emergency room. Shaunna blanched at the blood all over him. "My God, Sam, are you hurt?"

Sam reached for her. "Shaunna, I'm so sorry," he sobbed. His eyes filled with tears of exhaustion and shock, brimmed with compassion. "There was nothing anyone could do. It all happened so fast."

"What happened? No, never mind. I don't care what happened. Where is he?"

Sam's grip on her arm tightened. "The doctor's with him. Let him tend to him first."

Shaunna jerked from his grasp and turned her back against the anguish etched in his face. "Where is he? I want to see him. If you don't take me to him, I'll tear this place apart with my bare hands. I'll find him, Sam."

He nodded. With a ragged exhale he led her into the room where Joe lay.

Shaunna gasped in horror at the paleness of her husband's face. She walked over to him. With trembling hands, she ran her fingers through his thick, blond hair. "Joe," she whispered, knowing in her heart he couldn't hear her. She traced his features, his jaw, the eyelids covering his beautiful blue eyes, his firm lips. A sob caught in her throat.

"No! Oh, God, please, no," she whispered her voice harsh with despair. Cupping his face in her hands, she pressed her lips to his, hoping to infuse some of her warmth into his lifeless body.

Pain and anger sliced through her. Hurt and confused she backed away, recoiling at his coldness.

"He's a hero. He probably saved my life. Oh, God, Shaunna, I wish it were me," Sam sobbed.

Shaunna gazed helplessly at the man in front of her and realized Joe's blood, *his life force,* still covered Sam. She felt no compassion for the man standing, *alive,* in front of her. She felt nothing, nothing at all. She stood in a numb state of shock as his words seeped into her consciousness.

Hero? A bitter little laugh escaped her. "Funny, most heroes end up dead."

Sam took her by the arm and led her out of the room. Joe's coworkers filled the waiting area. No one said much, just offered a hug or a whispered, "I'm sorry," as each tried to convey the sorrow he felt at the senseless loss of their friend.

Shaunna stood mutely among the throng of men, listening to their apologies and condolences until she thought she would vomit. Sure, they were sorry—but they were *alive.* Anger swept through her. She turned to Sam and asked him to take her home.

He nodded, then turned to one of his friends and asked to borrow the guy's truck. The man protested until Sam assured he was OK to drive. He led Shaunna outside, guided her into the truck, and buckled her in.

Once underway, he reached over, touched her shoulder, and said her name in a ragged voice. Shaunna turned to face him.

"Before...uh, after." He cleared his throat, obviously struggling with whatever he had to say. "Uh, Joe said to tell you he loves you, and Joey."

Shaunna gasped. "You talked to him?"

Sam nodded. "Yeah, I was there." A sob escaped him. "Oh, God, Shaunna, I tried to save him, to stop the bleeding, but I couldn't. It all happened so fast."

Shaunna patted his arm, smiled a little. "I know," she consoled, her voice devoid of emotion. "At least he wasn't alone. Thank you."

He frowned in confusion. "You're thanking me? You should be crying, no, howling with pain and anger."

"A lot of good that'll do," Shaunna mumbled then sat in a numb state of shock. In her heart she screamed. Pain, anger, and confusion battled within her soul, but her mind checked off a list of things to do. She had to tell Mary and Joey, make funeral arrangements, call Mike and Buddy...the list went on and on until she was dizzy. She swallowed hard and fought down a wave of nausea. "Pull over Sam," she urged, fumbling with the seat belt.

Sam pulled the truck over with a screeching halt and she baled out. Stumbling to her knees she puked, retching until she had nothing left but a huge gaping hole where her heart once was. She felt his hands on her as Sam tried to help her up. She shook her head.

"Don't touch me," she whispered. "You still have his blood on you." A horrified sound escaped her as he hauled her to her feet anyway. She struggled with the urge to hit him.

It's not fair you're still alive!

She grabbed his shirt, wanting to rip if from his body, to throw it away, out of her sight.

"Oh, God, Sam, what am I going to do?" she asked, her eyes dry and aching from holding back the tears threatening to engulf her. But she couldn't cry. Not yet. She had to be strong for her son and Mary. Someone had to be strong, to keep it together. She had too much to do to cry.

Compassion filled his eyes, but Sam offered no words of comfort or advice. Helping her back into the truck, he drove her home, walked her to the door, and asked if he could do anything else for her.

Shaunna shook her head. "I'm sure you've had about enough of this whole ordeal."

"Yeah, but I'm sure it's just beginning. Please know I'm here, for whatever you may need."

"Thanks, Sam. Go home to your family and take care of yourself."

Shaunna watched him walk toward the truck. He turned and she answered the question before he could ask. "I'll let you know the arrangements as soon as they're made."

She entered the house as he climbed in the truck, closed the door, and started the ignition. Mary met her at the door and nearly fainted at the news. Shaunna held Mary while she sobbed. Mary cried, but Shaunna didn't. She didn't shed a single tear, didn't utter the first cry of anguish. Or pain. She just stood there. No one realized Joey had crept down the stairs, or that he heard Shaunna tell Mary Joe was dead, until his horrified scream rent the air. "No! You're lying! My daddy's not dead!"

Shaunna turned to her son, every feature of her face tense with pain. Tears stung her eyes—tears she couldn't shed.

She held her arms out to him, and Joey flew into her embrace. A horrified moan escaped her as she clasped him to her breast. With little effort she picked him up and carried him to his room. Cradling him, she rocked, answering his questions as best she could.

He sobbed hysterically. She didn't. She sat, numb, silent, and held him the rest of the night.

* * *

Sunlight, dull and subdued, had started to filter its way through the blinds when Mary entered Joey's room with his favorite breakfast of cinnamon toast and hot chocolate. He lay asleep in Shaunna's arms while she sat stiffly, her eyes wide and gritty. Mary brushed the hair off Shaunna's face and urged her to put down her son and try to eat.

"I'm not hungry."

Her voice roused Joey who woke up sullen and uncommunicative. He agreed to eat if Shaunna would.

In an attempt to appease him, Shaunna took a piece of toast and a cup of chocolate. Her face paled and her throat convulsed with each bite, but she managed to eat half a piece. With a tender smile to her son, she excused herself to take a shower and urged him to do the same after he finished eating.

His lips trembled, tears filled his brown eyes. "I don't want to go to school, Mama."

Shaunna hugged him to her, smoothing the hair off his

forehead. "You don't have to, baby. I'll go by the school on my way to town."

"I want to go with you."

"Not this morning."

"But you promised," he protested. "I want to see my daddy!"

Shaunna rocked him. "I know. I'll take you to see him later. But for now, you stay with Mary. OK?" She held him until he reluctantly agreed.

Mary took Joey in her arms and urged him to finish his breakfast while Shaunna walked stiffly to her bedroom. Emotions raged through her. Her nerves were raw, her head spun, her stomach churned. She stared at herself in the mirror and saw the signs of hysteria in her eyes, the pain and anger etched in her face.

Leaning over the sink, she vomited.

The hot shower she took did nothing for the way she felt but helped a great deal in preparing her for what lay ahead.

Chapter Twenty-Six

"Hey, Mike old man, what brings you to this neck of the woods?" Todd greeted his friend with a hearty handshake.

Mike frowned. "I'm here to see about Shaunna."

Todd's smile wavered. "What about Shaunna? What's wrong, Mike?" Suddenly aware of the pain reflected in his friend's gray eyes, fear clutched his heart.

"You haven't heard from her?"

Todd shook his head. "Not in a while. Why? What's wrong?"

Mike sighed. "Her husband was killed night before last. The funeral is tomorrow. Haven't you heard? It's been plastered all over the news for the past two days."

Todd groaned and with a shake of his head, sank into his chair. "Oh, no. How is she? That's a stupid question," he chided himself. "She must be going through hell."

Mike shrugged. "She's for sure not having any picnic. I don't know, Todd. She won't eat and looks as though she hasn't slept at all. She hasn't shed a tear that I'm aware of. She's just there, like some kind of zombie. I don't know, but I'm worried. I'm surprised you didn't know, even more surprised she didn't call you."

Todd raked his hands through his hair. If pain was tangible, then he could feel hers, gnawing at his soul and he had to force himself to concentrate on Mike's words. It took every ounce of self-control he possessed to restrain himself from tearing out of the room and rushing to her side. "I've been out of town the last couple of days, visiting other ROTC programs, getting ready for the new semester. You know I don't watch the news or listen to news reports. I overheard folks talking about the incident, but never a name. I wasn't here even if she tried to call."

But he knew she hadn't, and it cut to the core.

"Are you going to the funeral?" Mike asked.

Todd shook his head again. "I don't know if that's a good idea," he replied, his tone grim.

Mike's frown deepened. He gave Todd a puzzled look.

"Last I heard you two were visiting on a regular basis."

"Yeah, well that changed a few weeks ago."

Tension coiled through the room. Mike's eyes flared with a sudden flash of insight. "Are you two sleeping together?"

There was no accusation on his friend's face, only concern. "No," Todd replied in an agonized voice. "We've come close, but, no."

The full impact of the news cut into his heart, and he sighed. "Oh, man, Mike! She's hurting so much. I can feel it!" He pushed himself out of his chair and paced the floor.

Mike put his arm around Todd's shoulder. "I know how you feel guy, just hang tough. She's going to need you, or someone, when she comes to grips with what's happened. I wish I could be there when the time comes. Maybe at the funeral tomorrow she'll face it."

But she hadn't. She buried her husband with the same blank look on her face that had been there since she found out about his death.

And now he had to leave her.

Mike leaned back in his seat on the plane, his time was up. As much as he hated it, he had to go home. The last thing on earth he wanted right now was to leave Shaunna alone. He groaned inwardly thinking about the past week. *Shock.* Nothing else explained the emotionless state she walked around in, the numbness surrounding her, and the fact she hadn't shed a tear in the past five days. In fact, the only time she showed any emotion was when he and the Fredricks tried to convince her to return to Georgia, if only for a visit. Adamant about not taking Joey away from his father, she refused.

Mike closed his eyes and sent a silent plea to God to watch over her. He knew Todd would do his best to watch over her too. *If she'd let him.*

* * *

The days slipped by with Shaunna barely aware of the passing of time. As if in tune with her emotional state, the days grew shorter and the evenings cooler. Fall approached. Then winter. Deep. Dark.

Like the hole in my life.

She only found relief by hiding from the truth. Joe was dead. So was she. She felt empty, lifeless. Nothing helped.

Nothing mattered.

The anti-anxiety pills the doctor prescribed that night in the emergency room, and some blessed soul had filled for her, provided escape. Sometimes she took two or three so she wouldn't have to wake up too soon. Wake up and face the truth, the fact that Joe was not coming home in a couple of days, or ever.

He was never coming home.

Mary noticed the prolonged state of shock Shaunna dwelt in and the effect it had on her son. He missed school more than he attended. He desperately needed his mother, but she resided in her own world of misery, too consumed by shock and grief to notice his needs.

Despite the situation, the child's question, "Is Mama going to die too?" startled her. Her heart sank into her stomach, but she pasted a smile on her face.

"Why no honey. Why do you ask?" she replied in as normal a voice she could muster.

Joey shrugged and Mary knew he had no idea how to express his fear and concern.

"I don't know. She just walks around like some kinda robot. She won't talk or cry." A tear dripped from his eye. "And I can't remember the last time she kissed me. Or smiled. Or tucked me in." He fought back a sob. "And I miss her. And Daddy." The dam broke, he burst into tears.

Mary took him in her arms and rocked until his sobs subsided. "I know, baby. It's hard on her. She's having a difficult time accepting what happened. Just hang in there, Joey. Be strong a little longer. Say an extra prayer for her. And remember," she looked into his frightened brown eyes, "your mama loves you very much. She'll be fine, I promise. OK?"

He nodded, a faint smile on his handsome little face.

"I love you, Mary," he whispered.

She hugged him. "I love you, too." She sat with him while he said his prayers and had to force back tears when he asked God to please help his mama. "Cause I need her, and she needs me. Take care of Daddy, God. Tell him I love him and that I'll take care of Mama."

Placing a kiss on his silky head, Mary tucked him in and went to Shaunna's room. She sat in the middle of her bed, wrapped in a cloak of misery. Mary ignored the emptiness in her eyes and went over to the bed. There was no easy way to say what needed to be said. Taking a deep breath she plunged right in.

"Shaunna, you're going to have to pull yourself together. Get through this. Joey needs you now. He's worried, asked me if you're going to die too."

The words made little impact on her. She raised dull, listless eyes to Mary's. "I wish I could," she mumbled.

Mary put her hands on Shaunna's shoulders, wanting to shake the truth into her. "Well, you can't. Your son needs you. You need each other. Come on, Shaunna. Get a grip. Joe is dead, and there's nothing you can do to bring him back! Killing yourself won't solve anything either. You have a son, be thankful for that!"

A solitary tear dripped from Shaunna's eye. She ignored it. Her hands curled into fists, and she visibly struggled with her emotions. Mary knew the battle well and why Shaunna fought so hard not to cry. If she cried, then she'd be forced to admit why she was crying.

"Oh, Mary, I don't know if I can go on without him. I'm not sure I even want to."

At least she admitted that much. It was a start. Mary steeled herself against the pain she knew all too well. "You have to. You have no choice. Joey needs you. He's more than reason enough to go on." She breathed a sigh of relief when the light of acceptance dawned in Shauna's eyes.

Shaunna nodded realizing the truth in Mary's words. "You're right. But how?" she asked, terrified at the prospect of living without Joe, of not having his strong embrace or seeing his smile.

Of raising her child without his father.

Mary shrugged. "I don't know. You just do. You pray, a lot, and you just do it."

Shaunna nodded. "I guess so...I don't know. I don't know anything right now except I have to get out of this house. I'm going for a walk. Thank you, Mary." She reached out and took Mary's hands. "For everything, for caring and for looking after Joey. I don't know what I would have done without you, without everyone."

Mary hugged her. "It's OK. Go for your walk now. Put a

sweater on," she admonished.

Shaunna slipped on her shoes and a sweater and tiptoed into Joey's room. She watched him, so peaceful, in his sleep. She brushed the hair off his forehead, kissed his brow. "I'm sorry. God, forgive me," she whispered then left his room. She locked the door on her way out, and then slipped her house key into her pocket. Aware of nothing but the turmoil in her soul, she walked.

She didn't realize how long or how far she walked until she stood on Todd's doorstep. The chill in the air seeped through the numbness which had surrounded her since the night of Joe's death. She trembled. A welcoming light peeped through the window. The warmth of the cozy little house beckoned her. She knocked. Within moments the door flung open.

"Good grief, Shaunna! What in the world?" Todd yanked her into the house. "What are you trying to do, freeze to death?"

The numbness lifted. Blinding reality and searing pain filled its place. Tears rushed to fill her eyes, spill over onto her cheeks. "He's dead, Todd," she stated in a flat, expressionless voice. "Oh, God," she wailed as a tremor shook her slender frame. "He's dead!" She began to tremble and sob. "What am I going to do?"

Heart-wrenching sobs wracked her body and tore at Todd's gut. With a groan he drew her into his arms, hoping to comfort her. "I know," he whispered. "I know and I'm so sorry."

He held her, helpless to do more as she soaked his shirt with hot tears and ached with empathy. It killed him to see her cry.

When her sobs subsided into soft, hiccupping sounds, he pushed her gently away from his chest. "Come on, sit down. I'll get you something to drink." He led her to the couch he'd just vacated, and she looked up at him, a confused expression in her eyes. Dark circles surrounded them, making them appear huge in her ashen face. He rubbed her cold hands. "We need to get you warmed up."

She nodded. Fresh tears gushed forth. He groaned, brushing them away. "I'll be right back," he whispered, then placed a soft kiss on her forehead as she trembled again.

Todd paced the kitchen floor waiting for the milk to heat. The minutes seemed like hours as he doctored it with brandy and honey. Taking the glass, he headed toward the living room. He stopped in the doorway, his heart clutching in his chest. She sat where he left her, holding a handful of pills. The empty bottle lay on the table before her. In less than three strides he reached her.

"That's not the answer, Shaunna," he growled slapping her hand.

Shaunna gasped in shock at his actions. "Now look what you've done," she sniveled. "You've spilled them all over the floor, and I need them to sleep."

"You don't need them," he ground out and scattered them with a curse. He slammed the glass down on the table. "Have you taken any tonight? How many?"

Bewildered, she shook her head.

"Answer me," he ordered giving her a slight shake.

"No!" She jerked out of his grasp. "What's the matter with you?"

Three weeks frantic with worry, he fought not to go to her, and now, she shows up on his doorstep, pale and hysterical. It was the overload to his emotions. He lost it.

"Me? You walk here in the middle of the night, not dressed to be out in this weather, crying, hysterical, and then sit here with a pile of pills, and you ask what's wrong with me? You scared the hell out of me!"

Shaunna stood. "Well, I'm sorry I bothered you," she said and pushed away from him.

He grabbed her by the arm. "Where are you going?"

"Home."

She began to tremble again. Her eyes reflected a turbulence of emotions. Sensing her panic, Todd strove to calm down. He picked up the glass, held it toward her.

"You're not bothering me," he said, his tone gentle. "Here, drink this. It'll warm you up. Then I'll take you home."

She sniffed, a stubborn lift to her chin. "No, thanks."

His patience snapped, breaking the tenuous control he had on the situation. He thrust the glass toward her. "Damn it, Shaunna, don't be hardheaded. I said drink it."

His anger must have frightened her for she flinched then reached a tentative hand toward the glass.

"What is it?"

"Warm milk."

"Ugh, I hate warm milk," she replied in a petulant little

voice and slapped his hand away.

The glass shattered as it hit the floor.

Todd clenched his fist, bit down on his tongue and held to his temper with dogged determination.

Shaunna stared down at the splintered glass, bemused. Her life had been shattered worse than that glass, and Todd was angry over spilled milk. The irony of the proverbial phrase tickled her, and suddenly everything took on an eerily funny quality.

"I'm sorry," she whispered with a little giggle. A tear dripped down her cheek. "I didn't mean to break it. Really," she said between hysterical giggles and heart-wrenching sobs.

Todd reached for her. "It's OK, Shaunna. It's OK," he said, his tone soft. He shook her slightly when she began to struggle, laughing and crying at the same time. "Shaunna, stop."

She struggled harder, fought his embrace. "But it's not OK," she whined. "Don't you see? It'll never be OK again."

Her hysteria tugged at him like a giant vortex, sucking them both into a whirlwind of pain and anger. Todd mustered up his courage and slapped her. A hint of sanity crept into her eyes. She gazed up at him in surprise then fainted.

Todd caught her as she slumped toward the floor. He picked her up and carried her to his bed. He'd let her rest awhile then take her home.

He returned to the living room and cleaned up the mess. His mind replayed every moment of the incident. Tired, disgusted, drained, he poured himself a drink then sat on the couch, stared at the fireplace, and wondered at the ironic circles fate played in their lives. An hour later he still sat, the brandy soured on his stomach. He walked into the kitchen, placed the glass in the sink and gazed out the window. "What now, God?"

Silence.

He walked into the bedroom to check on Shaunna. She hadn't moved. He wondered how long he should let her sleep. One thing was certain; he couldn't let her stay there forever, like he wanted. Not yet anyway. A shiver shook him as he realized the full impact of Joe's death on his life. Shaunna was free. As much as he hated to see her in the turmoil she was now in, he couldn't suppress the small thrill of hope that she would finally be his.

He shook his head and chided himself for getting too far ahead of the situation. He sat on the bed and gazed down at the woman he'd loved for so long. He ached for her. She looked frightened and hurt. A tear slid from the corner of her eye. She whimpered. Even in sleep she couldn't find peace. Todd swallowed the lump in his throat and brushed the silky strands of hair off her cheek. He loved her so. Taking a deep breath, he whispered her name.

Shaunna opened her eyes and gazed up at Todd in sleepy confusion. The events of the evening crashed in on her. Her lips trembled and tears filled her eyes. She choked on a sob. Todd took her into his arms but said nothing. No words were needed. The dream was over, the nightmare just beginning, the only thing left was reality—cold, hard, brutal reality.

Joe was dead.

When her sobs subsided once more, Todd offered to take her home. The ride began in silence then she turned to him. "What now?" she asked in a frightened whisper.

He took her hand and raised it to his lips. "I don't know, love," he replied. "But Shaunna, I'm here. Remember that. I'll always be here. If you need me, call."

Shaunna clung to his hand as if it were a lifeline, then, just as desperately she pushed away. "I feel so guilty."

"Why?" Although he knew.

"For coming to you."

He took her hand again in silent dare for her to pull away. "Don't. That's what I'm here for. You've done nothing wrong. We've done nothing wrong. I'm your friend," he insisted. *And I love you*, his heart added silently.

"I know...I'm just...it's just..." She choked back a sob. "I don't know what I'm going to do. I can't think straight. I can't even believe it's real. I keep waiting for him to come home." She began to cry in earnest, not protesting when he stopped the car and put his arms around her. "But he's not. He's never coming home again."

Shaunna cried until she thought there were no tears left, only a dry, aching hole in her chest where once her heart had beat. She pushed herself out of his arms, placed her palm on his cheek. "Thank you," she whispered.

Todd grabbed her hand, kissed the palm. "Anytime. Please call me, Shaun. Don't make me go crazy with worry."

She nodded her promise.

Todd put the car in gear and within minutes, turned into her driveway. Shaunna climbed out and went into the house. She stopped in Joey's room and kissed him again. She cried herself to sleep with Joe's pillow clasped in her arms.

Chapter Twenty-Seven

The days slithered by. Shaunna began adjusting to the loss of her husband, reluctantly accepted the fact that he would not be home on his days off, or ever. Between school and Cub Scouts, Joey seemed to pull himself up by the proverbial bootstraps and get on with his life, for which she was grateful.

Shaunna, on the other hand, found it a little more difficult. Though she only talked to him, she leaned heavily on Todd's friendship, often keeping him on the phone all hours of the night, talking to avoid going to sleep. Alone. Knowing Joe would not be there. Tonight, or ever. She would never again sleep wrapped in his strong embrace.

David and his boys were constant companions, easing the pain and frustration for both she and Joey. Between the two men, Mary's constant support, and frequent calls to and from Georgia, Shaunna found relief in her worst moments.

October gave way to November without much difference. The ache was there, stronger at times than others. The weather changed about as often as Shaunna's moods and the approaching holidays were cause for dread.

Her days ranged between the good, the bad, and the ugly. On the good days, she reflected some of her natural buoyant personality. She prayed a lot on those days, depending on the Lord to pull her through. These were the days both Joey and Mary cherished, those when Shaunna was her true self.

The bad days were bad. She became depressed, even angry her husband had left her. On the bad days she stayed away from everyone, choosing to suffer alone. Those were the days when she clung to her faith, knowing no other way to get through it. As usual, when tears and sorrow came in the night, joy came in the morning, and everyone was glad when the bad day ended.

The ugly days were the worst and usually coincided with some obstacle she confronted in the everyday running of her, and Joey's lives. The days when she had to face circumstances head on and make decisions concerning their future. Decisions she was not ready to make. Days like those when she had to go to the Social Security office and file a claim so Joey would get benefits from his father's death, and when she had to argue with the bank over the accidental death policy they paid along with the service charge on their checking account. And the day she fought with the insurance company regarding the life insurance policy Joe had bought and maintained for the past six years. A policy he paid a slight fortune for but insisted on keeping.

The company agreed to pay the initial face amount, but refused to pay the double indemnity, claiming Joe perpetrated the accident when he picked up his stick.

This infuriated Shaunna, and she insisted Joe had reacted in self-defense. He made a mistake and paid for it with his life! As a result, she refused to accept the initial face amount and the battle was on, a fight she intended to win. Her son's future depended on it.

With all of the turmoil and Thanksgiving closing in on her, Shaunna welcomed the diversion when David approached her about a Cub Scout outing. Pain shone deep in his eyes. He reached for her hand.

"You know, Mr. Taylor's death affected a lot of people in different ways. Even my boys seem a bit subdued. Memories, I guess."

Shaunna blinked back tears and nodded.

"The weatherman says we'll be having a few days of unseasonably warm weather, and then it'll turn wintry again. Now might be a good time for the hike and a picnic I mentioned at Open House the beginning of school."

Shaunna brightened. "Have you mentioned it to the boys yet?"

David shook his head. "No. I thought I'd mention it to you first and see how you feel about it. I mean, it may seem kind of soon after Joe's death, but maybe it'll do Joey some good. I know my boys will love it."

Excitement curled through the ever-present sadness in her heart. *It would do me good too.* "When?"

"The Saturday after Thanksgiving." He hurried to continue as gloom once again clouded the air. "I've been feeling out the boys. Jimmy Bishop and Ryan Broussard will be here, but Scott LeBlanc is gonna be out of town. If it's OK with you, I'll set it up this evening."

Panic bubbled in Shaunna's throat, tightened her features, and she was sure, showed in her eyes when compassion and understanding flashed in David's. She touched his arm, suddenly desperate for a reason to make the day as festive as possible. "What are you guys doing for Thanksgiving?"

He shrugged. "The usual, I guess. Cook, eat, and watch football."

"Ya'll come here," she offered, hoping he would accept.

Pleasure lit his gaze. "We'd love to. It'll do us all good. Though each year does get a bit easier, you never get used to the holidays without the missing loved one. Now...what about Saturday?"

She hesitated, but only for a moment. "Sounds great."

David grinned and gave her a friendly wink. "OK, I'll set it up. We'll pick you and Joey up first thing that morning. Let's not tell them anything until it gets closer though, otherwise they'll drive us crazy."

Shaunna laughed and agreed.

Thanksgiving, though a bit subdued, was nice. Shaunna was grateful David, and his boys came, especially since neither Mike nor the Fredericks could get away. Mary, glad Shaunna, and Joey would not be alone, accepted an invitation with friends.

Saturday dawned bright and clear. A few white, puffy, clouds marred the bright blue of the cool morning sky. Everyone set out in jeans and t-shirts, with sweaters or sweatshirts over them. David drove to the closest state natural park where they walked down a nature trail discussing the different seasons and the habits of the sea and marshland animals. They laughed and picked at Shaunna, who screeched when they surprised a water snake out enjoying the warm sun.

She took their ribbing in stride and screeched on cue every time someone threw a stick and hollered "snake." At lunch, they spread blankets on the ground and feasted on fried chicken, biscuits, corn on the cob, and cookies. They returned after dark, tired but happy. As she helped him get ready for bed, Joey asked Shaunna a totally unexpected question.

"Did you have fun today?"

She smiled. "Yes. Did you?"

His eyes danced with delight. "It was great," he admitted then a frown marred his little forehead. "Mama, you don't think Daddy would mind us having fun, do you?"

The pain and fear in his eyes pierced Shaunna's heart. Life

was not fair! He shouldn't have to worry about something like that so young! She hugged him and chose her words with care. "No. I believe your daddy would want us to get out. He always enjoyed life, and I don't think he'd mind at all. In fact, I think he'd be more upset if we stayed home instead of going with your den today."

He sighed in relief and hugged her tight. "I thought so too, but I wanted to ask. I miss him so much sometimes, Mama." His little voice broke.

Shaunna stroked his silky head. "Me too, baby. But remember, Joey, I love you."

"I love you too," he mumbled, sleep coloring his tone.

Shaunna held him a little longer. When his breathing deepened, she tucked him in, kissed him goodnight, and went to her own bed. The next morning, she awoke groggy from lack of sleep. Joey's question incited a whole range of emotions ranging from guilt at having fun soon after Joe's death to relief that she and Joey could and should get on with their lives. It made her think. In fact, she'd lain awake most of the night thinking.

Shaunna dragged herself out of bed, stood a long time in the shower, and let the warm water alleviate her tired mind and refresh her lethargic body. She was in the kitchen with her second cup of coffee when Joey came downstairs.

"I'm hungry!"

She chuckled. "You're always hungry. What would you like for breakfast?"

"French toast. Can I..." His words trailed off at her raised eyebrow. He waited while she broke two eggs into a bowl, added sugar, a touch of cinnamon, some milk, and whipped it together.

"May I go to Mr. David's today?"

Shaunna placed the bowl next to the stove, turned a burner on and put a grill pad on top of it. "We spent the whole day with them yesterday. Maybe Mr. David and the boys would like a day to themselves."

Mary walked into the kitchen. "Mmm, something smells good."

Shaunna smiled and reached for the bread. "How many slices would you like?"

While she cooked and served breakfast, Joey continued

his plea to go to David's. Shaunna's protests ended when Jason called and invited Joey over for the day. Assured it was all right with David, she let him go. Mary offered to drop him off on her way to church when Shaunna declined her invitation to attend services with her.

Shaunna washed up the breakfast dishes and decided to go for a ride. Satan's agitation surpassed Smokey's, who was half wild from lack of exercise. Shaunna watched him rear and snort, running along the fence while she kept Smokey within the boundaries of his corral. Her heart twisted as she realized she would have to make another major decision so soon after Joe's death. Observing Satan in his current state, she realized she could not keep him tame. He was a one-man horse.

And that man was dead.

Tears clogged her airways when she realized she would have to sell him. The finality of getting rid of Joe's horse hurt as much as getting rid of her own would, but she knew she could not keep him. The fact became painfully clear as she continued to ride, and Satan persisted in acting up.

* * *

Todd drove up to Shaunna's house, relieved to see her out riding. He took it as a sign she was getting things together. It hadn't taken him long to make up his mind about going to see her.

He missed her.

Since the night she walked to his house, he hadn't seen her, only talked. Her calls, nightly at first, had cut down to a couple each week and awakened a whole new range of needs in him. The need to comfort and protect was more prominent than ever. Though he vowed to give her space and time, the fact she'd spent two days in one week in the company of another man ate at his heart.

She'd told him who David Farley was. He knew they were friends with a common bond, but he loved her, and there was no way on earth he'd lose her now. So, he came here today to see her, and touch her, and let her know, even subtly, that he was still around. Even if he could not come right out and tell her, he'd show his love and concern. He walked toward the pasture. Fear made him stop, momentarily immobilized.

"Oh, God," he muttered as a big horse, with an angry squeal, jumped the fence. Ears flat and teeth bared, he headed straight for Smokey. *And Shaunna.*

Todd's warning sounded too late. The two horses collided. Smokey reared. Shaunna fell off, beneath their angry hooves. Todd's immobility was short lived. He jumped the fence, whistling in an attempt to distract the fighting horses.

Smokey nickered in welcome and trotted toward Todd.

Todd grabbed his bridle, glad at least he got one of them away from Shaunna who lay, face down, very still, her arms covering her head.

The other animal was furious. Another angry neigh escaped him as he renewed his assault on Smokey—and this time, Todd.

Todd whirled Smokey around, getting him out of the horse's reach. His actions further infuriated the animal. He reared, his threatening hooves aimed at Todd's head.

"Oh, yeah?" Todd muttered as his fist connected with the horse's jaw. The blow turned him away. He released Smokey and sent him off with a slap on the rump. The big horse jumped the fence and headed straight for the barn, the other continued his aggressive tirade, running along the fence and neighing an angry challenge.

Todd ran to where Shaunna lay. Her sobs both relieved and worried him. He knelt beside her and rolled her over, careful to be gentle. "Are you OK?"

She nodded, but her sobs increased. "Oh, Shaun, are you sure? Talk to me," he urged and took her into his arms, stroking her hair.

"I've got to sell him," she sobbed.

He nodded, his cheek rubbing her silky head. "You should. I told you before he was too much horse for you," he chided, relieved she didn't seem hurt.

"Satan, not Smokey." She shoved herself out of his arms. Anger pushed past the raw terror in her eyes. "I'm not selling my horse."

Todd chuckled and cupped her face in his hands. "I don't care if you bring him in the house with you. As long as you're OK."

He brushed his lips across her mouth, cheek, and forehead then drew her back into his arms.

Shaunna's strained senses leapt in response to his tenderness. She trembled. "What are you doing here?"

He shrugged and continued to hold her. "I missed you. Your calls, the sound of your voice. You," he admitted, his voice soft, gaze tender.

Shaunna rolled away, afraid he would kiss her. Her reaction to him didn't surprise her. She'd always reacted to him that way, but it confused and angered her. She shouldn't feel anything this soon after Joe's death, especially desire or anything resembling it. She turned away and walked toward the patio, an embarrassed flush on her cheeks.

Todd rushed to his feet and grabbed her by the arm. "What's wrong?"

Tears filled her eyes. She shook her head. "Nothing. Everything." She shrugged. "It's just...I don't know," she admitted in a shaky voice, and continued her escape.

"Talk to me, Shaunna."

Shaunna had a feeling he wouldn't want to hear what she might say. She raked her fingers through her hair, heaved an exasperated breath. "I'm just not ready for this. I can't handle it. Not yet."

Anger flashed in his eyes. He choked it back. "Handle what?"

"What just happened between us."

"What happened?" At her defiant look, he continued. "I'll tell you what happened. I just saved your pretty little butt from being trampled to death by those horses!"

There was no disguising the hurt and anger in his voice. Ashamed, she reached for him. "Todd, please. Wait a minute."

"No! You wait a minute," he interrupted, boiling over. "I came by here because I missed you. I haven't seen you in almost two months. Just because we've talked doesn't mean I don't worry. That's what friends are for. And though you may have a new friend," he sneered, jealousy replacing the hurt in his voice. "Doesn't mean I don't care! You know how I feel about you and I'm not sorry about that. I am sorry if my coming here has bothered you, but I will *not* apologize for loving you." He turned on his heel and stormed away.

A sudden rage swept through Shaunna. "Just great! Walk away. You had your say so leave! How I feel doesn't matter anyway!"

Todd turned to face the angry beauty. And what a beauty! A flush colored her cheeks, her eyes flashed. Within seconds he stood before her. He did the only thing he could think of to convince her she did matter. His mouth swooped down, slashing across hers in a scorching kiss, his hands kneaded her back. At her soft moan of surrender, he pushed her out of his embrace. "Think about that when you start feeling like you don't matter," he muttered, and then walked away.

A furious hum escaped Shaunna, and he wondered if she might be reeling from the kiss as much as he. He knew for certain when a flowerpot whizzed by, missing his head by a hairsbreadth.

"Jerk!"

His anger spent, Todd chuckled. He turned with a wink. "I love you too, darling."

Shaunna glared at him and he watched her struggle to hang onto her anger. He imagined anger was safer for her at this point. His heart danced when her lips twitched, and a smile flitted across her features—although she tried to suppress it. Her chin jerked up a notch. Her eyes sparkled.

"Oh, go away."

He grinned and gave her a mock salute. "Yes, ma'am. See you again...soon."

Later, thinking over his visit, Shaunna couldn't help but smile. Todd was jealous. Though her mind chastised her for the thought, her heart smiled. She wasn't alone. She was loved. Those truths gave her new strength. When David brought Joey home, she offered him a cup of coffee.

"Looks like you've had a good day," he remarked.

"Didn't start out that way," she confessed. She told him about Joey's question the night before and what happened between the horses, omitting Todd's visit from her story. "Knowing I have to sell Satan and can do so, makes me realize I have to do something about getting on with our lives."

David nodded. "Whether we like it or not, life goes on. Our only choice is to go on with it."

"So," she continued. "I've made another decision. I'm going to see a lawyer about the runaround I'm getting from the insurance company. In fact, I'm going to see who all can, and will, pay for Joe's death."

David frowned, obviously surprised by the thread of steel in her voice. "What do you mean?"

"Well, Joe always told me if anything ever happened to him to sue every…" She blushed, remembering Joe's words. "Let's just say he had a crude but unique way of saying every company out there. Someone's going to pay for his death."

"I can imagine what the saying might be and he was probably right. Under normal circumstances."

"What do you mean?"

He reached for her hand, but it was obvious something about her plan concerned him. "Remember, *vengeance is mine said the Lord.*' There are a lot of crooked lawyers out there who will take advantage of your situation, and I'm not sure you're seeing things clearly enough to make the right choice. Don't let this decision make you bitter or rash. It'll make things worse if you do, and I'd hate to see you end up broke instead of vindicated."

Shaunna thought long and hard about David's advice. She had her attorney talk to and negotiate with the insurance company. In the end they settled for two-thirds of the total death benefit—including accidental—half of which she put in a trust fund for Joey. At the attorney's advice, she didn't pursue a wrongful death suit. The company Joe worked for had come through, paying his burial expenses and the death benefit they carried on all their workers. If managed wisely, that, along with the insurance money, Joey's social security benefits, and her catering, would be sufficient to maintain their current lifestyle.

Relieved things worked out without a big hassle or fight, Shaunna thanked David for his advice. They would be all right now that Joey's future was secure. Now she could concentrate on healing her heart and soul and life.

Chapter Twenty-Eight

We made it through Thanksgiving, but can we make it through Christmas?

The question repeated itself in Shaunna's mind as the first weekend in December passed and no one, not even Joey, felt like putting up the Christmas tree.

Selling Satan and Joe's truck had been difficult. She and Joey clung together and cried when the man who bought both drove away. Hard as it was, the sale made Shaunna more determined to make a life for herself and her son. If only they could get through the remaining holidays. Try as they might, no one could get into the Christmas spirit.

Joey struggled with his belief in Santa Claus, knowing even if there was a Santa Claus, he could not bring him what he wanted for Christmas: *His daddy*. No one, nothing would bring him back.

Shaunna fought not to sink back into the pit of despair that had surrounded her before she accepted Joe's death. Finally, she made a decision and they all went to Georgia.

New Year took on a new meaning as Shaunna determined to build a new life for herself and her son. At the fireworks display in Thibodaux they ran into David and his boys.

"Hey! How was Georgia?"

Shaunna laughed. "The Fredericks and Mike outdid themselves to spread the holiday joy."

He grinned. "Good. Being with family and friends always helps."

"Yeah, it wasn't easy, but we made it through."

"What are y'all doing after the festivities?"

She shrugged.

"Why don't y'all come to the house? We've a tradition of ringing in the New Year by toasting marshmallows and drinking hot chocolate."

"We wouldn't want to impose."

He took her hand, arched a brow at her. "If it were an imposition, I wouldn't ask."

"Please, please, please," the boys added, jumping with excitement. "We haven't seen Joey in two weeks and school's about to start again."

David chuckled. "Can't argue with that, now can you?"

Shaunna laughed. "I guess not."

They had a wonderful time laughing and playing games. The boys roasted marshmallows in the fireplace and David provided the ingredients for smores. It was a great way for a new beginning and after two o'clock in the morning before she could drag a reluctant Joey home. While she helped him change for bed, Joey asked her a question she was totally unprepared for.

"Do you think you'll ever love anyone again?"

Shaunna chose to ignore the real question. "I love you."

"Nah," he insisted. "You know what I mean. Another man."

Todd's image swam before her eyes. She forced him from her mind and tried to answer Joey's question as honestly as possible. "I don't know, honey. Maybe someday, I guess. Why?"

He shrugged. "Just wondering."

Shaunna sensed a deeper reason. "Why would you be wondering such a thing?"

Again, he shrugged, his face red. A kaleidoscope of emotions flickered in his eyes. "I don't know. Jason and Josh said their dad hasn't dated much since their mother died. I just wondered if you intended to date, and maybe, date Mr. David?"

Shaunna felt a wave of relief. He liked David. Her heart constricted at the thought that he might already see David as a substitute father. But he was a child, a boy who wanted and needed a father. David was nice but she hadn't thought of him in that manner. "Would it bother you if I dated him?"

Shaunna saw the emotions on his face as he pondered her question. She wondered what his answer would be. He smiled a bit sheepishly.

"I guess not. I mean, he likes you and he's always asking about you."

Shaunna laughed and hugged him, relieved they could talk. "Well, we'll see. I'm not sure if I'm ready to date anyone yet, but when I am, I'll keep him in mind. But Joey, I want you to know no matter what happens, no matter who or when I start dating, I don't want anything to come between us. I want us to always talk, no matter what. Do you understand?"

He nodded. His eyes rolled a little. He yawned. She held

him to her breast and kissed his head. He reminded her so much of Joe it hurt. She whispered her love as his breathing deepened. He mumbled a reply as she tucked the covers around him.

January slid along peacefully. Shaunna and Joey spent a lot of time together talking about their future. She always tried to be honest with him whenever he brought up the subject of her dating David. She promised to think about it when the time was right, but it was too soon. Joe's death still hurt too much. They seemed to be adjusting until one wintry afternoon.

Joey was at his den meeting, and Mary had gone shopping in town while she waited for him. Shaunna sat by the fireplace, reading, when the phone rang.

"Mrs. Taylor?"

"Yes." A frown creased her forehead as she tried to recognize the voice on the line.

"This is Mr. Dugas. Jonathan Dugas. You don't know me, but..." he hesitated. "My son was involved in your husband's death. He's the one your husband hit over the head." He cleared his throat.

Shaunna grasped the phone before it could slip through her trembling fingers. What did he want? "And?" she breathed in a choked voice.

He took a deep breath. "Mrs. Taylor, I know talking to me isn't easy for you, but I had to call. My son woke up this morning and asked to see you. I don't know how he knew you existed, but he does. He wants to see you."

"What?" she gasped. "Why?"

"I don't know, ma'am. He hasn't been too coherent but keeps insisting I call you. Mrs. Taylor, I know what you're thinking, what you're going through..." He broke off at her harsh cry of denial.

"How can you know?"

He sighed. "You're right, I don't know. But I do know this...the doctors are amazed John woke up at all. In fact, they don't think he's gonna make it. I know this is hard for you. It's hard for me, too, but as a father, I'm asking you to come and see him. It may be his last request."

Anger surged through Shaunna. *How dare he?* "My son doesn't have a father because of your son," she informed him through teeth clenched as tight as the fingers clutching the phone.

"I know." Sorrow colored his tone. "And I'm sorry. I don't blame you for being angry. I'm really sorry I bothered you, but I had to try. Please try and understand. He's my son, I had to try."

Shaunna slammed the receiver back in its cradle and buried her head between her knees. Rage and pain sliced through her until she thought she'd be sick. Hands trembling, she picked up the phone.

Todd became instantly aware of the terror in her voice.

"I need you," was all she said, but it was enough. Within minutes he arrived at her house. He let himself in when she failed to answer the door. He found her in the living room, on the edge of a chair, staring into space.

Todd took the clacking telephone from her hands and hung it up. Kneeling before her, he took her cold hands in his and whispered her name. Her eyes were haunted when she looked at him.

"He's alive," she whispered. "He's alive and Joe's dead. He wants to see me."

Todd shook his head in confusion. Fear clutched at his heart. "Who, Shaunna? What are you talking about?" he asked, half afraid to hear her answer.

Reality dawned and with it tears, darkening her gaze, rolling down her cheeks. With a horrified moan she buried her face in her hands.

"Mister Jonathan Dugas called. His son is the man Joe hit. He's been in a coma." She began to cry. "He woke up this morning and he wants to see me."

Heart wrenching sobs wracked her small frame. Todd took her in his arms and hissed a curse. Why now when she had just started to pull her life together?

"I don't know what to do," she whispered.

"What do you want to do?" he asked, hoping she didn't want to go. He couldn't make that decision for her. As much as he wished otherwise, he couldn't protect her from the truth. All he could do was stand by her in whatever she chose to do.

"I'd like to kill him," she moaned, her fists clenched in suppressed fury.

"Well, I won't let you do that, but I will go with you, if you want."

Her eyes glistened with pain. "Do you think I should?"

He shrugged. "I don't know, Shaun, that's something you're going to have to decide. I just want you to know I'm here, no matter what."

Shaunna shivered. For some reason, she felt a strong urge to honor Mr. Dugas's request and to face his son, to face the man who had killed her husband and wrecked her life. She couldn't ignore the urge, nor suppress it.

"You'll take me?" she asked Todd in a soft whisper.

Resentment flashed in his eyes, but Todd bit back his arguments and nodded. He picked up the book which had slipped from her hands, put it aside, and helped her to her feet. They drove to the hospital in silence.

Shaunna asked for Mr. Jonathan Dugas. He greeted her warmly, took her hand, and led her to the room his son occupied. Security officers guarded the door. Numbly she consented when they asked to search her for weapons.

"I can't thank you enough," Mr. Dugas said. "I know this isn't easy for you."

Shaunna gazed up at him but refrained from comment. She reached for Todd, fighting down a momentary surge of panic. "You'll wait?"

He nodded, a ghost of a smile tugged at his lips, concern etched in every plane of his face. "Dynamite couldn't get me away from this door," he assured, giving her hand a gentle squeeze.

Shaunna choked back her tears as Mr. Dugas woke his son. Her heart constricted when she looked into the pained, frightened eyes of the man who had indirectly killed her husband.

"Thank you for coming," he rasped. "I wanted to see you."

A shudder shook his entire frame. John ground his teeth, grimaced.

"Rest, son," his father admonished.

John shook his head. "Can't, not yet."

He reached for Shaunna's hand which she jerked out of his grasp. Another shudder wracked his body. He closed his eyes for a moment, then opened them once more.

He held a beseeching hand toward her. "I am so sorry about your husband," he whispered, and coughed, moaning in pain. "Please forgive me."

Shaunna's knees threatened to buckle beneath her. He wanted her forgiveness? Her husband was dead because of him, and he wanted her forgiveness?

"Please," he whispered. "I don't know if God will forgive me if you don't."

Shaunna collapsed onto the chair beside the bed. This man had destroyed her life and now he begged for her forgiveness. Of all the nerve! Her heart hardened. She turned to see Todd at the door. Waiting. Watching.

He smiled. His eyes conveyed all the love and support he felt. Her pain lessened when she realized she was not alone. *She was loved.* And although her life had changed dramatically, she was still alive. She had family and friends and a lifetime to look forward to. What did this man have but a lifetime in prison if he lived that long? She felt his touch on her arm.

"Please, I promise you, like I promised God that if I get through this I will never, ever, hurt another human being in my life."

Shaunna felt her anger weaken. Still... "My husband is dead. My son is without a father." She wanted him to know the extent of what he asked. He emitted a tired sigh and struggled to stay awake. His eyes begged.

"I'm sorry."

The fight left her. He only wanted to hear her say three simple words: *I forgive you.* She could say it, but could she mean it? Shaunna knew she would have to forgive him if she ever intended to really get on with her life. In the past four months she went about the motions of getting her life together, but her heart had been bound by the fact that someday she would have to face this man, if only across a courtroom.

Deep down she knew she would have to forgive him sooner or later. Forgive and maybe, by the grace of God, forget the pain and anger and get on with her life. She knew what she had to do. She took his hand in hers and swallowed the lump of tears in her throat.

"I forgive you," she whispered, and felt her heart lighten; her burden lifted, carried by the Lord now, not her. Not any longer. Now she could get on with her life.

John smiled. Tears of relief streamed down his cheeks. He closed his eyes. A deep sigh escaped his pale lips.

Mr. Dugas walked with her to the door, opened it, and whispered his thanks. Shaunna nodded in response and allowed Todd to take her arm, lead her out of the hospital, and drive her home. The phone rang the minute she opened the door to her house. Mr. Dugas was on the line, sobbing.

"He's dead. He died in peace knowing you forgave him. Thank you."

The phone slipped from her hands, she slid helplessly downward. Todd grabbed her before she reached the floor and guided her until she rested against the couch.

"He's dead," she whispered. *It's over.* There would be no murder trial, only the judgment of God, and Shaunna was infinitely grateful she hadn't added to that judgment, and her own, with unforgiveness. Now she could move on in peace knowing she'd done what the Lord expected of her. She'd forgiven a man his sins and, in doing so, eased the sting of his death.

Chapter Twenty-Nine

January blended into February and Shaunna felt a sense of peace. The efforts she and Joey made toward rebuilding their lives were succeeding. They enjoyed each evening more than the previous—riding, doing homework, or playing games. Even her relationship with Mary deepened as they worked together to put their lives back into some semblance of order.

Valentine's Day arrived and Shaunna helped with the class party for Joey as she had since he began school. At the party, one of his friends invited Joey to his birthday celebration that same evening. Shaunna hesitated.

"Please, Mrs. Taylor. My mom said it would be over by nine," Jimmy begged.

Shaunna smiled, unable to resist the pleading eyes of the child. "I bet you were a nice Valentine gift for your mother."

He grinned. "She said I was her Valentine gift from God. Can Joey come? Please?"

"I guess."

David, who had been listening, agreed to let Josh and even Jason go if they wanted. Then he cornered Shaunna with a dinner invitation. All three of the boys as well as Mary encouraged her to accept. "Five to one are not very fair odds, David," she chided.

He acknowledged her admonishment with a cheeky grin. "Don't think I'd risk the chance of you turning me down, do you?"

After cleanup, Shaunna agreed to let David bring her home so Mary could go to a church meeting. He dropped her off with a promise to pick her up for dinner at seven.

Shaunna was getting ready to go to the cemetery when a knock sounded at the door. Opening it, she was greeted by the biggest bouquet of flowers she'd ever seen. Her eyes widened, "How pretty," she crooned, assuming they were from David. "Wait, I'll get your tip."

She reached for the flowers. Relieving the delivery boy of his burden, she turned to put the flowers down then looked over her shoulder and into Todd's mischievous grin.

"The only tip I accept from pretty ladies is a Yankee dime," he remarked, thrilled at the surprised expression on her face.

"Well, hi!" Shaunna glanced out the door, her eyes alight and brow furrowed in question. "These are from you?"

He chuckled, glad his ploy had worked. He'd never forget the surprise on her face. "You don't think I'd be delivering them for some other guy, do you?"

She grinned. "Guess not. Come in. How did you manage all this anyway?" Her wave encompassed the florist's van parked in her drive.

"Charm I'm sure." *And begging.*

He'd gone to the florist's right after work. They agreed to sell him the biggest arrangement he could carry. Getting the use of the truck proved a little more difficult. He outlined his plan of surprise to the owner of the shop. Jenny Granger, a romantic at heart, relented when he threw his military I. D. and a major credit card on the counter.

"How've you been?" he asked Shaunna. He hadn't seen her since the day they went to the hospital. He talked to her almost nightly but hadn't seen her.

"Good. Busy," she admitted, rolling her eyes for emphasis.

He laughed. "What are you doing this evening?"

"Right now, I'm headed to the cemetery."

His heart ached at the hint of sadness which still lurked deep in her eyes. "I won't stay long," he promised. "Where's Joey?"

She smiled. "He's at a birthday party. We're picking them up at nine."

Todd picked up on the "we" immediately. "We? Them?"

Shaunna suppressed a smile. "Yes, we. David asked me out to dinner in front of Mary, Joey, *and* his boys. I capitulated," she admitted. "Reluctantly but graciously, I might add."

Todd snorted. "I bring you flowers, and you go out with some other guy. I don't know why you're even bothering with this guy anyway," he insisted, unable to disguise the jealousy in his voice.

Shaunna grinned. "Why? Well, for starters he asked. Secondly, Joey adores him and has been after me to go out with him. And third, you're a fine one to talk, what about Lacey?"

Todd bit back a grin. She teased him, and Lord it felt good.

"Well, Miss," he began in as serious a tone as he could

summon. "I haven't asked you out because I'm trying to give you some space. As far as Joey is concerned, I haven't even had a chance to meet him, much less get him to *adore* me. And Lacey is just a friend."

"So is David," she argued, unable to hide her smile.

Again, he snorted.

She giggled and moved closer, peering at him. "My, my, Todd, I never knew how green your eyes are."

Her eyes glowed. Unable to keep up the pretense of annoyance, he laughed. "Well, you might as well set an appointment for me to meet your son. Since you've started accepting dates, I'm hereby informing you of my intentions."

She arched a brow. "And what are they?"

In less than a heartbeat his arms were around her, his lips on hers. Todd held his passion in check. The kiss was gentle but firm, tender yet demanding and totally devastating in its teasing innocence.

"Now," he remarked, his voice husky. "I'll accept that as a tip for the flowers, and I'll leave so you can do whatever it is you have to do before your date."

Unable to resist, he kissed her again.

"Have a good time," he added, hoping the kiss would bother her as much as it would him.

Shaunna smiled tremulously as she opened the door for him. "Call me," he ordered. At her nod, he added, "Soon."

Lifting her chin with his finger, he kissed her with all of the tenderness he possessed. He left wanting to scream because she was going out with someone else and yet, glad she was going.

* * *

At the cemetery Shaunna sat close to Joe's headstone. She felt his presence, gained peace from it. She'd wrestled with guilt ever since Todd left—guilt over her date with David and guilt over Todd's kisses.

She swallowed the lump of tears in her throat and whispered. "I miss you, but I can't stand being alone. That's the only reason I said yes to David, I didn't want to be alone all evening." She hoped he understood. She loved him, but he was gone. *Forever.*

She heard his voice in her heart. "I know. It's time. Joey needs a father."

"Well, I don't know about that," she hedged. "Not yet anyway. I like David and all, but he's just not..."

Todd.

She shook her head as if denying would change the fact.

"You," she insisted. She heard his chuckle, envisioned his laughing eyes, and felt her guilt ease.

"I know how much you loved me, Shaun, and that you were faithful. It's OK to move on."

She sat, amazed at the clarity with which she heard his voice and saw his face. She felt his warmth and strength in her heart and knew without a doubt he would want her to get on with her life and be happy. She secured the heart-shaped wreath she'd brought, whispered her love, and promised to return, then walked away with a smile.

* * *

David arrived promptly at seven. His eyes widened in surprise when she opened the door. "Wow!" he breathed. His eyes swept over her in appreciation.

Shaunna took his hand as he led her to his car. Their reservations were for seven thirty at the Oilman's Restaurant and Lounge, where you could have a drink and dance while waiting for your food. They enjoyed the music and quiet conversation. David placed their order and then urged her out on the dance floor.

Shaunna felt nervous, and awkward, and shy, but it didn't last long. David turned out to be a marvelous dancer. He led her smoothly across the floor and steered her thoughts with teasing banter then thanked her with a light squeeze.

His fingers trailed down her back as they turned toward their table. A flush warmed her cheeks, tremble skittered down her spine. Shaunna glanced around the room. Her eyes met and melded with Todd's. He made no outward acknowledgment he'd seen her, but his gaze burned clear to her soul and sent an answering shiver through her body. She blushed and turned away.

David heard her gasp, glanced in the direction which she

stared, and placed a protective arm around her. "Is he bothering you?"

She shook her head no.

"Do you know him?"

She nodded.

David held the chair for her and she sank into it. "Are you OK?" he asked as she slipped on her jacket. She avoided his eyes and nodded.

He returned to the chair across from her and took her hand in his. "Are you sure? You seem a bit surprised to see him."

Shaunna's other hand shook when she took a sip of water. Every fiber of her being hummed with the knowledge that Todd was right across the room. She prayed David couldn't see through her confused senses to the need bombarding her system.

Shaunna sighed gratefully when their food arrived. She and David contemplated their meal in silence until she heard his soft chuckle and looked up.

"It's a good thing that cow's dead otherwise you'd fork it to death."

Color rushed to her cheeks as Shaunna realized she'd been playing with her food instead of eating it. Instinctively aware of why she was so nervous, David asked how and when she'd met the man seated across the room.

"The first time or the last?" she asked with a self-conscious laugh.

"Oh no, that question begs for details. C'mon now, tell all."

She giggled. "Can't, it's classified."

David tossed his head back and laughed. "Guess you'll walk home then."

She eyed him a moment then put down her fork, took a sip of her wine, and told him a story of love at first sight and of two young people thrown together and torn apart by fate and circumstance more than once in their lifetime.

David gazed across the room, in the direction where Todd had been. "His companion must be deaf. They're speaking in sign language."

Companion? It had to be Lacey. Shaunna glanced across the room, surprised at the strength in which jealousy rose in her heart. She looked at her watch then back at David. He signaled the waiter for their check, paid, and they left. Goodnight was a kiss on the cheek under the watchful eyes of three livewires disguised as boys.

Shaunna thanked David for a lovely evening and ushered Joey up to bed answering questions as she went. Yes, she had a good time. Yes, she'd go out with David again if he asked. Alone in her room she forced herself not to call and see if Todd was home yet. She lay awake a long time wondering where they went and what they did after Todd and Lacey left the restaurant.

The next morning dawned bright and clear. Shaunna went riding and ran into Todd. She smiled down at him. "Hi!"

She waited for him to ask the questions burning bright in his emerald gaze. Instead, he inquired as to her plans for the evening. She shrugged.

"Good. I'll pick you up at six."

Shaunna arched an eyebrow at his authoritative tone. "You will?"

He nodded. "Yes, I will. Tonight's my night. Be ready," he ordered with a smile.

That evening Shaunna met him at the door and invited him in to meet Mary.

Todd urged Shaunna by his side as they got under way. She hesitated a moment then relaxed. He drove down to the Gulf shore. After parking the car, they got out and walked along the beach surrounded by sweet, companionable silence. They didn't speak. No words were necessary.

They were together.

When they did speak, they played and teased, laughed and splashed each other. Tired, relaxed, and happy, Todd withdrew two blankets from the trunk of his car. He spread one on the ground and draped the other around them to ward off the evening chill.

Held in his arms, Shaunna felt a sense of peace and wholeness she hadn't felt in a long time.

Todd felt her relax, heard her contented sigh, and tightened his embrace. His whole body throbbed at her nearness, but he didn't push. And though he wanted her with a hunger unlike any he'd known, he was content to hold her, and to have her body snuggled into his.

They sat in silence a while, sipping wine from the bottle he brought along. The numbness induced by the sweet drink was a welcomed relief from the ache in his body, but it couldn't stop the question rolling around in his mind, especially with the way she looked last night, in that dress, with legs all the way up to... He gave himself a mental shake.

"Did you have a good time last night?" He tried but couldn't hide the jealousy in his voice.

Shaunna nodded and smiled then hugged his arms around her waist.

"You don't have to worry about David, we're just friends."

"Who says I'm worried?"

He tried to be nonchalant, but it didn't work. She laughed.

"Well, if you are, don't be." She snuggled closer. "And I won't worry about Lacey."

He chuckled, cuddled. "Deal."

Chapter Thirty

February melded into March, then April. Spring was in full bloom with promise and new life. Shaunna felt her life coming together. There were still times when reality would slip past the wall she'd built around her precious memories of Joe and she ached for her husband, longed to hear his voice and see his face. She spent the bigger part of those days beside his grave...talking, crying, and mourning. Somehow she always left feeling better, and stronger, assured nothing would ever destroy her memories of him and the love they shared.

The worst were times which held special meaning to her, when the days were long, unbearable, and the nights longer, harder. With the love and support she received from her friends, both human and spiritual, Shaunna always managed to pull through. Resurrection took on a whole new meaning as she coped with the pain of death and conquered it with faith, love, and hope.

Her greatest source of comfort came from the Lord and thoughts of Todd's love. Since that night on the beach, they'd spent a lot of time together. He urged her to introduce him to Joey. When she didn't comply as quickly as he wished, he took matters into his own hands. He arrived on her doorstep one evening with Lacey in tow.

Shaunna answered the door with a smile which froze on her face. "Hi. I thought we'd agreed on lunch next week."

He grinned. "I was in the neighborhood. Thought I'd drop by..."

"Yeah, sure," she interrupted. "Come on in," she relented.

His gaze drifted to the tray of cookies and milk she'd placed on a table by the door.

"You have company?" The innocent tone of voice belied the smug gleam in his eyes.

"Like you couldn't tell," she muttered, knowing there was no way he could miss David's truck in the drive. She called Joey out from the den and introduced him to Todd as he stepped through the door.

"How do you know my mom?"

Todd chuckled at the question and raised teasing eyes to

Shaunna's. Her frown warned him to tread with caution. "I knew your mom when she was sixteen. We ran into each other a few months ago."

Joey accepted the explanation without question. "Is that your wife?" he asked and pointed to Lacey who had stepped in behind Todd.

Todd grinned. "No. This is a friend of mine. Her name is Lacey." He turned to Lacey and, using his hands, introduced her.

Shaunna's smile held greeting. She watched as Joey's eyes widened in surprise.

"I know sign language," he informed them while signing.

"Really?" Todd asked.

Joey's brown eyes danced with enthusiasm. "Yes, we learned in Cub Scouts. I got a badge."

"You're very good," he said with a smile as Lacey stepped over to Shaunna.

"Hello," she signed.

Her tender smile mirrored the light in her eyes. Shaunna felt a pull from deep within she didn't understand. A flush heated her cheeks. Her panicked gaze sought Todd's.

"I don't know sign language."

He took her hand in his. "It's OK. She can read your lips."

Turning back to Lacey, Shaunna smiled and extended her hand. "Hello."

Lacey took it in hers. At that moment a bond formed, as though their souls connected the moment their hands touched.

Shaunna invited them to join the others, picked up the tray, and led the way to the den.

"She's pretty," she whispered to Todd as Joey led Lacey by the hand.

"Don't think I'd be involved with an ugly woman, do you?" he teased with a wink.

"Jerk," she admonished. Shaunna introduced Lacey and Todd to David and his boys then stood mesmerized as the men in the room became totally captivated by Lacey. She couldn't understand their words, but she recognized the look on David's face.

Love at first sight.

Shaunna glanced up at Todd. "I don't know what they're saying but I sure know that look."

Todd's grin and raised brow indicated he knew it too, and the power of it was reflected in the gaze he shared with her.

"She needs a good man," he said with a nod of approval.

"You don't even know him," Shaunna reminded.

He shrugged. "But I know you, and if he's worthy of even the slightest bit of your affection, then he's a good man."

His voice was soft and so full of emotion it sent a shiver through her heart. She couldn't know what thoughts danced through Todd's head, but she had a feeling they were much like her own. Watching David—who was a true friend—find someone special was a profound joy. The glow in Todd's eyes pretty much said he felt the same way about Lacey.

* * *

Shaunna paced the floors. Her spirit raged with spring fever. Though early May, it was still too cool to swim. Spring hung on, refused to give into the subtle urges of summer. She decided to go for a ride and enjoy the early morning hours. She took extra care in grooming Smokey, who thrilled at the attention. The currycomb clearly felt good to the horse and eased the itch of losing his winter coat. Covered with horsehair, she took a shower first.

She wrapped a towel around her then sat at her dressing table to brush out her hair. Her whole body ached as she recalled the dream she'd had again last night, the same dream she'd had regularly for about a month now. A replay of Joe's last night home and the wild loving they shared.

Though it always started out the same, the man in the dream changed in the end. It wasn't Joe she shared the night of passion with, but Todd.

A groan of frustration rent from her. She tossed the brush on the table. "Please don't do this to me," she pleaded, begging her heart, mind, and body. She shook her head as if to banish the thoughts, then dressed and went for her ride, hoping the exercise would ease the tension in her body.

Todd also felt a touch of spring fever. He decided to go for a jog and slipped on a pair of running shorts and tennis shoes. Maybe, just maybe, he would stop by Shaunna's house. The thought of her sent a shiver of excitement down his spine.

His thoughts drifted back over the last couple of months. Every look, every touch, and every kiss he shared with her intensified in his mind. By the time he slowed to a walk, his breathing was shallow and labored. And it wasn't from the jogging.

The sound of hoofbeats roused his attention. He turned and watched Shaunna ride toward him. The sight of her induced a groan from deep within as another surge of desire shot through his system. She was obviously enjoying her ride. Her face flushed, her eyes shone with excitement.

He trembled with need.

She brought Smokey to a sliding halt beside him. "Hi!"

Todd looked up into her radiant face and felt an answering pull of excitement in his gut. "Where are you headed?"

"Anywhere. Nowhere. Everywhere," she answered with a laugh.

He grinned. "Where's Joey?"

"At David's, his home away from home."

"No doubt Lacey's there too," he remarked, unaware of the jealous note in his voice.

She grinned. "Probably. Jealous?"

His lips curved. "No. Yes. In a way. Jealous of the time they spend together." His voice lowered to a suggestive whisper. "Wish it were us."

Desire kindled then sparked to flame. His eyes glowed like firelight dancing off the polished surface of smooth, flawless emeralds. Shaunna gasped at the raw hunger in his gaze. She felt her own response and blushed. Desire crashed over her like waves against the shore. Her heart beat in hard jerks, mouth felt like sawdust. She licked her lips and swallowed hard.

Evidently Todd sensed the effect his heated gaze had on her. He took a step closer. His bare chest brushed her knee and burned clear through her jeans.

The thrill of contact rocked them both.

"Give me a lift home?"

"Todd, no," she croaked and shook her head for emphasis.

He ignored her feeble attempt to refuse and jumped up behind her.

He nuzzled her ear. "Yes."

A soft whimper escaped her as he slipped his arms around

her waist and took the reins from her trembling hands. "Todd…I…"

"Shh," he insisted. His hand moved slowly up from her waist to cup her face. He smoothed her hair back and nestled her head into his shoulder.

Shaunna leaned into him, bit back a groan. She heard his heart beat wildly, felt it pound beneath her cheek. She smelled the musky, male scent of him. All of her senses were fine tuned, to him, for him. Her nerves crackled with tension. She was a wreck. Her body screamed for his touch, his kiss. Her heart cried out in confusion. Her mind was no help. It too, wilted into a useless, jumbled mass of emotions. She tried to think.

This is not a good idea.

She turned to tell him.

He silenced her with his lips then urged Smokey toward his house, while his hand traveled over her body in a slow, torturous caress.

"Ummm, lovely," he murmured, and continued to tease with hands and mouth, until she nearly wept.

"Todd, please…"

"Please what?"

"Please stop, I can't think straight."

He ignored the plea in her voice and drew her more firmly against him. "What's there to think about?"

Shaunna grabbed his hand. She had to stop this! She tried again. "Todd…"

He tilted her face and kissed her again. His actions signaled 'stop' to Smokey. Todd took full advantage of the halt in movement, sent her nearly over the edge with grazing teeth and dipping tongue.

When the horse shifted, Todd loosened his hold on the reins and urged him into a walk. They stopped alongside the porch at his house. Shaunna felt an acute sense of separation when he dragged his body away from hers and dismounted. He loosened the cinch with a couple of quick jerks, draped the reins over the rail, and reached for her. Too weak to protest, she slid into his arms.

Todd carried her into the house, lowered her feet to the floor with an agonizing slide along his hard frame then turned to lock the door behind them.

Shaunna tried again to stop this from happening. "Todd, wait."

He pulled her firmly in his arms. "No," he rasped. "No more waiting. I've waited too long already."

Shaunna gave up all hope of reasonable thinking when he crushed her to him in another electrifying embrace then picked her up and carried her to his bed. Her flesh tingled where he gazed, burned where he touched.

His hand trembled over her skin. "So beautiful."

His velvety-rough voice sent shivers down her spine. Shaunna grabbed his hand while she still had the strength to do so. "Please," she pleaded. "Listen to me. This is not a good idea. Not today."

"Perfect time, perfect day," he countered.

She shook her head in quick denial. "No, it's not."

"Why not?" he queried.

"Because," she began. *How on earth could she tell him?* "You're all hot and sweaty."

He chuckled. "That's why showers were invented."

Perfect! "Just what you need, a shower. A cold shower," she insisted and pushed gently at his chest, trying to think of a delicate way to tell him the truth.

He shook his head, nuzzled her cheek. His voice lowered to a husky purr, "No way, a warm one, together."

"No. Besides..." she whispered in his ear.

He stiffened, glared. "Please, tell me you're joking."

Shaunna did her best to bite back a smile. "I'm sorry, I tried to stop you."

He rolled over, groaned in frustration. "Great, if that don't beat all!"

Shaunna squirmed. "Maybe I should go."

He shook his head, tightened his grip. "You will not. I may not be able to love you right now, but you're not leaving. Not yet. I want to hold you."

She snuggled closer.

He folded her in his embrace, rubbed her back. "No objections?"

"Not a one."

They lay together a long time, anticipating the day they could express their love fully.

Chapter Thirty-One

Todd called Shaunna and asked what she intended to cook for supper then laughed when she told him she hadn't thought that far ahead.

"I'll bring something over," he promised, then arrived a little after five carrying two large pizzas and several bags.

Shaunna shook her head as he and Joey unloaded the sacks of junk food. "Todd, you're going to ruin my son's health feeding him this way."

"Aw, shucks, Shaun, lighten up, nothing like a good old night full of junk food. Right, partner?" he added, and exchanged a high five with Joey.

"Yeah," Joey agreed. "Mom *never* lets me eat like this!"

"What about the stomachache that's very likely to follow?" she asked.

Joey grinned. "A good reason to skip school."

"Dream on, young man."

Todd couldn't help but tease Shaunna's sense of propriety. "You get a stomachache, just call me, Joey. I'll come and get you."

"Todd..." Shaunna warned.

He chuckled.

Joey noticed the package he'd stashed in one of the bags. "What's this?"

"I don't know," Todd remarked. "I guess they put it in there by mistake. What does it say?"

"Happy birthday, Joey." He gave Todd a puzzled look. "It's not my birthday."

Todd turned to Shaunna with a wink and grin. "It's not? Oh, well, must be for your mom then."

Shaunna shook her head, eyes wide and innocent. "It's not my birthday either."

Todd schooled his features into pure puzzlement. "It's not? Well, it must be Mary's. Mary!"

Joey bounced with excitement. "It's not Mary's either, let's open it!"

"Oh, no, can't. Must be a mistake. I'll take it back."

Joey put the package down, fingered the wrapping. "Aren't you curious?"

Todd shrugged. "Not really, must be for another Joey, a mistake. I'll take it back tomorrow."

"Oh." Joey frowned. "But surely... Don't you want to know what's in it, Mama?"

Shaunna shrugged and bit back a smile.

"OK," Todd relented. "Go ahead. Open it. We can always find out who it belongs to later."

Joey tore into the package, a combination checker & chess set. "Oh, boy, checkers!"

Todd chuckled. "You like checkers?"

"Love 'em!"

"Any good at 'em?"

Joey nodded. "Yeah, I beat Josh and Jason all the time. Haven't beat Mr. David yet, but I will."

Todd chuckled. "Set 'em up, partner, and I'll give you some practice so you can beat him."

"All right!" He pumped his fist in the air then rushed into the den to set up the board.

"Think he adores me yet?" His teasing query reminded her of the excuse she had for dating David the first time.

The only time.

Todd had seen to that.

She laughed. "If you keep spoiling him he will."

"He's a great kid, Shaun, easy to spoil." His voice lowered to a husky purr. "I think I'd enjoy spoiling his mom too." His mouth closed over hers in a tender kiss.

The kiss deepened, until both trembled, breathless with need.

"Geeze," he whispered with a chuckle. "I want you so bad I can't think straight."

"What's there to think about?" she taunted him with his own words.

He nuzzled her cheek. "About how wise it'd be to throw you down on this kitchen floor and..." He whispered in her ear.

A shiver shook her. She reached up to brush the hair off his forehead. "You're right, it's not a wise idea."

He groaned and forced himself away from her.

* * *

Shaunna slipped the rose-colored dress over her head,

zipped it up, and tugged it into place. Her mind replayed the sound of Todd's voice when he asked her to wear it. The past two weeks had been wonderful, blissful. Almost like having a husband again, she thought, remembering the evenings with Todd and the nightly game of checkers he and Joey played. She loved the way he treated her son, the way he laughed and teased and challenged him to use his mind and concentrate on the game. It took less than a week before Joey beat Todd.

Todd had admitted to defeat but issued another challenge—chess. He tossed Joey the rules. "Study them. Then we'll see who the best is."

They were still playing. Until last night. Last night Joey left with David, his boys, and Lacey for a weekend camping trip. And tonight...Tonight she and Todd were going dancing. Thoughts of the evening ahead filled her with a mixture of anticipation and trepidation. Ten to one they'd end up making love. A shiver of anticipation danced along every nerve in her body followed by a wave of guilt.

She'd wrestled with herself ever since Todd called this morning and informed her of their plans. Her body screamed for his touch. Her mind cried out in confusion. Her heart ached for the kind of love only he could give—a melding of hearts, minds, bodies, and souls.

She knew he loved her. He hadn't said it. Not since that day with the horses, and then in jest. But she knew, had always known, but still...

Todd's anticipation tripled when Shaunna opened the door to greet him. His plans to wine, dine, and romance her slipped from his mind as desire surged through his body, and obliterated all thoughts except how beautiful she was. He had to force himself to take her hand instead of pull her into his arms, and down on the floor to ravish her on the spot.

He lowered his gaze, lest she read his mind, and kissed her hand. Never in his life had he wanted a woman the way he wanted her. Nor had he loved with the depth of emotions he felt for this one girl, this woman, whom he'd loved forever. The thought of finally having her, and making her his, of being able to express his love fully, nearly made him sick with excitement. He trembled and chuckled. "I want you so bad I'll probably never get it right."

His teasing broke the spell, eased the tension. She giggled but refrained from comment.

"Ready?" he asked.

She smiled. "Do I look ready?" Before he could answer, she groaned and held up a hand. "Don't answer."

He chuckled again.

Later, while they danced, his mind went back over the past couple of hours...the dinner, the wine, the dancing. So far, the evening was a perfect success. He hugged her to him as the words of a typical country song about loving forever and always, and then some enveloped them. She began to tremble. He heard her soft gasps, felt her warm tears penetrate his shirt. He groaned and held her tighter. He brushed the hair off her face, and gazed into her beautiful eyes which swam with confusion. "You don't have to say anything," he whispered. "I know."

She tightened her embrace. "Do you? Do you really, Todd? Can you understand I will *always* love him and mourn the loss? Can you live with that?"

He tightened his arms around her. His response came in three, simple words: "I love you."

Shaunna didn't answer, but drew him closer still, and laid her head on his shoulder.

Todd swallowed his disappointment when she didn't return the endearment. *It may still be too soon,* his mind whispered. His heart argued it was long overdue.

When the song ended, he walked to the table, picked up her jacket and led her out the door. Taking her in his arms, he caressed her mouth with his, changed the angle and depth until Shaunna wound her arms around his neck and pressed her soft body into his, lost in the passion of his kiss.

Todd sensed her surrender and loosened his desperate hold. He guided her into the car, kissed her again then drove home. Inside, he embraced her once more. Each kiss became more passionate, more urgent. He cupped her face in his hands, gazed into her eyes, and trembled at the passion he saw there. "Shaunna," he whispered. "You know how much I want you?"

She nodded.

"There's not a doubt in your mind how I feel about you?"

She shook her head.

He groaned and kissed her. "I'm probably going to regret

this but here goes: If you don't want to be here now, I'll take you home."

A tiny smile tugged at her mouth. She didn't say a word but placed her lips on his.

He buried his hands in her hair. "I love you," he whispered then repeated the endearment, kissing her eyes and cheeks. "I've loved you for so long."

A soft moan escaped him when she wrapped her arms tighter around his neck. He fumbled with the zipper down her back, which seemed to defy his every effort.

He nearly sobbed in frustration, picked her up, and carried her to his room.

He reveled in each taste of her sweetness, stroked, and kneaded and felt her skin heat and quiver wherever he touched. His voice was thick and husky as he whispered sweet words of love and desire. A funny sound, part groan, part chuckle escaped when she urged him onto his back and took a turn at the sensual torture. He buried his hands in the luxurious softness of her hair and gathered her close for another kiss.

"I love you, Shaunna," he said, in a tone rich with emotion.

Todd trembled, ached to hold her closer, but waited for her to make the next move. He loved her. She knew it. She may not be ready to say it, but he could see it in her eyes, feel it in her touch.

It would kill him if she didn't say the words.

"I love you." She barely whispered, but the declaration screamed within his brain, echoed throughout his body, ricocheted in his heart, and settled with a warm glow in his soul. The breath he didn't realize he held, rushed through his lips on a sob.

He sat up, cupped her face in his hands and plundered. Love and passion erupted with violent force. His mouth molded and shaped hers to his until each breath he took robbed them of much needed oxygen. Loosening his hold, he ended the kiss in slow degrees.

"I love you," he whispered over and over as his mouth traveled across her cheek to tease her ear. He forcefully refrained from weeping from the onslaught of emotions screaming through him.

"I've waited so long for this day. Love," he breathed. "Say

it again, Shaunna. I've waited so long to hear you say it."

Gazing into his eyes, Shaunna felt as though she were drowning in a sea of emotions. His words echoed through her brain. *I love you.* Three little words which had the power to render a person helpless with pain, or ecstatic with joy.

I love you.

He loved her. She loved him, had for so long, but life got in the way. Now they were free to love, to be together. She only had to say three little words, and everything would be perfect. She ran her hand up from his waist, over his chest, and felt him tremble beneath her touch. She thrilled at the newly awakened power over his body.

She pulled him closer, slid her arms around his waist. Her hands traveled up the firm muscles of his back. She nibbled on his throat then lips. The intensity of his need made her nervous.

Todd dragged his mouth away from hers. "Please," he whispered. "Say it again."

She ran a finger down his chest, thrilled at the violent quiver that shook him.

"It again," she whispered, for some reason finding it difficult to say the words he so desperately wanted to hear.

His eyes glittered. "You're a witch," he said with a chuckle. "I love you. Say it," he urged. "Say: *I love you.*"

"I love you," she complied.

He rubbed his lips along her throat. "Again," he urged.

The words balanced on a sense of freedom. She cupped his face in her hands and gazed into his eyes. "I love you, Todd Jameson," she admitted. Still nervous at the depth of feelings between them, she kissed his chin, nibbled on his throat, nuzzled his chest, and teased, "And if you'd listened the first time I told you..."

He silenced her with his lips then chuckled. "Oh, shut up. The one thing I can't handle is a woman who says, 'I told you so.'"

She giggled and wrapped her arms around him. "Todd?"

"Hmmm?"

"You know how much I want you?"

He nodded.

"There's not a doubt in your mind how I feel about you?"

He eyed her, a curious lift to his brow, and she knew he was not going to enjoy her next words. After a full moment, he nodded.

"Then you also know I can't go through with this tonight," she said in a gentle tone.

"Why not?" he asked, unable to mask the frustration he felt.

"Because I'm not ready."

He arched an eyebrow at her. "Think not?" he challenged, a glint of determination in his gaze.

She smiled. "Don't go there, Todd. You know what I mean. Physically, I've always been ready. Emotionally, I'm not so sure."

He buried his face in her hair with a groan. "Shaunna, I love you," he said, disappointment evident in the velvety-rough voice she loved so much.

"I know you do. And I love you, but I just can't go through with this. Not yet. Please try to understand."

"I'm trying, Shaunna," he muttered and tightened his hold on her. With a sigh of surrender, he rolled away, but didn't loosen his hold.

"I'm not going to push you, Shaunna. I love you too much to pressure you. But," he hesitated then spoke. "Stay a while. Let me hold you. I promise we won't make love if you're not ready, but please don't rob me of the opportunity to have you in my arms."

With a tender smile she curled into him.

The next morning Todd awoke as Shaunna tried to slip from his arms. They hadn't meant to fall asleep but... He pulled her back into his embrace.

"Where are you going?"

The guilt and pain in her eyes tore at his heart. "Home," she whispered.

He shook his head. "Oh, no, you're not. Not yet. Not like this."

"Todd, please. I need to go home." She blinked fast and swallowed hard in an attempt to hold back the wave of guilty tears which threatened to engulf her.

To engulf them.

He tightened his hold on her. "Why, so you can beat yourself up feeling guilty? I don't think so."

Her lips quivered. Tears trembled on her lashes. "Oh, Todd, it hasn't even been a year and I'm in your bed."

Todd clenched his jaw in frustration but chose his words with care. "Your vows said till death, not death and a year. Not even death and a day. You have nothing to feel guilty about. You've done nothing wrong. We've done nothing wrong. We didn't even do anything," he insisted.

Another surge of guilt clouded her gaze. She nodded. "I know that. You know that. But who's going to believe it?"

"Those who really care will believe it. What difference does it make anyway if we love each other?"

She shrugged, stroking his arm. "I don't know. We've waited so long, and been so close, but..."

"But, what?"

"I don't know," she insisted.

She stopped stroking his arm. A panicked expression filled her eyes. Todd saw the wedding ring reflected in them and the pain. Slowly, gently, he removed it from her finger then kissed her hand. "I love you."

Her lips trembled then bloomed. She flexed her fingers. A teasing light filled her eyes. "Now I feel naked."

"Exactly the way I want you," he said with a laugh and nudged her cheek. "Someday."

He reached under his pillow and retrieved the item he hid there yesterday. "Maybe this'll help," he whispered and placed a ring on her finger.

Shaunna gasped as the tiny marquee diamond sparkled up at her. "Oh, Todd..."

He silenced her words with his lips. "I love you."

"I love you too," she whispered and surrendered guilt to the joy of love reborn.

Chapter Thirty-Two

The transitions from wife to widow, and friend to lover were bound to be rough on Shaunna. Todd opted to stay away, until she came by or invited him over. He talked to her often but didn't want to push her. He knew she needed time to deal with the feelings that raged so strongly between them. Then Joey called.

"What's wrong between you and Mama?"

"What makes you think there's something wrong?"

Joey snorted. "Well, you haven't been here in almost a week, and you're usually here every day. And she's been acting weird."

His words put Todd on instant alert. "What do you mean by weird?"

Again, he snorted. "Well, she's either laughing or crying or screaming. She never screamed at me before. And," he continued in exasperation, "she bought all new furniture for the guestroom and moved in it. That's what I call weird."

Todd chuckled. His heart soared with the knowledge she no longer slept in the bed she had shared with her husband. "It'll be all right Joey, I promise."

Joey sighed.

"Trust me, OK?"

"Yeah, I guess."

"Good, partner. I'll see ya'll in a couple of days," he told him, determined if Shaunna didn't come by soon, he'd get over there.

Two days later she called and invited him for supper. He arrived to find candles and wine. Music drifted from the stereo. He pulled her into his arms, closed his mouth over hers in a gentle embrace.

"I've missed you," he whispered. Soft, sensual conversation flowed between them as they shared the bottle of wine with supper. Todd urged her out of her chair and into a slow dance with him.

Bittersweet emotion clouded her gaze. "I've been wrestling with myself all week," she admitted. "I thought I'd have you over, you know, candlelight, wine, whatever. I hoped I wouldn't feel guilty if we made love. It's not working. I feel guilty even considering it," she confessed.

"Why, Shaun?"

"Because, Todd, as much as I love you, it's wrong. Even the Bible says fornication is wrong."

"You make it sound ugly," he argued. "I'm sure God would understand. After all we've been through."

"Maybe, but I don't think He'd approve."

Deep down Todd knew she was right. He too, had wrestled with himself, and God, over the difference between right and wrong, lusts of the flesh and works of the Spirit.

His heart cried out in frustration. *"But I love her; I've loved her for so long!"*

Then make it right.

There was no doubting the voice of wisdom.

"Marry me," he insisted.

"I'm not sure I'm ready," she whispered. "I do love you, Todd. Please, I just need more time," she pleaded. "Please try to understand."

He nodded. "Just so you know I'm not letting you go. Not again. Not ever."

* * *

Todd rushed home from work. Not stopping to change, he hurried over to Shaunna's. Fear clutched at his heart. His mind whirled in circles with the memo he'd received this morning: *The United States is invading Granada. You are hereby on standby for possible departure.*

Over the past four months their lives ran like well-oiled machines. He and Shaunna spent as much time together as their schedules would allow. As usual for the summer months, her catering business picked up, and he stayed busy teaching. In all that time, he honored his promise and hadn't rushed her into marriage. He was content having her in his life, in his arms. The most precious times in his heart were those when she came to him, sometimes shy, sometimes bold, but always with love in her eyes and fire in her touch. Today was different though, he had to know where they stood. Joey opened the door before Todd could knock.

"Where's your mom?" In his frantic state, Todd missed the sadness in Joey's eyes when he nodded and pointed to the door of a room upstairs.

* * *

Shaunna sat on the floor in what used to be her and Joe's bedroom. In the past few months, she'd experienced less grief over his death. When she had a rough day, she always found peace at the cemetery and in coming home to Todd's embrace. Today was no exception.

She and Joey stayed over an hour at Joe's gravesite. She talked to him in her heart, but he hadn't answered. She knew in her spirit he was at peace since they were getting on with their lives. Though she'd never forget him or the love they'd shared, it was time to say goodbye and to release Joe—emotionally, spiritually.

Then she intended to call Todd.

She sat with a picture of them taken on their wedding day in her lap. Their matching gold wedding bands and her heart shaped engagement ring lay nestled in her palm. Pressing all three items to her heart she sighed.

"Goodbye, Joe," she whispered. "Part of me will always love you." A soft sob escaped her. "It hurts, so much, but it's time to let go, to start over."

She pressed the items to her lips then put them in the same little trunk she'd bought after her mother's death. She closed the lid and wiped the tears off her cheeks. "Goodbye, my love."

She heard a gentle knock and turned as Todd entered the room.

"Shaun?" He walked over to her. "You OK?"

She nodded and accepted his hand. "It's been a year today, Todd," she told him as he helped her to her feet. "I was just saying goodbye," she whispered, welcoming his warm, *live* embrace.

Todd groaned and hugged her close. *Oh, no, a year. Today of all days. And now I've got to tell her bad news on top of it.* He lifted her chin with his hand and kissed her. "I need to talk to you, Shaunna. It's important. Can we go downstairs?"

She nodded. He led her out of the memory-filled room. When they reached the kitchen, he again took her in his arms. His lips covered hers. "I love you, Shaunna. You know that, don't you?"

There was no hiding the dread in his voice. Shaunna gazed into his eyes for a long moment. He saw when her world tilted, and her expression changed to one of fear and suspicion.

"What?" she asked in a terrified whisper.

Todd trembled. He had to tell her. No way around it. He may be leaving. "Shaunna." He hesitated, took a deep breath, and began again. "We've invaded Granada, Shaunna. I might have to go." His arms tightened around her as she swayed.

"No," she whined. "Not again. Not now."

Suddenly she was sixteen again. And he was leaving. Todd remembered that day nearly fourteen years ago. This time he said the words he should have said back then. "I love you, Shaunna. Marry me. Wait for me."

Shaunna jerked out of his grasp. "No!" She began to cry. "Oh, God, please, no."

Todd pulled her back in his arms and blinked back tears as she sobbed into his chest. "I love you," he whispered. "I love you so much. Please say you'll marry me."

"I couldn't bear to lose another husband," she wailed.

Todd's hopes and dreams died a slow, painful death as he continued to hold her. Lacey and David walked into the room.

"What's wrong?" David asked.

Todd turned to face them. "I received notice this morning I'm on standby for possible departure to Granada."

He reached a hand toward Lacey who shook her head in denial. She took his hand and pressed it to her cheek, then wrapped her arm around Shaunna.

"Let's go in the other room," she signed.

David reached over and hugged Todd as Lacey led Shaunna out of the room. "Oh, man, that's terrible."

Anger and pain hardened Todd's jaw. "What's even worse is she said no. I asked her to marry me, and she said no."

He swallowed the hot knot of tears constricting his throat.

"She's been through a lot," David reminded, his tone gentle. "She'll come around."

"Yeah, well I've been through a lot too," Todd muttered,

suddenly angry. Angry with Shaunna, angry with the Communists backing a revolutionary group in an attempt to overthrow the government on an island halfway across the world. Angry with the United States for sticking their nose in it.

Let the med students get out the best way they can, they knew the risks when they went there!

But most of all, he was angry at fate for doing this to them again. How much more were they going to have to go through before they could be happy? He felt David's arm around him as he urged him outside.

In the den, Shaunna sat with Lacey as she tried to pull her thoughts together. *Why? Oh, God, why?*

Lacey fingered the diamond on Shaunna's finger. "Are you and Todd going to get married?"

Shaunna shook her head. "He wants to. But I said no."

Lacey's face was a study of disbelief and shock. "Why?"

Shaunna cringed. "Oh, Lacey, I can't bear the thought of losing another husband."

"Listen to you," Lacey chided. A gentle, understanding light shone in her eyes. Peace emanated from her, not judgment or condemnation. "How can you deny him what he's waited for all of his life? How can you let him go, knowing you have denied him the one thing that will make him happy? How can you let him go, knowing he may not come back, and you robbed him of his dream? Don't you know he'll be so much more careful if he has you to come home to?"

Mary hesitated in the doorway, watched, and listened while Shaunna and Lacey talked, then walked into the room. She reached out and stroked Shaunna's head. "She's right. You have been so blessed Shaunna. Most people find that kind of love only once in their life. Because of the crazy circles of fate in yours, you've found it twice. Don't throw it away. He loves you. Show him you love him too. You said yes when you accepted that ring. Don't let him down now when he needs you the most. Don't throw away the chance of happiness y'all might have."

Shaunna felt the light of truth and love come alive in her heart. She had loved and lost. *And loved again.* She knew in her heart she could not rob Todd of the joy of being his wife, even if for a short time. She also knew if she did lose him, she could survive.

I won't lose him! she determined silently.

She stood up and grasped the hands of her two dearest and truest friends.

"You're right. Thank you!" She rushed out to an empty kitchen. She looked out the patio door and saw him and David leaning on the fence, talking. She flung the door open. "Todd!"

He turned. She flew into his arms. "Yes! If the offer is still open, the answer is yes!"

Todd hugged her to him then twirled her around. "You mean it? You'll marry me?"

She nodded.

He crushed her to him, his lips devouring hers.

"Under one condition," she breathed as soon as his lips released hers.

He grinned. "Anything."

She smiled and cradled his face in her palms. "That you'll come back to me," she whispered in a tremulous voice.

He chuckled. "Oh, darling, there's not a demon in hell that can keep me from you, and I doubt there'll be an angel in heaven not pulling for us."

He picked her up, pressed her body against his and kissed her again. They turned as the boys came barreling around the house.

"Ugh!" Joey remarked. "All this mushy stuff."

Todd and David chuckled when Josh and Jason chimed in their agreement.

Shaunna laughed. "You might as well get used to it young man. Todd and I are getting married."

They watched a range of emotions flit across his face—hope, happiness, fear, jealously. He masked them all with a stubborn look.

"You're an OK guy but you'll never be able to take my daddy's place."

Todd looked at Shaunna, a look of sheer panic on his face. She let all the love and encouragement she felt show in her smile.

He knelt and placed his hands on Joey's arms. "I know I can never replace him in your heart, partner. I wouldn't expect to, nor do I want to. But I'd sure like to try and be the next best thing in your life. I love you and your mom, Joey, a lot."

Joey looked over Todd's head at his mother.

"I love you," she mouthed with a tender smile.

He sighed then grinned. "OK, you can marry her."

Todd chuckled and tugged Joey into his arms. "Thanks, partner," he said and welcomed Shaunna into their embrace.

Later, over coffee, Lacey and David announced they, too, were getting married. Excitement and good cheer replaced the fear of war as the four friends celebrated and made plans, trading coffee for glasses of wine. Wedding plans developed as they discussed and rejected the idea of a double ceremony. It was Lacey's first wedding and she wanted it to be her day, just hers and David's. She also wanted Todd to give her away, which thrilled Todd. Shaunna agreed to be her matron of honor as soon as Todd got back from Granada.

* * *

Shaunna and Todd's wedding took place three days later; a short ceremony in the company of friends. They decided to spend their wedding night in the house where he'd lived the past year. He carried her over the threshold, amazed and humbled that he would not have to spend another night without her by his side. He breathed her name, released her from his embrace with an agonizing slide of her body against his. He reached back and locked the door behind them then embraced her once more. "You've made me the happiest man in the world this day."

She placed her palm on his cheek, ran a thumb over his lips, replaced it with hers.

He lifted her once more and carried her to his bed where, at long last, their love was consummated in a tender celebration.

Two days after, he left.

Part III

FAITH: Loyalty, trust. *Belief in God.*
The golden link between fate and destiny.

Chapter Thirty-Three

Lacey Farley was on her knees in prayer when she felt the first flutters of movement within her womb. She'd been there more than an hour, which was her custom. Her mind reflected over the last year and the many blessings of the Lord. So much had happened. Her life was so abundantly full!

A far cry from the deaf orphan raised in a convent.

She and David were married on Thanksgiving Day. Now, less than a year later she was four months into her pregnancy with their first child.

Todd and Shaunna were married before he left for Granada. Todd was gone less than a month then he and Shaunna stood up for them as promised. They too, were expecting a child.

A smile lent a glow to her already radiant countenance as she again felt the child stir within. An ache pierced her heart as she thought about the baby growing inside her.

"Lord Jesus," she signed the name with reverence. "There were times when I questioned You about the loss of my hearing, but I've always accepted Your will. I've never asked for much..." She hesitated and once again felt the flutter of life within her body.

"But Lord, I'm asking now. To hear my child say *"Mama"* would be the greatest blessing I could ever dream of receiving. Please Father, in the name of Jesus I pray for restoration of my hearing. I know nothing is impossible for You." She hesitated again, then continued as the tiny flutters became more noticeable.

"You made the lame walk, the blind see, and the deaf hear. You are the same today as yesterday and are faithful to Your word. According to Your word, by Jesus' stripes we are healed. So, therefore Lord, standing on Your promises, I thank You for my healing."

She knelt in silence, felt the presence of the Lord surround her, fill her. The child within her also seemed to sense His presence and once again became still within her womb.

Lacey felt sure God heard her prayer and would answer, in His time and according to His will. She vowed to say this prayer daily with faith and thanksgiving, and to never lose sight of the fact that the Lord was true and faithful to His word. He would heal her.

She also promised herself, for she knew you shouldn't bargain with God, that whatever the outcome, she would always give the glory to Him. When and if it was His will she hear again, and speak, she would not remain quiet or withhold the testimony of His blessings in her life.

At three o'clock, she rose from her prayers and went into the kitchen to prepare an afternoon snack for her husband and sons. She moved around the kitchen while she mixed and baked a batch of cookies. She went to retrieve a tray from the pantry and stumbled over Rex. Part golden Labrador and part German Shepherd, he guarded the house as well as his deaf mistress with a fierceness that pleased David.

But now, his tail wagged in anticipation. She put down the tray and with a snap of her fingers and a slap on her thigh, gestured for him to come. She hugged him then opened the patio door and offered him free rein of the fenced yard. He accepted with a joyful kiss. She had time to throw his Frisbee twice before David and the boys got home.

"How was your day?" David asked then leaned down for a kiss.

Lacey smiled and placed his hand on her rounded abdomen. "Wonderful. I felt the baby move."

His brown eyes lit with a merry twinkle. Lacey recognized the look she loved so much and geared herself for his banter.

"Really? It's kind of soon. I bet it was gas."

She shook her head. "No, I'm sure. He moved," she assured, wishing the flutters would occur again. They did. "Feel," she urged, and pressed his hand into her stomach. "Did you feel?"

He rubbed. "No. What did they feel like?"

She smiled. "Angel wings."

He chuckled. "Angel wings? Nah," he shook his head. "Just gas."

"Was not."

"Was too."

She turned up her nose with a dainty sniff. "You're just jealous because I can feel him move and you can't."

He chuckled again, took the turned up nose as an offering

and nibbled on it, then her lips.

Lacey gave herself up to her husband's kiss. The Frisbee missed them by a hairsbreadth. David shielded Lacey from Rex's precarious slide then frowned at Josh, who had the grace to look sheepish.

"Sorry, Dad." He apologized then grinned.

"Yeah, I bet. Just wait until you start dating. I'll get you back."

"I can't wait till he starts dating. Then I can pull all the dirty tricks on his girlfriends that he pulls on me," Jason chimed in.

Josh slid his arm around the stepmother he adored. "You won't let them do that will you, Lace?"

She hugged him then grinned. "Not without my help."

Outnumbered, Josh shrugged. "Well, I'm not going to date unless I find someone just like you."

"Suck up!" David and Jason accused in unison. Lacey stepped out of the way as the three began to horse around.

David escaped from the wrestling match, urged Lacey onto his lap, and cheered as the two boys and the dog chased each other around the yard. The boys' pent up energy dwindled, and everyone went inside. David worked on the account he brought home with him, while the boys tackled homework. Over dinner, Jason reminded them it was their turn to pick up Joey for Cub Scouts.

The two families took turns driving each other to events. The men would take the boys to the meeting. Unless there was something special going on, the women stayed home and visited or went shopping. The standard joke between Todd and David was that Cub Scouts cost them a lot more than necessary when the wives went shopping.

After dinner, showers, and dishes, they headed out for the evening. Lacey decided she'd stay with Shaunna if she did not feel like going out. She knew and understood how tiring it could be. A quiet visit with her and Mary would be perfect after the day's activities.

Concern entered her heart when Lacey thought about her friends. Shaunna seemed to be having a difficult time in accepting her pregnancy as well as adjusting to the difference between this marriage and her first. She had confided that Todd and Joe were very different, especially in what they wanted out of marriage. All Joe wanted was love and loyalty. Todd seemed to want the very breath of her. Though she loved him with all of her heart, he seemed to want her soul and gave his in return.

Joe had been a physical person, comfortable with the knowledge he loved and was loved in return. He didn't talk much about the past or the future, content to live for the day. Though he had a tender side, he was the typical strong, silent type, who showed his love to her and Joey in simple, physical ways. He taught Joey to be tough, believing strength made the man. Shaunna had Joe's strength and protection when he was home, but he expected her to be able to take care of herself and Joey when he was gone.

Todd, on the other hand, was emotional, passionate, tender, sharing everything with her, his hopes, dreams, and fears. He taught Joey to think and feel and to accept his weaknesses—something Joe would never do—believing that only by doing so, could a man venture to overcome them and then be strengthened. He believed real strength started in the mind, quoting scripture to substantiate his reasoning. He drew on her strength and shared his with her, imparting a sense of unity Shaunna never knew could exist between a man and a woman, and she was stronger for it. He wasn't ashamed to adhere to her love, to need it and ask for it, clinging to her warmth when he had a rough day or night. Though he too was very physical, demonstrating his love in a number of ways, she felt closer to Todd than she ever had with Joe. The very depth of love and need they had for each other scared her, and she often wondered if she could love him as deeply as he seemed to need and want.

When Shaunna had shared these fears with her, Lacey had prayed and encouraged her friend to open up and love Todd the way he loved her—completely and unconditionally.

Chapter Thirty-Four

Monday afternoon he neither taught nor attended class, so Todd took the afternoon off, anxious to spend time with his wife. He arrived home, disappointed to find Shaunna in a bad mood. Though he tried to be patient, she was irritable beyond belief. Her irritation increased when he took advantage of having the swimming pool all to himself.

"You're a fine one. I can hardly move and there you sit, all relaxed after swimming for an hour. Don't ask me to wait on you, I'm too tired."

He tried to ignore the accusation in her voice, but it grated on his nerves. "I don't recall asking. What's the matter with you anyway?"

"You mean besides being as big as a house?"

That did it. "I don't understand you at all. How come you're so upset? How can you claim to be so miserable when you're carrying our child? I thought you were happy about this baby?"

"It's not that I'm not happy, it's just..." Her voice trailed off, uncertainty clouded her gaze.

"What?" He knew the baby had been a surprise, but at almost seven months she should be used to the idea.

"I don't know." She shrugged. "Everything."

"What kind of answer is *'everything'*?" he asked, hoping she would explain her feelings.

Shaunna massaged her temples. "It's just so soon. Everything's happening so fast. It's always happened fast between us."

"I still don't understand. You're not making any sense, Shaunna. What do you mean? What's wrong?"

"I mean..." the tears came. "I mean, first Joe and then us and now—" Her voice broke. "Now, the baby. I don't know. I wanted to spend some time just us, and Joey. And..." A sob halted her words.

Every intention he had of being patient escaped Todd at the mention of her dead husband. "Well," he snarled, "had I known you didn't want my child, I would have prevented you from getting pregnant."

A flush filled her cheeks. Shame lit her beautiful eyes. She reached for him. "That's not it..."

Hurt, angry, and disappointed, he jerked away before she could touch him. "Then what is it?"

Shaunna gasped. Tears trembled on her lashes. "I'm sorry."

The pain and confusion in her eyes cut him like a knife. Her apology softened his heart. He cupped her face in his hands, brushed the tears off her cheeks with his thumbs. "Shaun, how can I be loving and supportive if I don't know what's bothering you? I know the baby was a surprise, but it's more than that, isn't it?"

She fought back another deluge of tears with a valiant sniff.

"You're going to think I'm crazy," she muttered. Embarrassment colored her tone.

He grinned. "I already know you're crazy. You're married to me. Talk to me, Shaunna."

She heaved a sigh, rubbed her eyes and whined. "I don't ever remember being this uncomfortable with Joey. This heavy, or this..." The tears started again. "This tired and emotional. I mean, I can't ride my horse or swim or anything."

He could sense more to what she said. Something akin to fear filled her tone and gaze. "You can walk. I walk with you every evening when it's cool."

She nodded. "I know, but it's so hot and I'm so big and..."

"And?"

"I feel so fat," she confided in an embarrassed whisper.

Todd wrapped his arms around her and ducked his head to hide a smile. So that's it! He kissed her ear and cheek and lips. "You are so beautiful to me..."

His warbled rendition won him a giggle. "For someone with such a beautiful voice, you can't sing worth a flip."

He tried to look offended despite the twitch of his lips. "I'm crushed you would belittle my efforts to cheer you up."

She smiled and his heart flip-flopped.

"I'm sorry. I guess I am being silly. But I'm allowed."

He grinned again but refrained from comment. He'd allow her anything. He kissed her and put his arms around her as far as they would go. "I love you. I happen to think you're very beautiful and very desirable, baby and all.”

His voice lowered to a husky whisper, “I'll be more than happy to show you every day how much I want you.”

She arched an eyebrow at him. “Every day?”

He chuckled. “Yep, twice a day if necessary.”

The baby stretched her stomach in an unnatural way. She groaned. “Just rub my back and massage my feet, OK?”

Todd heard the weariness in her voice. He massaged her abdomen until the child within her womb settled back into a more comfortable, more natural position.

“Anytime, love,” he breathed. “Anything else?” he asked and stroked her from shoulder to thigh.

Her groan turned into a soft sigh of pleasure but the desire in her eyes barely masked the exhaustion. He could almost read her mind: *If only I had the energy.*

“C'mon, little mama, let's take a nap.” Todd led her up the stairs, helped her undress and aided her into bed, then lay beside her and curled his body around hers. He stroked her from shoulder to hip until he felt her relax beside him.

“I love you,” he whispered.

She turned to face him and cupped his cheek with her hand. “Will you still want me when milk drips from my breasts? When stretch marks and after-baby fat cover my body? And when we can't make love for six weeks?”

He placed his hand over hers, brushed his lips across her palm. “You don't have to nurse her if you don't want to.”

Pain flashed in her eyes when he used that particular gender while referring to their child, but she didn't comment. From the moment they found out she was pregnant, she'd been adamant about not wanting a girl, another thing which puzzled him beyond comprehension.

“Nurse him,” she asserted through clenched teeth.

He nodded. “OK. Then yes, I will still want you when you have milk and stretch marks and baby fat. It's a temporary state, Shaunna. If I know you, you'll be back to your slim, sexy self in no time at all. As for making love, I've gone longer than six weeks without that pleasure before.”

He cuddled her until she relaxed once more.

“I'm sorry for being so silly,” she whispered between soft moans of pleasure.

He lowered his lips to hers for a long, leisurely taste of her mouth. "Don't ever think your feelings are silly to me. I love you, little mama. So much."

His lips tangled with hers again, tasting, teasing, and urging a deeper response. The kiss scorched, devoured until, with a soft murmur of acquiescence, she surrendered to the sweet ecstasy they always found in each other's arms. When she drifted off to sleep, he dozed beside her.

He'd been up about an hour when Joey got home from school. Todd sat at the table and read the paper while Joey did his homework. Mary puttered in the kitchen and Shaunna still rested. A thrill raced down his spine as his thoughts lingered over the intimate afternoon with his wife and the nap that had him feeling like...*He-Man.*

He suppressed a chuckle. *He-Man?* If there's any indication you're far too in love with your wife, comparing yourself to a fictitious superhero portrayed on Saturday morning cartoons had to be it, he thought, and forced his mind back to the newspaper in his hand.

"Hey, Pop?"

Todd's heart swelled when Joey called him Pop. It was a long time in coming. After they found out about the baby, Joey decided he couldn't call him, *Todd* when the baby would call him *Daddy.* But he couldn't comfortably call him Daddy either. Joe was his daddy. Todd understood. They decided on Pop. Todd was happy with Pop. "Yeah?"

"What's an adjective?"

Joey hated English.

"An adjective is a word which describes another word or an object."

"I don't understand."

"Well, like pretty describes a girl."

"Oh. What are some other adjectives that mean the same or almost the same as pretty? Like, if pretty isn't pretty enough?"

Todd had no problem keeping up with Joey's train of thought. He grinned. "Well, if pretty isn't pretty enough, there's beautiful or stunning."

"How would you describe Mama—pretty, beautiful or stunning?"

Todd gazed at Shaunna as she waddled down the stairs,

beautiful and relaxed in spite of her size, and grinned. "I'd describe your mom as drop-dead gorgeous."

Joey snorted. "I can't put that in my homework. What does that mean anyway?"

Todd chuckled. "It means when she walks in the room my heart stops beating, and if it didn't start up again, I'd drop dead," he concluded as she reached them.

Shaunna kissed her son's soft hair then put her arms around Todd's neck. "Thank you," she whispered in his ear.

He kissed her hand. "My pleasure."

Joey grunted with a frown. "All this mushy junk and I just wanted some help with my homework."

Todd laughed as Shaunna lowered herself into the chair between him and Joey.

"I'll help you, sweetheart."

Todd finished reading his paper and got up to leave. He paused beside Joey, whispered something in his ear, and winked at Shaunna. Joey grinned and scribbled.

"Todd, he's not going to learn anything if you give him the answers."

"Aw shucks, Shaun, a little help every now and then won't stop him from learning. He's a smart guy."

She rolled her eyes. "If this is any indication, I can imagine how rotten this child is going to be."

Todd leaned down and rubbed her stomach then kissed her lips. "I promise she won't be too spoiled. Huh, Joey?"

Joey grinned. "Yeah! I think it'll be neat having a baby sister."

"Maybe next time," Shaunna said. "I want another son."

Todd heard the edge to her voice and dropped the subject. He had no idea why, but Shaunna absolutely refused to discuss a girl. He figured it was a female thing, so he let it be. He went into the kitchen to help Mary with supper while Shaunna and Joey finished homework and discussed his day.

Mary welcomed Todd in the kitchen with a smile and accepted his offer of help with gratitude. While they worked, she asked him some questions about financial aide at the college.

Todd listened in earnest to her about her idea of going to school. A new bakery in town had put an end to the catering business and "Shaunna's Sweets" was no more. Though Mary worked part time at the bakery, she wanted to do more. She hadn't decided what she wanted to study yet, maybe culinary classes or business administration.

Todd thought it was a great idea. "Would you do me one favor, though? I know it's selfish of me to ask, but would you wait until after the baby comes. I'm worried about Shaunna. I mean, she's so tired all the time and Mary, I honestly don't know how she's going to react if this baby is a girl. Do you have any idea what's wrong?"

A pained expression crossed her face, yet Mary avoided his gaze when she answered. "I guess she just has her heart set on a boy."

He sighed, shook his head. "I guess."

They served supper, after which Todd helped Mary with the dishes while Shaunna sat with her feet propped up at the table, and Joey went upstairs to get ready for Cub Scouts. David and Lacey arrived, and the boys ran up to meet Joey while the adults visited.

"Lacey says she felt the baby move today. I told her it was just gas."

"Well, Shaunna says our baby is playing soccer in there. I say she's dancing."

A look of resignation crossed Lacey's face when she realized the battle was on, men against the women as they teased their wives in the normal ritual. Especially since Todd had remarked that she and Shaunna were so much alike they even got pregnant at the same time.

Lacey reached for Shaunna's hand and gave it a squeeze before answering. "Whether boy or girl, let's be grateful he's healthy."

Her eyes dared Todd to say more. She grinned when, with a look of surrender and a shake of his head, he turned to David. "Get up, Dave. Let's go before we get in trouble."

David chuckled and slapped him on the back. "Yeah, I guess we don't need to help each other out in that area. I get in trouble real easy all by myself."

Todd winked at Lacey. "Me too," he admitted with a laugh, and bent to kiss Shaunna. He whispered his love in her ear, and she rewarded him with one of her beautiful smiles as the boys barreled down the stairs ready to go.

Lacey waited until the door closed behind them and took Shaunna's hand again. She knew how Shaunna felt about having a girl and why. "You haven't talked to him yet?"

Tears rushed to Shaunna's eyes. "I can't, I don't want to hurt him."

"He's your husband," Lacey admonished. "He loves you. You're hurting yourself trying to deal with these feelings alone."

"I'm not alone. I have you and Mary."

"And I happen to agree with Lacey," Mary asserted. She too knew why Shaunna didn't want the baby to be a girl.

"Please," Shaunna whispered. "I don't need a lecture."

Empathizing with the depth of her pain, her friends dropped the subject.

Chapter Thirty-Five

"Military Science, Lieutenant Jameson speaking."

Shaunna's voice came over the line. "Todd, I think I'm in labor."

She sounds scared. "What's going on?"

"Well, I've been having contractions and I'm bleeding. Not much, but..."

Todd took a deep breath. *Stay calm*, he told himself. *Think.* "Where's Mary?"

"She went into town a while ago. Todd, it's too soon for this baby."

"Calm down, Shaun. Did you call the doctor?"

"No."

"Did you call an ambulance?"

"No, I called you." Her voice rose a notch then wavered. "Todd, I'm scared."

Stay calm, he warned himself again. She's *scared. One of us has to stay calm.* "Where are you?"

"I'm in the den."

"I'll call an ambulance. You stay put. I'll phone the doctor and meet you at the hospital. OK, Shaunna?"

"OK."

"I love you, Shaun. Stay on the couch. Make sure the door is unlocked then stay put. And prop your feet up."

"I will."

"Hang in there, love, and I'll see you in a flash."

"Be careful," she whispered.

By the time Shaunna arrived at the hospital, Todd paced the corridor. Her doctor was on his way. Paramedics rushed her into the emergency room. Questions flew. Answers wavered between pained gasps. Fear cloaked the room like a noxious cloud. The doctor on call examined Shaunna and barked orders for a baby monitor, charts, and vital signs. Finding her dilated, they administered something to calm her and stop the labor.

Three hours later the labor progressed. The doctors weren't able to stop the contractions, but Shaunna wasn't dilating on par. The medicine they administered to help her relax seemed to have the opposite effect. She worried to the point of hysteria. When the doctor came in to examine her again, Todd went out to use the phone. He called home and left a message for Mary. Then he called David. David promised to make sure Joey got home from school and said he and Lacey would be there as soon as possible.

The doctor walked out of Shaunna's room and grabbed Todd by the arm as he went in.

"We've given her another shot. If this one doesn't work, we'll have to take the baby."

The graveness in his eyes belied the gentle tone. Todd's heart constricted. "How soon?"

The doctor shrugged. "We'll watch them. As long as the baby's not in distress, we're safe."

Fifteen minutes later he wasn't so optimistic. The baby's heartbeat became irregular, and its movements slowed, but Shaunna's contractions increased. The labor room became a blur of activity as they prepared for an emergency Cesarean section. Todd refused to leave and followed her into delivery.

Shaunna mumbled incoherently. Todd did his best to calm her. His efforts doubled when the doctor sought his gaze.

"She has to calm down. Otherwise, she may feel a lot more pain than necessary. That could cause complications."

Fear sliced through Todd at the serious tone and expression. He brushed the hair off Shaunna's forehead. "Shh, love, calm down. Don't fight the medicine. Shaunna, you've got to relax."

Tears filled her eyes, dampened her cheeks. "I'm sorry," she whispered. "Please forgive me."

Those were the first coherent words she spoke since the whole ordeal began. He sighed with relief. Her eyes, dark with fear and glazed with pain, cut him like a knife. Todd jerked the mask away from his mouth, touched his lips to hers. "Anything, love, I'll always forgive you anything. I love you, Shaun. Please calm down. Please relax."

His words seemed to appease her. She nodded, her eyes rolled. "I love you, too," she whispered as the anesthesia worked its magic.

The doctor looked at Todd one more time. "If you want to leave, do it now."

He shook his head. "I'll stay."

Todd clung to his wife's hand and buried his face into the thick mass of her hair. He'd been abused, abandoned, arrested, alone, and at war, but never in his life had he been this afraid. The sight of Shaunna on the table, so pale, almost lifeless, frightened him. The only proof she lived was the pulse of blood through the veins beneath his fingers and it terrified him to think he might lose her, the baby, or both. He begged God for the safe delivery of his child and his wife's recovery. He didn't raise his head or lift his gaze until he heard a lusty wail. His eyes flew into the doctor's.

The doctor grinned. "It's a girl. She's perfect—tiny, but perfect.

Relief washed through Todd with shuddering force. *Thank you, God!* He choked back a sob and reached to hold his newborn daughter, allowed only a moment before the nurse whisked her off to be cleaned, weighed, measured, and placed in an incubator. The doctor urged him to leave while they stitched Shaunna up, and promised to let him know the moment she went to recovery. He walked into the waiting room to be met by anxious friends.

"How is she?" David asked.

"OK. We got the baby. It's a girl. She's small but seems to be healthy. Oh, God." He collapsed. "I've never been so scared in my life."

Lacey enfolded him in her embrace as tears slid unchecked down his face. David stood by with his hand on his shoulder.

"I could have lost them. I could have lost them both."

"But you didn't," David assured. "They're fine, and you have a new baby girl."

When the shock passed, Todd went to see Shaunna in the recovery room. David and Lacey waited by the nursery, anxious for a glimpse of the baby.

Todd sat beside his wife, held her hand, and urged her to respond. She stirred, mumbled. He leaned closer. She opened her eyes. A groggy smile tugged at the corners of her mouth.

"Hey, beautiful," he whispered.

"Hi. Where am I?"

"You're in the recovery room. Do you remember anything?"

Fear widened her eyes. "The baby, how's the baby?"

Todd smiled. "Perfect," he soothed. "Small, but perfect."

"Good," she whispered, dozed. "We'll name him after you."

Todd chuckled under his breath. He'd tell her tomorrow they had a little girl. For now, he wanted to relish in the relief that they were both fine. And he wanted her to rest. He closed his eyes and thanked God again.

* * *

Lacey arrived at the hospital to find Todd in the nursery feeding the baby and Shaunna in a near hysterical fit, in her room. Lacey embraced her until the sobs subsided.

"God's punishing me, Lacey. He's punishing me because of my feelings about a girl. That's why she came early. Now I have a scar for life reminding me of how selfish I've been. And to make things worse, I can't nurse her."

She began to sob. "I never wanted to hurt my baby. I know I was wrong, but..."

Lacey grabbed Shaunna's hands and shook her head. She buried her face on Shaunna's clenched fists. *Oh God, help me.* Peace filled her soul. She lifted her face, waited until Shaunna looked at her, dark eyes filled with anguish.

"You know the Lord better than that," she chided. The love of Jesus shone through her. "You know He doesn't punish us for our feelings. He doesn't have to punish you—you're doing a perfect job of doing so yourself. He loves you, Shaunna. He's not punishing you. For some reason you've forgotten or overlooked the blessing here. You have a beautiful, healthy, baby girl. Sure, she was premature, but He could have taken her. He didn't. Instead, He chose to bless your life and your marriage with a child. A perfect result of your and Todd's love. How can you say that's punishment? Granted, she's premature and had to be born by surgery and now you can't nurse her, but for Christ's sake, she's alive and healthy.

"Don't you know how very blessed you are? People everywhere would give their soul to be able to have a baby, premature, Cesarean birth, it wouldn't matter. God doesn't punish us; Satan does by manipulating our doubts and fears. That's what he's done here. Don't let him win," she urged.

The hope in Shaunna's eyes sent a thrill through her heart. "You think so?"

Lacey nodded. "I have it on good authority."

"Thank you," Shaunna signed, over and over, as tears drenched her cheeks.

Lacey hugged her. "Thank me by confiding in Todd. He's worried sick about you. He tries not to let it show, but he is."

"I will."

"Promise?"

Shaunna nodded and promised.

* * *

David got home from work to find Lacey in tears. He knew she'd been to see Shaunna and the baby, and she could tell by his expression he feared something was wrong. He gathered her in his arms, held her close.

"What's wrong?"

"I hurt so much for Shaunna."

"Why? She's OK, isn't she? There's nothing wrong with the baby?"

Lacey shook her head and told him about her and Shaunna's visit. David pressed her face into his chest.

She eased away, smiled up at him. "What did you say?" she signed.

He looked at her, puzzled. "How did you know I spoke?"

"I heard or felt the vibrations of your chest."

He grinned. "Oh. I asked if you think I should talk to Todd."

Lacey shook her head. She'd told her husband months ago about Shaunna's fear and confusion. "No, I'm sure she will now."

"OK, but you stop worrying. I don't like to see you this way and I don't want you upsetting this little one," he admonished and rubbed her stomach in a tender gesture.

"I love you so much, David."

His brilliant smile assured her he had no doubts or reservations about their love. Both knew they were soul mates. Now if only Shaunna would realize, and accept, she and Todd were too.

* * *

Todd and Mike met on the patio at dawn, their favorite time of day, and sat, sipping a first cup of coffee.

Mike put his cup down. "Well, I've decided to retire."

"Great! About time, too."

"Do you think Shaunna will mind if I stay with you guys until I find a place of my own?"

Todd shook his head. "Of course not, it'll be great to have you here."

"Do you think Mary will mind?"

"I doubt it." Something in his tone made Todd look a little closer, notice the twinkle in his old friend's gray eyes. His eyebrows shot up in surprise. He grinned. "Mary? You old dog."

Mike laughed. "I take it that means you approve?"

Todd chuckled. "Of course, as long as you don't take her away from us completely."

Mike shrugged. "Wouldn't dream of it, which is why I'm settling here instead of Georgia."

"Shaunna will be ecstatic."

Later, Todd walked up the stairs. Dread thickened his chest, slowed his steps. He paused in front of the one room he always avoided. After marrying his widow, he'd learned to live in his house and grew to love Joe Taylor's son as his own.

But he hadn't gotten past this room and the ghosts in it.

He knew Shaunna was in there. He didn't know why, though, and his imagination created the worst possible scenarios.

After the birth of their daughter, Shaunna slipped into a depression unlike anything he'd ever seen. The doctor told him this was normal after the shock her body and emotions went through. Physically, she recovered well, emotionally was a different story.

At first she didn't want to see the baby. Then she was afraid to hold her. She got over those feelings with one visit, but the depression deepened when she had trouble producing milk and couldn't nurse her. She seemed to improve after Lacey's visit three days ago but changed again when the doctor discharged Shaunna and the baby had to stay. The pain and fear in her eyes tore his heart out when she begged not to leave her child. They had no choice. Try as he may, he could not grant her that wish.

She hadn't stopped crying since he carried her to their bed yesterday.

He reached for the doorknob, hesitated, then laid his head on the cool wood and prayed for God to give him the strength to overcome whatever lay between them at this moment. He took a deep breath then opened the door of the bedroom she once shared with her husband and found her sitting in the chair where she'd once rocked her son. Her eyes were closed, cheeks wet.

He knelt at her feet and took her cold hands in his. "What's the matter, Sweetness?" His heart constricted when she opened tear-drenched eyes to gaze into his.

"Did I ever tell you Joe wanted another baby, a little girl with chestnut hair and blue eyes?" At the shake of his head, she continued. "We discussed it right before he was killed." Her chin quivered and she fought back a sob.

"So that's why you were so adamant about having a boy?"

She nodded. "For some reason I felt I would betray his memory by having a girl, or even wanting one."

Todd buried his face into her lap, fought pain and resentment. For lack of a better idea, he picked her up and carried her to the bed she once shared with her husband. He hated this room and the memories it held for her and if there were any way possible, he'd rip it from the house.

"If I could, I would make love to you right now, right here. I'd love you so much it would chase the ghosts right out of this room, and they'd never come back to haunt you. Or hurt you."

The love and tenderness in his voice couldn't mask the pain and frustration he felt. She smoothed the hair off his forehead with a tender smile.

"I'd let you," she whispered. "I love you, Todd. I'm sorry. I know God has forgiven me for my selfishness, but I can't forgive myself until I know you have also."

He kissed her. "Of course, I forgive you. But I want a promise from you. Promise you will never hide your feelings from me again. No matter how much you think they might hurt, nothing you say can hurt me as much as you've hurt yourself trying to bear this alone. I love you, Sweetness, more than life itself."

"Don't say that. Life is precious and I'm sorry I've wasted so much of it dwelling on the past. But I loved him, Todd. He was everything to me, my husband, friend, lover, and the father of my child. Everything he was, you are now, and more so. Believe it or not, I thank God every day I have you. And I promise, from this day onward, I'm going to make every conceivable effort to show you how much I love and appreciate you."

Todd hugged her, wishing he could hold her closer and make love to her until neither of them could move, or think, or breathe without the other. "I do love you, Mrs. Jameson. So much."

He brushed his lips over hers. "Do you think we could begin by deciding on what we are going to call little Miss Priss? I mean, don't you think she needs a name? We can't even bring her home from the hospital without a name."

He chuckled. "Joey's compromised, he calls her 'Sissy,' but she can't go by that forever. Can she?"

Shaunna's smile brightened. "I don't see why not."

"Sissy Jameson?" Todd shook his head. "Nah, she's much too beautiful for that."

Shaunna's heart lightened another degree as she thought about the little bundle of joy they would bring home from the hospital today. It was ironic she was born on the second anniversary of Joe's death. Now the day would be one for joy instead of sorrow. It was selfish and cruel not to think of a name for her baby daughter, and she silently thanked God for His forgiveness, the unconditional love of her husband, and asked for guidance in this decision. The name came to her in an instant.

"How about, Angel Dawn? Angel because she's a gift from heaven, and Dawn because dawn is the beginning of a new day and in this case, a new life, hers and ours."

"Hmm, Angel Dawn Jameson...I like it," Todd admitted and kissed her again. "It's as pretty as she'll be beautiful some day, with chestnut hair and *green* eyes."

Shaunna smiled, hoping he was right. If so, she'd have her father's beautiful eyes. "Well, if you like the name, I guess that's it. Besides, you can get up with your little angel at dawn when she wakes up with a wet diaper."

He chuckled at her teasing and promised to do just that. The love in his velvety rough voice sent shivers through her soul and Shaunna dozed.

Todd turned at the soft click of the doorknob and

welcomed Lacey with a smile.

"How is she?" she asked.

He reached for her hand. "OK. Exhausted but OK.

"Me too," Lacey admitted. Her hands rested on her bulging stomach. She and David's baby was due in about three months.

"Did y'all decide on a name?"

He nodded. "We'll tell everyone later. I'm going to let her rest awhile. Y'all?"

She placed his hand on her abdomen as the baby kicked. "Mary Katherine for a girl, David Todd for a boy."

Todd chuckled and stroked her stomach. "What does David say about that?"

She moved his hand to her face, nestled her cheek in his palm and smiled. "He's the one who suggested it. He knows how much you mean to me. He knows you're like the brother I never had, and he understands. He loves you too, Todd. I'm so glad we've both found happiness. God has blessed us so much."

Todd nodded, smiled. "Yes, He has. I never thought I could be this happy. Or love this much. I'm happy for you and David. You were right from the beginning, Lace; faith gave us victory over the circles fate played in our lives."

Shaunna stirred and smiled up at Lacey then accepted her husband's hand as he helped her out of bed.

"Let's go get our baby," he whispered. With an arm around each, Todd helped them down the stairs and thanked God for the three most important women in his life—his wife, his friend and his daughter.

Chapter Thirty-Six

Lacey fingered the envelope on the kitchen counter then laid it down. She poured herself a glass of milk, sat in a chair, and stared at the stark white object in contrast to the butcher-block countertop. Excitement curled in the pit of her stomach, caused her breath to hitch. A kaleidoscope of emotions shivered through her—anticipation, trepidation, need. She experienced them all as she wondered what the envelope contained.

From the first moment she held little Angel, an intense desire to know more about her birth parents grew in her heart. After weeks of thinking and dreaming, she discussed the issue with David. He encouraged her to write to the hospital where she was born. Another week of indecision tore at her soul before she dug out her birth certificate and wrote a letter to St. Francis Hospital in Rolla, Missouri.

The response lay in the white envelope atop her kitchen counter.

Now all she had to do was wait until David came home.

If that's possible, she thought with fresh insight to the definition of anticipation.

Sure, she could open the letter and read it herself, but fear of what it might *not* contain kept her from doing so. David would be home soon. Since her delivery date was less than a month away, he came home at noon every day.

As though sensing her turmoil, the baby began to kick and turn, not in his usual gentle movements, but in restless agitation. Lacey placed her hand on her abdomen, rubbed in a soothing motion and willed her thoughts into a semblance of peace. A lullaby echoed in her mind. Although she'd never heard one, nursery rhymes were some of the first words she'd learned to read. The music seemed to appear from somewhere deep in her memory, as though her subconscious remembered her mother humming while she was still in the womb.

She rose from her chair, put the glass in the sink then picked up the envelope and carried it with her to the patio. She placed it on the table, sat in the rocking chair and waited. At eleven thirty David walked through the house and found her there.

"Hi, love," he signed then leaned down to receive her kiss. "How's it going today?"

He rubbed her abdomen and gazed into her eyes, his alive with love and adoration. She smiled. "Fine."

She picked up the envelope and handed it to him.

David grinned. "Why didn't you open it?"

She shrugged, warmth flooded her cheeks. "Too nervous."

He sat across from her and took her hand in his. "I want you to know how much I love you. Nothing in this envelope can, or will, ever change that."

"I know."

"OK, here goes," he said and ran his finger under the flap to break the seal. He smoothed out the paper then set the letter on the table and read aloud while signing...

Thank you for your inquiry. However, we regret to inform you birth and death records are sealed. You can obtain them with a court order.

He stopped reading when she slapped the paper and buried her face in her hands. He hugged her close, rocked until her sobs subsided. He brushed the tears off her cheeks, kissed her.

"Don't cry, Lace. We'll work something out."

"How am I going to get a court order?"

"We'll wait until after the baby is born if we have to and fly up there. Let me do some checking. I have a friend in Missouri who's an attorney, maybe he can find out something."

Hope flickered. A smile broke through the gloom. "Do you think so?"

He hugged and kissed her again. "I don't know. I'll see. But you've got to promise me not to worry over this. We don't want to upset this little sweetheart," he admonished and patted her abdomen.

Though he hadn't said much, she knew he hoped and prayed this child was a girl. Lacey wanted a boy but he already had two boys. He wanted a girl. Lacey took his hand and cradled her cheek in his palm.

"I'll try not to," she promised, then turned her face and pressed her lips into his hand, teasing the flesh with her mouth.

Desire darkened his gaze. "Hey, stop that."

She tugged at the top button of his shirt, an impish grin on her lips. "I don't have to."

David chuckled and let her have her way. Caught up in the teasing demands of her hands on his flesh, he took advantage of having her so warm and willing, not that she ever wasn't. Later, he made a few phone calls and tried to work on some accounts while she rested. Work was impossible when all he could think about was how very much he loved his new wife and how different this marriage was from the first.

He'd loved his first wife, Judy, forever. They were high school sweethearts, married right after graduation. Both of their parents objected when Jason was born so soon, but they survived. David worked and went to college while Judy was content to stay home and have babies. Josh was born three years later and a year after, they found out about Judy's cancer. It began in the uterus and spread when she refused to abort the baby she carried at the time. She lost the little girl anyway. And the cancer spread. They held onto hope and faith. But it was not meant to be.

David questioned God a lot after Judy died, but never lost his faith. Now he was extremely grateful he hadn't, because now he had Lacey. Though five years separated their ages, he loved Lacey with a depth and passion he'd never felt before—deeper and with more appreciation. He loved her passion and sense of humor, her strength and loyalty, and he loved the way she gave herself so completely to him and the boys.

Now he hoped this need to know more about her roots didn't hurt her. This was a hurt he could not protect her from. Somehow, he knew it would work out. It had to.

He wouldn't have it any other way.

He closed his eyes and sent up a silent prayer.

* * *

David woke when Lacey tossed and turned, moaning in her sleep. He turned on the bedside lamp and shook her awake. "Lacey, what's wrong?"

She shook her head as she sat up. "I must have been dreaming."

The same dream as before, he thought with a frown. Two weeks had passed since she received the letter from Missouri, and he subsequently made his phone calls. Two weeks of coming home before noon to find her doubtful and depressed when the mail came and there was no answer.

Two weeks of bad dreams and sleepless nights.

Until today. Today, he came home to see her smiling and humming while she cleaned, polished, and scrubbed the already spotless house. The musical lilt to her voice had him asking questions.

"How come I've never heard you hum before?"

She smiled. "I didn't know I was."

"Where's the music coming from, Lace?"

She pointed to her heart and shrugged. "I just hear it in here."

Then she told him about her prayer for healing.

"Do you believe in miracles, Dave?" At his shrug she continued. "Well, since the first time I felt the baby move, I asked God for my hearing to be restored. I believe it will. Sometimes I think I hear whispers."

"Do you hear me now?"

She shook her head and shrugged. "Sometimes I'm concentrating so hard on reading your lips I block everything else out."

David hugged then kissed her. His lips traveled to her ear. He whispered.

She giggled. "I don't know if you spoke or not, but you're teasing me."

Desire shone bright in her eyes, caused him to forget what they talked about.

Now he remembered fully. Though he never experienced one, he heard of miracle healings. It didn't surprise him Lacey believed without a doubt she would receive one. He decided to wait and see and try not to deflate her hope with his uncertainty.

"What were you dreaming about?"

Lacey looked up. "What did you say?"

Her face contorted. She grabbed her stomach as her abdomen muscles contracted. She breathed a sigh of relief when the contraction ended and smiled. "I think it's time."

David grabbed his watch and waited. Excitement replaced the worry of moments before. Twenty minutes later she had another contraction. He jumped out of bed and slipped into his jeans. In the excitement David did not realize he'd neither faced Lacey, nor used sign language, when he asked what she'd been dreaming about.

* * *

Todd groaned when he heard the soft knock on the door. He held his breath and hoped whoever it was would go away. No such luck, the person knocked again, soft but insistent. He released Shaunna from his heated embrace, rolled out of bed, slipped into his jeans, and opened the door.

Mike smiled. "I thought I heard the baby."

Todd shook his head. "No, she's still sleeping."

"Oh. Well, is everything OK?"

Todd glared at him a moment before answering. "Fine."

Mike chuckled. "Sorry to bother you."

"It's OK." Todd ground his teeth in frustration when Mike blocked the door from shutting.

"You sure Angel's not awake? She should wake up any time now, shouldn't she?"

Todd sighed in exasperation, walked over to the bassinet, and picked up his daughter. "Wake up, little one. Go entertain Grandpa Mike so Daddy can get some peace."

She squirmed, yawned and opened huge, dark-lashed eyes to glare at him. Her lip trembled. Todd held her close, inhaled her baby-fresh scent and cooed. "I'm sorry, little love. It's Grandpa Mike's fault. Fuss at him."

He placed her in Mike's arms, shoved a diaper at him and closed the door then slipped back into bed and gathered Shaunna to him.

"Now," he breathed. "Where were we?"

Shaunna smiled and sank her fingers into his hair. Her lips met his in a hungry kiss.

"I don't know," she murmured, her voice husky. "Maybe we should start over."

Todd groaned as desire rekindled and roared out of control.

* * *

Mary walked into the den wrapped in a thick, fluffy, robe and found Mike in the chair by the fireplace. She smiled as the teddy-bear of a man cuddled the baby girl as though she were a tiny, fragile gift which might break at any moment.

"You're going to spoil that child beyond repair," she chided with a tender look. "No one will be able to stand her."

Mike chuckled and gazed down at the sleeping infant. "She reminds me so much of Shaunna. She's the closest thing to a granddaughter I'll ever have."

"Me too," she agreed and patted the soft, dark head of the child. She went into the kitchen then returned with coffee. She set the tray down within his reach and answered the phone before it could ring a second time, then hung up with a smile.

"Lacey's in labor. David said he'll call as soon as they get to the hospital. I'd better go wake Todd and Shaunna, they'll want to know.

"I wouldn't," Mike warned with a chuckle. "Unless you want a double dose of daggers aimed your way. Unless I miss my guess, they're very much awake at this moment."

His eyes lit with amusement, wicked amusement, and something else. Something which made her mouth feel like sawdust and her cheeks like fire. Something that made her feel things she hadn't felt in a long, long time. She avoided his gaze until he grabbed her hand.

"Mary Fontenot, you're blushing like a schoolgirl," he teased then pressed her fingers to his mouth.

"I like that," he murmured. He let go of her hand long enough to lay the baby in her playpen.

Mary trembled when he cupped her face in his hands and lowered his lips to hers as their friendship rose to a new level.

* * *

Todd bounded down the stairs sated, content, and ready for a hot cup of coffee. He sat at the table and picked up the newspaper. He hadn't skimmed the first page when Mike came in from the den.

"Who called?"

Mike grinned. "Oh, you heard?"

Todd grunted. "Better watch it Mike or you'll end up out

on your ear."

Mike chuckled. "Dave. They're on their way to the hospital. We didn't want to disturb you."

"What could you possibly disturb?"

Mike laughed at his dry tone as Shaunna bounced down the stairs and hugged him around the waist.

"Where's my daughter, you insensitive kidnapper?"

"Mary's got her in the den. I'll have you know I'm very sensitive. Aren't I, Mary?" he asked as she walked in and handed Angel to Shaunna.

Mary blushed red as roses but didn't answer. Mike winked at Todd and went to help her cook breakfast as Joey came downstairs and claimed he was starving.

Shaunna gasped. "Did you see what just happened between those two?"

Todd chuckled. "I'm surprised it took you so long to notice they're in love."

She smiled, her eyes warmed on his. "I guess I've been too busy being in love to notice them," she whispered and brushed his lips with hers.

Joey snorted. "I'll never fall in love. It makes even old men like Grandpa Mike act stupid."

Todd laughed. "We'll remind you of that in a few years."

David's call came during breakfast. A half-hour later they arrived at the hospital.

"Hi, guys." Todd greeted Jason and Josh who looked like ghosts. "What's happening?"

"We don't know," Jason admitted. We heard someone scream a while ago. Real loud. Don't know if it was Lacey or not."

Todd smoothed a hand over his head. "Might be, but I promise she won't remember one minute of pain as soon as the baby is placed in her arms. Come on you two, let's go get some coffee. Coming, Joey?"

They headed to the cafeteria as Shaunna, Mary, and Mike settled down to wait for news.

* * *

Lacey strained as one contraction led into another. David held her hand and brushed the hair off her forehead.

"Easy," he coaxed. "Breathe, Lacey. Breathe." He glanced at the doctor who nodded.

"Now, get her to push with this one."

David held up his hand, pushing one fist into the other palm. "Push, Lacey, push."

"I can see the head," the doctor said, and reached to help the child into the world. "Again. We're almost there."

David's smiled into Lacey's beautiful violet eyes. "I love you," he murmured even though she couldn't tell what he said with the mask on.

He made the pushing gesture again then held up a finger. "One more time, Lace. Push."

Lacey ground her teeth and pushed for all she was worth. In an instant the baby slipped from her body in to the doctor's waiting hands.

"It's a boy." The doctor grinned and held him up for them to see.

A smile broke through Lacey's tense lips.

"A boy! I can hear him! David, I can hear him cry." Though stilted, words burst forth between sobs.

David tugged the mask away from his mouth. "What? Are you sure?" he asked, signing anyway.

"I'm sure. I can hear him!" She answered between laughter and tears when the doctor placed the baby on her chest. "Praise God, I can hear him."

Tears streamed down David's cheeks. He lowered his lips to hers. "He's beautiful," he whispered. "You're beautiful. I love you."

"I love you too. And yes, I can hear you whisper," she assured him. "Thank you, God, I can hear," she mumbled then drifted into an exhausted slumber.

David took the baby to the nursery window as soon as the nurse allowed him to. Everyone gathered around as he unwrapped the baby to show off his son.

He placed David Todd Farley in his incubator then went into the waiting room to deliver the rest of the news. Everyone laughed and cried in unison when they heard of the second miracle, born that morning.

Chapter Thirty-Seven

Todd looked up from his desk at the knock on his classroom door then rose as Lacey stepped inside. He strode to her, took his namesake into his arms, and cuddled the baby. Little David Todd was the apple of everyone's eye. The fact that he preceded the miracle of Lacey's restored hearing endeared him to everyone he encountered.

"What's happening, Lace?" Todd asked, signing out of habit.

She laughed. "Nothing, we went to meet David for lunch and decided to surprise you."

The sound of her voice still astonished him and brought him great joy. "Wonderful. I needed a break."

They talked for a few minutes about family and children, then she brought up the situation which would puzzle him for weeks.

"Speaking of family, do you know anyone named Christopher Jameson?"

He grinned. "You mean besides me? No. Why?"

She leaned her hip against a desk. "Well, guess I'd better start from the beginning. The first time I held Angel I started wanting to know more about my mother and father. I wrote to the hospital where I was born, and they replied that birth and death records were sealed. David contacted a friend in Missouri who's an attorney. He wrote back and told us he'd tried everything, but all of the records were closed. However, I did get this."

She handed him a reproduction of a newspaper article. It told a story of a young woman and an old man who drowned in an automobile accident. Her name was Lucy Johnson, his, Christopher Jameson.

"What's weird is the Army sealed those records."

Fear, pure, raw, deep-seated fear curled in the pit of his stomach. "Lacey, I'm sure I'm not the only Christopher Jameson in the Army. I'm sure it's a coincidence."

"Maybe so, but do you think you can find anything out?"

The fear grew. "I doubt it. I mean, it'll take someone a lot higher up than me to get to those records, especially if the

Government had them sealed."

Disappointment flashed in her eyes. Todd averted his gaze and strove to tamp down the panic building in his gut. An awkward silence sprang up between them. Her face went from radiant to guarded. David began to squirm and whimper. Lacey shifted and took the baby from him. He quieted at once.

"Well, I thought maybe you could at least do some checking."

He opened his mouth to speak. No words came. Todd shook his head and turned away with the mumbled excuse he had to get back to work. He collapsed into his chair and let her show herself out.

What began as a simple request became a silent, insistent demand which lasted almost two months. Whenever they were together, Lacey brought up the situation. She enlisted David and Shaunna's help, and everyone wanted to know what, if anything, he could or would do to get the Army to unseal the records on Christopher Jameson.

The nightmares began. Dreams he couldn't remember. Dreams filled with violence, fear, and rage.

So much rage.

All that lingered were haunting doubts and pain—deep, raw, unexplainable pain—an ache which tortured his mind and soul.

The battle came to a tumultuous head one evening when the four of them played cards at David and Lacey's. Mike and Mary had taken the older boys out for pizza and a movie. The babies were asleep. David and Shaunna went to the kitchen for refreshments when Lacey brought the subject up to him again. Short on patience from weeks of sleepless nights, Todd exploded.

"My God, Lacey, give it a rest! I thought it was bad arguing with you when you couldn't speak, now it's ten times worse. You're driving me crazy with this!"

"You can be a real jerk sometimes, you know that?"

"Yeah, well I guess we all can."

Lacey's hands clenched, a low growl sounded in her throat. "Why, Todd? Can you at least tell me why you won't even ask around?"

Todd raked his fingers through his hair and suppressed a growl of his own. "I just don't want to go around digging up things better left buried."

"Better for whom?" Her voice rose toward hysteria. She burst into tears at his refusal to answer. "I never dreamed you could be so stubborn. And hateful," she said between sobs.

The sound of her crying and the sight of her tears shook his resolve. "Why is this so important to you?"

"I want to know. I want to be able to tell my son what his roots are." She walked over to him. "I want to know if we're related." Her voice softened. "Please, Todd."

Todd shifted. His gaze roamed the room, avoiding her's. That same deep-seated fear gnawed at his guts. "I don't understand why it's so important. What difference does it make? Your son is yours. Yours and David's, born of your love for each other. We're friends, couldn't be any closer. What's more important than that?"

"Don't you want to know? Aren't you curious to find out if we're even remotely related?"

The fear grew, tightening his chest until he thought he would suffocate. "No!"

"I don't understand why you're so opposed to this, to me," she whispered.

Todd raked his fingers through his hair. "I'm not opposed you, Lace. Never you."

"Then *why?*"

Anger he never thought her capable of erupted in violent force.

"Bastard," she hissed. Her hand connected with his cheek in a vicious manner. "You're a stubborn, selfish, hateful, *bastard.*"

Todd snapped her up by the shirt front.

"That's right, Lace," he ground out through teeth clenched as tight as the fists knotted in her blouse. "You're right on target. I *am* a bastard. I never knew my mother and I'm pretty damn sure she wasn't married to my father. In fact, my father was a bastard too, in the first degree." His voice hardened another notch. "One who drank too much and abused his child. Is that the kind of roots you want for your son?" He shook her by the shoulders. "Is it Lace?"

He released her and she sank to the floor in a helpless mass of emotions. The fight left him at her wretched sobs. He reached for her. "Lace, please don't cry like this."

She jerked away from him, slapped at his hands. "Don't touch me," she spat. "Just leave me alone, OK!"

Rex whined and growled and scratched at the door. Shaunna and David rushed into the room. Rex squared off with Todd, teeth bared. A low growl rumbled in his throat. David strode to where Lacey lay in a crumbled heap on the floor and lifted her into his arms. He whirled on Todd, eyes fierce, voice harsh.

"You've gone too far this time. Get out, Todd."

"David, look..."

His eyes narrowed. "No, *you* look. Look at what you've done. Go home, before something else happens, something we'll both regret in the morning."

Todd turned toward the door, angry, hurt, defeated.

Surrounded by tension, Shaunna stood helplessly rooted to the spot. The wretched sobs of her friend and the air of desolation surrounding her husband had her immobile with indecision. She blinked back tears. Never before had she seen Todd in such a state. She'd seen him hurt and angry, but *never* had she witnessed such utter defeat in a person. The door closed with a soft thud and spurred her into action. She reached for Lacey, smoothed the hair off her face.

"I'm so sorry, Lace," she whispered. Questioning eyes flew into David's, begging for understanding and forgiveness.

David nodded. "It's OK, Shaunna, go to your husband. Leave the baby, we'll tend to her. Get her in the morning, or Mike and Mary can pick her up when they drop off the boys."

Shaunna sighed with relief. "Thanks, we'll talk later," she promised and headed for the door. She reached Todd as he opened the car door and enfolded him in her embrace as he began to tremble in the aftermath of emotions. "I love you," she whispered.

His arms tightened around her. "I know."

His voice sounded harsh, raw. Shaunna ached to the core at the pain in his troubled gaze. "You want me to drive home?"

He shook his head. "I'm OK. What about Angel?"

"Mike and Mary will bring her home. Let's you and I go for a ride. You're not going to sleep tonight anyway."

They left in silence. Shaunna stroked his thigh, not

surprised when he stopped on a deserted road. "Damn it, Shaun, do you think I'm being unreasonable?"

Shaunna shrugged. "That's not for me to say when I don't understand why you're so resistant to it. What are you afraid of?"

He sighed. "That's just it, Shaun, there's not a bit of telling what I might find. And it scares me to death."

She heard the strain in his voice, and the fear, as he continued.

"Lacey has this romantic idea we're related and that it'll make everything perfect."

"What would be so bad?"

"Has everyone forgotten I was attracted to her?"

Shaunna still didn't understand. "Did you sleep with her?"

He winced at the question then shook his head. "No, but the only thing which kept us from crossing that line was the fact she was a student and I'm an instructor."

She couldn't stop the sharp stab of jealously, at his admission, but his reasoning still made no sense to her.

"Todd, you're a military man," she chided in a gentle voice. "You above all people know close only counts in horseshoes and hand grenades. Suppose your worst fear was true and you are related, would it change the way you feel about her?"

"No. Nothing could do that. I couldn't love her more if she were my sister."

His voice had softened, the light of truth glittered in his eyes. Shaunna cupped his cheek with her palm. "So what's the problem? What is it you *don't* want to know? What are you so afraid of?"

The pain in his eyes cut her like a knife. She turned, cupped his face in both hands and rested her forehead on his. "Todd, how can I be loving and supportive if I don't understand what's bothering you?"

He closed his eyes with a groan. "I hate it when you use my own words against me."

She giggled. "Ditto, love."

She waited a beat, kissed him. "You're going to have to open up to me, or someone, Todd. Otherwise, you'll go nuts trying to keep this all in."

"It's my father." His voice was a harsh whisper. He swallowed hard then continued. "It took me a long time to forgive him, Shaunna. I don't know if I can do it again. No matter what I find, for some reason or another, I'll have to. I'm just not sure I can."

Shaunna wrapped her arms around him and buried her face into his shoulder. Oh, how she wished she could take away his pain and fear, that she could, somehow, change his childhood. But she couldn't. All she could do was love him. She ran her hands over his chest, pressed tiny kisses along his throat and prayed her touch would somehow reveal the depth of her feelings for him. She pressed her lips to his when he shuddered. He opened his eyes. Shaunna saw the pain and fear in his beautiful green gaze and her heart broke for him. A question formed in her mind and grew until it all but burned her tongue.

"Todd, what's the worst thing you could imagine?"

He shrugged.

"Whatever it is, what good would it do to despise your father again? He's dead. You can't change what's happened. Is it worth throwing away what you might gain? I love you, not for what your father was but for who you are. Lacey loves you for who you are, not what you were, or he was. Is it worth throwing away the chance you have a family because of what he may or may not have done? Something you can't change anyway?"

"I have a family—you and Joey and Angel. Lacey is as close to a sister I'll ever have or need. Then there's Mike and Mary, David, and the boys. We are a family, maybe not of the flesh, but of the heart. I don't understand what could be more important than that."

"Maybe it's not enough for Lacey. I mean, she loves David and the boys, but this child is her flesh and blood."

"So? You have children but you've never been obsessed with finding your father's family."

"That's different. I had Mama and Uncle Mike. As far as I'm concerned my father's family rejected my children when they refused to acknowledge my mother and me. Joey had both a father and a mother. Now he has you. We've always had Mary and Mike and the Fredericks. Now there's David and the boys. Even you had your father. Painful as your childhood may have been, you still had each other. Lacey's had no one. She's been alone all of her life. It never bothered her before, but now that she's a mother, maybe she just wants to know the truth. Is it too much to ask, or so hard to understand?"

Todd gazed into the eyes of the woman he loved more than anything else on earth. He saw the love she felt for him shining back, felt it emanating from her touch, and knew he was loved—completely and unconditionally.

"I guess you're right." He lingered over another kiss.

Shaunna relaxed as the kiss changed from soft and tender to one of passion and strength. "I love you," he whispered. "How'd you get to be so smart?"

She shrugged.

"So, you think I should check into it?"

"That has to be your decision, my love. Whatever you decide, remember, I'm behind you all the way."

He urged her close for another kiss. "Let's go home."

She nodded, pressed her lips to his once more then slid over onto her seat. The ride home began in silence until he turned around without notice. "Where are you going?"

"Apologize."

She smiled and squeezed his hand.

David opened the door before Todd could knock a second time. He walked through without waiting for an invitation. "Where's Lacey?"

David grabbed his arm. "I thought I told you to go home."

Todd understood his feelings. He sighed, his eyes begging the same of his friend.

"Dave, please, I just want to apologize, and pick up my daughter."

"Apologize tomorrow. I don't want you upsetting my wife anymore tonight. And I told Shaunna the baby would be fine. Don't you trust us?"

Todd gasped, realizing for the first time how very much he'd hurt his friends. "Of course, I trust you."

"Then go home."

"OK." He nodded and fought the tears that rushed unbidden to his eyes.

"Wait." Lacey spoke from the doorway. "It's OK, David, I owe him an apology too."

Waiting for David's nod of approval, Todd walked over to her, cradled her face in his hands. "I'm sorry, Lace. Hurting you is the last thing on earth I want to do. You too, Dave." He turned to his friend. "You guys mean more to me than I can say."

"I'm sorry too, Todd," Lacey began. "I shouldn't push so hard. You have a right to your privacy. It's just..."

Todd pressed his finger to her lips, hushing her words. "Shh. It's OK. You have a right to know too. I'm just scared, Lace. I don't know what I'll find, and I don't want you hurt more by what might or might not be."

"What on earth could be so bad you wouldn't want to know? I love you. You'll always be the brother I never had. Nothing will ever change that."

"Promise?"

Pain-filled eyes searched his. "Do you really have to ask?"

He sighed. "I guess not. I'm sorry. I'll look into it."

Lacey's smile was brilliant. "You will?"

He nodded.

"Oh, thank you." She hugged him. "I promise not to harass you. Do it whenever you're ready. But, please, hurry."

He chuckled. "You're not going to harass me as long as I hurry?"

Lacey had the grace to blush at the contradiction of words.

* * *

Todd sat by the fireplace, poker in hand. He shuffled the wood and watched the sparks fly from the ashes as the fire blazed, bright, and hot. Last night was another in a long string of sleepless nights. It began with a hot shower and a full-body massage and ended when he slipped out of bed long before dawn. He loved Shaunna deep into the night, trying to rid his mind of the memories that had haunted him for the past several weeks and would continue to do so until the truth was revealed. He'd promised Lacey a week ago he would do some digging. Still, he put her off. She never asked, but the questions in her eyes had haunted him night and day.

Revelation came yesterday when he had an unusual conversation with Joey.

Shaunna had called for him several times to come in for supper when she approached Todd, a worried frown on her face. "Do you know where Joey is?"

He shrugged. "I think he went out to tend to the horses.

Why?"

"I've been calling him, and he won't answer."

"I'll go look." He didn't want her to be the one to find him if there had been an accident. He found Joey in the barn absently brushing his horse. "Joey, Mama's been calling you."

"Oh, I didn't hear her."

The expression on his face told Todd something went on in the boy's mind that needed straightening out. "What's wrong, partner?"

Joey shrugged.

"Come on now, it helps when you talk about your problem.

Joey dropped the brush on the shelf and sat beside him on a bale of hay. "Sometimes I feel so different from everybody."

"Well, we're all different. That's what makes us unique. You know, special."

"I guess."

The pain in his brown eyes stabbed at Todd's heart. "It's more than that isn't it?"

Joey nodded.

"Want to talk about it?"

"Everyone has the same last name but me. I mean, Angel's last name is Jameson like yours, and even Mama's is Jameson now. Davey's is Farley just like Jason and Josh and Lacey. I'm the only Taylor in the bunch. Sometimes I don't feel like I belong."

Todd hugged him. "That's not true, Joey. You belong as much as anyone else. I don't know what I'd do without you being here for your mom and Angel when I'm not around. Besides, I adopted you a long time ago. We just didn't change your name. Your mom thought it would be wrong to do so and you were too young to make that decision. One part of your father you have left, is his name."

"Sometimes I miss him so much," Joey admitted. "Sometimes I don't even remember what he looks like."

Todd held the boy close. "Well, anytime you're wondering, look in the mirror. Except for your mom's eyes, you look exactly like him."

"Really?"

"Yes."

"You adopted me, for real?"

"Yep, legally, you're my son, but I don't want you to even think about changing your name. Not now anyway. I still agree with your mom, you're too young. If you do change it, you may grow to regret it. Besides, it's not what a name is—it's the honor you bring to it that counts."

Hallelujah, Holy Lord, he thought as the truth of those words sank into his heart and mind. He knew what he had to do. "Do you understand what I'm saying Joey?"

Joey nodded.

"Good, partner, now, how about some supper?"

"OK. Thanks, Pop," he whispered.

Todd hugged him. "No. Thank you. You made me realize something important too. You see, sometimes discussing things helps the one you're talking to as well."

They went in together. While Joey went to wash up, Todd sought out Mike. They talked a while and Mike agreed to do the digging for him and some of his own as well.

Now he only had to stay sane until it was over.

Chapter Thirty-Eight

To appease himself as much as her, Todd rocked his daughter. Just shy of six months old, she was smaller than most babies her age, but her development was remarkable. She cooed and smiled and sucked her thumb. She knew her name and recognized voices when someone familiar spoke. She could sit up by herself and attempted to crawl. The deep baby blue hue of her eyes had evolved to a shade similar to his. Though dark, her hair shone with red highlights which were more noticeable when wet.

"Hey, little one." He cooed when she stopped sucking on her pacifier long enough to smile around it. "What's Daddy's angel thinking, huh? How about another smile for me?"

He brought her silky head to his lips and inhaled the sweet scent of her as she gurgled then laughed.

Mike had left within two days of their talk and would return today. Shaunna rode with Lacey and David to pick him up at the airport, along with a surprise guest whom he said, *"knew everything and was anxious to see Todd again."*

Soon the truth would be known, and it still scared him to death.

Angel dozed as he continued to hold her. Only with her in his arms could he find peace from the tension within. He hummed a lullaby, reluctant to put her down despite the fact Shaunna fussed that he held her too much.

With a reluctant sigh he placed her in her crib but continued to stroke her back. The action soothed his troubled mind and soul. His eyes lifted to meet Mary's when she entered the room. She walked over and hugged him.

"No matter what we find, you know everyone loves you. Nothing can ever change that."

Todd welcomed her embrace. "I hope so Mary. I hope so."

Turning, he picked Angel up and walked back to the rocking chair. He'd risk Shaunna's wrath. Not even when he heard the car drive up did he put her back in the crib.

Mary went to greet them at the door. Todd stayed put.

Shaunna walked in, her dark eyes bright with excitement. "Hi, love." She hugged and kissed him. "I'll take Angel up to her bed."

Todd held her for a moment, reluctant to release her.

"Everything's fine. I promise," she whispered with a kiss. Taking their daughter, she left him in the den to wait for Mike.

Mike walked in. "Hi, guy. How are you?"

He shrugged. "You tell me."

"Well, you look like hell," he teased, trying to ease the tension already crackling in the air.

Todd growled. "Thanks, just what I needed to hear. Out with it Mike. What did you uncover?"

"Well," Mike put his arm around his shoulders, "I think congratulations are in order. You have a sister."

Todd felt the blood drain from his features and collapsed in a chair.

"It's not as bad as you think. Honest," Mike added when Todd's tortured gaze lifted to his.

"Lacey is my sister? How?"

"I'll answer if you don't mind." They turned in unison at the voice from the door.

A smile broke through Todd's tense lips. "Father Champagne, Sir."

Darrell Champagne reached for Todd's hand then embraced him. "It's Bishop now, Todd, and sir no more. How are you? Turned out pretty good considering the hard-nosed kid I recruited. Not that I had any doubts you would."

"I'm not so sure now. You know about all of this?"

"Yes. And if you'll sit down and listen with an open mind, I'll tell you a story. It began a long time ago, Todd. Your mother's name was Lucille, Lucy for short. She was two when your father and her mother got married. Her mother died when she was eight, a shooting accident. Your father was cleaning his gun."

He held up his hand to ward off the questions before Todd could ask. "I'm getting there. An investigation uncovered no evidence to suggest anything other than an accident. Your father was not drinking too badly then. Anyway, having no next of kin, they left Lucy with him.

"Then, things began to go wrong. Your father started drinking, lost his job, his home, everything. Your grandfather, Christopher, took them in, mostly for the child's sake. He loved her, Todd, like a granddaughter. When your father's lifestyle changed for worse instead of better, he filed for custody of Lucy.

She was twelve.

"That's when your father raped her. He came home in a drunken rage, knocked the old man out and raped her, saying no matter what, she belonged to him. She was thirteen when you were born. Naturally, when the courts found out, they gave Lucy to your grandfather and that was the first time your father went to jail. He came out two years later a 'rehabilitated' man."

"Please," Todd interrupted. "Please tell me she found some peace and happiness."

"She did. For three years. Although your father was out of prison, he upheld a court order restraining him from contact with her. He did real well, for three years."

"OK, so that explains how I got here. What about Lacey?"

"You and Lacey have the same mother."

"Oh, God!"

"Let me tell you the whole story," he urged when Todd got up to pace. "You were three, almost four. Lucy was sixteen. She met a boy or a man perhaps. Someone she adored. She got pregnant. Your father forced himself on her again. Christopher was not home, just you and she. When she found out she was pregnant, after almost losing the baby, she somehow convinced your father it was his. That was the only way she thought she would be safe. The only way he might change, which he vowed to do.

"He checked himself into a rehab center and sobered up for a while, but he was jealous of her, Todd—real, sick jealous. He fought with his father over her often, even accused him of sleeping with her. Somehow, by the grace of God, they survived. Lacey was born very premature, lucky to have lived at all from the sound of it. Anyway, when Christopher picked Lucy up from the hospital, Lacey had to stay. It's a good thing too. They both drowned when the car went into a canal."

Todd knew the truth even before he spoke. "Another accident?"

"No one knows for sure. It appeared to be. By the time the authorities found the car, your father had taken you and left town. The police did some investigating, but again, they had nothing to go on except the diaries of a young girl. The diaries Lacey has now. Lucy hadn't written enough to charge him with murder. Even with his past history. They found no proof he tampered with the car. Anyway, the hospital kept Lacey until she was strong enough to go to an orphanage. The rest, as they say, is history. So, that makes Lacey..."

"My sister and me no better than him." Todd wanted to vomit with the truth.

Mike grabbed him by the shoulders and shook him. "If I ever hear you talk like that again, I'll beat you! Look at yourself and the life you've built. You're a hundred times the man he was!"

"Really, Mike? Hell, man, I held her in my arms like..."

"A woman?" Mike interjected.

"Like a lover," he snorted.

Mike's lips twitched. His eyes glittered with ill-concealed amusement. He shook his head. "I knew you'd say something like that and it's ridiculous. You—"

"You think this is funny?" Todd interrupted, forcing himself not to put a fist in his friend's face.

"I think you're overreacting," Mike replied. "Todd, you did what any red-blooded man would do. Lacey is a very beautiful woman."

"But I should have known somehow," he groaned, not willing to be let off the hook so easily.

"How? Look at her. She doesn't resemble you at all. How on earth could you possibly have known?"

Todd sighed. "I guess you're right. So, you don't think I'm like him at all? Not even deep down?"

Mike shook his head. "Not a bit."

Todd returned his gaze to Darrell's. "Do you?"

"I can't believe you'd even ask me that question."

"What I don't understand is why the Army had those records sealed."

"I had them sealed," Darrell admitted. "The Army started digging when you applied for Special Services. That's when we found out. You were so young, been through so much, and had so much ahead of you. I didn't think you were ready for the responsibility of a deaf sister. Neither did my commanding officers and you were too valuable to us at the time. Believe me, Todd; I've wrestled with myself for years over my decision. But I did keep tabs on Lacey. Up until she moved here and started going to college. I vowed, if and when she started checking, I would talk with her and help her to find you. I didn't know you two would meet, or become so close, but God has a way of working things out. I hope you can forgive me for not telling you sooner."

Todd shrugged too tired, confused, and relieved to be angry. "I guess you did what you thought was best."

"I did. Thank you."

Mike answered the soft knock on the door. He hugged Lacey and took the baby from her as she walked in the room.

Todd went to her, took her face in his hands. "My sister," he breathed. "Oh, Lace, I love you so much!"

He brushed the tears off her cheeks with his thumbs, brushed his lips across her forehead.

Lacey wrapped her arms around him with a happy little sound. "I'm so proud. My brother, a lieutenant! I knew you were special the first time I met you."

"Know what?" Mike interrupted, bringing the baby to them. "That makes you an uncle—a bonafide, flesh-and-blood uncle."

Overwhelmed, Todd took the baby and collapsed in the nearest chair. Pulling Lacey to him, he made room on his lap for her. Tears of joy mingled on their cheeks.

David and Shaunna walked in the room. "Hey, what's all the crying for? I thought this was a happy occasion. I brought champagne. The bubbly kind," he teased, and winked at Darrell who joined in the laughter.

Todd reached a hand toward him, swallowed the lump in his throat. "Oh, man."

David embraced them. "Welcome to the family, Todd. I'm glad this is settled. Getting pretty tired of you hugging up on my wife all the time. Now I don't have to worry."

Except for his wife, Todd had never felt so loved and accepted. Of course, they were all friends, but no one knew his past or his father's. Now it didn't matter. They were family.

Shaunna poured the champagne, and they sat around the coffee table sipping. Lacey took a worn leather book out of her back pocket.

Our mother's diary.

"I wonder who M. P. F is?" she said. "She talks about him a lot. I wonder if he's my father. I wonder if I can find out. Find him? Listen, here's something she wrote that includes you, Todd....

'I saw him again today. He is such a wonderful man. Even though I love the name Cecilia, I hate having to lie to him. I'm so tempted to tell him everything, especially after the way he looked at me when Todd called me 'Mama.' I picked the baby up and tickled him until he called me 'Sissy.' Guess it was convincing enough, 'cause M didn't question me. We left the bowling alley and spent the entire afternoon together....'

Mike felt his mind go numb. Amidst the excitement over the facts and worry over Todd's reaction, he never connected the story with his own past. He left the table, walked to the window, then turned and watched Lacey for a moment.

"She talks about him a lot," Lacey repeated. "I mean she only uses initials, never in the same order, sometimes she even drops one of them, but they're always the same. M. P. F. I wonder who he is."

The light of truth burst inside Mike. "Michael Paul Ferel," he said, his shoulders tense, eyes moist.

A collective gasp sounded from the table as five pair of eyes sought his. His gaze never left Lacey's. "I swear, Lacey, I never knew."

She went to him. "You? You're my father? How?"

He cradled her face in his hands. "I thought I felt something the first time I met you. I put it off as an old man appreciating a beautiful girl. You look exactly like your mother. You have her fragile beauty, the same petite features, that musical voice. Only, she had blue eyes."

"I don't understand," she whispered. Hope shone in her eyes.

"I had just enlisted and was stationed at Fort Leonardwood. A bunch of us went bowling in Waynesville. That's where I met her. She told me she was eighteen. I knew she probably lied about her age, but I didn't care. She was so beautiful."

He turned to Todd. "I've always felt something familiar about you, too. I remember now. She had you with her one day. Said you were her little brother. I had a feeling she lied then too but didn't press. Didn't care. All I cared about was her."

Turning back to Lacey, he continued. "Anyway, we saw

each other for a couple of months, and then I got sent to Korea. I never heard from her. The letters I sent to the address she gave me always came back with 'no such person' stamped on them. When I finally got a chance to get back to Waynesville, I found no trace of her. I searched everywhere. I learned about her death by sheer coincidence. One of my buddies came across the newspaper article and obituary while reading back issues on microfiche and put two and two together, but we never heard about you. Oh, God, she must have been so afraid, to lie about everything."

Tears poured from his gaze as he gathered her in his arms. "Lacey, I'm your father."

"I couldn't have picked a better man myself," Lacey said, holding him close.

Shaunna rose, walked to them and took Lacey's hand in hers. "I should be so mad at you," she whispered. "First you've a claim on my husband. Now, the only father I've ever known. I should be jealous. But I can't be. Oh Lace, I'm so happy for you. Now we really are sisters."

They were hugging when Mary walked in with Angel. Shaunna took the baby and handed her to Lacey. "Meet your niece."

Lacey hugged the baby to her breast.

Mike pulled Mary into their embrace. "Guess what Mary? I have a daughter." He tucked Lacey under his other arm. "And a grandson. If you'll marry me, I'll share them with you. We'll have more grandchildren too. Won't we, Lacey?"

"Several," Lacey promised.

Mary began to cry. "I feel like Job."

Mike knew she referred to the ancient patriarch whom God allowed Satan to test his faith. In the end he won, and God multiplied all Satan had taken from him. "So, you'll marry me?"

She put her arms around him. "Yes, I'll marry you."

"Great! Will you perform the ceremony, Darrell?"

Darrell chuckled. "I'd be honored to. I'll baptize these babies too."

Epilogue

Three Years Later....

Todd gazed down at his son—*a son*—the epitome of pride and joy. He never thought he could be so happy, or so proud. His homecoming yesterday was quite a surprise.

His final tour of duty in Okinawa turned into nine months instead of twelve. He'd been gone a very short time when Shaunna found out she was pregnant. She didn't tell him. Instead, she picked him up at the airport two nights ago, alone.

Though anxious to get home to the rest of his family, he reveled in the passionate embrace of his wife. Holding her luscious body after nine months, he couldn't help but chuckle when she blushed and admitted she'd put on a little weight in his absence. He held her close, his hands and lips assuring her he didn't care.

It didn't surprise him when they got home yesterday to find a house full of people. What did surprise him was when Angel screeched his name and flew into his embrace. Even though he talked with her whenever he could, he didn't know if she'd remember him or be afraid of him after his long absence.

"Daddy!"

He picked her up and held her close, reaching out to hug Joey also. Hugs and jostling from his friends drowned out her excited chatter. When everyone quieted down, she cupped his face in her tiny hands.

"Daddy, we got a baby," she said in a stage whisper.

"You've got a new baby?" he asked, misinterpreting her statement. In the excitement, he didn't see Shaunna reach into the bassinet until she walked up holding a snugly wrapped bundle. Her dark eyes shone.

"What she's trying to tell you is that *we* have a new baby. Meet your son, Todd," she remarked, holding the bundle toward him.

Shaunna smiled. "Don't you want to hold him?" she asked as the flash of a camera brought him out of his stunned trance.

"Mine? Ours?" he asked as Angel slid from his grasp.

Shaunna laughed. "Yes, ours. Who else's?" she teased and

placed the baby in his arms with a hug. "I took the liberty of naming him Christopher, after you and your grandfather and John, short for Johnson. I hope you don't mind."

He gazed down at the baby nestled in the crook of his arm, the shock of black hair undeniable and thought he'd die with happiness.

"It's perfect, he's perfect," he breathed, then gathered her close. "I don't know if I should beat you for not telling me or kiss you until you faint," he murmured against her lips. What he did was love her that night until neither could move or speak or breathe without the other.

Christopher squirmed and grunted and brought Todd's thoughts back to the present. He closed his eyes, still surprised at the depth of emotions coursing through him at the sight of his son.

Angel, a miniature of her mother, struggled in Shaunna's arms when she carried her into the room. She toddled up to Todd, arms outstretched to be held. At three-and-a-half, she was still very tiny, though healthy. He picked her up and tugged at the pacifier in her mouth. "I thought you threw out this nasty nook."

She grinned and clamped down on it with her teeth.

"Give it up," he insisted with another gentle tug on the rubber ring.

She giggled, shook her head, and then released it with a loud smack.

He tossed it aside then ran a finger along the soft skin of her neck. "What's that?"

"A shushar bowl," she said, and scrunched up her shoulders so he couldn't tease the tender flesh there.

He wondered how much of the ritual she remembered. "Ummm," he smacked his lips. "I want some sugar."

She shook her head and scrunched her shoulders tighter. "No, Daddy."

"I'm gonna get some anyway."

She eyed him, her expression wary as though anticipating his next move, then shook her head. "Nuh, un."

He tossed her to one side, exposing the tender skin of her neck. He growled and nibbled on her throat until she burst into a fit of little girl giggles.

Music to his ears.

He straightened her up. "Shh, we're gonna wake the baby."

Laughing eyes, a shade lighter than his, danced with joy. She pointed to his neck and moved on to the next stage of the game.

"What's that?" She asked in a stage whisper.

"A spot that needs kissing," he replied and arched his head so she could kiss him.

"And here." He pointed to another spot.

"Here too," he said, and touched yet another place, repeating the process until she grabbed his face in her tiny hands and planted sweet, wet kisses all over him.

Shaunna chuckled at the exchange. "All right you two, you're going to wake up the baby," she chided, though no trace of seriousness marred her tone.

Todd put his forehead on Angel's. "Good," he conspired in a loud whisper. "Then we can hold him."

Angel giggled and nodded.

Shaunna shook her head in exaggerated dismay. "Y'all are terrible. She did throw out the nook, but started taking it again while you were gone. I didn't think it would hurt." She wrapped her arms around them. "I'm so glad you're home," she breathed.

"Me too," he assured her.

Two months later, retirement was but a formality. Despite the lucrative incentives the government offered, Todd wanted out. He wanted to be around to watch his children grow up and he wanted to be there for Joey. Being a teenager was tough enough without being man of the house when he was gone and a child whenever he wasn't. Todd remembered his own childhood with an ache of regret and vowed to be the kind of father he never had.

He applied for a teaching certificate and now waited to find out what he had to do to obtain one. Until then, he would stay home and enjoy his family.

Lacey and David were expecting their third child. When little Jeremy was born thirteen months ago, Todd and Mike had teased David about not being able to follow the pattern before him. He assured them he'd paid close attention. They were recalling the incident last night when Lacey raised David's hand to her lips. "I promise this one will be a girl."

He chuckled then looked surprised. "Wait a minute. What do you mean this one?"

She leaned over and kissed him. "Do I need to draw you a picture?"

"Again?" He grinned. "I sure hope it is a girl."

She smiled and replied in a silky tone, "Yes, again. Didn't you once say you wanted to sire a basketball team?" she teased. "Besides, I promised my father several grandchildren."

"Girls can play basketball."

"It will be a girl. I promise."

Somehow Todd had a feeling if Lacey said the child would be a girl, it would be a girl. It turned out his sister was also good at more than having babies. She told the miracle of her hearing often and recounted her testimony of faith in the Lord.

A popular Christian magazine asked for her story, which resulted in a contract for a book. The book opened a whole new door while uncovering yet another talent. She wrote stories, books, and songs, often giving most of the proceeds to the poor.

Bound by no religion, Lacey taught sign language in the churches and schools, and never tired of sharing her faith in Jesus Christ to anyone who would listen.

Mike and Mary, ever the doting grandparents, bought a house nearby and were available to babysit anytime. Well, almost anytime. Mike enjoyed being alone with his bride of three years.

Much to everyone's surprise and delight, Buddy and Millie Frederick moved to Louisiana. A heart attack forced him into early retirement, so they sold the Feed Trough and moved to town.

"Why not?" They conceded when asked why they considered leaving everything familiar. "Home is more than a city. Home is where the heart is, and everyone we hold near and dear to our hearts is here."

The thought of his family brought new meaning to the phrase *joy unspeakable.* Once Todd thought he'd never have a family. Now, it continued to grow in size, strength, and love. He knew to count it all blessings. His mind wandered back over his life, his childhood and years as a young adult, his twenty years in the army. Times of war and strife and he knew, that only by the grace of God, had he survived and flourished, when so many others succumbed to the horrors they encountered.

Call it fate, call it destiny, call it what you will, but Todd knew faith in God was the golden link that bound the two as one.

The End

If you enjoyed **Circles of Fate** you may also like, ***My Heart Weeps*** ~ *When life takes everything, your world stops. Can a retreat heal the broken lives of two wounded souls?*

Dear Readers,

Often in our faith walk we feel as though we are going in circles. Or perhaps, taking one step forward then two back. We live, love, gain, lose and start over so many times we doubt we'll ever arrive at the place of peace and harmony.

If you feel as though fate is wreaking havoc in your life and running you around in circles, remember, the Bible promises us that *all things work together for the good of those who love God and are called according to His purpose.*

Seek after Him and His kingdom and you'll recognize His hand in every circle and circumstance in your life.

Until later, may God bless and keep you—and yours—in the palm of His loving hand!

Pamela S. Thibodeaux

"Inspirational with an Edge!" ™

About the Author

Pamela S. Thibodeaux grew up in the town of Iowa, Louisiana, and currently lives there. She is the mother of four (two by blood and two by marriage) and a grandmother. A deeply committed Christian, Pamela firmly believes in God and His promises.

"God is very real to me, and I feel people today need and want to hear more of His truths wherever they can glean them. People are hungry for practical (and real) Christian values, not some 'holier-than-thou' beliefs which are impossible to believe and impossible to live up to," Pamela says.

"I do my best to encourage readers to develop a personal relationship with God. The deepest desire of my heart is to glorify God and to get His message of faith, trust, and forgiveness to a hurting world."

Email Pamela at: pam@pamelathibodeaux.com
Visit her website: http://www.pamelathibodeaux.com
Or blog: http://pamswildroseblog.blogspot.com

Other Titles by Pamela S. Thibodeaux

Kyleigh's Cowboy

She's attempting to start a new life. He's roamed for more than a decade. Can they let go of the past and grab hold of the future?

Seven years after the death of her husband, Kyleigh Winters turned their old vacation home into a brand new guest ranch. Not willing to join the ranks of lonely women trolling the bars or online in search of a man, Kyleigh is sure if God wishes her to have another husband, He'll send the perfect someone in His own time. But will she be open to the possibility of new love when He does?

Searching for a place that calls to his soul, Lance Stevens has been a roaming cowboy for ten years since retiring from the Marines. He finds that sanctuary the moment he drives through the Silver Star's gate and meeting the lovely owner speaks to more than his soul. Will he open to the healing power of love?

Get Pamela Thibodeaux's second chance romance novella today and see how love and faith conquers all.

My Heart Weeps

When life takes everything, your world stops. Can a retreat heal the broken lives of two wounded souls?

Melena Rhyker's world shattered the day her husband died. Lost without the man of her dreams, she digs deep to find a path out of her sorrow. Discovering an artistic retreat, she vows to find a reason to carry on and focus her life in a new direction. Can she heal her own heart, and find her new beginning?

Garrett Saunders knows pain. He's spent most of his life hiding from his past. Regrets and lies haunt him, but he longs to leave them behind and embrace his true self. Will Melena's efforts to rebuild her life in the face of such grief encourage him to exorcise his own demons of guilt and shame?

Will two hurting people find peace, wholeness and perhaps love in the heart of Texas?

Get Pamela Thibodeaux's second chance women's

fiction novel today and see how love and faith conquers all.

Keri's Christmas Wish

Controversy and Inconsistencies are thieves of holiday joy for Keri...is there any hope for a happy holiday season?

For as long as she can remember, Keri Jackson has despised the hype and commercialism around Christmas—especially with the controversy over the time of Jesus's birth. Will she get her wish and be free of the angst to truly enjoy Christmas this year?

Jeremy Hinton thinks Keri is a highly intelligent, deeply emotional, and intensely complex woman and he's as fascinated by her aversion to Christmas as he is of the woman herself. A devout Christian at heart, he's studied all of the world's religions and homeopathic healing modalities. But when a rare bacterial infection threatens her life, will all of his faith and training be for naught?

Fans of near death experiences will enjoy this woman's mystical journey into spiritual Truth.

Love is a Rose (Devotional)

Music is the magical entry into the spirit world; the golden gate into the Kingdom of God. But we mustn't be of the mindset that God only uses Christian music to reach out and touch our mind, heart, and spirit. God uses any and ***every*** means available to speak to His children.

Our job is to be open and receptive.

In this devotional, Pamela S Thibodeaux shares how God opened her spirit to a deeper understanding of the abundance of His grace and mercy through the words of the song, The Rose sung by Country & Western artist Conway Twitty.

Pamela offers Seeds to Ponder and a prayer as she parallels the love of God and the Christian life to each verse of the song.

Lori Strickland (introduced in *Tempered Fire*) has always

been known as her father's "wild child" with no desire to change until she meets ex-bull-rider-turned-preacher, Rafe Judson. Her attempts to change her wanton ways come to naught until she realizes redemption only comes with true repentance. Can she find redemption and win the heart of the cowboy preacher? Find out in *Lori's Redemption.*

The Visionary ~ Will the ugly secret haunting the twins keep them from finding true love?

While most visionaries see into the future, Taylor sees the past. but only as it pertains to her work. Hailed by her peers as "a visionary with an instinct for beauty and an eye for the unique" Taylor is undoubtedly a brilliant architect and gifted designer. But she and twin brother Trevor share more than a successful business. The two share a childhood wrought with lies and deceit and the kind of abuse that's disturbingly prevalent in today's society.

Can the love of God and the awesome healing power of His grace and mercy free the twins from their past and open their hearts to the good plan and the future He has for their lives?

Fans of Redeeming Love will appreciate this contemporary story of the awesome power of God to heal the most wounded of souls.

Tempered Hearts (book 1 in Tempered series)*:*

Rancher Craig Harris and veterinarian Tamera Collins clash from the moment they meet. Innocence is pitted against arrogance as tempers rise and passions ignite to form a love as pure as the finest gold, fresh from the crucible and as strong as steel. Thrown together amid tragedy and unsated passion, Tamera and Craig share a strong attraction that neither accepts as the first stages of love. Torn between desire and dislike, they must make peace with their pasts and God in order to open up to the love blossoming between them. It is a love that nothing can destroy when they come to understand that **only when hearts are tempered, minds are opened, and wills are softened can man discern the will of God for his life.**

Dr. Scott Hensley (introduced in Tempered Hearts) has built a wall around his heart since the death of his wife and parents. Katrina Simmons is recovering from scars inflicted on her as a battered wife. Can dreams be renewed and faith strengthened? Can they find joy and peace in God's love and in love for one another? Find out in ***Tempered Dreams*** (book 2 in Tempered Series).

Amber Harris is a good girl on the brink of womanhood. Stanley Morrison is a young man at the start of his life. For each other, they have always felt the fireworks that two people in love should feel. But the questions about his past, his pride, and Amber's father might be the end of what could be a strong relationship. As the two try to protect their budding romance, some unlikely but powerful forces conspire to keep them apart. Will they survive the wishes of everyone around them with their relationship intact? Find out in ***Tempered Fire*** (book 3 in Tempered Series).

All around rodeo cowboy and heir to the Rockin' H Ranch, Ace Harris is determined not to fall in love. He's only loved one woman in his life, his mother, and no one can even come close to filling her boots. Lexie Morgan thinks rodeo cowboys have rocks for brains and a death wish for a soul. A broken childhood and the death of her father and best friend leave her doubting and questioning God (despite her years of religious upbringing) and afraid of love. Can two young people who clash from the onset learn to trust in the healing power of God and find love and happiness amidst tragedy and grief? Find out in ***Tempered Joy*** (book 4 in Tempered series).

Lori's Redemption (spin-off novella)

Lori Strickland (introduced in *Tempered Fire*) has always been known as her father's "wild child" with no desire to change until she meets ex-bull-rider-turned-preacher Rafe Judson. Her attempts to change her wanton ways come to naught until she realizes redemption only comes with true repentance. Can she find redemption and win the heart of the cowboy preacher?

Tempered Truth (Book 5)

Fate declared them neighbors. Scandal insisted they were brothers. The fact that they looked enough alike to be twins only added fuel to the rumors flying about their parentage.

For fifty-plus years Craig Harris and Scott Hensley have enjoyed a bond nothing can sever.

Not the insinuations that they share the same father.
Not the years of strife and grief and heartache.
Not even death.

Will the truth set them free, or will it destroy the friendship that has lasted a lifetime?

Temperance Publishing